Praise for bestselling author Jill Shalvis

"Shalvis thoroughly engages readers."
—*Publishers Weekly*

"Shalvis's writing is a perfect trifecta of win:
hilarious dialogue, evocative and real characters,
and settings that are as much a part of the story as
the hero and heroine. I've never been disappointed
by a Shalvis book."
—*SmartBitchesTrashyBooks.com*

"A Jill Shalvis hero is the stuff
naughty dreams are made of."
—*New York Times* bestselling author
Vicki Lewis Thompson

"Jill Shalvis has the incredible talent of
creating characters who are intelligent,
quick-witted and gorgeously sexy, all the while
giving them just the right amount of weakness to
keep them from being unrealistically perfect."
—*www.RomanceJunkies.com*

"Witty, fun and sexy—the perfect romance!"
—*New York Times* bestselling author Lori Foster

USA TODAY bestselling and award-winning author **JILL SHALVIS** has published more than fifty romance novels. The four-time RITA® Award nominee and three-time National Readers' Choice winner makes her home near Lake Tahoe. Visit her website at www.jillshalvis.com for a complete booklist and her daily blog.

JILL SHALVIS

Room Service

Shadow Hawk

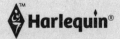

Harlequin®

TORONTO NEW YORK LONDON
AMSTERDAM PARIS SYDNEY HAMBURG
STOCKHOLM ATHENS TOKYO MILAN MADRID
PRAGUE WARSAW BUDAPEST AUCKLAND

ISBN-13: 978-0-373-68824-1

ROOM SERVICE & SHADOW HAWK

Copyright © 2011 by Harlequin Books S.A.

The publisher acknowledges the copyright holder of the individual works as follows:

ROOM SERVICE
Copyright © 2006 by Jill Shalvis

SHADOW HAWK
Copyright © 2007 by Jill Shalvis

CONTENTS

ROOM SERVICE

PROLOGUE

Los Angeles

EMMA HARRIS WAS PART Hollywood business shark, part Ohio farm girl, and though that might seem like an odd combination, it had always worked for her.

Until now.

Now she was a twenty-seven-year-old TV producer facing her last chance in this business. If she blew it, then goodbye job, goodbye career, goodbye to it all because she'd be washed up. Done, finished, finito, before she'd even hit the big three-oh.

But she was too determined, too stubborn, to allow that to happen. Of course, it didn't help that everyone at the production company she worked for thought her luck had run out, including her own assistant, who'd quit last week to go to work as a grip at an NBC sitcom. But Em would never give up.

Nope, she was made of sterner stuff than that. She'd grown up in Ohio, on a thriving family farm, which she'd left to go to college and then produce television shows. Her parents were still horrified, certain that a girl like her, with strong morals and ethics, couldn't possibly make a go of it in Hollywood, but she was dead set on proving them wrong.

She *loved* this job. She simply wouldn't believe she couldn't make it work, her way.

But she'd been summoned by the boss…reminding her that determination was not enough, not in Hollywood. Drawing a deep breath, she made the long walk from her office to his. Outside his closed door, she smoothed her skirt, decided there was no hope for her hair so she didn't even try and, after pasting a smile over her worried frown, knocked with every ounce of confidence and authority she had.

"Come in!"

Em opened the door. From the big leather chair behind his big, fancy network desk, Nathan Bennett scowled.

Em locked her smile in place. "You wanted to see me?"

"Emmaline Harris. Sit."

Great, her full name. Never a good sign. She entered and sat where he indicated—a smaller, far less comfortable-looking chair, which was there, she knew, to make people feel inferior.

She wouldn't let it work. After all, she'd been raised with her mother's words ringing in her ears. "Em," she'd say, hands on her hips, her jeans dirty from hard work. "No one can make you feel inferior without your consent."

A quote from Eleanor Roosevelt, of course, and Em had always believed it. She *was* tough enough for this town!

Nathan looked at her for a long moment, as if measuring his words carefully. "Do you know why you're here today?"

To be fired. Unless she could fast-talk her way back. Which she could do, she told herself. She could fast-talk with the best of them. It was lying and manipulation she had trouble with. "I'm pretty certain."

Nathan nodded, looking stern and unhappy, and Em felt as if she was sitting in front of the principal, only this was worse, far worse, because being ousted here meant so much more than a few days suspension without homework. It meant bye-bye paycheck.

But she would not be saying bye-bye to her self-respect. Nope, if she was going down, then she'd go down with pride intact.

Nathan steepled his fingers. "We hired you, Emmaline, in spite of your utter lack of experience in this business, because we thought you were a bright star on the horizon, just waiting to make her mark."

"Sir—"

"We thought you'd do great things for our production company."

"And I hope I'm just getting started." She tried the smile again.

It still wasn't returned.

Instead, Nathan rearranged his already perfectly arranged pencil and pen set to the right of his spotless blotter. "Emmaline, can you explain the last three shows you produced here?"

"Well, I—"

"And why each failed?"

Her smile faltered. Yes, she could. But she wouldn't. Because that would mean hurting others. When she'd first come to town, she hadn't understood the rules—or, rather, that there were no rules. She got it now, the challenge being to make that work to her benefit without compromising herself. "I'm sure everyone here has had some trouble at one time or another," she said. "Three failures in the whole, big scheme of things—"

"These were your *only* shows, Em. You're batting zero here."

They both knew she was a hard worker, that wasn't the problem. In fact, she'd been throwing herself headlong into every project from her first set of LEGO at age three, and had been told time and time again by her family and teachers that she was made of pure tenacity and grit.

Unfortunately she had a soft heart to go with that drive, which often threw a wrench into being the best of the best. Because she wouldn't lie, nor would she hurt anyone or anything on her way to the top. She couldn't live with herself if she did.

Which was why she couldn't explain to Nathan about the failures of her three shows. "I know my record looks bad, but I can do this, Nathan. Please, just give me another shot. If I could just have the reins of a show from the very beginning—"

Already shaking his head, he leaned back in his chair. His hair was black, devoid of any gray, and with a similar comb-over style to Donald Trump's. His face was tanned from his last vacation in the Bahamas with the third wife, and he wore diamond studs in his ears that could pay Em's salary for at least five years. He'd probably never been fired in his life. "You've had your shot," he said firmly. "*Three* of them."

Sure. First up had been the exciting reality show involving two brothers, both sweet and adorable inventors, with IQs off the map. Em had thought Ty and Todd so wonderful, and because they'd been struggling to make ends meet, too, she'd made it her personal mission to get the word out on them. Only as it turned out, Ty and Todd had failed to mention the word had been out once before, and that they were in court for patent infringements. By the time the first episode aired, both the network and Nathan had been sued.

With failure ringing in her ears, Em's second attempt had been her chance to prove the previous disaster had been an unlucky break. But right from the beginning, the crew on the safari-adventure-themed reality show had fought viciously amongst themselves, backstabbing and sabotaging at will. Because Em hadn't been allowed to hire them in the first place, she'd been left in the position of being unable to control them. That, coupled with the fact that not one of them could read a map, and it had been a "lost" cause before they'd even begun.

Em's third and last effort had been a talk show where, not-so-coincidentally, the host had been Nathan's niece by marriage. A lovely, funny, sharp woman making her way up the ranks in the comic circuit, a woman who'd had an incredibly unlucky streak in life culminating in a horrific car accident the year before and was now, secretly and unfortunately, addicted to her prescription meds. A secret, of course, that could ruin her. When Em had discovered it, the woman had begged and cried and pleaded for Em not to tell.

Of course Em didn't tell, it wasn't in her genetic makeup to do such a thing, but when the comic had self-destructed—on live TV—the decision had cost Em the show, garnering her the knowledge that she didn't want to work with relatives of her boss ever again.

Now she had three failures like balls on a chain around her neck. Each had occurred, Em was certain, not because she was a bad producer, but because she'd been handed the cast and crew instead of picking them herself.

The stakes had never been higher, she knew this. But she also knew anything was possible, including making it in this business. Her way. "I can do this, Nathan," she said again. "I know I can. You just have to give me a real chance to do so."

"Emmaline—"

"A *real* chance." She stood, putting her hands on his desk, leaning in, desperate to make him see how badly she wanted this. "If I could pick the crew and the host this time—"

"You don't have any experience in that area."

True enough. Until college, she'd driven a tractor, she'd run a hay barn and she'd managed the books for the dairy division of her family's farm.

Having graduated from college with a business degree in TV development, she knew it was time to hold down a job in her field, not a hay field. And she wanted it to be *this* job. "You saw something in me, you just said it. Please, let me try again, just one more time."

Nathan twirled a mechanical pencil in his fingers and did that long silent pause that always made Em want to squirm. Finally he let out a long sigh. "I know I'm going to be sorry, but...yeah."

"Yeah?" In shock, she laughed. *"Really?"*

Looking unhappy about it, he nodded.

"Oh, my God, thank you thank you thank you," she cried, running around his desk to throw her arms around him.

Awkwardly, he patted her on the back. "Okay now."

"I'm sorry." She dropped her arms and stepped back, but she still couldn't swipe the wide grin off her face. "You won't regret this, not for a minute."

"Just promise me you're really going to make this work," he said solemnly to her face-splitting smile, though if she wasn't mistaken, his eyes did actually twinkle. "Because, trust me, Em, if you screw this up, you're done in this business for good."

"Oh, I'm going to make this work." She inhaled deeply to keep from hugging him again. "So tell me... what kind of show is it going to be?"

She envisioned another talk show, or maybe a well-written, sharp, witty sitcom. Yeah, that would be so perfect, something that would make people laugh—

"We want a cooking thing."

Em stared at him, some of her elation fading. "A cooking thing."

"With a dynamic chef who can really entertain. You know, juggle knives, toss the ingredients around. Like those chefs at the Japanese restaurants, only without the ethnicity. You'll cook everything across the board on this show, from burgers to beef tartare."

Tartare? She didn't even know what that was. "A cooking show," she repeated, thoughts racing. Unfortunately, she didn't know the inner workings of a kitchen any more than she understood the aerodynamics of a plane.

"Cooking shows are hot right now," Nathan said.

A cooking show, when Em could burn water without trying.

"You should start with the chef. He'll be the key to your success. I actually have one in mind—"

"But you just said I could hire—"

"The staff to *support* the show."

She fixed her smile back in place, adding an easy nod that she hoped covered up the panic hurtling through her veins instead of blood. *Cooking* show… "I was hoping you'd trust me to hire everyone for the show."

"I do. Just go check out the chef I have in mind. He has charisma in spades. He'd draw the audience right in. Women think he's sexy as hell, too."

"Who is he?"

"Chef Jacob Hill, currently running Amuse Bouche, the world-class restaurant inside Hush, an equally world-class hotel in New York."

"You mean that new hotel that's themed for…"

"Sex? Yep, that's the one. You can leave ASAP." Nathan stopped and looked at her. "Oh, one more thing."

She was still reeling from the fact that she wasn't fired, that she was doing a cooking show and that she was headed to a hotel that specialized in sexual exploration and adventure.

"I know your potential, Em. It's why I'm doing this. But listen to me. You're going to have to…"

"What?"

He sighed. "Harden that ridiculously soft heart of yours. Toughen up."

"I'm plenty tough."

"Not in the way I'm talking. It'd help if you learned to conform to the way we do things around here."

"You mean like lie and cheat?"

He offered her a smile, his first. "Exactly. If that chef won't come willingly? Hire someone to find a hair on their plate at Amuse Bouche. In a place like that, he'd be ruined instantly. He'll be begging to do the show."

She stared at him. "That's despicable."

He shrugged. "That's life."

"I would never do something like that."

"Yeah." His smile faded and he scrubbed his hands over his face. "Here comes number four."

"I am *not* failing a fourth time."

He didn't look convinced, but to his credit, he didn't say so. "You've got yourself one month to get this show off the ground. Go break a leg."

She moved to the door when he opened it for her, feeling a little stunned, a little overwhelmed, a little excited and a lot sick.

"Good luck," Nathan said wryly.

No doubt, she was going to need it.

CHAPTER ONE

New York

THREE DAYS LATER EM stood in the gorgeous lobby of Hotel Hush, looking around in marvel. The carpet beneath her feet was a pattern of blacks, greens, grays and pinks, and felt so thick it was like walking on air. The grand furniture and artwork on the vast walls brought to mind the great old salons of the roaring twenties.

She knew from Hush's Web site that the place catered to the young, wealthy and daring. It was eighty guest rooms of fun, flirty sophistication and excitement, with additional offerings such as designer penthouse suites complete with personal butlers, an "it" bar named Erotique that attracted the glitterati of New York, a luxurious spa, a rooftop swimming pool…

And every available amenity was geared toward Hush's hook: erotic fun. Guests could use their room's private video camera complete with blank tapes, or any of the "toys" in each armoire. And downstairs in the basement was a discreet entertainment parlor where couples could engage in semiprivate exhibition fantasies, and more.

"More" being sensual pleasures that only those with an extremely open, worldly point of view would dare experience. According to the info Em had gotten online, anything could be obtained here, tried here, seen here. Anything at all.

Em couldn't even imagine the half of it. Not that it

mattered. She wasn't here for the pleasures. She was here to see Amuse Bouche, and its chef. Nathan had chosen well. It was rumored that Chef Jacob Hill was unparalleled in the kitchen, any kitchen, and that he was a virtual modern-day god.

And wildly, fabulously sexy to boot.

People said that his food was out of this world, that once you ate something he cooked, you fell for him hook, line and sinker. They said that his waitstaff had to guard the doors to the kitchen, beating women off with a stick every night.

She hoped that translated to great TV.

She'd tried to learn more about him, but interestingly enough there wasn't much to learn. She'd found several lists of impressive credentials, but with an odd omission— anything prior to five years ago was a complete blank.

Which meant either Chef Jacob Hill was relatively new to his field, or he had a past he didn't care to advertise.

An enigma.

And the last piece to the puzzle of Em's success.

Hopefully he had one element common with the rest of the human race, that he could be coaxed, by either the promise of money or fame, all the way across the country to L.A.

"Look at this place," Liza said in awe. Liza was Em's oldest friend and newest assistant. That she looked like Barbara Eden circa *I Dream of Jeannie* had turned out to be invaluable in the industry as far as getting things done her way. Which was good, as Liza, never a warm, fuzzy sort, never one to back off from a good fight, liked to get her way. This made her an extremely efficient assistant, if a rather fierce one.

"They sure take the art deco theme seriously, don't they?" She looked all around them. "This stuff is all museum quality."

"Yeah, I'm sure that's why the male guests come here." This from Eric, Em's second-closest friend, and new location director. He was looking at a bold, bright painting of a very beautiful and very nude woman stretched out on a luxurious daybed for all to see—and he was enjoying the view greatly, if the smile on his face was anything to judge by. "The *quality*."

Liza rolled her eyes. "We're here for the restaurant."

"Yeah, and trust me, as a chef, good restaurants hold a special place in my heart, but we're really here to save Em's ass— *Oomph*." Rubbing the ribs Liza had just elbowed, he glared at her. "What? It's true."

Liza shook her head in disgust. "It's not true, and you're not a chef."

"Am so."

"Are not."

Em sighed. The two of them possessed a unique talent for getting a reaction out of each other, be it annoyance—or sexual tension.

Eric went back to ogling the nudes.

"You're a dog," Liza said to him. "Men are dogs."

"Woof, woof," Eric said.

If Eric was a dog, he was a good-looking one—tall and very Californian in his casual chinos, untucked polo shirt, tennis shoes and sunglasses shoved to the top of his blond mop. He had eyes the color of an azure sky, and could stop traffic with a single smile.

Also handy when it came to getting his way.

Em couldn't do this without either of them.

"I'm going to check in," Liza said. "I'm getting a room as far from yours—" she pointed at Eric "—as possible."

"Works for me." Eric gave a careless shrug. "Last chance, Em. Save yourself all the trouble and use me as your chef. You know I'm good."

He *was* good, but not formally trained, and such a goofball that no one ever took him seriously. She was afraid that would be apparent on the TV screen. "Eric—" Emma said.

"Yeah, yeah. I'm going to the bar."

"Works for me," Liza snapped, and with a mutual growl, both of them were gone, leaving Em standing in the lobby alone. "Well," she said to herself. "This is going to be fun."

The three of them together had always been fun before. They'd made their way through college, existing on fun.

That is, until last year. That had been when Eric had been stupid enough to tell Liza he loved her, then given her a diamond ring and married her.

The marriage—based on fun and lust—had lasted for two wild, sexually charged months before they'd had an explosive fight. And because neither of them had ever had a real relationship, neither of them had known what to do with real love. Now, with all that emotion still pent up inside them, with no way to deal with it, they snarled and growled and bickered.

Em loved both of them, but if they didn't realize that they just needed to trust themselves—and get back in the sack—then she was going to lock them together in the same room until they figured it out for themselves.

Another time, though. Because right now, Eric was right. She had to save herself. To that end, she walked toward check-in. The front desk had the same sexy sophistication as the rest of the lobby, with its chest-high black marble counters. The wall behind matched, broken only by the neon-pink *HUSH* blazing in the center.

The check-in process was handled by a pretty woman wearing a black tux with a pink tie and a friendly smile. "Twelfth floor, same as your friends. Room 1212 for you. It's got a great view of the city and should have everything you need. Feel free to call us for anything."

If only it were that easy. Just call the front desk for Chef Jacob Hill… She took the room key with a wry smile and caught up with Liza and Eric at the elevators.

Eric held out a beer, lifting it in a toast. "This place is really something. You can actually smell the excitement in the air."

Liza inhaled and shrugged.

Eric laughed. "This place is for people who want a rush, who want to feel cosmopolitan, exotic. *I* feel it."

"Since when did you ever want cosmopolitan, Mr. Beer-on-the-couch-with-the-remote?" Liza asked.

"Since two women in Erotique practically lapped me up just now."

Liza's eyes fired with temper but she merely inquired, "Erotique?"

"The bar. You should have seen me in there. Hot stuff, baby." He waggled his eyebrows. "You should have kept me while you had the chance."

"Ha."

Appearing happy to have irritated the thorn in his side, Eric smiled at Em. "Here's to phase two," he said and lifted his beer in another toast. "To getting our TV chef."

Liza nodded. "To Em's success."

"Absolutely." Eric's eyes locked on hers and went warm, his smile genuine.

Liza's slowly faded.

"What?" he asked. "What's the matter?"

Liza shook her head. "Did we just…*agree* on something?"

He laughed. "Doubt it."

"No, we did."

"Mark the calendar," he said softly. "Hell must have frozen over."

"You're a funny guy."

"No, it's true." He stepped closer to her. "When we were

married, you'd disagree with me no matter what I said. I'd say, 'honey, the sky is blue,' and you'd say, 'nope, it's light blue. Maybe dark blue. But not just blue, because I wouldn't want to agree with you on anything, even a frigging color thing.'"

Liza took a step toward him this time, her body leaning forward. "That's *not* what I did."

Their noses nearly touched. "Truth hurts, doesn't it, babe?"

The two of them were breathing heavily, tension dripping off them in waves, and not all of it anger.

"Guys," Em said.

"You know what's the matter with you?" Liza asked Eric.

"No, but I'm guessing you're about to tell me."

"*Guys?*" Em said again.

"You think you're God's gift to women," Liza said to Eric. "It's obnoxious."

"I'll try to keep it to myself then," Eric said lightly. "Thanks."

"This was stupid," Liza said. "Being here, the two of us."

"Right. Em, you want to give up on this whole chef search and just use me? Seeing as I'm God's gift and all? Then we can all go home."

"We're doing this," Em said. "You guys can do this. Please."

Eric looked at Liza. Liza looked back. Both sighed and nodded.

Em let out a breath. She'd done her research. She was as prepared as it got. They needed Jacob Hill, and she intended to get him.

Her way.

As they waited for the elevator doors to open, Liza scoped out a gorgeous man walking through the lobby.

Eric watched her, eyes shuttered.

Em sighed, then bent to pet a sleek black cat who'd showed up out of nowhere, wearing a bright pink collar with a tag that read Eartha Kitty. With a purr, Eartha Kitty wound around Em's ankles until the elevator doors finally opened.

Em stepped on. The inside was as plush as the rest of the place, lined with mirrors and decorative black steel. As she contemplated the row of glowing pink buttons, the doors began to close—without Liza and Eric, who were facing each other and once again bickering over something or another.

Fed up, determined to do this with or without them, Em pushed the twelfth-floor button. The doors slid all the way closed, and blessed silence reigned. With a sigh, she leaned back against the mirror, closing her eyes. If Liza and Eric didn't kill each other by sunset, she'd happily do the deed herself.

No, better yet, she'd lock them up in one of the rooms here and let them work out their frustrations.

Unfortunately, Em had no outlet for *her* frustrations. Most of the men in her life had turned out to be toads. Okay, *all* of them had turned out to be toads, and though she'd kissed quite a few while looking for her prince, he hadn't yet showed up.

Opening her eyes, she caught a glance of herself. Yikes. Hair wild, eyes tired…if a prince showed up today, he'd go running at the sight of her. She closed her eyes again, opening them only when the doors slid back, revealing… the second level?

How had that happened?

A man stepped into the elevator. He wore black Levi's and battered boots, and a black long-sleeved shirt with the pink *HUSH* logo on his pec. His eyes were covered with mirrored aviator sunglasses, and when he shoved them to the top of his head and looked at Em, her heart stopped. Not because he was drop-dead gorgeous. No, that description felt too neat, too pat, too...*GQ*. In fact, he was the furthest thing from *GQ* she'd ever seen.

He was tall, probably six-four, all tough and rangy and hard-muscled. His hair was cropped extremely short, and was as dark as his fathomless eyes, which were set in a face that could encourage the iciest of women to ache. And that face told the tale that he'd lived every single one of his years as fast and hard as he could.

Which wasn't to say he wasn't appealing. In truth, she couldn't tear her eyes off him. But she could tell he was the kind of man who would worry his mother, the kind of man who would worry a father with a daughter. He seemed...streetwise, tough as nails, edgy, possibly even dangerous.

And then he smiled.

Yeah, big and rough, and most definitely badass. This was a man who'd seen and done things, the sort of man who could walk through a brawl, give as good as he got, and come out unscathed.

A warrior.

Em would have sworn her heart gave one last little flutter before it stopped altogether.

But the most surprising thing was what he said.

"Good, you're here."

Um...what? *Her?* Em looked behind her, but they were alone. *Me?* she mouthed, pointing to herself, nearly swallowing her tongue when he nodded.

"You." His voice wasn't hard and cold, as she might have expected, but quiet and deep, and tinged with a hint of the South, which only added to the ache in her belly.

What was it about a man with a hint of a slow, Southern drawl?

Before she could process that thought, or any thought

at all actually, he slipped an arm around her and turned to smile at the two women who followed him onto the elevator. "See?" he said to them. "Here she is."

Both women were very New York, sleek and stunning, and...*laughing?* Whatever the man had been referring to, they weren't buying it. "Come on, Chef," one said, shaking her head.

Em stood there, not quite in shock, but not quite in charge of her faculties, either, because the man had her snug to his body, which she could feel was solid muscle, and warm, so very warm. Her head fit perfectly in the crook of his shoulder. At five foot nine she'd never fit into the crook of anyone's shoulder before, not a single one of her toads, and feeling—dare she think it?—petite and delicate made her want to sigh. The feminist in her tried to revolt, but was overpowered by her inner girlie-girl.

Then the man holding her tipped his face to hers. He had a day's growth of dark stubble along his jaw, a silver stud in one ear and the darkest, thickest eyelashes she'd ever seen. He could convince a nun to sin with one crook of a finger, Em thought dazedly.

He was still smiling, only it wasn't a sweet, fuzzy smile but a purely mischievous, trouble-filled one.

My, Grandma, what big teeth you have. Really she needed to get herself together. But he was so yummy she hadn't yet decided whether to smack him or grab him. And then he leaned in, brushing that slightly rough jaw to her ear, the friction of his day's growth against her soft skin making her shiver.

"Do you mind?" he whispered, his voice low and husky. "If I kiss you?"

Kiss her? She wanted to have his firstborn!

"Just for show," he murmured, drawing her in closer as if she'd already agreed.

Em's mind raced. He didn't look like the toads she'd been with lately. He didn't feel like a toad. But would she ever really know unless she kissed him...?

No, it was crazy; it was beyond crazy, letting a perfect stranger touch her, much less *kiss* her, but something about his mocha eyes, about what she saw in them—places and experiences she'd never even dreamed about—made her let out a slow, if unsure, nod.

He rewarded her with a smile that finally met those eyes of his. And then he lowered his mouth.

The two women behind him, the ones who'd been laughing at him only a moment ago, both let out shocked gasps.

That was all Em heard before her mind shut itself off and became a simple recipient of sensations. His lips were firm yet soft, his breath warm and delicious, and on top of it all, the man smelled so good she could have inhaled him all day long.

As a result, her lips seemed to part by themselves, and at the unmistakable invitation, her prince let out a rough sound of surprise and deepened the kiss, his fingers massaging the back of her head at her nape, his other hand sliding down, down, *down*, coming to rest low on her spine, his fingers almost on her butt, anchoring her to him.

Oh, my.

And the kiss...it didn't make any sense. She didn't know him from Adam, but somehow she felt as if that weren't really true, as if maybe she'd always known him, as if her body recognized the connection even if her brain couldn't place him. Confusing, bewildering, but she held on to him as if it didn't matter. And he kept kissing her, kissing her until she felt hot everywhere, until she was making little sounds in the back of her throat that would have horrified her if she could have put together a single thought.

It was as if he knew the secret rhythm that her body's needs responded to, as if they'd been lovers before.

And yet it wasn't real. Logically Em knew this, even through the sensual, earthy haze he'd created, but it also seemed shockingly profound. And nothing, nothing at all, like a simple toad's kiss.

Then he lifted his head, her perfect stranger, and for one beat in time looked every bit as flummoxed as she.

But the moment passed and he smiled—a smile that was sin personified. She tried to respond in kind, she really did, but all she managed was to open her mouth, and quite possibly drool.

With one last stroke of his hand up her spine, a touch that conveyed a carefully restrained passion, he pulled his arm free, and when the elevator doors opened, he pushed his gaping friends off the elevator.

Then turned back to Em.

She stood there blinking like an owl, unable to shift her tongue from drool mode into talk mode.

"Thank you," he said.

Thank you?

"I'm in your debt." His voice was far tighter and more tense than it had been before the kiss. Interesting.

And then, just like that, the shockingly sexy, charismatic man walked away.

Still gaping, body still pulsing, Em became vaguely aware that the elevator doors closed again. Her heart pounded, her knees shook, and she stood there like a stunned possum until the elevator doors once again opened.

A few people got on.

At least she finally managed to close her mouth, then leaned back against the mirrors, happy for the support.

There was some talking around her but her brain couldn't process the words.

When the doors opened again, everyone got off and she had to laugh at herself.

She was back on the lobby floor.

"Get it together, Harris," she told herself, and even hearing her voice seemed funny. She sounded shaky, a little off her axis.

A little? She'd fallen right off her world, that's what she'd done.

Shrugging, she once again hit the button for the twelfth floor, wondering when the doors had opened there and she'd missed it.

During the kiss?

Or after, when she'd been rendered a mass of sensual nerve endings incapable of doing anything but reacting?

Because of that kiss. The mother of all kisses. The kind of connection a woman dreamed about but was never really certain even existed, except in romance novels or the movies.

How did a man learn to kiss like that?

Given her reaction to it, that sort of ability should be registered as a lethal weapon.

And she didn't even know his name...

When the doors opened on the twelfth floor, *again*, she stopped hugging herself and stepped off, still in enough of a daze to do so without her roll-on luggage.

She ran back onto the elevator and grabbed her belongings.

Then she headed toward her room, unable to help but wonder if the rest of her trip was going to prove as adventurous as the first few minutes had been.

And that's when it came to her, what the women had called her glorious stranger.

They'd called him Chef.

CHAPTER TWO

To: Maintenance
From: Housekeeping
Check the air vents and temp regulator on elevator
2A. Guest seen coming out of it today looking dazed
and flushed.

JACOB HILL WALKED THROUGH the employee quarters, located on the second sublevel. Employees were treated well at Hush, probably because the creator of the hotel, Piper Devon, was a genuine, caring people-person, no matter that the press liked to call her the original Paris Hilton. That was because they saw only a gorgeous blond trust-fund baby. But anyone who'd ever worked for Piper knew the truth. She worked her ass off, especially on Hush.

Jacob moved through the cafeteria toward the locker room. There he received a few whistles and catcalls, and when he got close to his locker, he saw why.

A pair of black satin panties hung off the lock.

"Another thong." Jon, one of the doormen, stood at the locker next to Jacob's, changing for his shift. He was young, in his early twenties, and staring at the panties as if they were a choice cut New York steak. "It must be two times a week you get them," he said, bemused. "All I ever get is dumped."

Jacob gingerly removed the thong and tossed it to him. "Merry Christmas."

"Seriously, Chef, I want to know." Jon looked down at the satin in his hands. "What's your trick? I mean you get phone numbers, presents…give up the secret, man."

Jacob opened his locker and said nothing. There was nothing to say. After all, he didn't purposely do anything to gain women's attention—it just happened. A lot. He'd enjoyed it far more when he'd been young and stupid, when he'd happily worked his way through the line of women that had come his way.

He still enjoyed a woman's touch, her scent, her body, her everything, but lately, something had changed. He didn't seem to have quite the same patience for the game.

Was he getting old at thirty-four? Scary thought.

"I mean, I've done everything right," Jon said. "I call a woman when I say I'm going to. I listen to her ramble on and on and on. I take her dancing. I sweet-talk her."

Jacob grabbed his gear, shut his locker and then looked at Jon. "I'm going to sound like a first-class ass here, but the truth is…no. Never mind."

"Tell me. Whatever it is, I can do it."

"Okay, but listen. I should add a disclaimer here. I really don't recommend—"

"Dude. Just tell me."

"You're trying too hard."

The kid stared at Jacob. "Huh?"

"I know." Jacob lifted his hands. "It doesn't make any sense, but women seem to go for the guy who steps all over them, a guy who doesn't call, doesn't listen—"

"*That's* your secret?" Jon asked in disbelief. "Treat them like shit?"

Jacob shrugged. "I didn't say I condone it. I'm just giving you my observation."

"Wow." The young doorman stared down at the panties in his hands. "*Wow.*"

Jacob patted his shoulder and took the stairs back to the main level, entering the leaded glass doors of Amuse Bouche from the lobby.

Fresh flowers had been put out, as they were every day, making the place look warm and welcoming, and casually elegant. Unlike anywhere else, he never tired of being here, of the familiar black tables and funky black chairs bathed in the soft pink light, the gorgeous art deco paintings on the walls.

Inside his kitchen, he did as he always did—took a moment to survey his domain, the best money could buy in both design and appliances. No complaints here, either. The place had been cleaned during the wee hours of the night, to a spotless, disinfected, lemony-smelling shine that he never failed to marvel at. He could probably serve his food right here on this floor. Hell, he could probably serve out of their trash bin and still pass code, the place was so immaculate.

He marveled at that, too. There had been years when he would have happily eaten off this floor, or gone through the trash for scraps to fill his aching belly. Long, lean times, his growing-up years.

And now here he was, sous-chef of all things, reporting only to the executive chef who showed up on-site maybe once a week, leaving Jacob to handle the day-to-day operation of the place.

A slow, satisfied smile crossed his face. Not bad for a street urchin who'd grown up wild and feral, who'd wandered his way across the South in his youth, living hand to mouth, lucky to have a shirt on his back half the time. God, he'd been such a little shit, a real know-it-all. The one time that social services had managed to get hold of him, their diagnosis had been attachment disorder, which had cracked him up. Attachment disorder, bullshit. He could have attached. He'd just chosen not to.

Still did.

In any case, it was true that Amuse Bouche was everything he once would have scoffed at: posh and sophisticated, valuing quality over quantity. Odd then how very happy he was here, when his surroundings were far more elegant than he could ever be.

Ah, well. There it was. And eventually, he knew, the wanderlust would take over, as it always did, and he'd shrug and move on, never looking back.

But for now, things were pretty damn fine. He had all this incredible space, with the best equipment available, and the freshest ingredients money could buy. In a couple of hours' time the dining area would be filled with people wanting to taste his food. *His.*

Yeah, not too shabby, for a hard-ass punk kid from Podunk.

He moved toward the three industrial-grade refrigerators, thinking there were two things worth doing well in life. Both required passion, concentration and skill, and both gave him great pleasure: cooking and seducing a woman. Combining ingredients to create a masterpiece had always been a great source of entertainment. In the same way that the weather changed, without rhythm or plan, he liked to adjust his menu.

Women were no different. Same as a good recipe, they were meant to be played with, thoroughly explored, and devoured, but would undoubtedly spoil if kept too long.

So he never kept anything too long.

It simply wasn't in his nature. It was why he held the sous-chef position instead of executive chef, which he could have had if he wanted.

He didn't want.

He liked keeping his options open, liked keeping one foot out the door, liked knowing he could pack up and go at a moment's notice.

Hell, he didn't even have to pack if he wanted, he had nothing that couldn't be replaced in another town, another restaurant.

But for now, for right this very minute, Hush was a good place to be. A very good place. He smiled as he remembered the episode in the elevator, with his pretty stranger and her mind-blowing kiss.

"What are you grinning about?" This came from Pru as she entered into the kitchen behind him. She was Amuse Bouche's sommelier. The wine expert position fit his friend to a tee, given that she was a complete snob and had been since her first day here, even though, like Jacob, she'd arrived in New York with only the clothes on her back.

But she was extremely sharp-witted, and never failed to amuse him. They'd bonded immediately, of course, recognizing kindred spirits. The two pretenders, they called themselves.

Oddly enough, they hadn't slept together.

A first for Jacob, being friends with a woman, not lovers. But though Pru, with her curvy, lush body, creamy porcelain skin and startlingly blue eyes, was exactly his type on paper, in reality she batted for another team entirely.

An all-girl team.

After the initial disappointment, Jacob hadn't cared. He liked her, and that in itself was enough of a novelty that he put up with her less attractive traits—such as the one that made her get some sick enjoyment out of constantly trying to set him up with "the one."

The one. Why did there have to be just one?

"Do I need a reason to be grinning?" he asked.

"Yeah, when you're smirking like that." Pru studied him

thoughtfully, her dark brown hair carefully contained in some complicated braid. "You're thinking about sex."

He laughed. *Caught.* "Why do you always assume that?"

"Because guys think about sex 24/7. You're probably thinking about that poor woman you accosted in the elevator."

"I didn't accost her." Nope, after a brief startled moment on her part, she'd kissed him back. Quite eagerly.

"Who was she?"

A stranger, one who happened to be at the right place at the right time. A stranger by whom, for those sixty or so seconds, he'd been transfixed. As for who she was, he had no idea. He could have found out, of course, but it had been just a kiss.

Just a helluva kiss.

"My date."

Pru set down her Prada briefcase, overflowing with wine catalogs and food magazines, and put her hands on her hips. "You don't really expect me to believe she was your date."

"Why not?"

"Because she looked too sweet to have slept with you."

She *had* looked sweet in that long, flowery dress that had hugged her curves in a way that had made his mouth water. Sweet and yet hot. Extremely hot. "I don't sleep with all my first dates."

Pru laughed. "Yes, you do."

"I didn't sleep with you."

"In your dreams you did," she said smugly.

Okay, she had him there, and he had to laugh. "I'm not that big of a slut."

"Honey, if the shoe fits…" She pulled a California

winery brochure from her bag, tapping the label with a perfectly manicured finger. "We want their stuff."

He glanced at the cover, which showed wine country in all its fall glory. "What makes it different?"

"You'll have to taste it. It's out of this world. I want to make an order. All right with you?"

"You know I trust you."

"Uh-huh," she said dryly. "Which is why you date only the women I tell you to."

"Correction. I trust your judgment in *wines*."

"I have great taste in women." Pru waggled her brow. "I'm going to find you the right one yet, you'll see."

"We've been over this, Pru."

"I know, I know. The thought of just one woman makes you shudder, yadda, yadda. That's only because you don't know, Jacob. You don't understand how great it can be."

The kitchen doors slammed open and another woman entered. Tall, willowy, olive-skinned and gorgeous, Caya was part of the waitstaff, and Pru's platonic roommate. If Pru was the sedate and elegant lady, Caya was the happy-go-lucky party girl. The perfect odd couple.

Caya divided a glance between the two of them. "Having a fiesta without me?"

"Just reminding Chef of all his faults," Pru told her.

"Hey, now." Caya slid her arms around Jacob, setting her head on his shoulder. "Silly Pru. Our Chef has no faults."

Jacob laughed. "That's right, I don't. And don't either of you forget it."

"We were talking about the elevator scene," Pru told Caya. "The woman."

"No, *you* were talking about it." Jacob opened the meat refrigerator and pulled out a container of fresh mussels.

"So." Caya leaned back against the counter and watched him. "You going to tell us?"

"Sure." Jacob dumped the mussels into a huge pot and carried it to the sink. "I'm creating an island blue mussel with sweet potato chowder." He began to fill the pot with water. "I've had a lot of requests—"

"Not *that*, you very annoying man." Pru moved close. "Although an excellent choice," she murmured, peering into the pot. "You should serve a light to medium-bodied off-dry wine with that, you know. Maybe even a lightly sweet white, like a Chenin Blanc or Vouvray—"

"Oh, my God, Pru," Caya said with a laugh. "Stop being the workaholic for a minute. Let's stick to the subject, okay? The cutie in the elevator?"

"Forget it. He can't tell you anything because he was just kissing some stranger again."

Jacob rolled his eyes.

"By the way, I met this woman in the spa today," Pru said to him. "I was getting a Swedish massage—which by the way, was *heaven*. Anyway, she'd be perfect for you."

Jacob lifted up the heavy pot of mussels. "You know, I see your lips moving, but all I hear is blah blah blah blah blah."

"Funny."

"I thought so."

"Jacob—"

"Hey, how about this? When you're not single, we'll talk." He carried the pot to the huge stovetop. "Meanwhile, go find 'the one.'"

He saw Pru's quick longing glance at Caya—Caya?—but before he could assimilate it, the door opened and Jacob's two assistants entered.

Timothy and Daniel had been picked by him personally, and after going through at least ten previous assistants, each worthless, he had high hopes for these two. They were clueless, of course, and both far too young, but he'd been young and stupid once, too, and since they had a genuine love of cooking and were eager to learn, he'd given them a shot.

Timothy leaned over Jacob's shoulder, looked into the pot and let out a slow smile. "Island blue mussels. *Sweet*."

"It will be," Jacob promised. "Get out the whole dried bay laurel leaf and the coriander. Oh, and the fennel seed. Start grinding." To Daniel he said, "Get what we need for the soup. You know the ingredients?"

Daniel looked excited and terrified at the same time. "Yes."

"Then go. Oh, and stir frequently." He leaned in. "That means often, whether your girlfriend calls you every three minutes or not."

Daniel blushed at the reminder of last week, when he'd inadvertently burned the bottom of the pot and ruined an entire batch. "I won't screw it up this time."

"See that you don't."

"I was thinking," Caya piped up to Jacob. "We should all go out tonight."

By "all," Caya could mean anyone and everyone. While Pru batted for that all-girl's team, Caya had never limited her options by choosing a side.

"I'll bring that woman from the spa for Jacob," Pru said.

"Don't bother, I'm busy tonight," Jacob told her, and before they could object, he put an arm around each of them, steering them toward the door.

Laughing, Pru dug in her heels. "You are not busy."

"I am *extremely* busy."

"Fine. I can easily party without you guys," Caya said breezily.

At the flash of disappointment on Pru's face, Jacob sighed. Ah, hell. The Ice Queen had a thing for the carefree, spirited Caya, who went through sexual partners like water. Not that there was anything wrong with that, but Pru was the monogamous sort, always in it for the long haul. She'd been dreaming of her own special "the one" since he'd known her.

And now she was bound for Hurt City. "Maybe we could go out," Pru said to Caya. "You know, just the two of us."

Caya stared at her, then laughed. "Right. The sommelier go out with the lowly waitress. That's sweet, Pru, but you don't have to do that." Leaning in, she kissed each of them on the cheek. "See ya later, guys."

With that, she took her most excellent behind out of the kitchen.

Pru watched her leave the kitchen and Jacob shook his head. "Pru, what the hell is this?"

Pru swiped all expression from her face. "What?"

"You were looking at her."

"So? I was looking at you, too."

"Yes, but not like you wanted to lap me up with a spoon."

Pru reached for her briefcase and, taking a page from his own book, said nothing.

Jacob shook his head. "You should just come right out and tell her."

"Tell her what? There's nothing to tell."

Her face was pure stubbornness, and after a second, Jacob lifted his hands. "Fine."

"Fine." Pru left, too, shutting the door just a little too hard behind her.

Jacob shrugged it off and strode back toward his waiting ingredients with the same anticipation he would have had striding toward a woman in his bed.

CHAPTER THREE

EM, ERIC AND LIZA looked up as Amuse Bouche's maître d' came toward them. "We can seat you now," she said with an easy smile.

Amuse Bouche turned out to be casually elegant and extremely eye pleasing, with slender black urns holding arrangements of a variety of flowers that matched the art deco vibe of the rest of the hotel. The tables were well spaced and gorgeously done, each with its own discreet partition, so that while voices and laughter were audible, there was an illusion of intimacy for each party.

Em could use some privacy to obsess over what she thought of as the E.I.—elevator incident. Not going to happen with Eric and Liza just behind her, side by side and yet ignoring each other—well, if ignoring meant staring and pretending not to be.

Granted, Liza looked amazing in a tiny scrap of a red cocktail dress, which probably accounted for the glazed look on Eric's face. He didn't look too shabby in his finery, either, turning the head of more than one woman.

"Here you go," the maître d' said and gestured to their table. "Tonight you'll be experiencing Chef Jacob Hill's renowned cuisine creations. Enjoy."

"I'm starving," Liza said and lifted her menu, which she used as a shield so she could covertly stare at Eric with the unguarded longing she sometimes got in her eyes.

Eric got the same look while pretending to watch the crowd, though really checking out the long length of Liza's bare, smooth legs.

It drove Em crazy—how could they not see they belonged together? *Everyone* knew it.

Everyone but them.

Em didn't look at her menu yet. She was still trying to find her own balance, and while she did, she looked around, too. Each place inside Hush had turned out to be more exciting and different than the last, full of a spirited energy and yet somehow also a Zen-like peace.

Not much of a hotel person herself, this one had won her over. Her room was large by Manhattan standards. Beach inspired, it was done in creamy blues and greens and earth tones, with a mural of the sun rising over the Atlantic on one wall, and a mounted waterfall on the other, giving off the soothing sounds of water running over rocks. Her California king bed had lush, thick bedding she couldn't have afforded at home, and her bathroom came with a huge sunken hot tub she could happily drown in, with scented candles lining the edges. The towels were Egyptian cotton, and on the counters had been lotions, bath oils, scrubs—a virtual day spa.

There had been more, as well: the TV channels that were exclusive to the hotel and showed an array of erotica, the beautifully illustrated copy of the Kama Sutra and a selection of self-heating lubricating oils in the bedside table. But the coup de grâce…in the tall closet outside the bathroom hung a long, intricately braided leather whip. She'd fingered the thing in amused shock, had even tapped it against her palm.

Ouch.

Em would have called herself sexually adventurous.

Okay, maybe not quite, but she was at least sexually game. Now she had to admit, maybe she wasn't nearly as game as she'd thought.

This hotel had certainly been an eye-opener. A costly one. She thought of her expense account and winced as she stared at the elaborate but somehow elegantly simple, menu of Amuse Bouche. And yet, she reasoned, if coming here got her Chef Jacob Hill, then every penny spent would be worth its weight in gold.

Or so she hoped.

Logically she knew that even if she somehow managed the miracle and convinced him to come to Hollywood to star in his own TV show, it was only half the battle.

She still had a successful show to make.

One crisis at a time.

Liza set down her menu, took one look at Em and nodded. "Alcohol," she said. "We need some."

"Not until I talk to him," Em said, determined, but getting nervous. "I need all my wits about me for that."

"Honey, with this guy there's no chance of having your wits at all. The guy'll charm the pants right off you without trying."

"You don't know that."

"I've heard. And then what happened today proves it."

Em was already regretting that she'd told her friend about the E.I.

Liza waggled her carefully waxed eyebrows. "Personally, I think you should go for it, you could use the cookie."

"Cookie?"

"Orgasm," Eric explained, checking into the conversation. "She calls orgasms 'cookies'. She thinks it's cute."

"*You* used to think it was cute," Liza sniffed.

Eric's blue eyes sparkled. "Maybe I still do."

Liza stared at him, then reached for her water as if parched. Em eyed the door to the kitchen. "What's the best way to approach him, do you think?"

Liza was still staring at Eric. With what looked like great effort, she tore her gaze from him, her thumb rubbing her ring finger where her wedding band used to be. She turned to Em. "What did Nathan suggest?"

Nathan wanted her to play hardball from the start, offering Jacob standard money, and when he balked, adding small slices of the profits. And when all else failed, she was to resort to hair in the food.

As if she'd ever really do such a thing. "Maybe I could ask the waitress if I could talk to him."

"Jeez, at these prices, he oughta come with the meal. Maybe sing and dance, too." Eric tossed down his menu and smiled as the waitress came close. "Excuse me, do you know the chef?"

"Of course." The waitress smiled back. "Wait until you taste his food, it's out of this world."

Liza leaned close to Em. "And according to you, his food isn't the only thing that tastes out of this world."

"Stop." Em felt the blush creep up her face.

The waitress rattled off the specials. "Everything is fabulous. Trust me, you'll love everything you taste."

"Including the chef himself," Liza murmured for Em's ears only.

"Could we have another minute before deciding?" Em asked the waitress.

"Oh, you bet. Take your time."

Em waited until it was just them and turned to Liza. "I shouldn't have told you about the elevator incident. I don't even know for certain that it was him."

"Well, it was somebody named Chef. You sure you don't know *why* he kissed you?"

"No, he just said 'do you mind?' and then he was doing it."

"And you didn't think about kneeing him in the 'nads?" Eric asked.

At the first taste of him, Em hadn't thought at all. In fact, she'd been the one to deepen the connection. "It wasn't like that."

"Uh-huh." Liza looked at her speculatively. "Must have been some kiss."

Oh, yeah. "It was…interesting."

"Interesting? Honey, this menu is interesting. The decor is interesting. But a kiss? A kiss is either hot stuff or not worth the trouble. No in-between."

Worth the trouble. Times ten. Times infinity.

Eric was studying Liza thoughtfully. "Which was it with us?"

"What?"

"Those two months we were married. Was it hot stuff or not worth the trouble?"

Liza opened her mouth, then closed it.

Eric's amusement faded, replaced by an unmistakable hurt. "Right."

The waitress came back and took their orders by memory, and then offered the services of their sommelier, who could come to the table and make wine suggestions if they'd like.

The sommelier turned out to be one of the women in the elevator, though if the tall, elegant, beautiful brunette recognized Em, she gave no indication of it.

When they were alone again, Liza set down her drink and looked at Eric. "It was hot stuff."

Now it was Eric's turn to blink in surprise.

Liza seemed just as taken aback and abruptly turned to Em. "If you don't approach the chef tonight you'll have to make an appointment," she babbled. "By all accounts, this guy is media reclusive, and not interested in a career path other than what suits him personally. I bet he wouldn't easily grant you an interview."

"I know." Em had worried about this. She worried about a lot of things. But mostly facing the sexy, gorgeous Jacob Hill now that she knew he lived up to his reputation. "I need to make contact tonight—" She broke off when the waitress came back and set down a plate of appetizers that they hadn't ordered.

"From the chef," the woman explained. "Vegetable spring rolls with chili oil and teriyaki mustard sauce. They're a favorite here."

Eric looked around at the other tables. They were all filled with people having conversations, sharing food, all enjoying themselves greatly, if the happy buzz in the place meant anything. "Does the chef always give away his food?"

"For his friends, or special guests, yes."

Liza looked at Em.

So did Eric.

Em laughed nervously. "Uh, thank you."

"Enjoy."

"Oh, boy," Em whispered when she'd left. "Do you think he sees us here?"

"*You*, you mean," Liza said. "Does he see *you* here. Of course he does. He sent the food over."

Em stared at the appetizers, then looked around her. Waitstaff moved easily and discreetly around the crowded room. No chef in sight.

"Must have been a helluva kiss." Liza dug into the spring

rolls, then moaned. "Oh, my God. Em, you've got to taste this."

"Oh, yeah," Eric said when he'd popped one in his mouth. "This guy knows his stuff."

"The man's a god," Liza moaned.

"Are you sure all you did was kiss him, Em?" Eric reached for his second. "Because this isn't a thank-you for a kiss. This is a thank-you for a good fu—"

"Eric." Liza glared at him.

Eric just popped another appetizer into his mouth.

"Men," Liza muttered. "Dogs."

"Woof woof," he agreed happily.

Em shook her head and tasted a roll herself. It did melt in her mouth, made her stomach rumble happily, and actually brought a helpless smile to her face, just as a movement caught the corner of her eye.

A tall, broad man stood at the back of the restaurant, leaning against the doorjamb of the kitchen. Seeming extremely comfortable with both himself and his surroundings, his posture and manner spoke of a quiet, rock-solid confidence.

A confidence she'd experienced firsthand.

Unlike earlier in the elevator, he wore a white chef's hat and jacket, which only accentuated to his height and well-built body. His staff moved around him like a well-tuned army, most of them taking the time to say something to him, or at least cast him a smile, which he always returned.

"That's him?" Liza whispered. "Because *wow*."

"Yeah." Suddenly Em felt hot in the cool room, and reached for her water. Even from this distance she felt the weight of his quiet, assessing stare, and wondered what he was thinking.

Then his lips curved oh-so-slightly, and she knew.

He was thinking about the kiss, the one that would have knocked her socks off if she'd been wearing any, the one that had rendered her deaf, dumb and blind.

And made her wet.

Even now, her thighs tightened with the memory, and she squirmed.

And his not-quite-smile went just a bit naughty.

Oh, God. Her glass nearly slipped out of her hand, and she set it down with such awkwardness on the table that water sloshed over the edge.

"Easy," Liza murmured, putting a hand over hers. Then she smiled at the chef, pointing to the appetizers, and gave him the thumbs-up sign.

Chef smiled and gave a slight nod of his head.

Nope, no trouble in the confidence arena.

"He is pretty yummy," Liza noted, and Eric craned his neck to check him out.

"Not that yummy," he said.

Liza laughed and patted Eric's arm. "Don't worry. You're yummy, too."

"Yeah?" He turned a suddenly extremely interested face toward her. "You still think so, huh?"

Liza shrugged. "You have a mirror."

He grinned and leaned in close. "If I'm so yummy, why did you let me go?"

They all knew why. Because Liza's crappy childhood memories of her mother's eight marriages had made her afraid of commitment.

Eric, who'd grown up without a mother at all, had the same issue. Together, they hadn't trusted their love enough, and they'd had two collective feet halfway out the door at all times.

Now Liza, more mature in many ways, strove to keep

it light and tapped him playfully on the nose. "I let you go because you're an ass."

"Yeah, maybe, but I'm a yummy ass." Eric grabbed her hand and ran his thumb over her bare ring finger. "Now tell me the truth. Why did you let me go?"

"An ass is an ass, Eric."

"Right." Eric nodded, and sat back. "That explains it. Clear as mud, thanks."

Across the room, the sommelier handed the chef a champagne bottle and gestured to a table. Jacob Hill nodded, then walked over to the couple seated there, where he began conversing with them as he smoothly, easily, opened their champagne for them.

"Just look at him," Liza murmured. "Do you suppose he makes love to a woman the same way he opens a bottle of champagne? I bet he does."

Em thought about that and felt her body heat up even more.

The waitress set their dishes on the table, momentarily blocking Em's view of the other table. By the time she moved away, Jacob Hill was gone.

She didn't see him again during the scrumptious meal during which the three of them shared two bottles of wine. They turned down dessert and once they'd settled the bill, Liza stood up first and visibly wobbled.

Eric surged up and slid an arm around her. "Whoa there, tiger."

Liza grinned and set her head on his shoulder. "You're so pretty."

Brow raised, Eric looked at Em.

"Three glasses of wine," Em explained.

"That's right. I'm a cheap drunk." Liza grinned, sliding her hand down Eric's back to pinch his butt.

Eric narrowed his eyes. "What was *that?*"

She waggled her brow. "What did it feel like?"

Eric shook his head. "You are *not* coming on to me."

"Okay, I'm not." She laughed and patted the butt she'd just pinched. "But I am," she whispered extremely loudly.

"You said you'd rot in hell before you slept with me again," he said, confused.

"Silly man." She went to pat his cheek, missed, and nearly poked out his eye. "Never take a PMSing woman seriously."

"Okay." Eric caught her hand, saving his other eye, and nodding agreeably as he pulled her close. "I can work with this information."

"Eric. She's tipsy," Em admonished. "You can't take advantage of a tipsy woman."

"Sure he can." Liza bit his throat, eliciting a rough sound from Eric. "Take advantage of me all you want."

Eric let out another sound, this one of regret. "Em's right. Knock it off."

"Fine. I'll go to my room," Liza said. "Where I plan to eat everything in the minibar. Did you see that thing? It's completely stocked with stuff from Dean & Deluca."

"You just ate," Eric reminded her.

Liza waggled a finger in his face, this time almost poking it up his nose. "Do you know nothing of women?"

"Apparently not."

"Just take me to my bed, superhero."

Eric's eyes darkened. "I like the super part."

"Eric," Em warned softly.

"Right." He frowned at Liza. "I'll put you to bed, but that's all I'm doing."

"Oooh, playing hard to get." Liza sighed and again set her head to his chest, staring up at him adoringly. "You're good at that."

Eric looked over her head at Em helplessly.

She shook her head.

Eric's jaw ticked. "I'll get her to her room. You going to be okay here by yourself?"

"I'll be safer than you," Em assured him, watching as he led Liza out of the restaurant.

Alone, Em looked around her and decided if she sat for much longer, she'd just begin obsessing again. Maybe instead, she'd walk around the city for a little bit to clear her head. Make a plan of action that involved more than drooling after the man she needed to talk into saving her sorry butt.

She got as far as standing up and reaching for her purse when a low, husky voice drawled in her ear, "Leaving without dessert is an insult to the chef."

Her heart kicked once hard, and she turned her head, coming eye to chest with Chef Jacob Hill. At the sight of him, the rest of her kicked. The man exuded a raw sexuality that made her feel her own sexuality in ways she hadn't in a long time, if ever. "You."

"Me," he agreed. "You look beautiful."

"Oh…thank you." She tugged at her black cocktail dress, modestly cut, but snug and—she hoped—relatively sexy. "I wasn't sure of the dress code here—"

"I didn't mean your clothes." When he smiled, as he did now with a dash of wicked intent, he flashed a single dimple on his right cheek, and she had the sudden, shocking urge to run a fingertip over the spot.

He hadn't shaved, and the slight stubble on his jaw was nearly longer than the short hair on his head. She wondered if it would be soft to the touch, then wondered why she wondered.

Because she was losing her mind, that was why.

He was younger than she'd imagined, but there was something about the way he held himself, and the way he took her in, that spoke of a much older soul. His mile-long legs were encased in black trousers instead of his Levi's, his feet in much cleaner, much newer black boots than the ones he'd had on in the elevator.

Chef Jacob Hill cleaned up real nice.

"Crème brûlée or white peach cobbler?" he asked. "Or maybe a cheese plate with an imported selection of artisanal?"

She slid her hand to her belly, which was jumping nervously. *Ask him. Ask him to be your TV chef.* She was afraid if she opened her mouth she was going to ask him something else entirely.

Come to my bed.

"I'm full."

"Are you kidding? You're never too full for dessert."

His voice was somehow extremely arousing, which she told herself would be great for the show, and that was why she'd noticed.

A lie.

She'd noticed because she was a woman. A woman who'd felt his voice all the way to her toes. In fact, the tingling effect began deep in her womb and spread, and she squirmed some more.

He noticed. His eyes cut to her body as she wiggled, and then back up to her gaze, something new there besides the curiosity and wry amusement.

Heat. Lots of heat.

Oh, boy. Resisting the urge to fan cool air in front of her hot face, she searched around for something else to lock her gaze on, for something to occupy her mind, because ever since that elevator kiss, nothing else but this man had.

The tables were all hopping with activity, everyone enjoying themselves. Waiters and waitresses moved around, serving with easy charm and personality, all so beautiful Em could have hired any one of them for her show and the cameras would have been thrilled.

One particularly beautiful waitress was serving a table

of elderly gentlemen with professionalism, even when the oldest of the bunch reached out and patted her butt.

In return she shook her head and patted the top of his head with a smile. The old man adjusted his toupee and smiled with only a hint of regret.

Oh, good. *Everyone* had sex on the brain, not just Em. Maybe it was the hotel. She reached for her water and gulped it down.

"You okay?" he asked her, bringing her attention back to him.

As if she could possibly forget he was there.

Not quite sure she trusted herself to speak, she nodded her head. *See? See how fine I am? And by the way, will you come with me to Hollywood and save my sorry career?*

"Please, sit," he urged, putting a hand on her arm.

Just like in the elevator, his touch electrified.

"I'd really love to bring you dessert," he said. He smiled a little. Could he see how he turned her on without even trying? "I owe you."

"No, that's okay. Really. I—"

He put a finger on her lips, yet again touching her, and yet again causing her every hormone to stand up and take notice.

"Wait here," he said in quiet demand.

Wait here, repeated those hormones, and quivered. She nodded, and he gave her another little knowing smile that told her he realized exactly what he did to her. She watched him stride off, tall, sure…confident that she'd wait simply because he'd commanded it to be so.

She didn't understand it, but he had this unsettling way about him of getting her to do what he wanted.

What was that?

She had no idea, but she waited. But only because she wanted to.

CHAPTER FOUR

HE'D MADE HER SQUIRM, Jacob thought, intrigued. He walked into the restaurant kitchen, grabbed a plate and loaded it himself, intending on sitting with her to watch her eat, and to see if he could make her squirm again because it was damned arousing.

She was arousing, with her wide, expressive eyes, her full lips that she kept licking nervously. Her voice. Her taste. The way she looked at him. As if he was some forbidden treat tempting her to the ends of her restraints.

He moved back into the dining area, which was filled with contented diners, and felt that same surge of fulfillment he got every single night. She was still sitting there, watching him approach with both wariness and something else, something he recognized well. Awareness.

Let the dance begin, he thought, and smiled as he sat. "Try this. Bouche S'mores. House-made marshmallow, fresh graham crackers and imported semisweet chocolate, all melted over an open flame."

"House-made marshmallow?"

"Yes." He met her gaze. "We get a lot of requests for marshmallows via room service, melted of course."

She stared down at the plate, a lovely flush working up her cheeks.

"People are very fond of melted marshmallow," he said. "Specifically, they're fond of licking them."

She gave a slow blink. "Oh. Um—"

"Off of each other," he clarified. "Not the plate."

She reached out to touch the stack of marshmallow. Felt the soft, warm, gooey texture. She cocked her head as if considering exactly how to lick it off another person and, just like that, the tables turned, and Jacob was the one squirming.

"Interesting," she said, throwing him further off balance. "Seems a bit fattening, but I'm sure it's worth it." She bit her lower lip, each of her thoughts chasing another across her face.

She was picturing it. With *him*.

He sank a fork into his fun creation and leaned across the table, touching the marshmallow to her lips. She opened her mouth, tongue darting out to catch a dollop.

Their gazes locked, and when she moaned in delight at the taste, he nearly moaned, too, at the look of rapture on her face.

"Delicious," she said when she'd swallowed. "But I have a feeling you already know it."

Ah. She was quiet but not shy, and that in itself was another unexpected turn-on. "Yes. I know it." When she laughed, he decided he liked the sweet, musical sound because it wasn't silly, it wasn't fake. It was real.

She was real, and damn if he didn't want to know more about her.

"I don't even know who you are," she murmured, clearly having some of the same thoughts. "And yet here we sit, discussing your marshmallows and their incredibly diverse uses here at the hotel."

A conversation he most definitely wanted to have, but… "You don't know who I am?"

She slid him a self-deprecatory smile. "Okay, so you're Chef Jacob Hill."

"Which leaves me at a disadvantage."

She smiled. "I doubt you're ever at a disadvantage."

He laughed and relaxed, realizing his instincts had been right. He was going to enjoy himself with her, immensely. "What's your name?"

"Emmaline Harris. Television producer."

"Emmaline," he repeated, liking the way her name rolled off his tongue. "Are you enjoying your stay here at Hush?"

She seemed surprised that he hadn't jumped on her profession. But they were nothing if not discreet here at Hush, where they hosted celebrities and movie stars all the time, and she guessed he wouldn't bring it up again unless she did.

"Yes, I'm enjoying myself," she said. "It's very lovely here."

Lovely. Not a word he'd have used to describe the more adventurous and eclectic services the hotel had to offer, which meant she was either being coy, or she hadn't experienced any of it. "Are you staying for business or pleasure?"

At the word pleasure, her tongue darted out again and nervously licked her lips. "Business."

"That's a shame."

She laughed, a little nervously now. "Yes."

It should have given him pause that he'd flustered her, but instead, it excited him. He was thinking of all the ways he could fluster her some more when she spoke again.

"I'm here to find the next new reality TV star."

Reality TV. The genre appealed to him about as much as a trip to the dentist. "Hmm."

"You don't like reality TV?" she asked.

"Actually, I'm not into any kind of TV," he admitted. "Not my thing."

"What about if you could be on it?" she asked. She was watching him carefully. "On your own show."

"Sounds like a nightmare."

"Oh." She looked at him for a long moment, assessing for God knew what. Speculating on the mysteries of the female mind was always a bit like tiptoeing through a minefield. "Tell me something," she said. "Do you kiss every strange woman you meet in the elevator?"

"Ah." He'd been waiting for her to broach the subject. "That."

"You must have known we'd have to talk about it."

He lifted a shoulder.

"What if I'd been married?" she asked. "Or attached?"

"Are you?"

"No."

"Then no harm, no foul."

"Is that a life motto for you?"

"Pretty much." He smiled.

She returned it, but he could still see the wheels spinning. Her eyes were clear on his, such a mossy, pretty green. The rest of her was pretty, too. Shoulder-length brown wavy hair with long choppy bangs that she kept shoving out of her eyes, a narrow strong face, with a most lovely mouth, as he had reason to know. She had good height on her—another bonus for him at six foot four—and plenty of curves, he was happy to note. He didn't approve of skinny.

"Why did you do it?" she asked, taking another bite of the s'mores, which meant that while she might be a tad shy, she went after what she wanted. He liked that. "Why did you kiss me?" she pressed.

"Because I wanted to."

She laughed, and took another bite. "Do you always do whatever you want?"

He thought about that. "Mostly."

"There was another reason you kissed me," she insisted.

"Okay, yes."

She waited, a brow raised.

"You see, I have these two extremely nosy, bossy, interfering people in my life," he admitted. "They're very annoying."

"Then why are they in your life?"

He sighed. "They're my friends."

That wrangled a laugh out of her. "Okay, I'll buy that. I have two of those myself."

"They think because I'm single that I need to be fixed. In their mind, that fixing requires a woman."

"So? You're a big boy. Say no."

He smiled. "Tell me something, Emmaline."

"Em," she said softly, staring at his mouth as if maybe she liked his smile.

He hoped so, because he liked hers, very much. "Em, then." Yeah, that suited her even better. Em was even softer, more feminine. It fit her to a tee. Which didn't explain why he wanted to sit here with her all night. "You ever successfully say no to the people in your life?"

"I'm a sucker when it comes to the people I care about."

Why the hell *that* attracted him, too, he had no idea. "Exactly."

She was still shaking her head. "You're no one's sucker, Jacob Hill."

"No, I'm not. But I still care about my friends."

Her eyes softened. "That's very sweet."

"Actually, I'm the furthest thing from sweet you've ever met."

Her gaze searched his for a long moment, while all around them the restaurant continued to buzz with life—talking, laughing, music. There were a few celebrities here tonight, as well: a big movie star, and also a national newscaster, both being left alone thanks to his discreet staff. There was also a rock star at the center table, *not* being left alone, but then he'd come here to be noticed and fawned over. The guy undoubtedly had his pick of the women here tonight.

Emmaline kept her gaze locked on Jacob's. "Something's not adding up."

"What?"

"Why would you need to be set up?" The moment the words left her mouth, she looked embarrassed. "It's just that you don't look like you'd need any help in that area."

"Thank you."

"Actually, I didn't mean it as a compliment."

He grinned. Yeah, he liked her. "My friend Pru, the sommelier who helped you pick out your wine, she thinks I need to experience a 'real' relationship. That's because hers have all been so important to her—she's convinced I'm missing out by not experiencing that."

Em shook her head. "See, now this should be in the friendship handbook. When you fall in love, you should be required to contain your happiness and not try to spread it around."

"No one's in love."

"Your friend…."

He was shaking his head.

"What was she doing in *her* 'real' relationship then?"

"Having lots of sex, I imagine."

Her brows vanished beneath her bangs. "So you both have something against love?"

"I didn't say I did."

"You didn't have to. It was in your tone."

He just eyed her while she smiled at him, seeming quite

amused at his expression. "So we've just discovered something you *don't* do," she said thoughtfully. "That's good, actually. I'm relieved to find out you're not perfect."

A shocked laugh escaped him. How long had it been since someone challenged him? Too long, if this was giving him a thrill. "I have a thing against the way people fling the love word around," he said, knowing this area was a deal breaker for most women, who wholeheartedly bought into the love myth, to the point that it tainted their every date.

Not him. There wasn't a single dab of naiveté or innocence left in him, and he hadn't believed in something as elusive and unattainable as the Easter Bunny or love since he was four years old. Truth was truth. Love was nothing but a big, fat pain in the ass. "I'll tell you one thing," he said.

"And what's that?"

"The night's too good to waste it philosophizing on some emotion that may or may not exist."

"True enough."

He had to get back to the kitchen. They both knew it, and yet Jacob wanted to stall longer, keep her talking. Or at least smiling at him like that.

But she pushed her now-empty plate away. "That was heavenly. Thank you so much."

When she stood, he did as well, taking her hand and bringing it up to his mouth. "Have a great night," he murmured, his lips against her skin.

She looked up into his eyes, hers a little dazed as she shook her head. "You're probably the only man I know who could pull off that ridiculously romantic gesture."

Lightly he scraped his teeth against her knuckles, taking the "romantic gesture" straight into raw sexual mode. He noted her sharp inhale. "Enjoy your stay," he said softly, and let her pull her hand free.

Still staring at him, she brought her hand up to her cheek, the movement oddly tender and vulnerable. But instead of feeling as if he had the upper hand as she turned and walked off into the hotel, he felt as if he needed to sit down.

Or touch her again.

EM TOOK THE ELEVATOR without incident. Meaning no gorgeous stranger stepped on, pulled her into his arms and kissed her senseless.

She told herself the vague disappointment in her gut was about the cooking program. He'd said the thought of being on his own show sounded like a nightmare.

God. What now? When the doors opened on the twelfth floor, she looked down the hall at her door, decided she wasn't ready to be alone and headed toward Liza's room instead. Hopefully Eric had gotten her tucked safely into bed and—

And Eric was sitting on the floor right outside Liza's room, head back against the door, looking miserable.

"Eric?" She crouched before him and took his hand in hers. "Honey, what's the matter?"

"Nothing." His smile didn't reach his eyes. "I tucked her in. She's out like a light. Did you know she snores?"

"Like a buzz saw. But what are you still doing here?"

"I…" Closing his eyes, he lightly thunked his head back against the door. "Nothing. Never mind." He rose to his feet. "'Night."

She caught his arm before he got away. "Eric."

He shoved his fingers through his hair, tousling the golden ends. "I brought her up here intending to…" Now he scrubbed a hand over his face. "I wanted to…"

"I know." She laid a hand on his arm. "But she was drunk. You did the right thing by walking away, no matter how much in love with her you still are."

Eric's gaze flew to hers. "I'm not…"

Em just looked at him.

"I'm really not…"

Em smiled gently and stroked her hand up his tense arm.

"*Shit,*" he said. "I am. Tell me she doesn't know."

"Are you kidding? Our Liza? She's pretty much only thinking about her own feelings at the moment."

"Yeah." He sighed. "She couldn't even get out of her clothes—she insisted I unzip her dress. Then the little fool tripped over it and I had to—" He groaned, walked down the hallway and stalked back. "I had to strip her down and shove her into that bed, and the whole time she was teasing me, asking me if I wanted to kiss her, touch her—"

"She was drunk," she reminded him softly. "She didn't mean to be a tease."

"Yes, she did."

"Okay, well, she didn't mean to be cruel about it."

"Which is the only reason I didn't—" He scrunched up his face. "*God.* She's going to be the death of me."

"Have you thought about telling her how you feel?"

"Oh, yeah." He laughed harshly. "That'd go over well. I'm the one who cried uncle and walked, remember? I can't tell her now. She'd just use it against me."

"I think you're wrong." She hugged him. "Look, if you can't handle this trip, I totally understand." She needed him, but his happiness meant a lot to her. "You can fly home and I'll—"

"I can handle this." He straightened with great resolve. "Trust me, I can handle this."

"If you're sure—"

"Very. Did you get the chef tonight?"

"Uh…not yet. Soon. Just get some sleep, okay?"

"Yeah. 'Night."

She went to her room and sighed at the glorious beach-themed decor that instantly instilled her with a sense of calm peace.

Or would have if tonight had gone off the way it should have.

She kicked off her shoes, her toes sinking inches into the opulent carpet. If she had to be stressed, at least this was a damn fine place to do it. After stripping, she took a long bath in her hot tub, and though she didn't mean to, she stared at the flickering candles and let her thoughts drift to Jacob Hill—to that first moment when he'd stepped onto that elevator and stolen her breath, to the way he kissed her, to how he'd looked at her after he'd done so.

Silly as it seemed, in that beat of time, she'd lost a little part of herself to him. And whether he admitted it or not, he'd lost a little piece of himself to her, too. She'd seen it in his eyes.

And it hadn't been just that. He'd gotten hard. She'd felt him when he'd pressed up against her, and remembering, alone in the tub, her body heated, tingled.

The carefully placed jets didn't help ease any of that but only heightened the arousal, leaving her aching and unfulfilled and…hungry for far more than a kiss, damn it.

She could imagine it, the two of them in bed. Given the way the man walked, talked and cooked with such utter confidence and effortless ease, she knew he would do things to her that would be out of this world.

"Ridiculous," she muttered, ruthlessly draining the tub before she could relive dessert, before she could picture how he'd looked at her as he'd fed her, how his eyes had flared when she'd licked her lips.

She was here to get him on the show! No more sex on the brain!

She had to figure out how to reach him, how to prove that her show would be different from whatever he was thinking it would be. Drying off, she climbed into the glorious bed, sliding against the silk sheets and thick comforter, her body still humming with lingering pleasure from the bath. It took a long time before sleep finally claimed her.

The next morning, after a night of Jacob-filled dreams, she sat up and laughed at herself. "No more," she said out loud. He was her job's salvation, which was far more important than a quick toss in the sack. Repeating it to herself like a mantra, she got dressed and called Liza.

"'Lo," came a very grumpy, sleepy voice.

"I need caffeine," Em said. "You with me?"

"I need someone to turn off the jackhammer inside my head," Liza groaned.

"Meet me downstairs. I have the next best thing."

"What's that, a lobotomy?"

"Aspirin."

"SO YOU DIDN'T TELL HIM you wanted him for the show." Liza shook her head at Em and downed the aspirin.

They sat in a corner of the lobby, watching the world go by on the other side of the hotel windows, where pedestrians and cars whipped busily past them with the rushed sense of urgency characteristic of Manhattan.

"I tried to bring it up," Em said. "But he wasn't interested."

But Nathan was plenty interested, as proved by the ring of her cell phone. After looking at the ID, Em rolled her eyes at Liza, and answered.

"Sign the chef yet?" he asked.

"Working on it." She wondered if not mentioning that she was close only in her dreams was playing the "Hollywood game" the way he wanted her to.

Whether Nathan caught on, or if he was just worried, he paused. Then said, "Remember, Em. Do whatever you have to do to get him. Hell, use your feminine wiles."

Em looked at Liza in disbelief as she shook her head. "You did not just say use my feminine wiles."

"Why not? By all accounts, he's not bad to look at. You're single. Sleeping with him wouldn't be a hardship."

No, sleeping with Jacob wouldn't be a hardship. Too bad she'd be doing it for reasons entirely separate from the show. "Goodbye, Nathan."

"You're thinking about it," he said.

She growled.

He laughed. "Seriously, stay tough. Remember the hair-in-the-food trick."

Em hung up on him. She sighed and looked at Liza. "Here's the problem."

"You mean besides Nathan being a complete ass?"

"Yeah. I don't think Jacob's all that interested in his career at all, other than he enjoys what he does."

"Wait a minute." Liza narrowed her eyes. "Since when are you on a first-name basis with the chef?"

"Since that's his name."

Liza let it go, which meant her head still hurt, because it was unlike her to let anything go. "Are you *sure* he's not interested?"

Interested in the show? Or Em herself? "He runs the show here. He likes that. I don't see him happily letting a show run him."

Liza carefully rubbed her temples, her beauty looking a little strained this morning. "This aspirin needs to hurry up and kick in. Look, Em, just put it out there on the table for him, see what happens."

"I know."

"Today."

"I will. Eric," she said in surprise when he walked by.

He stopped, then with his eyes locked on Liza, came up to them. "Hey."

"What's up?" Em asked. "Want to have a seat? We're coming up with my plan of attack for approaching Jacob."

"I know an approach," Liza said as Eric sat. "Offer to have a wild fling with him. He wouldn't turn you down. No man who finds a woman attractive would turn her down." After having carefully avoided looking at Eric, she purposely turned her head to him. "Right, Eric?"

He cleared his throat. "Maybe he'd have his reasons."

"What reason could possibly be more important than making that woman feel good?" Liza pressed. "Than helping her out in her time of need?"

He glared at her. "Look, I didn't turn you down to insult you."

Liza snorted.

"Okay." Em stood up. "I'm going to leave you two alone—"

"Don't go," Liza said, snagging Em's wrist without taking her eyes off Eric.

"All I'm saying is that there *are* reasons," Eric said to Liza.

"Name one."

Em tried to pull free.

"I said don't go!" Liza snapped.

"Okay, that's it." Em gently but firmly extricated herself. "You two need to work this out, preferably by yourselves, without killing each other. Personally, I think you should work it out upstairs, maybe even in bed…."

Eric made some sort of strangled sound.

Liza just lifted a shoulder. "Can't. Eric has an aversion to getting in my bed these days."

Em put a hand on her friend's tense shoulder. "Stop torturing him."

"Tell him the same thing."

Eric shook his head.

Em kissed his cheek, then Liza's. "Be kind," she whispered to Liza, and walked off.

Caffeine, she decided. Now. A few other people were moving around, sitting on the black sofas talking, taking in the incredible artwork on display. She stopped in front of a large painting near the elevators, done in the bold strokes and colors of an early art deco piece. It was of a woman, nude, her hands outstretched, a look of ecstasy on her face as a man and another woman, also nude, attended to her. From their positions, one could assume the man took pleasure at a breast, the woman between her legs.

It should have been lewd, should have made the heat rise to Em's face, but instead she couldn't tear her eyes off the thing, not off the bright colors, or the boldly painted, beautiful bodies. In fact, she found herself just standing there, surrounded by the tranquility around her, absorbing it, breathing it in, trying to find her own center, her own sense of self, which was all tied into her job, into getting Chef Jacob Hill. She had to do this. "*I have to do this.*"

"Really?" It was the same low, husky voice as last night.

Jacob had come up to her side to look at the picture, too. "Which woman did you want to be?"

Just his proximity made everything within her react, tighten in anticipation, leap to attention. A little shocked at the effect he had on her, she turned her head and looked into his caramel eyes.

Yum, thought her body.

Watch out, thought her remaining working brain cells, and there weren't many.

He looked great, more than great, more like gorgeous in his work trousers, wool and gray and fitted to that long hard body, and a black dress shirt. His short, short hair seemed glossy beneath the lights. The scent of him alone should have been bottled and marketed as an aphrodisiac.

He arched a brow, waiting for an answer to his question, amusement swimming in his gaze. That look released something inside her.

She thought maybe it was the last of her resistance. "I didn't mean..." Damn it, she felt herself blush as she gestured to the painting. "I didn't mean I have to do *that*."

"No?" Tipping his head back, he looked at the two women in the picture again. "Now that's just a damn shame."

CHAPTER FIVE

To: Pastry Chef Ed Mohr
From: Sous-Chef Jacob Hill
Tonight send a basket with fresh makings for Bouche
S'mores to room 1212, with my compliments.

JACOB WATCHED EM SHIFT her weight from foot to foot as she glanced again at the bold art deco painting of the threesome. It made him want to smile. God, he loved to ruffle her feathers.

"I really was talking about something else," she said.

"Like I said, it's really too bad."

Embarrassed or not, she met his gaze straight on. "So it's true. Men really do fantasize about two women in their bed."

"Doesn't have to be in bed." She rolled her eyes, and he laughed. "You asked."

"I thought it was a myth. That men couldn't really be so…so base."

"'Fraid not, and that we are."

She cocked her head and studied him thoughtfully. "What's the draw? Two women? Seems like a lot of work."

"You mean 'cause there are two of every body part, and in some cases, four? Not work." He grinned.

"Women don't fantasize about two men."

"Never?"

She squirmed just a little, went a touch red, and he knew she was torn between lying or admitting a truth she preferred not to.

A minute ago he'd turned in the staff schedules for the week, and had planned on spending the next few hours on his own before he had to get started in the kitchen, but he'd seen her standing here and had been drawn to her like a metal rod to a magnet.

What was it about her? He wished he knew. He'd always been attracted to beautiful women, the more outspoken and unabashedly sexual the better. Em was beautiful, no doubt, but neither outspoken nor unabashedly sexual, and yet she fascinated him. She stood there in a long floral skirt and cream angora sweater with a row of tiny buttons down the front, looking very together despite her blush and wry smile. She'd made an attempt at taming her hair, which amused him. The sides were pulled up in clips, but her long bangs had escaped, framing her jaw on either side. She wore gloss on her lips, something peachy, and he was hungry for it, for her.

Then there was the way she was looking at him, with a repressed yearning that stopped his jaded heart. Damn, her eyes were intoxicating, and suddenly, or maybe not so suddenly at all, he wanted to know what made her tick, what her bare skin felt like, what it tasted like, every inch of it. He wanted to see her lost in him, coming for him, wanted to feel her wrapped around him, panting his name.

No, make that *screaming* his name.

Em turned back to the erotically charged painting, but he put his hands on her arms and pulled her around to face him. Her eyes were a little dilated now, the pulse at the base of her throat racing. She was every bit as turned-on as he was, which made his condition worse. "Let's go."

"What? Where?"

He looked into her wary, but undoubtedly excited, eyes. "You up for an adventure, Emmaline Harris?"

"An adventure? I don't know…"

"Say yes."

She stared at him for a long moment. "Yes," she said softly, then hemmed when he led her to the front doors of the hotel. "Where are we going?"

"It's an amazing day out there, have you seen it?"

"I haven't been out yet."

"Can't stay inside all day. Not on a day like today." Jacob nodded to the doorman. It was Jon, who grinned and gave Jacob the thumbs-up sign behind Em's back.

As they stepped through the doors, a gust of wind wrapped around them in a chilly caress, and Jacob took a moment to admire how it molded Em's clothes to her belly, hips, legs and breasts, which were not big but not small, either, just right.

Unaware of his perusal of her body, Em tugged a rioting strand of hair out of her mouth. "Jacob, there's something I really wanted to talk to you about first. My work—"

"No work. Not yet. Look at that sky." It was a brilliant, shimmering blue, and when Em tipped her head up, it brought a slow, beautiful smile to her face.

He stroked another wayward strand of hair from her cheek just for the excuse of touching her. "Come on. It's too perfect a day to waste." Taking her hand in his, he began walking.

Keeping up with him, she said, "Do you ever ask?"

"What?"

She shook her head. "I don't think you do. You just do whatever you want."

"Is that a problem?"

"I just can't believe women let you get away with it. Why would they? Wait, don't answer that." She looked baffled and just a little off her axis at the same time. "You are a very spoiled man, Jacob Hill."

"Spoiled?"

At that, she actually laughed at him at that, a sound he thoroughly enjoyed.

"I'm sorry," he said.

"You are not."

That tugged a grin out of him. "How about some coffee?" He spread his hands. "Hear that? I'm asking."

"You're teasing me is what you're doing. But yes. Coffee would be great."

He loved that, quiet or not, she spoke her mind. No pretense. No games.

Traffic was a bitch this morning, nothing new, so he steered her through a throng of pedestrians, easily weaving her across the street between bikes and cabs and honking cars.

"Oh, my God," Em grumbled beneath her breath when a car came close. *"Crazy."*

"It's New York."

"In L.A.," she gasped breathlessly, as she kept up, "cars actually stop for people."

"Here, cars use pedestrians for parking spaces." He grabbed her arm and tugged her to him when a cab nearly did just that with her toes. "Stick close."

"Yikes," she muttered, but stayed against him. Now the strands of her hair stroked his face, the scent delicious enough that he wanted to breathe her in. As her long legs moved in tandem with his, he enjoyed the feel of her thigh brushing against his every step they took. Her breast was pressed up against his ribs and he wanted to turn her to face him, to savor the full experience, but when traffic slowed, she pulled away.

Where was a speeding cab when he needed one?

They walked through the gorgeous Bryant Park, an oasis in the midst of chaos, and were only one block from their destination when a bicyclist came out of nowhere, barreling down the middle of the sidewalk, without any apparent concern that they were in his way.

Perfect. Jacob turned toward Em, put his hands on her waist and pushed her back against the wall of the building at their right.

The bicyclist sped past, swearing at them for good measure.

Em lifted her head, blew a strand of hair out of her mouth and blinked at him. "That man should get a ticket."

"Not likely, not here." He touched her chilly cheek, letting his finger linger on her soft skin. "Em."

Her eyes flickered with something far more than irritation at the cyclist as she licked her lips and slowly raised her gaze to his. The pulse at the base of her neck beat like a poor overworked hummingbird's wings.

"I'm not going to ask if you mind this time," he said softly.

Understanding lit her gaze as he lowered his mouth toward hers. In spite of his words, he gave her the chance to stop him. Even a slight pressure from the hands she'd set on his chest would have done it. Instead she did the opposite, slowly curling her fingers into his shirt.

He smiled then, and as he kissed her, he thought, *That's the first time I've wanted to smile and kiss a woman at the same time.*

LOGICALLY EM KNEW this was a mistake but once Jacob's mouth touched hers, logic flew right out the window, and her body cut off all circulation to her brain cells, including the one that was supposed to say, "Don't even think about it!"

With a low, rough murmur deep in his throat, his hands came up and framed her face, sliding into her hair to palm her head, changing the angle of the kiss, deepening it.

Oh. My. God.

Helpless against the onslaught of pure lust, Em did as any woman who'd already tasted heaven and wanted to savor it some more would have done—she pulled him even closer and held on for all she was worth. But it was more than just his kiss, his touch. He aroused her physically, no doubt, and yet her need for him came from her heart, too.

If she could think, she'd have been terrified. But she couldn't think, couldn't do anything other than feel.

When his tongue slid to find hers, she heard a throaty, desperate sort of growl and realized it came from her.

Oh, boy. She was a goner.

It wasn't her fault, though. The man was the best kisser she'd ever been with. The best kisser on the planet. She shouldn't have been surprised. He was a walking dream.

And she didn't want to wake up.

So she tuned out the sounds of the streets around them—the talking, the footsteps, the honking of impatient drivers—and did what she knew she didn't do enough: let the experience wash over her. And it did wash over her, everything, his scent, deliciously male, the feel of his long, hard-muscled body pressed to hers, her soft thighs spread by one of his, and his hands…the way they slowly, knowingly glided up and down her arms, then up her throat to hold her face. It all simply undid her.

Finally, when he'd thoroughly ravished her with the kiss, he raised his mouth a fraction and opened his eyes, filled with a searing heat and desire and that ever-present wry amusement.

"What could possibly be funny?" she demanded, her knees still shaking.

"It's just that you kiss like you think."

She blinked. "I *what?*"

Again, that fleeting smile, the one that flashed his dimple and crinkled his drown-in-me eyes. "You, Emmaline Harris, are a series of contradictions. You dress like a businesswoman, for instance."

"I *am* a businesswoman."

"But you have a very carefree, come-what-may streak. It's sexy as hell, you know." He ran his thumb, rough with work calluses, over her lower lip, which was still wet from his mouth. She had to stifle the urge to suck the pad of it into her mouth.

What was happening to her? She'd always managed to go for stretches of time without thinking about sex. Or having sex. She'd slept with her last boyfriend—what had it been?—only four months or so ago. Not so long. Surely not long enough for this overwhelming longing, this heart-breaking ache to be sweeping through her body at the mere touch of his mouth or thumb.

"I see," she said, but she didn't. She had no idea where he was going with this, or where she wanted him to go with this, and yet when he spread his fingers over her jaw, she turned her face into his palm, pressing her lips there.

"I'm not sure what it is about you," he murmured, his voice a little husky now. "You talk like a schoolteacher. A little uptight, a little reserved."

Uptight? Reserved? She lifted her face away from his touch to look at him.

He smiled. "And yet you think things, things that have your eyes smoldering, things that bring heat to your face. Things that make me hot, Em."

She stared at him, no longer sure what she was feeling,

though it caused her tummy to quiver and an embarrassing dampness to gather between her thighs.

"A contradiction," he whispered in that Southern honey of a voice that, along with his knowing smile, made her think of Matthew McConaughey in *How to Lose a Guy in 10 Days*. "Still up for caffeine?"

"Please."

He took her hand. As they began walking again, his long-legged easy stride eating up the sidewalk, she risked a quick sideways glance at him. *What was she doing?* She needed to get across the fact that she wanted him to host her TV show, and yet all she'd done so far was stare at him dreamily.

And kiss him. *Let's not forget that. Sheesh. Good going.*

"Here we are," he said, and stopped in front of a small hole-in-the-wall Irish pub called Patrick's.

Em stared at the Celtic sign swinging from the eaves. "But…it's ten in the morning."

"Yep." He opened the door for her.

She stepped inside, and was surprised. Even at this hour, the pub was filled, and with the mahogany bar and raw-wood floors and ceiling, the place felt warm and welcoming, exuding a natural charm. The conversation that greeted them was a good-natured mixture of gossip, wit and discussion. She could imagine sitting here comfortably with a drink, and when she looked at Jacob, could also imagine him perfectly at home in the middle of a brawl right there on the floor.

As if he'd read her mind, he grinned. "I've been known to escape here now and then."

"Isn't there a bar right in the hotel? Erotique, right?"

"Yes, but I feel more at home here." He pulled her up to the bar.

A woman came out of the back, sixtyish, with hair the color of a bright red crayon piled high on top of her head. She wore jeans and a T-shirt, with an apron that read, If Your Order Hasn't Arrived Yet, It's Probably Not Coming.

"Jacob, my love," she said with a heavy Irish accent and a surprised wide smile. "You came to cook up me day's special again!"

"That was for your birthday, Maddie."

"Damn." She sighed mightily. "I had a real hankering for one of your omelets…" Only someone with great love for someone else could lay on the guilt so thick.

Jacob looked at Em. "Em, meet Maddie. She owns this place and runs it with an iron fist, so watch out."

Maddie tossed back her head and laughed. "I'll iron fist you, boy. And don't think I can't." She hugged him hard, her head barely coming up to his chest. Then she pulled back and smacked his chest. "Now how about that special?"

Arm still around Maddie, Jacob looked at Em.

"I don't mind," she said, curious at the obvious great affection between the two of them.

"See, the girl doesn't mind." Maddie smiled innocently. "And then there's the added bonus of letting her see your soft side." She laughed again, and so did Jacob, as if they both found the possibility of Jacob having a soft side extremely funny.

"Come on, then," Jacob murmured to Em, leading her behind the bar, to the back. "Since you've let her get her way, there'll be no living with her."

Making himself right at home in the postage-stamp-size kitchen that had to be poorly equipped compared to what he was used to, he grabbed a pan and set it on the stovetop. Then he opened the refrigerator and said, "Heads up."

Em barely caught the red pepper he tossed her, and then the green one. And an onion— *"Hey."*

He straightened, his hands full with a carton of eggs and a hunk of cheese. Before her eyes, he chopped and diced and mixed it all up, hands moving quickly and efficiently, like a well-honed machine. God, was there anything sexier than watching a man in the kitchen? He caught her looking, and flashed her a dimple and a wink as he tossed the ingredients into the sizzling pan. And in less than two minutes, he was flipping an omelet in the air and then back into the pan.

Em couldn't tear her eyes off him. He wasn't just regular sexy, but beg-him-to-take-her sexy.

Maddie came into the kitchen in time for Jacob to hand her a loaded plate. Her carrottop hair wobbled as she leaned over the plate and took a bite, then grinned broadly. "Jacob, me boy, you've outdone yourself. I don't suppose you're going to do the dishes?"

Jacob laughed and led Em back to the front to her bar stool.

Maddie followed them out, still chewing. "Well, hell. I suppose I have to serve you now."

"We'll have two coffees," Jacob said. "Unless I need to brew that, too?"

"Smart-ass." Maddie moved back into the kitchen.

Jacob looked over at Em, his eyes full of laughter and mischief and memories of their kisses, maybe? Just thinking about them made the heat rush to her face, and to other parts of her body. "Jacob."

"Em," he said with mock obedience.

"I, uh, might have given you the wrong idea back there."

"Back there…"

"Outside."

He just looked at her.

Damn it. "When we kissed."

"Ah." He nodded seriously. "And what idea would that have been?"

"That I intend to sleep with you."

He arched a brow. "And you don't."

"No. I'm sorry." *No matter that you've made me so hot my skin is steaming.* "I don't."

Maddie came back with two mugs of coffee. Jacob didn't say anything while Em doctored hers up with sugar, lots of it, and cream. Not sure what to say, or how to get back to broaching the subject of her TV show, Em looked around her. The place had mismatched chairs and flooring that had probably been there for fifty years, yet was scrubbed to a shiny clean, as were all the surfaces. The crowd was much older than Hush's, and most were eating, not drinking. Two men past retirement age were playing cards in the corner. Others hunched at the counter over their mugs, some talking, some not. All the while Maddie ran the show with her boisterous voice and easy laughter. It was curious to Em that Jacob came here.

"Taste your coffee," he said with that uncanny way he had of reading her mind. "It'll make better sense to you."

She looked into Jacob's eyes, which matched the color of her coffee, thinking it'd be nice if he would read the rest of her mind, at least regarding the hosting gig. She took a sip of her drink, and the brew melted a delicious path all the way to her belly. "Oh. *Perfect.*"

"Yeah." He smiled.

"No, I mean it. This is almost better than your food."

"Careful."

She laughed. "You been coming here a long time?"

"Oh, yeah." He looked at Maddie. "A long time."

It occurred to her how much she wanted to know him.

Not the chef, but Jacob Hill, the man. "Tell me," she said quietly.

"The first time I showed up here, it was raining. Pouring, actually. It seemed like the skies had just opened up. I was cold and wet and hungry and, quite frankly, lost." His mouth twisted wryly. "At night, that hanging sign out front flashes like a beacon. Maddie harassed and badgered me, but she finally let me in."

"Why wouldn't she have?"

"I was fourteen."

Em gasped. "Fourteen? What was a fourteen-year-old doing alone on the streets of New York?"

"Ah." He sipped his coffee.

"Ah? What does that mean?"

"You probably had a curfew at fourteen."

"Well, of course I had a curfew at fourteen."

"And a bunch of rules."

"Yes."

"And you followed them."

"Well, not *always*." But mostly. Her parents had been wonderfully warm and loving, and yet even she had done her share of chafing at the teenage bit.

"Which means what?" he said. "That maybe you didn't always do your homework, or once you stayed out an extra five minutes?"

"I was basically a good kid," she admitted. "Big surprise, huh?" Their worlds couldn't have been more different, and yet those differences fascinated her. "Kids need boundaries. Where were your parents?"

"Never really had any."

Em couldn't even imagine, and her heart squeezed.

"Typical story," he said. "Young girl grows up in a trailer park outside of Nashville, dreams of getting out, gets herself knocked up by the first sweet-talker, who then vanishes at the special news. The unwanted baby grows up to be a kid who looks just like his daddy and the girl can't handle it."

He spoke easily enough, but Em's throat tightened at all he didn't say about those young, impressionable years when he'd thought of himself as the "unwanted baby." "What did you do?"

"Oh, I had a thing for cooking, even back then, and a wanderlust spirit that made the whole thing an adventure. I left when I was ten. Never went back."

"Ten. My God, you were just a kid," she breathed, unable to even fathom it. "On your own like that…no one should be alone that young." She could hear the angry tears in her voice. "You should have been taken in by—"

"Social services? Hell, no." He let out a harsh laugh. "Happened once. It didn't work so well for me." Reaching out, he ran a finger over her temple, pushing her bangs from her eyes. "You have such beautiful hair."

She caught his hand. "We were talking about you."

"Then get that pity out of your pretty eyes. So I was young, it's no big deal."

"I'm not feeling pity," she said around the ball of emotion still lodged in her throat. "It's empathy. Anger for that kid you once were. How did you survive?"

"By cooking for traveling fairs across the South. I was pretty good. I did all right."

Having tasted his talents firsthand, she nodded. "Yes, you're extremely talented in the kitchen."

He shot her a wicked look. "Actually, I'm extremely talented in a number of areas."

Her stomach did a flip. "Finish your story." She'd intended a dry tone, but sounded more like Marilyn Monroe on a particularly hot summer day.

He touched her nose, looking amused. He knew what

he did to her, and he liked it. "From the fairs, I progressed to hole-in-the-wall diners. Then I caught a train and ended up here in New York for a while. It's where I met Maddie. Her uncle took me in for a year—he worked at a culinary school uptown. I learned a bunch there but didn't have much loyalty in me then. I didn't stay."

"Where did you go?"

"Everywhere. I'd worked my way up to restaurants by that time." Shoving up the long sleeves of his black shirt, revealing corded forearms that made her mouth water, he picked up a set of knife, fork and spoon, and began to juggle them.

She just stared at him. She would have been no more surprised if he'd grown a set of horns.

"I was a real hit at the Japanese places, where they toss the ingredients and knives for the customers." Much to her disbelief, he added a plastic jam packet to the juggling items, leaning back a bit, craning his head up to keep everything in sight.

Maddie whooped her encouragement. The two old men in the corner stopped playing cards to watch.

All the other customers did the same.

Jacob grinned, then added yet another knife, a sharp one this time, his finely tuned body working effortlessly.

Em put a hand to her pounding heart.

"Don't worry," Jacob said. "I hardly ever miss and lose a finger."

Maddie wrapped her hands around her mouth. "Show-off," she yelled.

Jacob just kept up the amazing feat, his arms and hands moving so fast they were a whirl, his eyes carefully trained on the task as he continued his story. "Now I'm in the posh Amuse Bouche, happy to be there, of course, but…" With a grin, he leaned forward and planted a quick, hard kiss on Em's lips, all without dropping a single thing.

She could only stare at him.

He merely winked. "But I'm not nearly as sophisticated as people think."

Mouth dry, body not, Em could believe it.

CHAPTER SIX

JACOB WALKED EM BACK to the hotel, and though he realized she couldn't possibly know it, they walked right past his own building, where he kept an apartment.

He'd have loved to take her up there, show her his place. And his bed.

And his shower.

And his table.

And anywhere else where he could stretch out her willowy, warm body and take her.

This yearning for a beautiful woman wasn't new to him. But despite the long, hot, deeply sensual kisses they'd shared, and all they'd implied, she'd held herself back, leaving him aching for more.

And that *was* new.

When was the last time he'd had to work at getting a woman naked and mewling his name? He couldn't even remember. He just hoped she was worth the wait.

They were just outside the hotel when the phone at his hip vibrated, signaling an incoming text message from Pru.

Ended up going out last night, met the perfect woman for you. She's "the one," I swear it this time.

Delete.

JON OPENED THE DOORS for them with a professional, friendly smile for Em and another wink for Jacob.

They stepped into the stunning lobby and Em sighed. "It's so lovely in here. Warm and quiet, yet…exciting."

Jacob liked the exciting part, and might have pursued the comment but his cell phone vibrated to life again.

Stop deleting me. Pru.

With great satisfaction, he hit Delete again.

"Problem?" Em asked.

"Remember the two women from the elevator yesterday?"

"Your friends?"

"Soon to be ex-friends? One of them is at it again."

"Tell her you're otherwise occupied."

"Am I?"

That put an extremely kissable look on her face but before he could lean in, his phone went off yet again. "Excuse me," he said grimly, and, ignoring the incoming message, entered one of his own.

Pru, goddamn it, tell Caya how you feel about her instead of bugging the shit out of me. In fact, you tell her, or I will.

There. That ought to do it. He waited a moment, but his phone remained still and blessedly silent. With satisfaction, he shoved it deep into his pocket. "Where were we?"

"Well…"

"Ah, I remember. You were going to tell me if I'm otherwise occupied."

She stared at him, with those mossy-green eyes. "You're teasing me."

"Yeah." Even though it was time for him to be getting into the kitchen to begin preparing, he walked her through the lobby toward the elevators, where he pushed the button for the twelfth floor.

"I can get myself back to my room," she said, clasping her hands together. "Really. But thanks."

He eyed her with amusement. "Are you afraid to get on the elevator with me, Em?"

She tilted her chin up. Her bangs were stabbing into her eyes, and she'd long ago nibbled off any lip gloss. A shame because he'd have liked to have nibbled it off himself.

"Don't be silly," she said.

When he just looked at her, she caved. "Not afraid. Let's call it…off balance, and you don't have to look so pleased," she said, putting a finger to his chest. "Or smug."

He couldn't stop his smile from spreading, which in turn had her letting out a rough laugh herself. "It's just that I'm not used to the way you leave me deaf, dumb and blind every time you kiss me, if you must know."

The doors opened and he gently nudged her inside, following close behind.

She eyed him with an arousing mix of wariness and excitement. The doors closed and he stepped toward her, closing in on her space.

She backed up.

His phone vibrated at his hip. He didn't even glance at it. Another step had her against the mirror.

She looked down her nose at him. "Intimidation?"

"Nope." He had no idea who was really seducing whom when he hauled her up on her toes and kissed her softly. "Just helping you get used to me leaving you deaf, dumb and blind." And then he kissed her again.

Not so softly.

THE MOMENT HIS MOUTH touched hers, Em knew she was in trouble. She'd begun to know him now. She admired what he'd done with his life, and she liked the man he'd become. Those things, combined with the sensual hold he had on her—figuratively as well as literally—made him damn irresistible, as evidenced by her low sigh of acquiescence.

At the sound, Jacob slid his hands into her hair to hold her head as he plundered. He'd been right, it was another deafening, muting, blinding kiss, but she wasn't going down easily. She tore her mouth free and gasped, "I don't think—"

"Perfect. Stick with that." He came at her again, cutting off any other words she might have come up with, weak excuses for why they shouldn't, why they couldn't, and she might have managed an excuse or two if she hadn't been drowning in pure, unadulterated lust.

This was a taking kiss, an I'm-the-man sort of kiss that might have pissed her off if it had been anyone other than Jacob Hill. She was so aroused she could hardly stand. No matter, he had her pressed back against the wall, holding her up with his delicious, hard body, and if that hadn't been enough, he had his tongue deep in her mouth with a hungry, urgent stroke that took her breath away.

When air was required by them both, he lifted his head and stared at her. The elevator rolled to a stop, and, without breaking eye contact, he reached out and slapped a hand over the close-door button.

His eyes beamed with intent. "Where were we?"

Oh, my. "Um…"

"Never mind. I've got it." And still holding the button down, he again lowered his head.

With the cold, hard mirrors at her back and the warm,

hard man at her front, she hesitated for one beat of her poor, overexcited heart, and then sank into the kiss.

He murmured his pleasure, deepening the kiss. She met him halfway, sinking her fingers into the defined muscle of his shoulders and holding on for dear life.

"God, you taste sweet," he murmured, shifting his mouth to nibble at the corner of hers, then her jaw, making his way to her ear, while his free hand stroked languidly up and down her back, squeezing her hip, then lower, palming her bottom.

When his fingers danced down and touched bare skin, she jumped, realizing he'd skimmed the hem of her skirt up so that he could caress the backs of her thighs.

And then between them.

"So sweet," he murmured again, spreading hot, open-mouthed kisses down her throat, nudging her sweater aside as he traced her collarbone with his tongue.

Panting, her head thunked back against the mirror, determination and all thoughts of her show gone. "Jacob."

"Yeah, right here." With his hands occupied, one still on the close-door button, the other beneath her skirt, he couldn't open her sweater, so he merely worked his way around that by sucking it into his mouth along with her breast.

She felt his tongue, hot and wet through the thin layer, and gasped. Then gasped again when he gently sank his teeth into her. And yet again when he pressed a finger against her, slowly tracing the edge of her panties.

Oh, God, she thought in a sudden panic, *am I wearing granny panties? Do I even care?* It shocked her how much she wanted to let go, how much she wanted to slap her own hand over the close-door button to free up his, so that he could put *both* hands on her body and take her, take her now, here, in an elevator, a semipublic place, where they could be seen, where maybe there were even cameras...

"Stop."

He went still, then slowly lifted his head, blinking those sleepy, sexy-lidded eyes at her.

"We can't," she said. "Not here."

He blew out a careful breath, looking hot, and just a little bothered.

"There are probably cameras..." Feeling silly, she trailed off. After stepping clear, she smoothed down her clothes, staring ridiculously primly at the closed doors, which slowly began to open. She exited quickly, then whirled back to face him, only he'd followed her off and she plowed right into him. "It's just that I never got to tell you. And you..."

"What?" he asked, his hands coming up to her arms.

God, it would sound so wrong now. She'd waited too long. Whirling again, she headed toward her room, fumbling through her purse to find her room card. He took it from her fingers and opened her door, waiting for her to go inside before following her.

The beachy elegance of the room cut through some of her tension, which came back full force when she caught sight of her reflection in the wide seashell mirror over the dresser.

Her hair, wavy on the best of days, had rioted, curling around her flushed face. Her eyes seemed huge and misty, dreamy, and her lips—still wet from his kiss—were full and puffy. Her sweater had a wet spot over one breast, and her nipples pressed against the material. She looked as though she'd just been thoroughly ravaged, which of course she had.

Jacob came up behind her and ran his hands up her arms. "Look at you."

She was looking. She couldn't look away. She blinked, but the same image presented back to her: one Emmaline Harris, rumpled and tousled, and smiling. No, that wasn't right. No smiling. Not until she told him. She swiped the ridiculous grin from her face. "Jacob."

"Uh-huh." His mouth was skimming her neck again, and the reflection of his dark head bent to her, eyes closed. Those long dark lashes against his cheeks, his tongue touching her flesh, made her shiver.

"Jacob," she said again, stronger this time, and turned to face him.

But Jacob Hill in the flesh was even more compelling than his mirror image had been. His eyes were very hot, and his mouth curved in a little knowing smile that said *I can make you come in less than three minutes.*

Given how close to that orgasm she actually felt, he could probably do it in three *seconds.* She took a big gulp of air.

His eyes cut to her bed, freshly made by housekeeping, with what appeared to be a small basket in the middle of the mattress.

With compliments from Sous-Chef Hill the note read, and she looked at him. "You sent this to me?"

"It's the makings for s'mores. You'll love them."

She had to laugh. "Do you ever doubt yourself?"

He frowned, thinking. "Sure."

"When?"

"Well…" He strode closer, tracing a finger along her hairline. "Now, for instance. Because somehow I know you aren't going to invite me onto that mattress with you."

"No." Her voice was far weaker than she would have liked. "No," she repeated. "I'm not. Jacob…" God, this was harder now that she'd touched him, kissed him. Now that she knew him. So much harder. "I've told you I'm a TV producer."

"Yes."

"What you don't know is that I have one month to get my show off the ground or I'm fired."

"Some reality show, right?"

"Yes." She'd never wanted to say anything less than what she had to say now. "A cooking show."

A little furrow appeared between his eyes as he digested her words. "As in a chef in front of a camera whipping up cookies kind of cooking show?"

"I was thinking something a little more interesting than that." Nerves fluttered in her belly. She'd wanted to recruit him, but now she just wanted him.

"Like what exactly?" His voice had cooled, the drawl thickened. He was irritated, with good reason.

"Well…"

"Should I guess, Em?" His eyes grew icy, too. "You heard about Amuse Bouche, and the success we've had."

"Actually, I heard about you."

"And you thought I'd, what? Drop everything and come running to Hollywood to smile for a camera on some cable show? Did you really?"

"It's a prime-time show, on a major network." She offered him a weak smile, which faded when he just looked at her. "I'm doing this all wrong," she said quickly. "I meant to woo you, to make it sound really appealing and interesting, which it should be. It's TV, Jacob. A show of your own. Your input would be welcome, of course, and—"

"My input would be welcome," he repeated slowly, then shook his head. "Let me get this straight. You want me to go to Hollywood and cook in front of a camera like…like a caged animal."

She didn't know how to respond to that.

"Jesus," he breathed, backing up a step, shaking his head. "You're serious. You're completely serious."

"Jacob—"

"Wow." He prided himself on his street smarts, on his worldliness, on the fact that he was sharp enough never to be taken. But this sweet, beautiful woman had walked right through his defenses with one kiss.

He was saved from having to admit that by a knock on the room door.

"Em?" came a female voice. "Open up."

Em jumped, then whipped around and stared at herself in the mirror. "Oh, boy." She stroked a hand down her sweater and shot Jacob an indecipherable look. "That's Liza, my assistant, and also close friend." She looked good and flustered, and distractedly shoved at her bangs.

Jacob felt his body stir just looking at her, and had to back up another step. No. She'd pissed him off, so no more thinking about her that way.

"I know this is crazy," she whispered, putting her hands on his chest. "But please, give me a chance to explain everything to you."

No need. That first kiss in the elevator had been his own doing, an amusing coincidence he could see now, fate playing a joke on the both of them. But she'd had plenty of opportunities between then and now to explain her business here. That *he*, in fact, was her business here.

But she hadn't.

The thing was, he didn't blame her. He knew desperation, and he recognized it well, so the thing to do here, the only thing to do here, was cut his losses and get over it, and over her.

Liza knocked again, louder now. "Emmaline!"

"Give me a minute," Em called to the door.

"Why?" Liza demanded. "Are you having wild monkey sex in there with the hot stud-muffin chef?"

Jacob choked back a laugh.

Unbelievably, Em glared at him, as if this was *his* fault, and scrubbed a hand down her face.

"Em, come on, I'm standing out here in my slut outfit," Liza said urgently through the door. "I tried it on and I want you to see if it's good enough to drive Eric out of his mind with crazed jealousy. I'm going to drag him to Exhibit A tonight, the basement bar where there's nude dancing. People supposedly do it in the booths, can you believe it? Now I need you to take a look at me and make sure I'm not too over the top, so open up."

"Oh, my God—" Looking as if she'd hit the boiling point, Em broke off, moved to the door and hauled it open.

Liza stood there in a canary-yellow micromini, cut nearly up to her crotch. A matching crop top, do-me lipstick and go-go boots designed to stop brain cells in their tracks completed the look.

"Oh, my God," Em repeated, looking her friend and assistant up and down. "Did you look in the mirror after you put that horror on?"

Liza opened her mouth, but then at the sight of Em looking the way she did—as if she'd just had that "wild monkey sex" Liza had mentioned—she shut her mouth again. "I don't think the subject here should be my outfit," Liza finally said.

"It's not what you think," Em said.

"Really?" Liza moved into the room, nodded to Jacob and then looked back at Em. "Because what I'm thinking is that you just got thoroughly laid. So does this mean you're in?" she asked Jacob.

"In?"

"Are you going to do the show and save Em's ass, cute as it may be?"

Jacob looked at Em.

Em sighed. "We were in the early talks."

"Yes, well, talks are officially over." Jacob moved toward the door, where he made the mistake of brushing past Em. He stopped.

She tipped her head up and stared at him with regret and embarrassment, and lingering arousal. Lifting a finger, he stroked it over her jaw—God, he loved her skin. "'Bye, Em."

"Jacob—"

Nope. Never look back. A mantra he was particularly fond of. With a shake of his head, he walked out of her room, shutting the door behind him.

"Tell me everything," he heard Liza say.

"You'd better sit down," Em replied, which threw Jacob off his stride just a little.

She'd gotten to him. No doubt, she'd gotten to him.

CHAPTER SEVEN

To: Sous-Chef Jacob Hill
From: Concierge
Maddie from Patrick's just delivered a pot of coffee
here for you, on request of the guest in room 1212.
Odd, since as you know, we have our own excellent
blend right here at Hush. Call when you come in.
We'll deliver it to you.

JACOB STOOD IN THE LOBBY, in front of the concierge desk, holding the memo that had been taped to his locker.

"I'd have brought the coffee to you," Deidre said. One of four Hush concierges, Deidre was his personal favorite. Not only could she get any answer anyone ever needed, but with her bright pink hair, multiple piercings and pixie face, she looked damn good while doing it.

The two of them had dated once.

Correction. They'd slept together once.

At the time, Deidre had felt the same way as Jacob, more than one night constituted something far too close to a relationship, and they'd happily gone their separate ways.

Since then, Deidre had gone on to other things—meaning other men. But now she was looking at him again, with that once-familiar heat. "Busy tonight?" she asked, handing over Maddie's large thermos.

"I thought you were dating some purple-haired guy." There was another note taped to the thermos.

Deidre lifted a shoulder. "I've moved on."

He cut her a glance. "He got too serious, huh?"

"Damn men." She sighed. "They always do."

"Maybe you're just irresistible."

She grinned. "Don't you know it. So tonight…? There's a new band playing at Erotique. Want to meet me there for a few drinks?"

He was about to reply but he'd just scanned the note— from Em—and it sidetracked him.

Jacob,
I know, I know. Coffee as a forgiveness bribe— tacky. But please believe me, I never meant to keep my reason for being in NY a secret. It's just that you're quite different from anyone I've ever met, and, well, potent. Please let me make it up to you. However you'd like. There, I bet that got your attention. Come see me anytime, anywhere. I'll be at Hush all day. Enjoy Maddie's incomparable coffee, Jacob.
Best, Em.

"Yoo-hoo, earth to Chef." Deidre waved a hand in his face. "Come in, Chef."

"Yeah." Jacob crumpled up the note. Deidre lifted her small black trash can so he could toss the note in. But he held on to the paper, which, if he wasn't mistaken, actually smelled like Em.

When he looked back at Deidre, her smile slowly faded. "Wow."

"What?"

"That look on your face." She stared at him in disbelief. "Who's the gift sender?"

"It's just coffee."

"Yeah, but that's not just a smile on your face."

He did his best to swipe off the grin.

She slowly shook her head. "The remnants are still there."

He snatched up the thermos, shot her a long look and began to walk away.

"You can run," she called after him. "But you can't hide, not from me. I have a responsibility to the rest of the staff to spread the correct gossip about you. Talk to me! *Chef!*"

He lifted a hand and kept going.

"Damn it," he heard her mutter, and any other time he might have laughed, but he didn't feel like laughing.

He felt like… Hell, he had no idea what he felt like. Unused to the feeling, he walked through the lobby, past Erotique, thinking a drink would be a great thing—if it hadn't been so early.

He entered Amuse Bouche. Pru met him just outside the kitchen door, also unusually quiet and subdued as she balanced her briefcase and a box loaded with four bottles of different wines. "You're early, too," she said.

He took the box from her. "What's wrong with being early?"

"It's a rare phenomenon, that's all. In fact, you're usually late enough that someone has to page you out of some woman's bed to get your ass in here."

"Well, good day to you, too."

Eyes unhappy, she shrugged.

"What, don't have the phone number of that woman you want me to call?" he teased when she failed to continue with her usual pestering. "No blind dates for me?"

When she only sent him a halfhearted smile, he stopped. "What's the matter?"

"Nothing."

He looked at her closed, miserable face. "It's something."

She shrugged, and walked ahead of him into the kitchen, setting her briefcase down on the black granite counter and taking the box from him.

"Pru."

Another shrug. Woman-speak for *Drag it out of me, please.*

He again took the box and set it next to her briefcase. "Where did you and Caya end up last night?"

"Erotique. We met up with some of her friends from before."

Before was any time before Caya had come to live with Pru. Pru liked it when the world revolved around her.

"Then we went down to Exhibit A," she said.

Jacob arched a brow, signaling his surprise that Pru would want to take Caya there, the place in Hush that was undoubtedly the most uninhibited, wild and adventurous. Possibly in all of Manhattan. "Did you tell her how you feel?"

"About what, that I don't like her wild friends? That I don't like how much she goes out? That I especially don't like the way she tries to lose her problems in casual sex?"

"No," Jacob said. "That you want her for yourself."

"Of course I didn't tell her that. It's going to ruin the friendship."

"No, it's not."

"This can't be happening to me," Pru said softly, pacing the room. "Love sucks, remember?"

"Hey, I didn't say anything about love."

"Oh, my God." Pru stopped and covered her face. "Oh, my God. I love her."

Shaken now, Jacob stared at her. "Okay, let's not get carried away."

"No, it's true. I love her." Stricken, Pru dropped her hands, then whirled on her heel.

"Where are you going?"

"To think. To obsess. To have my nails done before I chew them all to the quick."

"Pru—"

"Don't talk to me right now."

Suited him just fine. He didn't like talking anyway. What the hell was wrong with him, trying to help?

Or spending so much time thinking about Em when he had plenty of other women in his life to screw it up?

When he could no longer hear Pru's heels clicking angrily away, he leaned back against the counter and poured himself a mug of Maddie's finest from the thermos. Sipping the brew, he reread Em's note.

Twice.

When he caught himself reading it a fourth time, he crumpled it up again and tossed it in the trash. And reminded himself he never looked back, not ever.

EM, LIZA AND ERIC were having an emergency meeting. Because she'd screwed up. The thought made her wince, because it was true, she'd blown it. She'd lost herself in Jacob and had forgotten the goal. Now he felt used, and she couldn't blame him.

They were having the meeting by the pool, which was on the glass-covered roof. The area had scattered wrought-iron benches and freestanding fountains, and was warmed with tall gas-powered heaters designed like lanterns. All this was surrounded by lush greenery and wildly colorful blooms, despite the fact that in the real world, it was February in New York. The incredible beauty had a calming effect on Em's frazzled nerves. The pool itself was Olympic-size, with a large hot tub next to it, and a fully stocked bar for their drinking pleasure.

She lay on the cushiest white lounge chair she'd ever enjoyed, in a bathing suit. From here they were going to move their meeting into the spa. Liza had insisted, claiming they were far too busy back in Los Angeles for such foolishness, and that they should experience the full scope of what New York had to offer.

Especially now that it looked as if they were all headed toward the unemployment line.

Liza had booked them all for a variety of spa luxuries, a few of which Em had never even heard of. It seemed surreal, lying here, sunning as if they were lizards on a rock, being served their every wish by attentive, professional personnel.

While guilt and regret fought for space in her belly.

Liza had a drink in her hand, a pretty-colored something with an umbrella sticking out of it. Eric was facedown on his lounge and had a lovely attendant rubbing lotion onto his shoulders.

Every time he moaned his pleasure, Liza took a long sip of her drink.

Em leaned close to Liza. "You could just tell him he's getting to you," she whispered.

"Are you kidding?" she whispered back, adjusting her bikini top so that her breasts were plumped up and practically falling out. "Never give a guy the upper hand. Besides, I've got him just where I want him."

Em eyed Eric, who was still very much enjoying his massage. "If you say so."

"Oh, forget him," Liza said with a sniff, but she flipped

over, revealing her thong bikini bottoms. Or more to the point, her extremely perfect yoga-tightened butt.

From Eric's chair came a choking sound. When they looked over at him, he turned his head away.

Liza sent Em a smile. "See? Right where I want him."

Em shook her head.

"So tell me again why we sent coffee to a man who could probably get any coffee in the city that he wanted, especially from his own hotel?"

Em sat back against the cushy lounge chair and sighed. "Because I'm trying to apologize to him."

"Because why?"

"Because he deserves it. I should have told him sooner, Liza."

"Really? When, exactly? When he was kissing you in the elevator?"

"Yes, well, certainly by that second kiss."

Liza's eyes nearly bugged out of her head.

Even Eric sat up for this one.

"*Second kiss?*" they both asked together.

Em rolled her eyes. "Look, this isn't exactly the time to discuss how many kisses there were."

"When exactly would be a good time then?" Liza asked. "The next time I find you two having wild monkey sex in your room?"

"We were not having wild monkey sex," Em said with exaggerated patience.

"What about regular sex?" Eric asked hopefully. "Because you could tell us about that."

Liza shoved him back to his lounge. "Perv."

"I'm just saying she should get it off her chest," he said innocently. "That's all."

"There's nothing to get off my chest," Em assured the

both of them. "And we're here to talk about the real issue, that being the chef for the show."

"Or the lack thereof," Liza pointed out.

"Yes, thank you, Liza. Or the lack thereof. A situation that needs to be fixed, immediately. I'm going to find a way to talk to Jacob. I'm not giving up there, but…" Em's stomach clutched yet again. She felt funny opening her briefcase and pulling out a pad of paper in her bikini, but desperate times… "Any thoughts just in case?"

"Hire me," Eric said.

Liza laughed.

Eric turned his face toward the sun, his expression unreadable. "Well, if that's so funny, audition for other chefs." He sprawled facedown on his lounge again, stretching his long, lean body as he sunned. "Right here at Hush."

Liza and Em looked at each other in shocked surprise. "You know," Liza said, "once in a while he actually has a few productive thoughts."

"I've got a few more," Eric assured her with a naughty tone in his voice. "Want to hear them?"

"No," Liza said.

Eric shrugged and lay back down, facing away from them.

This left Liza free to openly study his slicked-up, smooth back and butt, with such an expression of longing it hurt to look at her.

"Tell him you want him," Em mouthed.

Pride blaring from her gaze, Liza shook her head.

Em sighed and began to make her list. "We'll need to book a conference room."

"And get the word of the auditions out," Liza added.

"I can do that." Eric mumbled this into his lounge pillow. "I've got agents I can call. Don't worry, I'll get you a decent showing."

It had to be done, Em thought as Eric and Liza continued to come up with good ideas. They had to have a viable backup if Jacob truly wasn't interested. She could do that, find someone else with the charisma and talent she needed. Because she couldn't lose sight of the real issue—this was her last chance. If she screwed this up, by this time next month she'd be standing behind a counter in a silly hat, asking customers if they wanted red or green sauce with their tacos.

"Excuse me," came a low, soothing female voice. "We're ready for you in the spa."

Eric and Liza jumped up eagerly. Em wrapped herself in one of Hush's thick towels and followed the woman through the gorgeous garden that someone worked very hard on. The moment they entered the spa, Em let out a deep, tense breath she hadn't even realized she'd been holding.

She could smell a myriad of special scents, mostly lavender, and the walls glowed with a gentle light that was nearly as soothing as the scent. In the reception area there was a wall of cascading water that both looked and sounded incredibly appealing. It was so beautiful in here it made her ache, and the quiet surrounded her, a calming balm on her shaky spirit.

They were each led into separate rooms. Em's had a freestanding waterfall similar to the one in her room. There was incense burning, and the soft sounds of a jungle coming from speakers she couldn't see. An attendant told her about an Indo-Asian hot oil treatment. "A delight to the senses," she promised in a soft, quiet voice that went with the atmosphere. "When you're ready, remove your suit, stretch out on the massage table and just concentrate on relaxing."

Braving the moment, Em stripped out of her bathing suit, covered herself with a sheet so soft it felt like a cloud and lay down. The attendant came back in and started the massage, using heated oil that had Em melting into the table. Her skin soaked up the oil, and by the time it was over, she didn't think she had a single bone left in her body.

Then she was wrapped in warm, herb-soaked strips of linen and covered with the sheet, left to bake pleasantly under a heat lamp. Once alone, she listened to the sounds of the water hitting the rocks, of the faraway jungle, and nearly forgot all about her troubles. In fact, her entire being began to let go for the first time in a very long time.

The door opened. "Look at that," someone said in a very low, husky Southern drawl. "Just what the doctor ordered—Emmaline Harris, bound and stretched out for my perusal."

Em, flat on her belly, trussed up in her herb-soaked linens and sheet like a mummy, barely lifted her head. It was all the movement she could manage.

Jacob's mouth was curved in a smile, but it wasn't necessarily a friendly one. It held things, naughty, wicked things, and made her tummy tremble.

"What are you doing here?" she asked, struggling to sit up.

He held up a piece of paper. Her note, written to him in her own hands, inviting him to please come see her today, anytime, anywhere.

Admittedly, not her smartest idea. An open invitation.

Interestingly enough, the note was crinkled, as if he'd balled it up, then smoothed it out.

And if she took a good look at him, she could see his jaw was tight enough to tic, that those broad shoulders seemed tightened as hard as rocks.

Chef was looking a little tense.

"Jacob," she said, still fighting the linen. "I'm so sorry I hurt your feelings."

"You didn't." He moved close, watching her tussle with the sheet for a moment before he gave her a hand, helping her to a sitting position so that her legs hung over the edge.

She kept a hold on the sheet wrapped around her body—her only armor—clutching it close, hoping not to expose any body parts. "I wanted to talk to you," she said, "about the show."

He hadn't backed up. His thighs bumped her knees. "I'm not here to talk about the show."

"Oh." She smoothed the sheet over her legs, feeling the strips of linen beneath beginning to loosen. "But—"

"No business in here." Reaching out, he stroked a finger over her shoulder—her bare shoulder—making her painfully aware that her sheet had slipped. With only the strips of the herb-soaked linen beneath, she wasn't completely bare, but she felt pretty damn naked all the same.

Jacob was just looking at her, his eyes dark and unreadable, leaving her feeling like Little Red Riding Hood staring into the eyes of the hungry wolf. She fought with the sheet a minute, tugging, letting out a sound of vexation because it was trapped under her butt.

Jacob watched, a slight smile on his lips.

She finally managed to pull some of the sheet free from beneath her so that she could cover her shoulders, only she pulled too much.

And felt nothing but table beneath her.

Oops.

To complicate her situation—and this was most definitely a situation—her linen strips were loosening. Feeling extremely naked now, she squirmed about some more, trying to get herself completely covered, but it just wasn't happening. "Maybe you could give me a hand here…"

He just slid his hands into his pockets. "You're doing just fine."

Oh, yeah. If fine was giving him a show! With some fancy maneuvering, she got her bare butt covered again—

A sound escaped Jacob at the exact moment she realized she felt cool air brushing over a breast.

Oh, God. She'd created her own Nipplegate. She told herself he couldn't possibly be able to see in the dim room, and dared a quick peek at him.

His eyes were seriously smoldering. She heard the rough breath whoosh out of his lungs.

He'd seen.

"Damn it." Leaping off the table, she pulled the sheet tight around her and prepared to lie back down, but it was too late. Beneath her, the herb-soaked linen began to slide down her body, hitting the floor. *Plop. Plop. Plop.* "This is all your fault," she said.

He lifted his hands. "I'm not doing anything."

"You don't have to. That's the point."

"Except become a cooking show host."

She let out a breath and hugged the sheet closer. "Look, if you believe nothing else, believe that I'm sorry about that."

With characteristic bluntness, he let his gaze roam over her, from her out-of-control hair, to the sheet she was hugging around her for all she was worth, to her bare toes. Without a word, he again stepped closer, staring into her eyes while the pad of his finger stroked over the very base of her throat, at the pulse she knew was drumming there. An innocent enough touch, but it felt intimate. Forbidden. And she wanted more, a realization that made her swallow hard.

His gaze locked on the movement her throat made, and his finger trailed down, over her collarbone.

Her nipples hardened.

In reaction, he let out a very male sound and slowly ran a finger over her bare shoulder, leaving a line of tingly awareness she didn't know what to do about. She stood there without a stitch on except the sheet, painfully aware of herself and the picture she must make, completely naked while he was fully clothed and yet…yet so aroused her skin felt too tight.

His finger retraced its trail, everywhere he touched creating a path of fire. She sucked in a breath.

So did he. "Tell me what you feel," he said.

You, making me shaky with lust. You, taking me to a place I'm not ready for. "I don't—"

"Tell me."

"Heat." Her voice cracked so she cleared her throat and said it again. "I feel heat."

"It's the oil," he told her, his hand smoothing slowly up and down her back. "It's seasonally blended to create a warming effect in cool weather. It works the opposite way when it's hot outside."

"Oh." An embarrassed smile escaped her. "I thought—"

"What?"

"That it was you." Her eyes drifted shut. "Whenever you're touching me, I feel so…"

"Aware?"

"Yes."

"That's the calamus root and sandalwood powder." His voice was low and quiet, and incredibly arousing, as much as the oil and his manipulation of it on her body. The man would be a huge asset to any spa, his presence alone making it millions of dollars.

"The combination is meant to stimulate." His gaze held hers as his finger kept moving over her, lower than her collarbone now, just barely skimming the upper curve of her breast, right at the edge of the sheet. "But I'm very much enjoying that you thought it was me making you feel so aware." His finger slipped just beneath the edging of the sheet.

"Jacob," she gasped.

He used the backs of his fingers now, his knuckles brushing over her.

She couldn't help it, she watched his fingers on her breast, mesmerized by the erotic sight of his big, tanned hand on her pale, creamy skin. Though her nipple was still covered by the sheet, barely, it poked against the material, begging for equal attention.

Other parts of her body were clamoring for attention, too.

He kept giving it, until she was a quivering, anticipatory wreck.

"I can't stand any more," she whispered. "*Please…*"

Putting his hands on her shoulders, he slowly turned her away from him.

She stood there wondering what he was going to do to her, the wondering made more all the overpowering because she could no longer see him.

"Onto the table," he murmured, wrapping his fingers in her sheet at the base of her spine.

"Hey." She grasped it between her breasts, held on to it for dear life. If she moved, the sheet would stay with him, falling away from her body.

She was *not* ready for that.

"Lie back down," he said softly from just behind her, his breath rustling the hair over her ear. "I'll cover you."

Unable to let go, she shook her head. "I can't."

"Go on," he said with a tone she hadn't heard from him before: tenderness.

Craning her head, she looked back at him. His eyes flickered with a tenseness that matched hers, but in a blink it was gone.

"Lie back down," he said. "You don't want to waste all the relaxing you've done."

"Too late," she muttered.

With infinite patience, he waited her out.

Closing her eyes, she took a deep breath and then let go of the sheet.

He surprised her, holding the sheet up between them, blocking his view of her as she lay down. Then it fluttered over her, covering her from midback to midthigh, and she let out a breath, only to have it clog her throat when he stroked a hand down her back, reactivating the oil, heating her up in an instant.

She kept her eyes tightly closed, concentrating on what he made her feel, but unable to let go of the tenseness she'd seen in his expression when he'd first walked in. "Jacob?"

"Hmm?"

Over the sheet, his fingers moved on her lower back, pressing lightly in just the right spot to make her want to stretch and purr like a kitten. "Are you…okay?"

Ignoring her question, he moved up her spine and then back down again. "You smell like something a man might want to gobble up."

"You're changing the subject—" She broke off to moan when he got to her shoulders and dug in.

"Good?" he asked.

So good she'd beg if he stopped. "Please talk to me."

He sighed as his fingers made their way back down her

spine, slowly, with unbelievable talent. "You have a one-track mind."

And so, she was willing to bet, did he. "Talk."

He skimmed over her bottom, which had her clenching her cheeks, but he didn't stay and linger, not until he got to the backs of her thighs. While he worked there, another helpless moan fluttered out of her lips before she could stop herself.

"Why don't you just concentrate on the pleasure?" he asked. "Stop holding back."

"Not until you talk to me."

"You're not going to like it."

She already knew that. "Try me."

One finger traced a silky path up the back of her thigh to the very edge of the sheet, and then a little farther. "I can't stop thinking about you."

She tried to turn over so she could see him but he held her down with one big, warm hand at the middle of her spine. "No, don't move. Just stay on your stomach. I'll go. Your attendant will be back in a few."

"But…"

But nothing. Whether it had been her reaction, or that he felt he'd said too much, he was gone.

Letting her cheek touch the table again, she lay there, mind racing, body aching, heart pounding, pounding, pounding.

He couldn't stop thinking about her.

Well, that made them even.

CHAPTER EIGHT

To: Spa attendants
From: Spa manager
Re: Herbal wraps
New as of today! Stay in room once herbal wrap is applied to keep guest relaxed and immobile. Otherwise, the linens apparently may unravel and fall off.

"THEY'RE HOLDING open auditions here today for some new cooking show."

This was what Jacob heard the next day when he got to his kitchen. Pushing open the doors, he found Caya and two other servers gathered around, talking.

Caya grinned at him. "Did you hear?"

"Yeah," he managed to say without a grimace. "I've heard." Though due to his own stubbornness, he knew none of the details. He didn't want the details. He wanted things to go back to normal.

"Maybe I should try out," Caya said. "I could become famous, and give you a run for your money."

"No one gives me a run for my money," Jacob said.

Everyone laughed, and they all got to work, but late that afternoon, he sneaked out of the kitchen and headed to the conference level. There he found a long line of chef hopefuls in the hallway holding résumés in their fists, wearing eager expressions on their faces. He moved past them, ignoring the softly muttered grumblings when they thought he was cutting in line to get his shot at stardom.

Not a chance.

But as to why he was there, he couldn't have said. He honestly had no desire to be on a TV show, to be the "it" boy of the week, to have people watch his every move as if he were performing brain surgery.

He loved what he did too much to turn it into a spectacle. He loved all of it: the physical skills, the easy joy, the variety and the choices. It fed his heart and soul. And after too many years of being forced to prove himself, being evaluated at the blink of an eye, never knowing how long his job would remain his, he just couldn't imagine willingly putting himself there again, this time at the mercy of an intangible thing like ratings, or the invisible Powers-That-Be.

No, he was here merely to satisfy his curiosity and nothing else, and with that in mind, he walked to the double doors of their largest conference room.

Standing there was a man holding a radio and a clipboard.

Jacob recognized him as one of the two people who'd accompanied Em to dinner at Amuse Bouche two nights ago. "Eric," he said, remembering.

Eric looked up from the clipboard and raised a brow. "You want an audition?"

"No."

"So then why are you here?"

Hell if he knew. "Is Em inside?"

"Yep." But Eric stepped in front of him. "Sorry, man. Only people who are auditioning can get in there."

"I want to talk to Em."

"I don't think so."

"Why not?"

"Because whatever you've said or done to her already has left her feeling shaky. Now she's in there trying to save her career and I'm not going to have you screw with her head."

"You do realize she's the one who lied to me, right?"

"Not lied exactly," Eric corrected. "Just a slight omission is all."

Jacob raised a brow.

"Look, just leave her alone to do this, okay?"

"Are you her husband?" Jacob asked.

"What? No, of course not."

"Boyfriend?"

"No."

"Boss, then."

"No," Eric said, looking annoyed. "Not that it's any of your business."

"Then I'm going in."

"I already told you why you're not."

"Only if I was auditioning, right? Then you'd let me in."

Eric slapped the clipboard against his thigh as he studied Jacob. "If you wanted to audition, none of this would have been necessary."

"I don't do performance cooking."

"Someone here in line today is going to be extremely thankful for that."

"I just want to talk to her."

Eric sighed. "You know what? Fine. Talk to her. But mess her up, and I'll mess you up."

They sized each other up for a moment, then Jacob sighed. "I'm not going to do anything to hurt her."

"Sure it's not too late for that?"

What the hell did that mean? Jacob had no idea, and with a muttered "thanks," he stepped inside the conference room. There was a long table set up, and behind it sat Em and a blonde, both watching the man standing in front of them.

The man was short, fat, bald and toting a whip. Instead of a white chef's hat and coat, he wore all black. "First, you must determine if the lettuce is dirty," he said in a deep, strict voice. He snapped the whip through the air for emphasis. "Is it dirty? Is the lettuce dirty? If so, naughty, naughty."

Jacob, who'd seen it all, just shook his head.

The blonde's mouth fell open.

Em looked equally flabbergasted.

"Are the tomatoes bad?" the auditioning chef asked sternly. "Are they very, very bad? If so, you slice them up real nice, or no food for you!" Another swoosh of the whip.

Em jerked to her feet. "Thank you," she said quickly. "That's enough."

The man pointed the whip at her. "You, quiet. I am not finished."

"Oh, yes, you are." Liza jumped up next to Em. "Get out."

The man "hmphed," then stormed past Jacob, his squat figure barely coming up to his shoulder.

The blonde reached for her drink. "Well, that was interesting."

"Yes," Em said, and looked at Jacob. Relief filled her gaze.

She thought he'd changed his mind, that he wanted to be her chef.

Jacob shook his head, and the disappointment in her eyes nearly killed him. It had been a hell of a long time since he'd disappointed someone he cared about.

It had been a long time since he'd cared like this at all.

Liza turned to see what had caught Em's eye, and put down her drink. "Tell me this is our lucky day," she said to Jacob.

Again he shook his head.

"You're killing me," Liza muttered. "*Next!*"

The doors opened. A woman entered, dressed in nothing but a string bikini. A string bikini with strings sorely tested by her considerable girth. Her large breasts were pushing precariously at their restraints, and the bottoms of the bathing suit were strained to the point of being frayed. She'd topped this off with pink polka-dot stilettos.

"My turn!" she cried, waving a carrot of all things. "I plan to be the Great Loss Chef! Together, me and America are going to lose twenty-five pounds!"

Jacob thought she could have tripled that and been closer to the right number.

She began gyrating, dancing to some music only she could hear, her body jiggling and shaking, and not in an attractive fashion.

"Uh, thank you," Em said. "But…"

The woman didn't stop. In fact, she kept dancing as she began to eat the carrot.

"That's all," Em called out politely.

"No, don't say stop," Bikini Woman pleaded. "I can do this! I'm your next amazing chef!"

"I'm sorry." Em shook her head. "I'm going to have to ask you to—"

"Not yet! I'm not finished—"

"Yes," Liza said firmly. "You are. *Next!*"

Bikini Chef threw her carrot to the floor. "This is nothing but a bunch of crap! I'm an excellent chef. You're all making a *big* mistake. You hear me? I was meant to be a star—my mother told me so!"

Em pressed her fingertips to her eyelids.

"Look," Em said firmly, dropping her hands. "You haven't shown me what I wanted to see, which was talent for cooking."

"That's because I can't cook," she cried.

"Then try one of the other reality shows," Em told her as patiently as she could.

Bikini Woman sighed, nodded and headed toward the door. Once she was gone, Eric poked his head in. When Em shook her head to another contestant, he shut the door.

"It's going to be a hell of a long day," Liza said. She came around the table and eyed Jacob. "Unless you want to…"

Jacob shook his head.

Liza sighed. "Right." She glanced at Em, who hadn't taken her eyes off Jacob. "I'll give you two a minute. I'll just go get a coffee, maybe torture Eric with my beauty and wit."

"Liza—"

"Just kidding." She grinned. "Sort of. In any case, don't give me another thought."

When she'd left, Em said to Jacob, "Did you come for a good laugh?"

"I don't know, that S and M chef was…interesting."

She just shook her head. "God. I'm in big trouble."

"Maybe you should make a show of the auditions. A sort of preshow show. That'd be some good entertainment."

She laughed, only there wasn't much amusement in the sound, and he walked around the table to stand close to her. "You didn't really expect to find someone your first day."

She lifted her gaze to his and he saw the truth there. "You didn't expect to have to audition at all," he said.

She slowly shook her head.

"I'm sorry." He was shocked to find his apology genuine.

"I know." She smiled. "And it's okay. But if you're not here because you've changed your mind, I need to get back to it." She gestured with her head toward the closed door, and the line of people waiting. "Just tell me there are no more whips or bikinis out there."

"No, but I did see a monkey."

She closed her eyes.

"And a set of triplets singing a cappella."

She opened her eyes again. "That's not funny."

"Not even a little bit?"

She tried to remain stern and unsmiling, but gave up. "A monkey? Ah, hell." She pinched the bridge of her nose. "Okay, yeah, maybe it is just a little bit funny. But it won't be next month, when I'm in the unemployment line."

Because he didn't want to picture that, he kept it light, leaning in to kiss her jaw. "I've got a plan to keep your mind off your troubles."

"I just bet." She eyed him warily but didn't pull away from his touch. "What is it?"

"Come out with me tonight after my shift."

"To…"

If he told her what he really wanted to do with her, to her, she'd probably pass out on the spot. "To see New York."

"I've seen the city."

"Come see it my way."

She was already shaking her head. "Ooooh, no. *Bad* idea."

"Actually, it's a great idea. It'll help you relax."

"Yeah? And how will being with you help me relax?"

He let out a slow grin, and she pointed at it, shaking her head. "Don't do that."

"Do what?"

"Turn on that charm. Because, damn it, I'd follow you anywhere when you smile at me like that, and that's bad. Very bad. I have a job to do, I have to—"

"You'd follow me anywhere?" he asked.

She looked at him for a long moment. "Let's just say, I have few survival skills when it comes to you."

He wasn't sure what to make of that, either, and suddenly he was uncomfortably warm. Was it hot in here? He took a step backward, toward the door, startled anew when she grabbed his hand, and at what he had in it.

Her note.

Unwrinkling it, she studied her own words. "I did promise to make it up to you," she said quietly, then lifted her face to his. "I guess I'll see you tonight."

Since he'd apparently lost his tongue, he couldn't come up with the words to tell her that she was right, this was a bad idea, that being with her wasn't good for his mental health.

Eric opened the door. "The natives are getting restless."

"Okay." Em smiled at Jacob. "See you later."

He looked into her beautiful face, with her thoughts chasing each other across her features. When he saw one particular thought—that she wanted him—he said softly, "Yeah, see you later."

HE WENT TO THE ONLY PLACE that ever made him feel better and completely at home.

His kitchen.

Pru was already there, brooding, too. After listening to her slam around in her wine cabinet for five tense, silent minutes, he sighed. "*What?*"

"You're not going to like it."

"Okay, then never mind."

She turned to him, her eyes wet, the emotion on her face stabbing directly into his heart. "I told Caya how I felt about her."

He backed up a step. "Okay."

"Yeah, that's what *she* said."

"What?"

Pru sighed. "She said okay. She said thank you. She said that it made her feel good. What she didn't say was 'I love you back, Pru.'"

"Why the hell would you tell her such a thing?"

"Because you told me to!"

"I told you to tell her you wanted her. I didn't say anything about love."

"But I do love her." Pru shut the cabinet hard enough that the bottles rattled, and crossed her arms, glaring at him as if this was all his fault.

"You scared her," he said.

"Take a peek into the dining room."

She tugged him to the kitchen door and cracked it open enough to reveal the front room. The waitstaff was out there having a meeting at one of the large dining tables. Caya was sitting on the lap of Michael, headwaiter. Her head was thrown back and she was laughing her cute ass off.

"Does that look scared to you?" Pru asked.

Uh, no, not exactly. He pulled Pru away from the door and looked into his usually calm friend's face. No calm there now. Just a panic he'd never seen before, and hurt. Damn it. Worse, looking at her expression, he saw something else. *Someone* else.

Em.

There had been pain in her eyes, too, and *he'd* put it there. "I tried to tell you this was a bad idea."

She let out a disbelieving sound. "That's it? That's all you've got? I told you so?"

"What else do you expect?" Honest to God, he didn't know. But he did know this: he had an ache in his chest that had better be heartburn and not emotion. What was wrong with everyone? Why couldn't it go back to the simplicity of before?

"Thanks, Chef," Pru said sarcastically. "Thanks ever so much."

"What do you want from me?" he asked helplessly.

"To make this better. Can you do that?"

If he couldn't help himself, how the hell did she think he could help her? "Pru..."

"Yeah, forget it." She sighed. "I'll be fine."

Jacob hoped so. And he hoped he'd be fine, too.

THE REST OF THE AUDITIONS were predictably horrible, but Eric promised Em they'd have a better selection tomorrow, and she chose to believe him rather than panic.

Tomorrow. Tomorrow her future would figure itself all out.

But first she had to get through tonight, and the evening with Jacob, without losing anything important.

Like her heart.

Nathan had called. Did she have him yet? She'd promised she was working on it and hung up.

Unable to find either Eric or Liza, she got ready alone, trying not to think too much.

Was she working on Jacob? No. She wouldn't do that. She couldn't. So what *was* it that she was doing?

She had no idea.

And what did one wear to go out on the town with Jacob Hill? She had no idea what to expect, much less how to prepare for it. Finally she settled for her favorite red cashmere hoodie, and a black skirt and boots. Comfort clothes that just happened to look decent enough for any adventure that came her way. Taking a peek in the mirror, she shrugged. Not bad, she supposed. *Hoped.*

He'd left her a message to meet him in the lobby at ten o'clock. She took the elevator, half expecting him to be on it already, where he'd start their evening off with a wild kiss.

But no Jacob.

Instead she rode the elevator with another couple who couldn't keep their eyes, mouths or hands off each other, leaving Em standing in the corner trying to pretend she couldn't see them, trying not to think about how she'd been kissed just like that woman was being kissed, trying not to remember what it had felt like to have Jacob's eyes, hands and mouth all over her.

She began to perspire.

God. The man could make her hot when he wasn't even anywhere near her. When the doors opened, she nearly ran off the elevator. Stepping into the lobby, her eyes locked on the life-size art deco painting of the threesome.

Perfect. Now even artwork was mocking her.

All around her, the place was hopping, people coming and going, some from Erotique, some from other areas of the hotel, others from the street.

Then she saw him standing in the center of the lobby, and everything else seemed to fade away. How cliché, how ridiculous, but the voices, the people, the sights and sounds, all of it vanished except for the sight of Jacob wearing all black, looking big, bad and extremely dangerous to her heart and soul.

And all she could think was…*God, I hope he kisses me again tonight. And touches me.*

And makes love to me.

The thought alone was enough to douse some of the excitement. No way. She was not going to sleep with him, not when she knew she was going to get on a plane in a matter of days and never see him again. She wasn't equipped for an affair.

Was she?

From across the lobby, through the people and the chatter of conversation and laughter, he smiled at her, one of his slow, heated smiles that rattled her knees and liquefied her bones.

Then he was walking toward her. With that long-legged stride and sense of purpose. Other women watched him, wanted him, and yet he didn't even look.

And despite what she'd told herself about her heart, it tipped on its side and began the fall.

"Hey," he said when he reached her side. He took her hand. "Ready?"

If he only knew just how ready she was, he'd go running into the night, putting as much distance between them as he possibly could. "Ready," she said, and put her hand in his. "Where are we going?"

"Anywhere. Everywhere."

He was true to his word. They walked through Soho, looking at art displayed on the street. Not pretty, neat museum art, but dark, deep stuff that she'd never experienced before, from artists who looked as if maybe they'd lived by train tracks their whole life, or out of cardboard boxes.

Jacob didn't say much, just waited for her reaction. She didn't know for certain but thought maybe this was his way of testing her—could she understand his world?

She studied the art, while Jacob studied her, appearing to be watching her for any signs of revulsion or discomfort, but she felt neither. In fact, with his big, tough body at her side, she'd never felt more comfortable, or safe.

And the art honestly captured her, entranced her. She told him so, and felt more than saw some invisible string of tension break free.

After that, he took her for a very late dinner at a tiny Thai place with only three tables, where no one spoke English, where it was possible that everyone here had just gotten off a boat from Thailand. The place was clean but dark and furtive, as if the entire staff was ready to pick up and run at a moment's notice of the immigration authorities.

It was some of the best food she'd ever tasted.

It was Jacob, she knew, still trying to scare her off his world, which was so incredibly different from hers, but he didn't know that while she might look sweet and act sweet, even taste sweet, she could dig in her heels with the best of them. She didn't care that he'd had a vagabond, wanderlust life, and that hers had been relatively sheltered. She didn't expect anything more than what they could have in this moment right here, right now.

So the test continued.

They browsed through a magic shop for fun, then went through the back and ended up in a porn shop. Tasteful as the interior was, with lace and silk curtains dividing the DVDs from the whips and chains, Em still blinked in surprise. Dildos and vibrators and cock rings, oh my.

Jacob just watched her in that way he had of never hesitating, never fumbling, never looking flustered or confused.

God, to have half that confidence.

"Need anything?" he asked, deadpan.

"Um…" She eyed a row of anal plugs, each bigger than the last, and swallowed hard. "No, thanks."

"Sure?"

"Yes." She cleared her throat. "I'm good." She managed to look him in the eye. "You?"

For the first time all night, he tossed his head back and laughed, the sound real and rich and warming her belly.

And in that moment, she knew. Whether he liked it or not, whether he even knew it yet or not, she'd passed his test.

CHAPTER NINE

EM LOOKED AROUND HER at the porn shop. She was going to do it, she was going to buy something, just to see the look on Jacob's face when she did so with mature ease and without embarrassment.

Oh, he was standing there, so positive that he'd shocked her, so confident that she'd never have the guts to actually do it.

Ha! Watch her.

She stalked right up to the counter, telling herself she'd purchase the first thing she saw that she could name, heart racing at the selection of vibrators right in front of her. Gulping, she pointed to the one called The Rabbit—*the rabbit?!?*—and said, "That one."

Behind her, Jacob choked, but when she looked at him, he'd pulled himself together.

"Problem?" she asked loftily, taking out her credit card.

Jacob put his big, warm hand over hers and pulled out his wallet. "No way. This baby's on me." His eyes locked on Em's as he said to the woman behind the counter, "Add batteries."

Em was too mortified to argue with him, and the next thing she knew, she was walking out of there with a brown bag heavy with The Rabbit, and a body zapping with sexual energy.

Unbelievable, but she was twenty-seven years old and had just bought her first vibrator.

"Don't worry, you'll like it."

"I wasn't worried."

His dimple flashed. "Were, too."

Damn it, did he have to read her mind, and then toss her own humiliating thoughts back at her?

He leaned in. "If you need any help with that thing, you just let me know."

Before she could formulate a response to this, he directed her into a bar.

A live band played with more decibels than talent, and the youthful, free-spirited crowd danced and laughed and talked over them. The servers wore jeans and suspenders— and no shirts. Including the women.

"Thought you could use a drink after that last adventure." Jacob gestured for the bartender, then looked at Em.

"A beer," she said, definitely needing it.

Jacob lifted up two fingers. When the drinks came, he looked at her over his bottle as he drank, his eyes filled with laughter and heat, God, so much heat.

She downed her beer. "I could probably use another."

"It's supposed to bring you pleasure," he said.

"The beer brought me plenty of pleasure."

"The vibrator."

"Oh."

"Gotta have trust, Em. There's easy pleasure there."

"Fine for a man to say. It's simple for you to—" She clamped her mouth shut. Had she just been about to say it, really? That it was easier for a man to masturbate?

Interested, he cocked his head. "What is it easier for men to do, Em?" His expression assured her she was still providing him with great entertainment. "Jerk off?" Leaning in so she could see nothing but that sinfully perfect face and yummy mouth, he whispered in an extremely naughty voice, "If you can't say it, how do you expect to be able to do it?"

"I can do it," she said, then wished she hadn't, because his grin widened.

"Sure?"

"*Yes.*"

"Because like I said, I could help—"

"I said I'd be fine! Now I need another beer. Please," she added in a more civil tone.

He tossed down the money to cover the beers they'd already consumed. "If it's serious drinking you're in the mood for, let's hit Patrick's."

She had no idea what exactly she was in the mood for, but it would be nice to assuage the odd ache deep inside her belly.

The one between her thighs was another story.

Patrick's was busy, too, with a very different crowd than the morning one. This crowd was tougher, younger, and looked far more apt to cause trouble. As they sipped their beers, Em noted that the trouble always seemed to be started by Maddie's two sons, who were bartending, when they weren't brawling.

After a lull in the noisy wildness, Jacob surprised Em by asking about the auditions.

"They went well," she said.

"Is that the line you gave your boss, or the truth?"

"The line I gave my boss." She sighed. "I'm hoping to get luckier tomorrow."

"And if you don't?"

"Maybe you'll change your mind."

"Em—"

"Just kidding." She shot him a half smile. "Sort of. Listen, what's so bad about being a TV chef anyway?"

"Other than the fact it's all a sham?"

"A sham?"

"Sure. The TV chef easily whips up some tasty-looking dish, impressing the viewers. He should, he's a trained pro. But you and I both know, due to time constraints and the boring factor, he'll skip all sorts of basic steps that the viewer has no idea how to perform, then tries it at home and experiences complete disaster trying to replicate it. I don't want to do that to people."

He'd really thought about this. "You wouldn't have to—"

"It's the advertising dollars that'll matter, or product placement, or something. Not the art of cooking."

She opened her mouth again, then slowly shut it in silent admission that it could be true.

"I'm just not interested," he said more gently. "At all. I've been there, done that, as far as cooking for performance, and I don't want to go back."

She nodded, remembering the juggling act he'd demonstrated. She knew how he'd grown up now and completely understood. And because she did, she would never want him to do this, either.

"So what are you going to do?"

She lifted her head with determination. "Hold auditions in Los Angeles. It'll give us more of a pool to choose from."

"Listen, I'm sor—"

Reaching out, she put a finger to his lips. "It's okay, I get it." And that was the thing, she really did. She knew Nathan wouldn't, but she did. "I'll make this work another way. I'm determined."

"You know," he said, watching her, "I believe you will."

"You do?"

"Oh, yeah." He stroked a finger over her jaw. "You've got something I recognize and know well."

Her breath caught at the touch. "What's that?"

"Determination. Passion. Hunger to succeed."

She understood him, and loved the feeling. But he understood her, too. Was there anything more sexy than that, a man who really knew her? She found herself fighting a broad, stupid smile. "You, Jacob Hill, are a very kind man."

He stared at her, then let loose with a laugh. "First you think I'm sweet, and now kind. Who are you looking at?"

"You."

"I'm not either of those things," he said with a slow shake of his head. "In fact, ask around." He shifted his weight on his bar stool, and suddenly his legs, long and hard were entangled, with hers.

Leaning in, he insinuated a muscled thigh between hers. His lips brushed against her ear as he spoke. "In fact, I'm probably the furthest thing from kind—or sweet—you'll ever meet."

His low, husky voice brought a set of shivers to her spine. But she couldn't think past the feel of his thigh between hers, or the hand he'd set against the bar at her back, ostensibly to hold his balance, but in reality trapping her within the confines of his body.

His gaze dropped to her mouth as he slowly pressed his thigh higher between hers. A rush of arousal surged through her. They were in public, anyone could see, and yet this excited her. She had no idea what that said about her, but she wanted more.

He moved again, just a slight shift that put him in direct contact with the V between her legs, shooting bolts of sexual yearning to every erogenous zone in her body. And apparently there were more than she'd known about.

No one around them paid any attention. And anyway, if anyone had happened to glance over, all they'd see was a couple who appeared to be in deep conversation, with his head bent attentively to hers, his arm at her back.

Then he rocked his knee again and she actually had to close her eyes, clutching the bar stool at either of her sides, seeking balance as everything within her clutched, as well. "I can't think when you do that," she whispered, and yet she didn't try to push his leg away.

"Do what?"

Her eyes flew open and she stared at him, prepared to tell him to stop teasing her, but he wasn't teasing at all. His eyes were dark, so very dark, and filled with honest curiosity.

He wanted to hear her say the words, that she couldn't think when he touched her, that she couldn't think with his thigh between hers, and that when he moved that thigh against her, she saw stars. Forget the vibrator, she wasn't going to need it.

"Em?"

Right. The words. Only she'd never been good at them. It was why she worked behind the camera and not in front of it, but she'd especially never been good with *sex* words. In the bedroom, on the rare occasion that she actually got there with a man, she was quiet, hoping he'd just guess what she wanted.

But suddenly she didn't want Jacob guessing. She didn't want to be coy. She wanted to be honest, and see where it got her. "I can't think when you touch me. When your leg is between mine, pressing against me."

Naturally he did it again, and her eyes drifted shut again. "Well, maybe I can think," she admitted softly. "But it's not the kind of thoughts made for mixed company."

"See, that's where you're wrong," he murmured in her ear. "Those thoughts spinning through your head *are* for mixed company. They're for me." He invaded her space a little more, making her suck in her breath because he felt so solid and smelled like heaven. "They're for you, too," he told her. "For what we do to each other."

She opened her eyes at that. "Which is what, exactly?"

"Make each other feel good."

Yes. Yes, she knew that, but she'd thought…for a minute she'd let herself think…hope… "Is there more than that?"

His gaze met hers. Again, openly honest. Brutally honest. "More than that isn't something I do."

"I know."

He looked at her for a long beat, then pulled back a little, and sipped at his beer, continuing to watch her thoughtfully. "How about you?"

"What?"

"You get involved with every guy you sleep with?"

"I'm afraid so, yes."

He nodded, and sipped some more, and by the way he'd backed off physically she got the message that he didn't intend to take it any further. Which in a strange way was a compliment.

He didn't want to hurt her.

But damn, she wished she'd let him take it a little further before they'd had that conversation, maybe even as far as his bed.

As if he could hear her thoughts, he smiled a little, and touched her hair, but he didn't try for more than that, and eventually they began the walk back to Hush. The streets were dark, quiet. There was no moon and a low fog lent an odd intimacy to the night around them.

The brown bag in her hands crinkled, reminding her of what she held.

And what she could do with it. "I can't believe I let you buy this for me."

The man beside her smiled but didn't speak. He never seemed to feel the need to fill an easy silence, and she'd gotten used to that. And nearly, but not quite, used to the way he touched her at every opportunity, a hand low on her spine as he guided her through a door, the way he bent close to her when he wanted to whisper something for her ears only, so that his jaw would brush hers and his lips graze the sensitive skin beneath her lobe.

"Tired?" he asked when they stood in Hush's lobby.

It was late, and given the stress of the few days she'd had here, she should have been past exhausted. But just peering into his dark, dark eyes banished any exhaustion. He was looking at her, his hands in his pockets, giving her an unusual amount of physical distance for a man who typically had no problem with body contact.

He was holding something back. Looking at him, she could see his shoulders tense with strain. His jaw was locked tight.

And that heat in his eyes was a carefully banked fire, and it nearly brought her to her knees.

He was holding back his desire for her.

Because of their conversation at Patrick's? If so, the man had been wrong about himself, he *was* sweet, and kind, so much so that she felt a lump catch in her throat.

He wasn't the type of man to let a woman close. He didn't want the burden or the responsibility of her feelings, much less his own. He'd learned young to count on no one but himself, and that wasn't a habit he would break lightly, if at all.

But she understood even more than that. This wasn't simply about her becoming attached to him.

But vice versa.

And he didn't like it. It scared him. That anything could scare this big, tough man was almost beyond comprehension.

But she'd scared him, and scared him deep. The tenderness that welled up nearly choked her.

"Why are you looking at me like that?" he asked, taking a step back, and she suspected, an even bigger mental one.

"Like what?" she asked softly.

His gaze searched hers. "Like maybe you're seeing me for the first time."

She was, and because of it, she smiled.

He did not. If anything, he looked more tense, and with his hands still in his pockets, the tendons and cords of muscle in his arms stood out in bold relief. The waistband on his pants gaped away from his flat, hard, tightened abs. She wanted to touch him there. Everywhere.

God, she wanted this man. She wanted to hold him, soften him, soothe him. She wanted to give him what he'd probably never let any woman give him: gentleness. Reaching up, she cupped his jaw.

He actually flinched. "What are you doing?"

"Touching you."

"Don't."

His voice sounded low, almost harsh, but she didn't take offense. Not when she'd just figured him out. "You touch me all the time," she told him. "Why can't I touch you?"

He didn't seem to have an answer for that.

So she smiled again and said, "Thank you for tonight, Jacob."

"I didn't do anything."

She lifted the brown bag. "You showed me a side of New York I might not have gotten to see."

His eyes darkened. The muscle in his jaw leaped. But he said nothing.

"I imagine it's still early for you," she said. "What are you going to do now?"

"I have to go up and look in on one of the suites. There's some VIP coming in tomorrow, and I'm cooking a private dinner for him and his fiancée. I want to check the kitchen."

"I heard the suites in this place are designer created and have to be seen to be believed."

He just looked at her.

She looked back, heart racing. What the hell was she doing? Baiting a tiger. Poking the bear.

"You want to come up to the suite with me," he stated rather than asked.

"Yes," she whispered quickly, before she changed her mind. She was insane, crazy—

"You know what toys the suites are equipped with?" he asked in a voice that left no doubt as to what category of "toys" he was referring to.

She'd read the brochures, and took a big gulp. "I think so."

"You think so." He shook his head and muttered something to himself that sounded like "Don't do it, Hill."

She just waited breathlessly.

He stared at her, the kind of deep, dark, edgy look that might have sent her running if it wasn't him. But she knew him now, and his bark was far worse than his bite.

At least she hoped so.

"There are video cameras and blank tapes," she said, "to be, um, used however the guest wants."

"They're not for filming the kids at the park."

"I know."

He stood toe to toe with her, not touching her in any way, but her body tingled nevertheless. "The camera is there to film the sex adventures the guests find here. Threesomes, hot tub adventures, S and M…"

She took another gulp. "I know. I want…I want to see."

"See? Or do?"

"I'm not sure yet."

He groaned at this, and turned in a slow, agitated circle, rubbing the day-old growth on his jaw.

The scratchy sound of it made her shiver. She wanted to feel it against her skin. "Show me," she whispered.

"I must be insane. *Insane*." He walked away a few feet, then stalked back, taking her hand. "Come on then."

He said this grimly, resignedly, and she wanted to tell him not to worry, it would be okay. But of course it wouldn't. Nothing would ever be okay again.

They took the elevator in silence, except for the brown bag in her hand, which crackled when she nervously tightened her grip.

Jacob's gaze met hers, and there was so much in it she swallowed hard. Before she could come up with something to say, he was leading her off the elevator and to the penthouse suites.

When he opened the door, she couldn't help but gasp. "Wow."

"Yeah." But he didn't seem to notice the surroundings as he nudged her inside enough to shut the door.

She gaped. She couldn't help it. The foyer was as large as her hotel room.

"It's called the Haiku Suite and was designed by Zang Toi. High-end Asian luxury."

There were floor-to-ceiling windows, and where there wasn't glass, the walls were upholstered in silk, the molding done in sycamore.

"The furniture is antique, the Oriental rugs handcrafted." He shook his head. "It's amazing to me that someone would put such expensive stuff in a hotel, but people like to be pampered. Especially here."

She looked at the lovely antique furniture polished to a high shine and the low couches arranged in a way that encouraged socializing. "There's still something different…"

He turned and looked at her. "Do you mean because it's meant for sex?"

"Um…" She bit her lower lip and clutched her brown bag. "Well, yes."

"You don't know the half of it." He pointed to an enclosed bookcase. "There's the video selection. Let me be specific. We're talking erotica. The best out there. Specifically designed for each guest." He pulled open the doors and revealed a stack of DVDs all geared toward spanking. "This particular guest's favorite fantasy."

She swallowed hard. "Um, how does Hush know what they'll want?"

"Questionnaires."

"The questions must be interesting."

"You know it." He pulled out a DVD. The cover showed a woman over a man's knee, her skirt pushed high on her waist, her panties to her knees, her bottom extremely red.

She struggled not to react but she felt her eyes widen.

"What do you think?" Jacob asked her, sounding darkly amused.

She looked at the man's big hand, raised above the woman's bottom. "Um…"

"Let me guess. Not your cup of tea?"

"Not quite," she managed.

With a rough laugh, he put the DVD back and took her into the bedroom, opening the closet there.

This time her mouth just fell open.

"A selection of costumes," he said, holding up a leather bustier, complete with whip. "This one is for a dominatrix fantasy." He arched a brow at her choked laugh. "No?"

"No," she said, shaking her head.

He pulled out another hanger. "How about a French maid?"

"Uh…no. Thank you."

Shrugging, he put that one back and opened the chest at the foot of the luxurious bed. Inside was a selection of… oh, my.

More toys, some of which she couldn't even identify. "Quite the education," she managed, leaning over him, touching a set of what she assumed were hand and ankle cuffs, in braided leather, lined with fur. She caught his eyes and nearly stopped breathing.

He was watching her finger the handcuffs, his eyes so dark she couldn't differentiate the iris from the pupil. "Well?"

"I've never…um."

He lifted a brow.

"I've never been bound before," she whispered.

"A fantasy?" he asked, his voice a mere whisper of a breath.

She touched a set of silk scarves, a leather harness, a riding crop, and shivered. "I didn't think so…" But now she could see herself bound in the cuffs, the scarf over her eyes, her body stretched to its limit on the bed as he leaned over her, taking her to helplessly aroused heights....

"Jesus, Em." Backing away from the closet, he shoved his fingers through his short, short hair, heat and sexual frustration coming off him in waves. "I'm just a man here."

Yeah. She was counting on that.

He turned toward the bathroom, which was bigger than her condo at home. An open sitting area sported a set of cushy, leather massage tables side by side.

"Wow," she murmured.

"You've said that."

She looked at him. He had carefully kept his distance, which in itself was extremely telling. Setting her brown bag down on the flawless polished granite counter, she nodded to the massage tables. "For couples?"

"You can get a masseuse in here, or just do each other. Everything needed is in the cabinets at the side of the tables."

She opened one and saw oils, lotions, candles... "I used to do manicures," she said. "I gave the best hand massages in Hollywood."

A dimple flashed. "I'm not going to touch that one."

She just gave him a long look.

"And here I thought you were just a producer."

"Now." And hopefully also next month. "But when I was in college, I worked wherever the money was. People gave great tips for my hand massages." She patted a lounge chair. "I could show you."

He stayed across the room, his hands in his pockets. "I don't think so."

And the hunter became the huntee. This was too good to pass up. "Chicken?"

His eyes reflected how he felt about being called a

chicken, and she nearly backed off. And she would have backed off if she hadn't seen other things there as well, like—it couldn't really be—uncertainty?

And want. There was no mistaking that one.

Good Lord, it was the sheer magnitude of that want that had her trying again to reach him. "Sit," she said again. "Try it." *Try me.*

He hesitated for one beat, then strode over to her and did as she'd asked, sitting on one of the massage tables. "Turnaround is fair play," he said so silkily she got goose bumps.

"You mean you want to massage my hands, too?" she asked.

"Not your hands, no."

Oh, boy. She took his wrists and turned them. Ran her thumbs over the work-roughened skin and calluses of his palms. "You haven't been moisturizing."

"No," he agreed, his gaze still locked on her face.

"Your hands are your treasure, Jacob."

"Actually, I think of my treasure as another body part entirely." Another flash of that dimple. "Want to moisturize and massage that part?"

CHAPTER TEN

To: Chef
From: Deidre
Hey, I'm at Exhibit A having way too much fun. Nothing you're doing can possibly compare, so get your gorgeous ass down here and join me.

EM SWALLOWED HARD and looked into Jacob's challenging eyes. "Let's start with your hands," she managed.

She had the pleasure of seeing those eyes glaze over, of watching *him* swallow hard, of rendering *him* speechless for a change.

About time.

The sheer womanly power of it made her want to toss her head back and laugh. Or rip off all her clothes and offer herself to him.

She did none of those things, just smiled in what she hoped was a daringly sexual way, and reached for a bottle of oil from the cabinet. She poured a little on her palm, its mixed scent sweetening the air. Then she reached for his hands and began to rub them.

At first, he remained silent, though she could feel him looking at her. She dug in, taking her time, hitting every muscle, every tendon, working each finger, his palm, his thumb. "Good?" she finally murmured, lifting her head.

His eyes were dark, his face taut as he gestured with his chin. She followed his gaze down.

He was unmistakably hard, the proof of it pressing against the buttons of his black Levi's.

Yep. It was good.

"My turn," he said thickly when she was done.

Oh, boy. He rose from the table and eyed her in a way that had her backing up. "You know what? That's okay," she decided. "My hands are good. I don't work them nearly as hard as you work yours—"

"Get on the table, Em."

"Well, I—"

"Chicken?"

She looked into his daring eyes, reminding herself she'd wanted this. She'd egged him on, played the game, and now she was going to follow through. "Okay, fine." She sat primly, legs swinging off the sides, hands in her lap. "I'll have you know, massaging hands takes quite the technique, not everyone can—"

"I'm not going to massage your hands. Lie down."

"Um—"

He clucked like a chicken, and she had to laugh. "Fine." She wasn't afraid of him.

Or not much, anyway.

Swallowing again, she contemplated the situation and tried to decide whether to lie facedown or faceup, because if she went facedown she couldn't see what he was up to, but if she went faceup then that left him with some fairly obtrusive areas to touch….

"You're thinking too much again," he said, sounding amused. At her expense.

"Yeah." Was that her voice, all breathless and wispy? Good Lord. She shut her mouth and lay down. Facedown. Then she scrunched her eyes shut and pretended she was Alice, going down the rabbit hole.

"I'm not sure what you think I'm going to do to you."

He still sounded quite amused as she felt him slip off first one of her shoes and then the other. "But if you want to be nervous, go ahead and be nervous." His hands slid beneath her long skirt to her calves, massaging lightly over her tights. "I'll promise you this, though."

My God, his hands were heaven, she thought dazedly as he dug into her calf muscles with a gentle firmness.

Leaning over her, he spoke into her ear in that voice that could bring her to climax all by itself. "You're going to like it. You're going to like it so much you'll be begging me for more."

Even if that were true, she'd never admit it. "I never beg."

He only slid his hands farther, past the backs of her knees.

"Uh—"

"Shh." Still higher his hands went, until his fingers hooked the elastic edging of her tights and tugged.

"Jacob—"

"I want to touch bare skin." After stripping the tights down her legs, he dropped them to the floor. She watched them hit and told herself he'd seen her far barer than this. Just as she also told herself he was going to take liberties that she wasn't altogether sure of, liberties that would put her far past her comfort level.

But everything about this man took her past her comfort level and she couldn't seem to get enough.

"Relax," he said, reaching for the oil.

Right. She'd just relax.

BOTTOM LINE FOR JACOB, he was fascinated by Em and her layers: the way she loved her friends, the way she'd responded with empathy to the story of his childhood, the way she'd laughed when he'd gotten silly and showed off his juggling skills.

Everything about her drew him, and that was quite possibly the most unsettling thing he'd ever felt, because it left him wanting more, more of her, more of this.

More of them.

Just the thought made him wish he had a drink, a hefty one, when he no longer drank the hefty stuff. What the hell had happened to a woman being just like a recipe, something to try and then move on to the next?

Nothing, he assured himself. He was just playing here, and so was she. To make sure of it, he poured the scented oil in his hands, slicked them up and touched her, because touching her made him forget everything else.

He started with her feet, pressing into the arches, rubbing all of the tension out, working his way over her ankles to her calves, which were smooth and creamy. This California girl didn't tan. She had her legs pressed tightly together, her muscles working overtime to keep them so. For whatever reason, that made him smile as he slowly worked his way past her knees, beneath her skirt to the backs of her thighs.

He wasn't kidding before. He knew exactly how good he was with his hands, and before much longer, he expected her to cave, and he expected her to beg.

Her soft, helpless moan swiped the smile right off his face, jerking him out of his smug complacency. She was right on schedule and yet he hadn't expected the sound to reach him.

Nor had he expected that having his hands beneath her skirt, out of view and yet on her bare skin, would seem like the most erotic thing he'd ever seen.

Her muscles were knotted and he worked them, dragging yet another moan from her. Utterly arousing.

"Shh," he said, not ready to give in to it, in to her.

But as he pressed the knotted muscles high on her thighs, she squirmed and then shifted slightly, her legs no longer pressed so tightly together, allowing him better access.

He took the opportunity, skimming his fingers higher, then higher again so that they just touched the elastic edging of her panties.

Silk.

Aw, man, they were silk and flimsy. One little tug and he'd rip them free. Because he couldn't actually see them, he wondered what color they were. Black? Red?

She lay on the table utterly motionless, holding her breath, he guessed, and slowly—so slowly he had to grit his teeth—he traced the edging of the panties to the string over either hip.

String bikini. His favorite.

"What color?"

"Wh-what?"

He almost didn't recognize his own hoarse voice. "What color are they?"

She remained still for a beat, then let out a breathless laugh that shook her shoulders. "I can't remember."

He ran his finger over the very tops of them now, drawing a line low on her spine.

Her breath caught. "They might be peach."

Now it was his turn to hold his breath.

"Or black." She said this in a whisper.

His body tightened. His fingers wrapped around the material of her skirt and slowly pushed it up, past her knees, revealing a gorgeous set of legs he wanted wrapped around him. Her thighs were every bit as taut and creamy smooth as he remembered from the spa, and his mouth went dry.

Then he pushed the skirt up even farther, to her waist

now, and exposed her ass, covered in a silky pair of barely there bikini panties.

Black.

His heart was drumming in his ears, all the blood in his head draining south. Reaching out, he traced his finger over her hip, then curled his finger around the string.

She squirmed again.

One yank, he thought, just one yank… His knees actually wobbled.

"It's…warm in here," she murmured very softly, making him realize he'd been staring down at her like a sixteen-year-old virgin with his first glimpse beneath his girlfriend's dress.

Hell, he felt like a damn virgin, a clumsy one. "You're wearing a sweater."

"I could take it off…"

Great idea. Reaching up, he pulled the sweater over her head.

Beneath, she wore a pale pink camisole, spaghetti straps, one of which had slipped off her shoulder. He nudged the other one, helping it to the same position, absorbing her caught breath, getting a surge of possessive desire at the sight of her flat on her belly, gripping the sides of the table, her shirt shoved high, straps off her shoulders, face turned away.

God. He had to stand there and purposely drag air into his lungs. Massage. He was here to give her a massage, and drive her as crazy as she drove him.

And to make her beg. Let's not forget that. Teeth clenched, he poured more oil into his hands, and with her skirt still bunched at her waist, worked on her bared shoulders, dragging more soft moans from her. "How are you doing?" he murmured, moving inward, to the back of her neck.

"Mmm," was her only answer, so he took his hands down her shoulder blades, and when the top of the camisole got in his way, he merely tugged it down to her waist.

On her belly, gripping the edges of the table for all she was worth, she gasped.

He smiled grimly and went back to work.

After a stiff moment, she let out a breath and relaxed into his touch, and when he'd removed every bit of tenseness from as much of her back as he could reach, he leaned in, kissed her jaw, and said, "Turn over."

Her eyes flew open. "Um—"

"Unless, of course, you're afraid I'll actually do it."

"Do what?"

"Make you beg."

She squeezed her eyes shut again for a beat.

This was it, he thought with mixed feelings of relief and regret. He'd pushed her past her boundaries. She was going to tell him to take a flying leap. She was going to run back to her room, then back to Los Angeles, certain she'd met the worst of the worst.

And then she did the unthinkable.

She turned over.

She bared her body, and given the way her eyes held his, open and vulnerable, she bared her heart and soul, as well.

Shit, he thought, feeling something deep inside him give. Crack. Break.

Desperately afraid it was his heart, he shoved it out of his thoughts by letting his gaze gobble her up. And there was a hell of a lot to gobble; the woman was a walking wet dream. Her bare breasts were perfect handfuls. No, make that perfect mouthfuls, with their soft curves and rosy nipples, hardening for him into two tight buds that made his jaw ache because he was holding it so tight.

Her ribs rose and fell quickly with her accelerated breathing, and though her camisole and skirt blocked a strip of her belly, he could see enough to know that it was softly rounded and pale and so smooth he wanted to rub his jaw right there.

Just below her bunched-up skirt were those heart-stopping panties. Black. Silky. And riding high enough to fully outline her.

His little L.A. producer was waxed or shaved or whatever mysteries it was that a woman did there. Her long, long shapely legs beckoned, and he ran a hand up one, feeling her tremble. "Cold now?"

Eyes never leaving his, she shook her head.

Holding her gaze, he added his other hand, dancing his fingers up both her thighs, past her panties, skirt and camisole, settling his palms on her ribs.

Again her breath caught, an audible sound in the room.

He stroked over her flawless skin, the very tips of his fingers just barely brushing the undersides of her breasts.

Her nipples tightened even more.

She licked her lips, swallowed hard, but kept looking at him, even when he shifted his hands, gliding them up to cup her beautiful breasts in his palms.

"Oh," she breathed, startled.

His thumb brushed her distended nipples, then he bent his head to take one into his mouth.

Arching her back, she gripped the sides of the table and let out a soft, erotic hum.

And he was a goner. Lifting his head, he looked down at her, then put his mouth to her jaw, her ear, inhaling her, the scent of her shampoo, her skin. Had he really believed he could just tease her, tease himself, and then walk away without sinking into her body? "Em…"

Her eyes fluttered open, filled with heat and need and something that nearly brought him to his knees.

Affection. Her eyes were swimming with it.

So he closed his and concentrated on the intoxicating scent of her, the feel of her glorious body. "We're going to do this."

"Yes," she shocked him by saying, reaching up, fisting her hand in his shirt, holding him over her, leaving him no choice but to look deep into her eyes. "Now. Please, now."

As if he could possibly resist. Bending, he kissed the heavy underside of her breast, licked his way to her nipple, and sucked it into his mouth.

Crying out, she arched up again, reaching for him, her warm hand running up his torso and then down again, her fingers tracing the ridges of his ab muscles.

With her breast in his mouth, her nipple pebbling against his tongue, and her hand warm and soft beneath his shirt now, he couldn't have walked away to save his life. She murmured his name on a sigh as her hand stroked over his bare belly now, then lower, toying with the waistband of his jeans.

It was both heaven and hell. Heaven because touching her like this, looking at her, felt so good. Too good. Hell because he already knew one time with her would never be enough.

Knowing it, pushing it out of his mind, he slid his hand down the length of her arm, twining his fingers with hers, lifting her hand over her head so she couldn't keep touching him, because if she did, this was going to be over before it started. Apparently with her, he couldn't control himself. So he took her other hand, pulling it out from beneath his shirt, bringing it up, as well, squeezing lightly.

Her response was a rocking of her hips, a soft wordless

plea, which he answered with a kiss. Leaning over her, he opened his mouth on hers and claimed her as his.

Hot, wet, deep, the kiss said it all, sending waves of need and desire to pool behind the buttons on his Levi's.

"Jacob," she whispered into his mouth, her breath sweet and hot, the little catches in her throat the sexiest thing he'd ever heard, making him forget the suite, his job, her job, the reason they'd even met, making him forget everything but how soft and giving her mouth was, her tongue just a little shy until he coaxed her with his. It was a kiss that left him wanting a hell of a lot more than what he could get in this position.

He broke contact, his body hardening even further at her low, mewling protest. Moving around from the side of the massage table to the foot, he put a hand on each of her hips and tugged, bringing her up flush against him, her legs sprawled, her black silk-covered crotch snug to his denim-covered one.

Blinking up at him, she smiled, and if his heart hadn't clutched hard before, it did now. She sat up and reached for his shirt, pulling it over his head, tugging him forward to catch his mouth with hers while her fingers danced over his flesh, making his muscles jerk and bunch with each stroke over his chest, over his stomach, then lower.

Again she toyed with his waistband, and this time didn't stop there, but pulled hard until the first button popped open. And then the next.

His body surged; his toes curled. He was going to lose it before they'd even started, something that had never happened, even when he'd been young and extremely stupid. He was quickly spiraling out of control here, wanting nothing more than to sink hard and fast into her body, forget finesse.

Again he bent over her, pressing her back to the table,

stroking his hands up the undersides of her arms, bringing them back over her head, leaning down to kiss her long and hard, until he felt her writhing against him, until she was panting with the need for more, until she was lost in the passion. There. He had her now. He trailed hot, wet, open-mouthed kisses down her torso, flicking his tongue over one nipple, then the other, swirling past her belly button, past the bunched-up clothes in his way.

Standing between her legs as he was, she couldn't close them, but given how she wrapped them around his hips, she didn't seem to want to. He curled his fingers into the elastic strip of her bikini panties and tugged.

They ripped free.

At the sound of the silk giving way, she blinked up at him, and he thought, *Now I've finally pushed her too far and she'll shove me away.* He was even braced for it, the apology ready on his tongue.

Instead she arched up again, her bare flesh against his denim, and whispered, "Oh, please."

He looked down to where her legs were opened, wrapped around his hips.

She was wet, and at the sight he groaned, slipping a finger into her.

Her breath came in short, desperate pants that went into overdrive when he added a second finger, slicking his thumb over ground zero.

"Jacob." She sounded panicked, her hips oscillating. "Please…"

"Come," he murmured, watching his fingers sink in and out of her creamy heat. "I want you to."

She brought her hands down and gripped his, holding his thumb to the right spot, and as she cried out and began to shudder, he bent over her and drew a nipple into his mouth.

It seemed to draw out her climax, or restart it. Watching her, listening to her, feeling her, made him crazy for her. While she was still lost in the throes, he shoved his jeans to his thighs and grabbed a condom from the still-opened drawer.

She opened her eyes and wrapped her fingers around the biggest, hardest erection he'd ever had, leaving him to stifle his groan as he helplessly pushed into her hand. She squeezed, and stroked him, and somewhere in the back of his mind he recognized that she was wrestling his control from him again, and that he was powerless to stop her this time. Everything she was doing, every touch, every sound she made, every look she gave him, drove him closer and closer, until he was standing on the edge.

She leaned in and kissed his pec, stroking him, and again his hips rocked to meet her, a base reaction he could no more have stopped than his next breath. Too good, this felt too good, and he was too far gone to be teased. He wanted to be inside her when he came. "Em."

Her busy fingers were exploring him, and there was a sexy little catch in her throat as she touched his body, as she looked up at him with everything she felt in her eyes. "Hurry, hurry, hurry," she said. "Oh, please, hurry."

It was all far too much for his poor, aching body. Unbelievable as it seemed, she was going to take him right over the edge with nothing more than her touch. *"Wait."* He heard the shocking desperation in his own voice. Later he could kick himself for letting it get so out of hand.

For now he tore open the condom packet and did his best to get it on.

Her fingers covered his. "You're shaking," she murmured.

Yeah. Shaking. *Shaken.* To the bone.

Pulling his head down, she smiled into his eyes, tugged

a little harder and kissed his tense jaw. He figured if he got any more tense his teeth would shatter.

Then she kissed her way to his ear. "I love your body," she whispered, and gave a damp lick to his lobe, along his throat.

He groaned. She was going to devour him. Kill him. *"Em."*

"I know," she murmured softly, soothingly, cupping his face, touching her forehead to his.

Christ. Tenderness. He didn't want tenderness. It brought a shocking lump to his throat, and made his eyes burn. Unable to handle either, he pushed her back to the table. Grabbed her hips. Gave a hard yank so that her wet heat slid over him, making his vision double and his knees wobble again. "Hold on," he grated out. "Goddamn it, hold on to me."

But she already was, and as he thrust hard into her body, she cried out, a sound of pleasure, of surprise, of need, her groan mingling with his.

"Kiss me," she whispered, and he did, leaning over her, thrusting inside her again as his mouth touched hers.

Her body tensed. "Jacob…"

"Again," he demanded. "Come again," he growled, holding on to her as she did just that, his name a sigh on her lips.

He was lost then. Lost in her body, in the feel of her, lost in her eyes.

Even as he was found.

CHAPTER ELEVEN

MUCH LATER, JACOB WALKED Em to her hotel room. She didn't know what she expected but it wasn't for him to follow her inside.

The light on her phone was blinking, so she picked it up to retrieve her messages, feeling a little self-conscious and a lot aware of the big, bad, silent man behind her, watching her every move.

What they'd just shared had been so intense, she didn't know how to react. Just remembering how she'd cried and panted, and damn it, *begged*, had the heat rushing to her face. Plus she was fairly certain she'd embedded her fingernails in his most excellent posterior, which meant that he had ten indentations in there.

Did he even know? If he didn't, surely he realized she'd bitten him on the shoulder in those last few seconds, when she'd practically burst out of her own skin. She'd left teeth prints; she'd seen it herself when he'd put his shirt back on.

God. She'd turned into a wild animal.

She had no idea how she was going to look him in the eyes ever again. *You won't have to tomorrow, when you leave.* Her heart clenched at that but she ruthlessly shoved the thought aside as she accessed her messages. She had two, the first from a desperate-sounding Eric.

"Your assistant has lost her mind," he hissed. "She's pounding on my room door, wanting in. Do you hear her?"

Indeed Em could hear some sort of knocking.

"I can see her through the peephole," Eric said desperately. "And good Christ, you should see what she's wearing. Nearly nothing, if you're wondering!" His voice cracked. "I know I promised you I'd resist her but that was when she was drunk. She's not drunk now, and I don't think I'm going to stay strong, Em. Either call me and remind me why I'm not having sex with her, or don't be upset at the consequences."

Click.

Em stared at the phone and made a sound of worry. She'd wanted them to get back together, but only if they were both ready. The past few days had told her Liza wasn't, and might never be. The fool.

"What's wrong?" Jacob asked.

"Nothing." Except her best friend was going to gobble up her other best friend, and then spit him out like yesterday's trash. It was Liza's MO: love them and leave them before they did the same to her.

Until Eric, no one had ever gotten hurt.

But now Liza had the poor man ensnared for the second time. Eric had a heart of gold behind all that sarcastic wit, and Em was worried.

The next message was Liza herself. "Don't bother coming down here and saving him," she said. "I've got him right where I want him, and let me just say all these toys in the closets here at Hush are coming in handy."

Em listened to this and felt the impending train wreck.

"I've found some silk scarves in the armoire here, and I don't think they're meant to wear for a walk in the park.

I've got him tied to the bed. He's a willing captive, though, so don't worry. I'm going to take good care of him."

Click.

Em hung up the phone and told herself they were both grown-ups. They could handle the consequences...

"Em?"

She turned to Jacob, and while she didn't quite manage to look him in the eyes, she settled her gaze on his chest. "Liza has Eric tied up in his room. Literally."

His eyes heated.

In response, something happened deep in her belly. To cover the confusing reaction, she laughed a little nervously. "What is it about this place? It brings out the animal in people."

"Is that what you think happened upstairs?" His voice was as intoxicating as whiskey. "The ambience got to us?"

"I'm not sure," she admitted.

He came toward her, tossing her brown bag onto the table—she'd nearly forgotten her purchase!—and put his hands on his hips as he looked at her and said, "Again."

"Wh-what?"

"Again," he said, and made her nipples hard and her panties wet.

Yes. Oh, yes, she wanted him again.

And again.

But he was talking about right here, right now. She also wanted him tomorrow. And the next day. And, she was beginning to realize, the tomorrows after that.

But what did he want? Certainly not that kind of tie, and knowing it should have given her pause, should have stopped her.

It didn't.

Her heart nearly burst as she tossed her room key aside and flung herself at him, sighing with pleasure when he caught her up in his arms. She could feel the barely restrained need in him, and thought maybe, just maybe, he wanted more, too.

It was enough for her.

"Let me," he said, dodging her fingers when she reached to get his shirt off. Instead he kissed her until she was dying for more, holding her hands behind her back while he decimated her with his mouth, his hands, his body.

"Let me," he whispered again, when finally, finally, he stripped her down to her skin. This time, he murmured with pleasure over every inch he uncovered, taking the time to touch her, to taste her.

And then he just took her, which he did in the hot tub.

"Again," he repeated later when he took her on the counter.

Then the rug on the floor.

And then even later, on the chair by the window overlooking the bright lights of the city that never sleeps.

They finally fell onto the bed somewhere around three, where Jacob pulled her against his warm, hard body and fell instantly asleep.

She stared into his face, relaxed as he slept, and felt her heart click into place. She could love this man. She could love him forever, if he'd let her.

But she already knew he wouldn't. He might think he'd kept the reins tight on his emotions tonight, hiding from her how he was starting to feel, hiding his fear of letting go, of giving her control and losing his, but he hadn't really kept a thing from her.

A surge of emotion for him welled up and filled her heart and her eyes. Leaning in, she put her lips softly to his. "'Night," she whispered.

He hummed in pleasure and tightened his grip on her without waking all the way. With a dreamy sigh, she snuggled in and let sleep claim her, too.

AN ALARM WENT OFF and Jacob jerked awake. He was in a bed, a strange bed, with a delicious, warm, naked female body plastered to his side.

Not just any bed, and not just any woman.

Hush.

Em.

He had a handful of breast with a nipple pebbling in his palm, his other hand cupping a warm buttock. *Nice.* Rumbling approval deep in his throat, he rolled her to her back, settling his weight on her, thrusting a thigh high between hers to spread her for his pleasure.

"The alarm," she gasped.

Reaching out, he knocked the clock to the floor and it went mercifully silent.

"Auditions," she mumbled, eyes still closed. "I have to— *Ohmigod.*"

Having sucked a nipple into his mouth, he teased the tip with his tongue, smiling at her moan, at the way she clutched at him with her hands, her legs.

"Jacob—"

Lightly he bit down on her nipple, then flicked it with his tongue.

Her fingers dug into the muscles of his shoulder, her body arching up into him.

Oh, yeah. Good. His slid his hand down her side, spreading his fingers wide to touch all that he could, her ribs, her belly, her hip. "Wait," she gasped.

He palmed her sweet ass, then dipped his fingers in—

"*Jacob.*"

For the first time he heard the tone in her voice. The

reluctant tone. The tone he'd used often enough the morning after when he'd had enough of a woman and needed out.

That was when he woke all the way up and smelled the news.

She was done with *him*.

She was done with him before he'd been done with her. That had never happened, not once, and a feather could have knocked him over he was so shocked. "Right." Without looking into her eyes, he rolled off her and off the bed all in one move. Reached for his jeans.

"Jacob."

Where the hell were his shoes?

"Jacob."

"Don't get up," he said, shoving his legs into his jeans and grabbing his shirt. "I know my way out."

Did he ever. He always knew his way out, and was pissed he'd stayed.

Sex with a woman, he could do that. He knew how to do it, extremely well.

Sleeping with one, not so much. In fact, he rarely did it at all, and never on a woman's turf.

Seems he'd broken all his own rules last night.

That's what he got for thinking with the wrong head.

The paper bag on the dresser mocked him. It was open, the packaging of the vibrator strewn over the glossy wood.

They'd put that thing to some fun, sexy, outrageous use, and if his heart hadn't been pounding heavily, uncomfortably, the memories of what they'd done would have made him smile.

As it was, they made him hard.

Because after her initial shyness, Em had gotten into it. Very into it. The batteries were close to dead.

Damn, he was thinking again.

He made it to the door before he felt her hand on his arm, trying to tug him around. He stared at his own hand on the handle. "Don't, Em."

"Look at me," she said softly, her hand rising to glide over his back. He felt his muscles quiver at the touch.

"Please?" she whispered.

Gritting his teeth, he turned only his head and met her eyes. They were deep and full not of discomfort or irritation at him still being here but hope and joy and, damn, that knee-knocking affection again.

She hadn't run off like a scared little bunny at the depths of his passion. Hadn't run from anything he'd shown her, as he'd assumed—and half hoped—she would. He didn't understand what drew him to her, why he suddenly wanted to toss her back into that bed and follow her down, why he wanted to keep her.

Keep her.

He couldn't keep her. Even thinking it was the stupidest thought he'd ever had. He'd never managed to keep anything in his life, not a place, not a thing, and sure as hell not a person.

"Last night," Em said, searching his gaze for something, God knew what. "It was…different."

He let out a harsh laugh. "Yeah. I'm guessing not a lot of guys would take you to a porn shop."

"That wasn't all that was different."

"You probably don't do a lot of barhopping, either. At least the kind of bar I took you to."

"I didn't mean different bad." She looked at him as if she could see right through him, damn it, into the very black depths of his soul. "I meant different…scary."

Scary? He'd scared her? Christ. "Em…" He squeezed his eyes closed tight. "I didn't mean to… I wouldn't—"

"No." She turned him to face her, both hands on his

arms. "No." She smiled. "Scary good. I'm trying to tell you that I had the most amazing time, and yes it was different, and yes it scared me because it was different. Different as in more meaningful. What we shared last night when we made love—"

"Wait." He shook his head. God, he couldn't let her finish. "I think you should stop right there. Before you say something you're going to regret in the name of lust."

"It wasn't just lust."

"Yes," he said. "It was. It was just a normal night of lust."

"Oh." She blinked once, the hurt in those depths unmistakable. "I see."

Hell. He should have left last night. He was a complete idiot. "I don't want to hurt you—"

"No. No, it's okay. I understand. It was a casual thing."

"That's right. Just a normal night out—"

"I get it." She nodded. She took her hands from his arms. Backed up a step. Even curved her mouth into a smile.

Though it didn't come close to reaching her eyes.

"Don't worry," she said, trying to soothe him, which made him feel even more like slime. "I'm fine."

From somewhere behind them her cell phone rang and she jerked as if she'd been shot. "Excuse me, I've got to get that—"

"Yeah. Uh…good luck with your auditions." At his own lame words, he winced. *Good luck?* Could he be a bigger ass? "Em—"

But she'd already turned away.

Just as he'd wanted.

EM PICKED UP her ringing cell phone. When she heard her hotel room door close behind Jacob, she closed her eyes. He was gone…

Just a normal night out.

She was such a fool, such a damn fool, she thought angrily as she flipped open her phone. "Hello?"

"Em."

"Eric." She let out a breath and concentrated on the here and now. "I take it you're not still…tied up."

"Uh, no." He lowered his voice. "Look, it was great. But…"

"But what?"

"Afterward…" He sighed. "She cried, Em. It broke my heart."

"Why are you whispering?"

"Because she's asleep right next to me. Why did she cry?"

Em sank to the bed. "Did you ask her?"

"She denied doing it, but I saw the tears."

"What happened after that?"

"We, uh, did it again. It was…well, words fail," he said in an awed voice. "Not the sex, the connection, you know?"

Yeah. She knew.

"I fell in love with her all over again."

Em let out a long breath. She was falling, too.

"God," Eric whispered. "I think she's just screwing with my head. What do I do?"

She laughed a little harshly. "Eric, what in our history together makes you think that I have any clue when it comes to love?"

"Because your heart's always in the right place. You're all about heart and soul, Em, making memories, shit like that."

"Yeah, well, I'm really a pretty big screwup in that area. Right now all that matters is that we're going to be unemployed and eating canned soup for the rest of our lives if I don't get downstairs and get going on the auditions—"

"She cried, Em."

Em rubbed her aching temples. Other things ached, too. Between her thighs.

But the biggest ache of all came from her heart, which she reached up and rubbed now, though it didn't help. "If I had to guess, she cried because she loves you, too."

Utter silence greeted this.

"Eric? You there?"

"She told me she doesn't."

"Even you are not that clueless as to believe her."

"Look, I'm just a guy," he pleaded. "We were *born* clueless."

"Okay, listen, I haven't had caffeine, and my night was… well." She drew a deep breath. "But I think she just doesn't know how to deal with the love she feels for you, or even how to show it. Tying you up was symbolic. You get it? You're hers. You're tied to her. You see?"

He was quiet for a moment. "I guess."

"You know what happened before. The two of you were too hot, too heavy. You didn't share the stuff that scared you. You didn't do the things you need to do to make it last."

"Yeah."

"You burned it out."

"I know." He sounded terrified. "I don't want that to happen again."

"Then do more than the wild sex. Talk. Communicate. Listen to each other. Be there for each other."

"I can do that. But pinning Liza down is hard. She's not exactly the communicative type."

"Well, turnaround is fair play," she said, quoting Jacob.

He paused. "You mean…tie her up?"

"Give the boy an A."

He laughed softly. "Gotcha. Now tell me about your night. You have a bad one?"

Bad? No. Good? No. Try the best night of her entire life. "Hard to explain." Especially since, for Jacob, it had all been…"normal." Heat filled her face at that. *Bastard.*

From its perch still on her floor, the alarm clock went off again, and she sighed. "We've got to get a move on. Get up. Get Liza up. Meet me in the conference room for round two."

"Oh, boy," Eric said. "Here we go again."

Yeah. Here we go.

THOUGH HE COULD HAVE showered and changed at Hush, Jacob went back to his apartment. Right now he wanted to be in his own space. But as he climbed the three flights of stairs, he knew the problem wasn't the outside world, but the thoughts racing inside his own head.

He wished he was still in bed with Em. He wished she was tucked beneath him, while he was buried deep inside her, taking them both to that nameless place of abandon they'd been to several times in the night.

How many women had he been with? Many, and not once when a woman had called out his name while lost in passion had he stopped just to watch her.

With Em, he hadn't been able to tear his eyes away. He loved the way she arched up, her throat open and vulnerable, the way she panted his name in that serrated, husky voice that always sounded so…surprised.

Yeah, that was it. Every time she'd come, she'd been honestly surprised.

Watching her unravel had the been the sexiest, most erotically charged experience of his entire life.

Then morning had come and she had wanted to obsess and tear it all apart and look for the meaning.

And he'd hurt her.

Damn it, he knew he had, but at the time he hadn't cared. He'd been choking, panicking, as he'd stared at her, wanting nothing more than to haul her close, bury his face in her hair, and not let go.

Never let go.

He scrubbed his hands over his face but the longing remained. And he didn't know what to do with it. Why wasn't it gone? Why hadn't one night been enough? One night *had* to be enough.

He came to the landing outside his front door and stared in surprise at Pru, who was sitting there waiting for him. "I'm going crazy," she said, and rose to her feet.

Jacob unlocked his door, shaking his head when Pru pushed ahead of him and entered.

"Come on in," he said dryly.

"Did you hear me?" She whirled to face him, her neat, long braid nearly blinding him. "I'm losing it here."

"Join the club." He stood in the middle of his living room, glancing toward his shower with longing.

"Jacob."

He sighed. "What's happened?"

"Everything. Nothing."

Jacob squinted at her. "Is that in English?"

"We went out last night, Caya and I. And at the end I kissed her. Caya kissed me back, and I'm telling you, it was real. It was love—"

"Pru—"

"It was," she insisted.

"How do you even know the difference between lust and love?"

She looked startled at the question. "I just do."

"You're going to have to do better than that."

"Okay, well…lust can be sated. Lust is gone when you

wake up the next morning. Lust doesn't have those bone-deep terrifying feelings, like you *have* to see that person again or your life is never going to be the same."

Something pinged deep in Jacob's gut. It felt like worry, but that couldn't be it because he never worried. Nothing had ever been worth worrying over. "Sounds like nothing another night of sex wouldn't cure."

"No." Eyes sad, Pru shook her head. "See, you'd think so, but then you get there, and you do it again, and it's only worse."

Shit. *Shit.* She was wrong. She had to be wrong. "Maybe some lust is just more stubborn than others."

"Honey, lust is a fickle bitch, but one thing she isn't is stubborn."

He stared at her, dread clawing its way up his throat. "I see."

Someone knocked at his door. Turning his back on Pru, he opened it and found Caya.

She had wet eyes and a matching misery on her face. Aw, hell. "I suppose you want to join—"

She stuck a finger into his pec, poking hard. "Did you tell Pru she should tell me how she felt about me?"

"Uh—" He glanced back at Pru over his shoulder, but she'd moved out of sight from Caya, flattening herself back against the wall, shaking her head *no,* looking panicked that Caya might see her.

He'd known this was going to come back and bite him on the ass. He turned to Caya, still on his doorstep. "Look, I don't think I should get involved—"

"Well, it's too late now!"

"Caya—" He stopped helplessly when a tear spilled over. "Aw, no. Don't—"

She burst into tears.

"Goddamn it." He pulled her in for a hug, turning her

away from seeing into his apartment, though it didn't matter because Pru had vanished into his bathroom. Now that she was out of sight, he moved Caya inside because he figured there was no chance in hell either of them was going away anytime soon.

"See, you do care," Caya sniffed against him.

"Just a little."

She pulled back and looked into his face. "Look at that, admitting it didn't make you choke."

He frowned. "What is that supposed to mean?"

"It means you're just as screwed up as me when it comes to letting people love you, and loving them back." Caya swiped at her wet cheek. "I'm sorry. I know I'm freaking out here, and taking it out on you." She covered her eyes, then dropped her hands to her sides. "Pru said she loved me."

"I know."

"She wants me to tell her how I feel back, but what the hell do I know about this stuff?"

"You're asking me?"

Caya laughed. "Yeah. Fine mess, huh? So do you think it's screwed up that I…sort of love her back?"

"Well, I—" Jacob broke off when the bathroom door behind them opened.

Pru stepped out, hand over her mouth as she stared at Caya.

At the sight of her, Caya jerked as if shot. "Y-you're… here."

Pru nodded, her eyes filling.

"You…heard me," Caya whispered.

"'Sort of'?" Pru whispered.

Caya swallowed. "More than sort of."

Pru's eyes filled. "Oh, my God."

"I didn't want to love you," Caya said. "I tried not to. But you're it for me."

Pru's eyes overflowed, and there was so much hope on her face, it hurt Jacob to look at her. "What about men—"

"They're great, but not what I want."

"Caya, my God. Are you sure?"

"Very. Besides, most men are maturity challenged. Sorry," she said to Jacob. "No offense intended."

"None taken," he said dryly.

Caya turned back to Pru. "I've been out there, I know what's waiting. I don't want any of it, men or other women. Just you."

They reached for each other in an embrace so real, so raw, Jacob had to close his eyes.

When he opened them, they were kissing.

"So." He cleared his throat. "I guess you can both go now."

They kept kissing, passionately. Jacob figured it was a fantasy of men everywhere but for him it only felt like salt on a wound he couldn't see. "You know what? Never mind. I'll go."

They just kept at it, as if they didn't need air, didn't need anyone but themselves.

Jacob grabbed his keys and walked out of his own damn apartment.

CHAPTER TWELVE

Note to Housekeeping:
Refill the sensual massage oils and the condoms in
the Haiku Suite.

THE AUDITIONS were worse than the day before, if that was
even possible. *American Idol* rejects had nothing on the
people they saw today, and after several hours, Em had her
head in her hands and Liza had a drink in hers.

"This isn't going to work," Liza said after they'd seen
an eighty-year-old woman from Russia, who could indeed
cook but couldn't speak a word of English.

"No, it's not going to work." A heavy dread was making
itself at home in the pit of Em's belly. "Well, it's been fun
working with you while it lasted."

"You could talk to Jacob."

"No."

"You could beg Jacob."

"Double no."

"Okay, then." Liza put her drink down and picked up
her purse.

"Where are you going?"

"You saved my life. Now I'm going to save yours."

"What do you mean, I saved your life?"

Liza looked at her. "I wasn't asleep when Eric called
you this morning."

"You weren't?"

"I was faking it. I've always been good at faking it. I've had to fake it with every man I've ever been with—except Eric."

"Oh, Liza."

"It's because he loves me. I can believe it because he told you. He has no reason to lie to you."

"Honey, he has no reason to lie to you, either."

"I know, but…well, I just couldn't be sure. Love has never been good to me."

Em knew that. Liza's parents hadn't been warm and fuzzy but cold and impossible to please. Liza had been acting up all her life to prove she didn't care. "Eric's the real deal," Em said quietly.

"I'm getting that." Liza's eyes shimmered with emotion. "And that's my point. I can let go, let myself *really* love him, you know? No games, just the real thing. And it was you who helped me see it, that this thing between us can really last for the long haul." She hugged Em tight. "I'll never be able to thank you enough for that. But I'm going to try like hell. You'll see. I'm going to fix this for you."

"You can't—"

"I'm your assistant. It's my job to solve your problems, and I'm going to go solve this. Let's go."

"Where?"

"Just come on." Liza opened the conference door.

Eric stood there with his clipboard monitoring the short line of hopefuls left. There were only two, a girl who looked to be about twelve and an old man who, if she wasn't mistaken, was napping on his feet.

"We need you," Liza said to Eric.

Without question, Eric turned to the two candidates left. "I'm sorry, that's it for today. Thanks for coming."

Liza looked at him as if bowled over.

"So what do you need?" Eric asked her.

Still looking unbearably touched that he'd blindly follow her simply because she said she needed him, she cleared her throat. "Let's go. You'll see when we get there."

As soon as they hit the lobby and walked toward the main entrance of Amuse Bouche, Em hesitated. "He already said no, Liza." Her heart tightened at the memories of last night and this morning. Memories he'd sullied when he'd looked at her as if she'd been any of the other women he'd let in, and then out, of his life.

She hadn't expected that, she could admit, though what she *had* expected, she couldn't exactly say. She'd known who he was, what he was. She'd known his past. She'd known he was wildly, fabulously sexy, with an edge, with a wanderlust spirit, a man who rarely settled in one place for long.

And she'd slept with him anyway, just as she'd also begun to fall for him.

That made her the crazy one, not him.

"Let's just talk to him," Liza said.

"I can't."

Liza frowned. "You look pale."

"Just tired."

"Long night?"

Aware that both Liza and Eric were watching her carefully, she lifted a shoulder.

"I knew it," Liza said. "Oh, honey. Did he break your heart? Because if he did, I can break him. I can—"

"Liza." Em smiled. What else could she do? "Let's just fix one thing at a time."

"Yes. Starting with the show." Liza looked through the empty dining room toward the kitchen, jaw tight, eyes determined. She was a bulldog when it came to this stuff. "Humor me. Give me five minutes."

The restaurant wasn't open yet. No one greeted them

so they moved toward the kitchen doors, where they could see lights and hear talking.

Liza knocked.

A pretty brunette poked her head out. Em recognized her as the sommelier from the other night. "Can I help you?" she asked, looking greatly stressed.

"Yes," Liza said. "I heard both of your assistant chefs were out with the flu and that you're in a real bind."

Both Em and Eric looked at Liza in surprise.

The sommelier sighed. "It's true. But I don't know how you heard such a thing—"

"Oh, you'd be surprised what I hear." Liza smiled and offered her business card. "I'm just a guest here, but you can see I'm an assistant producer, so I know how to get things done. Our location director here—" she pointed to Eric "—is an amazing cook. No formal training, but he's doing research for a show. Maybe he could help you out today. You could call our studio for his references."

The sommelier looked Eric over with hopeful curiosity. "Really?"

Eric, as confused as Em, nodded.

"Well…" The sommelier glanced down at the card in her hand, then back up into their faces. "You could come in, meet Chef. He'd have to approve this, of course, which, truthfully, he's not likely to do. He doesn't work with strangers," she said, though her gaze turned bemused when she looked over at Em.

"Oh, we're not strangers to Chef," Liza said with a smile.

Em added her own weak smile. Nope, not strangers.

"Just a sec." The sommelier shut the door.

Em turned to Liza. *"What are you doing?"*

"A favor for a favor. We do something for Chef, and then he'll do something for us."

"Liza, those are not equivalent favors!" Em cried. "One day of Eric's services is not going to make Jacob come across the country—"

The kitchen door opened again, and there stood Jacob himself, looking tall, big, and gorgeously rumpled in his battered jeans and boots and a T-shirt that said Smile, It Confuses People.

"Em," he said in surprise, for one brief beat his face unguarded, allowing her to see the pleasure before it was gone in a blink, carefully masked.

It made her sad to think that what they'd shared last night was going to be just a distant memory.

"Chef," Liza purred. "Eric's an amazing chef. He's offering to help you out today."

"Thank you," he said. "But I don't need—"

"It's a Friday. We both know what this place is going to look like tonight, and that's full to the gills. You can't do it alone."

Jacob looked at Eric. "You cook?"

"Yes."

Jacob turned to Em. "What's the catch?"

Em looked into his eyes and felt her throat tighten. He knew she was here for some reason, and not the goodness of her heart. All his life he'd had to scrap and fight to get by, nothing had ever been handed to him, not friendship, not love, nothing.

She wouldn't do the same thing. *She wouldn't do this Nathan's way.* "No catch."

He crossed his arms, disbelieving.

"I'm sorry," she said. "Coming here was a mistake." And grabbing both Liza and Eric, she turned away.

"Wait."

She went still, then turned back.

Gaze still inscrutable, he'd relaxed marginally, and she

knew with a sudden clarity that he'd lied to her. Last night hadn't been the norm for him, it had been just as special, just as amazing, as it had been for her.

And he'd pushed her away because of it. It had been his right to do so, and she understood it all too well.

"Help would be welcome," he said, surprising her.

Eric shoved up his sleeves. "Just tell me where and what."

Em nodded and took a step back to let Eric through. "Okay, then. Good luck tonight—"

"Where are you going?" Jacob asked.

"Out of your hair."

Jacob rubbed his nearly hairless head. "No worries there."

Em stared at him. "What are you saying?"

"I think he already said it," Liza said, looking at Jacob as she rolled up her sleeves. "He needs help. From *all* of us."

EM ENDED UP with a ponytail keeping her hair back and a white jacket over her clothes. But it was the knife in her hands concerning her as she contemplated a stack of vegetables that might as well have been Mt. Everest.

Jacob was moving around, lifting big pots, wielding equipment, working near the hot, open flame, mixing up something that smelled like heaven. Eric was on the other side of the kitchen at the open flame, smiling and joking with Pru, while Liza surreptitiously watched them from her corner, mouth grim.

They'd promised Jacob an hour of prep work. Correction. She and Liza had promised an hour. Eric would stay as long as Jacob was needed, the rest of the night if necessary, because, as he said, the experience would be fun.

From the range, Eric laughed at something Pru said.

Liza pretended not to notice.

Em wasn't as good at pretending. Ignoring what had happened between her and Jacob last night, even for an hour, was beyond her, but she gave it the ol' college try as she reached for a carrot and began slicing. How could he look at her and not remember?

Even as she thought it, Jacob glanced across the room at her, nothing showing on his face.

Was he thinking about what they'd been doing only a few hours before? How he'd touched her, kissed her? How when he'd been buried deep in her body he'd met her gaze and had been unable to tear his away?

Eric laughed again.

Liza set down her knife and walked toward them, a look of intent on her face.

Eric turned to her, smiling until he saw her expression. Then his changed, softened, filled with a look of such hope Em wanted to turn away, but she couldn't.

At the look, Liza suddenly broke into a smile, as if Eric was her everything.

Eric returned it.

Pru moved away, and Eric gently touched Liza's face, kissing her softly before going back to his station.

Liza brought her hand up to her lips, sighed, then went back to her station, as well.

And Em swallowed the inexplicable urge to cry.

"You trying to lose a finger?"

When she nearly jerked out of her skin, two arms reached around her, hands settling over hers. "Easy," Jacob murmured.

Easy? Was he kidding? She could feel his warm, hard chest against her back, his heat, his strength. And she could smell him, some complicated mix of soap and man that was so intoxicating she felt dizzy. "What are we making?"

"Spicy Szechuan noodles with grilled Indonesian tiger prawns for the first course, snapper with tamarind-coconut sauce and bamboo rice for the main course. Then tempura bananas with caramel sauce for dessert."

She didn't even know what half of that was. "Sounds interesting."

"Liar."

Craning her neck, she looked up into his eyes. Despite the tension in his body, his eyes were smiling.

"Do you ever just make burgers?" she asked.

"Yep."

"Burgers tonight would be good," she said. "I could forgo chopping all these veggies."

"Would you rather pick cilantro leaves for garnish?" he asked. "It's easier. Or you could prep spinach leaves for salads."

She'd had no idea how much work went into being a chef, the long hours, mostly on your feet, lifting heavy pots and pans, working near dangerous appliances at high temperatures. "I can handle this."

"I bet you can." His arms were still alongside hers, his hands guiding her fingers into the right position on the knife. "This way, Em, so you'll keep all your fingers, see? Nothing wrong with your way, other than I don't like blood in my kitchen." He spoke casually, showing her exactly how he meant for it all to be done, making it look easy. And having him surround her like that was, well…nirvana. It brought it all back, what it had felt like to be skin-to-skin with him, face-to-face, sharing their bodies, and more. Wanting to see him, to gauge if he was feeling any of the overwhelming emotions she was, she tipped her head up to look at him.

His eyes were on the knife and the carrot but they swiveled to meet hers. "You going to watch what you're doing? Or me?"

"You."

His eyes swirled with heat. "Em."

"The things you said to me this morning." She took a quick peek at the others. No one was paying them the slightest bit of attention. "I don't think you meant them."

"I never say anything I don't mean."

"Jacob." She pushed the carrots away and turned to face him directly. "We made love. We fell asleep together. And it was out of this world. I might not be all that experienced, but I know that much." He didn't say anything, and the first bits of doubt crept in. "Or I thought I knew that much," she muttered.

Beneath his breath, he swore. "You did know that much." She just looked at him, and he swore again. "It was insane how perfect it was," he said tightly. "How's that?"

She felt the smile split her face.

With a groan at the sight, he grabbed the knife and started slicing without her, his hands and fingers moving so quickly and efficiently they were a blur. "It doesn't matter, Em. It's not going anywhere, you know that. You're heading back to L.A., and I'm…"

"You're what?"

"I'm not sure. I'm never sure."

"Because you like to be free to walk when it suits you."

"That's right." He finished the huge stack of carrots and started in on the celery.

"Because contracts, even short-term television contracts for huge amounts of money, don't interest you any more than planning for the future interests you."

He set down the knife. "Thank you for your help."

She'd been dismissed. Well, didn't that suit her. She

turned away from him, and suddenly realized they were all alone. "Hey, where did everyone go?"

Equally bewildered, Jacob looked around. "You're stressing out my kitchen."

Em put her hands on her hips. "*I'm* stressing out your kitchen? Are you kidding me? You're the one giving me heart failure—"

"When did I give you heart failure?"

She shook her head and bit her lip so the rest couldn't come out.

He merely hauled her up on her toes and put them nose-to-nose. "Tell me."

"Every time you made me come," she whispered.

Still holding her, he stared at her. Annoyance faded, replaced by emotions that made her swallow hard.

"Is that right?" he asked in that silky voice that last night had driven her over the edge too many times to count.

"Yes."

He set her down. His hands left her. "Flour," he said.

"What?"

He gestured behind her, to what looked like a pantry door. "I need flour."

She narrowed her eyes. Was this yet another test? Or his way of changing the subject?

He just waited.

Fine. She'd get him the damn flour. And then they'd talk. She opened the double doors. Inside were shelves stocked with cans and dry goods.

And Eric and Liza. Eric's hair was wild from Liza's fingers, his shirt gaping, his belt open. He had Liza backed to a shelf, one hand up her shirt, the other down her pants.

As Em's mouth fell open, they jerked apart.

"Sorry," Eric said.

Liza smiled apologetically. "Make-up sex…well, you know."

No, Em didn't know. But suddenly she wished she did.

Jacob shut the door.

"Oh, my," she finally said.

Jacob looked into her hot face, then without a word, took her hand and pulled her back through the kitchen, down an employee hallway and through yet another door.

It was a beautiful room, quite obviously his office, with a black lacquer desk and matching shelving unit, and a large window looking out to the busy city.

A black cat sat on the desk, the cat from the elevator on her first day here. At the sight of them, she gave a soft "meow," rubbed around each of their ankles, and began to purr.

Jacob scooped her up, scratched behind her ears, and then set her down outside the office door.

"Yours?" she asked.

"Eartha Kitty belongs to Piper, the owner of the hotel. Sort of a mascot."

She tried a smile. "You have a nice view here."

"I guess. I look at you and I can't see anything else."

The words stunned her. Thrilled her.

"Em, I want to finish what we started in the kitchen."

"The fight?"

"We were discussing, not fighting. I believe you were telling me how it felt when I made you come—"

More heat flooded her body. "I don't feel like talking about that anymore."

"Really? Why's that?"

"Um…" She broke off when he took a step toward her. She took one back, but came up against the windowsill. She gripped it tight at her sides to steady herself.

He arched a brow.

She returned the gesture. "Because," she said, feeling immature as she crossed her arms.

And aware. Let's not forget extremely aware.

"*Because* isn't a complete sentence, or a reason," he pointed out.

"I don't feel like talking about it," she repeated a little shakily when he slid his body to hers, sandwiching her between the sill and his hard form.

"So what *do* you feel like doing?" His voice was amused, but looking into his eyes, he was anything but.

She bit her lip harder this time. No more blurting anything out! There was no point to it, no point in hashing this out.

"Then maybe we shouldn't talk at all," he decided, and slid his muscled thigh between hers, bringing it up high, making all her happy spots zing to life. While she was still absorbing that, he slid his hands in her hair, tugged her face close and kissed her.

CHAPTER THIRTEEN

To: Concierge
From: Housekeeping
Room 1212 has left a request for a pack of batteries.
Please make sure they're AAs.

EM PULLED BACK from Jacob's mind-blowing kiss. "Okay, maybe we *should* talk." *Before I let you take me right here on your desk.* She wanted him, so much, but realized that scared or not, edgy or not, Jacob was nothing but heartache waiting to happen.

When he stroked a strand of hair from her face and then left his fingers cupping her cheek she squeezed her eyes shut. "Jacob—"

"I loved watching you."

"Butchering the veggies?"

"When you came."

Her eyes flew open.

He smiled wickedly. "You always seemed surprised, every single time. The sexiest thing I've ever seen, watching you let go."

Just his words flooded heat in her veins. "Stop."

"Why are you always so surprised, Em?"

Nope. Talking was a bad idea, too. No more talking, no more kissing. In fact, no more staring at him, either, because he looked so good....

She shut her eyes again.

He stroked his fingers down her throat, then over her collarbone, pushing her sweater out of his way as he went.

Her nipples hardened but she nibbled on her lip and didn't make a sound.

"Haven't you ever come with a man before?"

That got her. Her eyes flew open. She shoved his hand away. "You are so full of yourself."

"Have you?" Undeterred, his hands took each of hers, bringing them around her back, holding them there low on her spine, which brought her entire front up against his.

"Yes, I've come with a man before." His gaze was so deep, so real. How could it be that he could let her in like this, and yet not keep her in? "But not like with you," she admitted. "Never like with you."

"What made it different?" His voice was low, husky. *Sweet.*

Damn it, he was sucking her right back in. "Are you sure you want to hear this?" she asked, and saw the truth. No, he didn't want to hear this. He didn't want to know any of it, but he was as deeply shaken as she. And listening to her was the only chance he had of understanding.

Her own understanding nearly rose up and choked her. God, he was something, all confident and sexy as long as things were on his terms, in his comfort zone.

But as he had with her, she, too, had taken him beyond comfort, and the expression behind his eyes opened her heart and made it bleed. "*You* make it different," she whispered. "There's something about you. About how I feel when I'm with you. There's something between us that I can't resist, even if you can. You take me out of myself, Jacob, whether we're laughing, talking, or making love. And because of that, you make me feel more than I ever have. An orgasm with you suddenly isn't this tiny little ping I have to strive so hard for. It's like…"

"What?" he whispered.

"Like the Fourth of July. A full fireworks display." She looked into his eyes and saw the acknowledgement, that he felt the same. "It involves so much more than just our body parts. For me, it involves my heart."

"Your two friends," he said. "Is it this way for them?"

"I think so."

"Seeing them like that made you hot."

And she wasn't the only one. She could feel him, heavy and hard against her. "They belong together, they have an undeniable connection. It makes me want such a thing for myself."

His eyes grew dark, if that was even possible. "I can give you a connection." Banding his arm around her, he lifted her. He sat her on the sill, then stepped between her legs.

"Jacob—"

"I want you again, Em. I can't think with all this wanting."

It melted her, and in spite of herself, she tilted her face up for his kiss, sighing as he met her more than halfway, leaning in, pressing his body flush to hers.

"I keep remembering last night," she murmured when he took little bites out of her on his way over her throat. "How good it felt…"

"If I say I can't remember, can we do it again?"

She let out a laugh—that backed up in her throat when he tugged her sweater down and exposed her bra, its front hook posing no problem for him. He just crouched in front of her, clicked the bra open, then let out a low breath of desire when her breasts popped free. Carefully, gently, he ran his stubbled cheek over one.

Her nipples puckered into a tight knot, wrenching another sound from Jacob's throat. "You are so beautiful, Em."

"Thank you, but I'm not sure—"

He sucked her nipple hard into his mouth and her thoughts skittered right out of her head.

"We probably shouldn't—" She broke off on a moan when he bunched up her skirt and slid a hand between her legs. "Um…well, maybe."

"Oh, yeah," he murmured roughly, slipping her panties aside to sink a finger into her. Then another. "You're already wet." His thumb spread that wetness around while his fingers stroked her until her vision faded.

"Jacob—"

"I'll buy you a new pair, I promise." Then he tore the flimsy scrap of material away from her and tossed it over his shoulder.

It landed on his desk lamp.

"Jacob—" she choked, but then his fingers were back inside her, his thumb teasing her sensitive nub with little slippery passes while his mouth found her breast again. "Oh," she whispered, unable to form words.

"I know." With his fingers driving her to bliss, she wrapped her arms around his neck and held on for dear life as he took her to orgasm in less than sixty seconds.

"Again," he demanded. He dropped to his knees. With wicked intent, he looked up at her, then stuck his head beneath her skirt. Holding her open with his fingers, he used his tongue to drive her right out of her mind.

Gasping, crying, she fell back against the window, her fingers digging into the wood sill as he took her to heaven and back.

And then again. *"Jacob."*

"One more."

"I can't—" But then he did something fantastically clever with his tongue and lightly clamped his teeth over her, as well, adding his fingers to the mix, and she completely and utterly lost it.

She came back to herself at the sound of the condom packet being ripped open. "My God."

"There's more." He spit out the corner of the packet and rolled the condom down his length. "Hold on to me," he commanded. His skin was hot and damp, the muscles beneath hard and trembling.

"Wait."

His gaze went to hers.

Her breathing was still ragged, but she had to say it. "This isn't…a normal everyday thing." She opened his shirt, ran her hand down his mouthwatering torso to wrap her fingers around his erection, gliding him against her. "Not for me."

He squeezed his eyes shut, gritting his teeth. "Em—"

"It isn't," she repeated in a shaky voice, and let him inside her, just an inch. "This is different, this is us…" Her body was still pulsing with pleasure, making talking difficult, but she forced it out. "This is *us* making it different."

He let out a ragged groan, his face a mask of pleasured pain, the cords in his neck standing out in bold relief, the muscles in his shoulders and arms as he held her so tense they quivered.

"Say it," she breathed, unable to tear her eyes off him.

"Christ. Yes. Yes, it's different with you." At that, he gripped her hips and thrust powerfully, sinking into her to the hilt, stretching and filling her, an action that ripped a helpless cry from her and a low groan from him.

Putting his forehead to hers, he panted for breath. "Wrap your legs around me. There. *There*." Using the sill as leverage, he thrust into her again and again, leaving her gasping for air, unable to say anything else, which she was certain he did on purpose, but with him filling her, sinking into her with each stroke so fully, so deeply, she didn't care. And with a helpless cry, she came again. He followed her this time, pulsing hard within her, his big body shuddering.

She held on to him through it, clinging, eyes closed, face pressed against his throat, her body absorbing the intimacy, the embrace, the closeness, never wanting it to end.

And he let her cuddle, the most endearing thing he'd ever done, holding her tight to him for a long time, as if maybe he didn't want the interlude to end any more than she did.

"And it's two," she whispered.

"Two?"

"Yeah." She smiled when she felt him kiss her neck. "You owe me *two* pairs of panties."

JACOB GUIDED Em into the private bathroom attached to his office where he soaped her up in his shower, then dried her off before helping her back into her clothes.

And all the while he wondered when she was going to say or do something to ruin the glow.

But she didn't say a word as she walked to his office door.

And in the end, it was he who couldn't keep quiet. "Em."

"I know." Turning to face him, she shot him a brave smile. "Don't worry, I know."

"Know what?"

"That even though what we shared was different for both of us, it's going nowhere."

Right. It wasn't. It couldn't. But just looking at her made his body twitch and his heart ache.

He still couldn't get enough, and more than that, he knew he might never get enough.

With one last smile, so sad it tore right through his heart, she patted his shoulder—comforting him!—and went out the door.

CHAPTER FOURTEEN

EM AND LIZA SAT in the lobby, on a corner couch, going over options. There weren't many. It didn't help that in spite of the shower in Jacob's office she could still smell him on her.

His shampoo, his soap… And it was orgasmically good.

Certainly the sex in his office had been.

She'd never come like that in her life, and she knew enough to be sure that she never would with another man.

He was it.

He was "the one."

After a lifetime of toads, she'd found her prince.

Not that he'd welcome her realization.

"Okay, speak."

Em blinked at Liza. "What?"

"I keep losing you to whatever thoughts are making you alternately grin like an idiot, or look as if your dog just died."

"I'm fine."

"You're in love with him."

"Don't be ridiculous. No one falls in love in just a few days."

"Of course they do. You can fall in love in a day, an hour, a minute."

"You've been with Eric for how long? And you can't figure out if it's love."

Liza smiled. "Oh, it's love. I'm pretty sure it always was. I'm going to tell him tonight. In fact, he wants me to wait for him in his room. I think he's going to pay me back for tying him up. Have you seen the toys in those rooms?" Liza shivered with delight. "I hope we use the fur-lined gloves and a blank tape—"

Em put her hands over her ears. "Not listening—"

Liza pulled Em's hands down. "I'll never forget how you helped me through this," she said fiercely. "I want you to be just as happy as I am."

"What I need is *not* to be picturing you and Eric using one of those blank tapes."

"Well, maybe we won't, maybe we'll just go through the Kama Sutra—"

Luckily Em's cell phone rang, cutting off that thought. It was Nathan.

"You've been seen with the chef," he said without preamble.

"What? How did you—"

"I know all. Now reel him in."

Em grated her teeth. "Nathan, you know I don't work that way."

"Are you or are you not sleeping with him?"

Em's heart clutched. "Whatever I'm doing on my off-hours has nothing to do with work."

"Perfect, you are."

"You're not listening—"

"Just keep at it, Em. This is going to be great." *Click*.

Em stared at her cell phone, dread and regret nearly overwhelming her.

Liza was watching her. "Forget him," she said. "He's an ass."

It helped to remember that but didn't make her feel any better to know that anyone on the outside looking in might assume the same thing as Nathan. That she'd slept with Jacob to convince him to take the job.

What if Jacob thought it?

No. No, he wouldn't. Couldn't. But still, the worry nagged at her. "I'm not going to do this the way Nathan would," she said out loud.

"Of course you're not," Liza said loyally. "You're not going to hurt Jacob. But, honey…is he going to hurt you?"

"No." Her eyes burned. "Maybe."

"Oh, Em—"

"Really. I'm okay." She managed a smile. "I'll see you in the morning. We fly home tomorrow."

"Yes, but—"

"Go. I'm fine." She waited until Liza had left to let her smile fall away. She wandered toward—where else?— Amuse Bouche. Nathan's words still echoed in her ears but she could care less.

She just wanted to see Jacob. It was late, far past the dinner hour, but the place was still buzzing, filled with groups of people.

No one, she saw, was eating alone.

Well, she'd start a new trend. She was seated at a lovely table, and as she settled in didn't catch a glimpse of the man she'd been with a dizzying amount of times in three short days.

Did that make him her lover?

No, she told herself. A lover implied some sort of relationship, loose as it might be. Lover implied emotions were involved.

Jacob Hill didn't want any of that. Jacob Hill wanted his freedom, he wanted no ties, he wanted—

"Look at you." In the flesh, he suddenly stood by her table in his chef's gear, looking so official, so authoritative, so…outrageously sexy. "Sitting here in my restaurant," he said, "looking like the best thing I've seen all night."

She didn't want to be moved, but damn it, she felt a helpless smile break through.

"Hungry?"

Uh-huh. For you. "A little."

He flashed a grin that was so naughty she felt her nipples go hard. "Well, I do aim to please," he said. "What can I get you? Something sweet? Something hot?"

"We are talking about your food, right?"

He waggled his brows. "Maybe." Then without asking, he pulled out the chair next to her and sat.

"Don't you have stuff to cook?" *Maybe other women to drive insane with longing?*

"We're winding down. It's late." He touched her, running a finger down one cheek. "And you're unhappy."

Turning her head away, she busied herself with the menu. Why had she come? To torture herself? Because if so, she was doing a good job.

"Em."

"You know what?" she said, shutting the menu again. "I'm tired. I should just order room service." She reached for her purse but before she could stand, he snagged her wrist.

Not looking at him, she fiddled with the strap.

"*Em.*"

With a sigh she glanced at him, then was sorry. He was no longer smiling, instead his expression had filled with things that made her want to melt into a pool of longing. "Don't," she whispered, closing her eyes.

"Don't what?"

"Don't look at me like that, like you want to hold me, like I mean something to you, like what has happened between us means something to you, because we both know that none of that is true. When I go home tomorrow, you'll go on as if nothing happened. And me, I'll—" She bit off the words, refusing to expose herself to him again, emotionally or otherwise. "Please. Just let me go."

He looked at her for a long moment, then slowly loosened her fingers. "I'm sorry."

Well, so was she. Sorrier than he could ever know. Letting out a frustrated breath, she stood up. She met his gaze for one long, helpless moment, during which she would have sworn time stood still, would have sworn that he wanted to tell her he felt everything she did.

Because she wanted him as a chef in her show, yes, but she also wanted him as a man. And not just in her bed. She wanted him to be hers. She wanted him to understand that love *could* happen, that it could even happen in a blink of an eye.

Or on an elevator.

It could happen in a year, a month, a few days, it didn't matter. She wanted him to know that when it was real, it was meant to be sought and kept.

Not tossed away.

But most of all she wanted him to understand that what they had, what they could have had, was as real as it gets.

In the end, she didn't say any of that. She just walked away.

And he let her.

THIRTY MINUTES LATER Em was in her room, in the white, fluffy, luxurious robe after a long, scalding shower, waiting for room service to bring the French fries she'd ordered, contemplating how stupid men were.

Because Jacob should be up here. Sighing, she brushed

through her newly washed hair. He should be in bed with her right now.

But he hadn't turned out to be much of a mind reader, and she was a grown-up. If she'd wanted him so badly tonight, she should have saved her little goodbye drama until morning.

Someone knocked at the door.

Tightening her robe, she put her eye to the peephole, then her body went as still as her heart went wild, leaping inside her chest, banging against her ribs.

Jacob stood there, still in his chef's uniform.

Em pulled back. *What was he doing?*

"Open up, Em."

Open up. Hadn't she done that? Hadn't she opened up her heart and soul? What more could she give him?

"Em."

She put her hand on the knob, drew a deep breath, then opened the door. "What are you—"

"You called for room service." He gestured to a covered tray at his side, then pushed it past her and into the room.

"But…" She stared at him as he shut the door and lifted the plate covers.

"Crisp pan-seared salmon," he said. "And from Pru I've brought a very nice 2001 Robert Stemmler pinot noir."

She couldn't help it, she laughed.

He raised his face in surprise. "What?"

"I ordered French fries." The ultimate comfort food.

He made a soft sound of disapproval as he looked over the meticulously arranged tray, and she laughed again. "You are such a food snob."

"I am not."

Oh, yes, he was, and he had no idea. Nor did he have any idea how absolutely, stunningly adorable he was. She had a feeling he'd never been considered adorable before.

"Will there be anything else?" he asked.

You on a plate. "No," she whispered, then remembered her little chat with herself. Be honest. Be open. "Yes."

"No or yes?"

"Yes."

"Name it."

She licked her lips and thought about how to tell him that if she couldn't have him in her life, she'd take him for the next few hours. "I want you."

His gaze flicked over her wet hair, her undoubtedly shiny, makeup free face, and then lingered on her robe-covered body.

For a long moment he just looked at her as she grew uncomfortably warm under the terrycloth.

"Well, we do aim to please here at Hush," he said finally, unbuttoning his chef's coat and tossing it to a chair, which left him in his black trousers and a snug white T-shirt that invited the general public to Bite Me in block letters. She smiled.

He wrapped his fingers around the tie of her robe and tugged her to him. "What's so funny?"

"I'd like to bite you."

He arched a brow. "Watch out. I bite back." His hands had easily unknotted her robe. Holding the lapels, he looked into her eyes. "What are you wearing beneath this thing?"

"Um—"

"A sexy thong?"

She shook her head.

"Flannel pj's?"

She gave him a weak smile. Thank God she hadn't put her flannels on. He'd have laughed his ass off. "No," she managed.

"Hmm…"

"Nothing," she whispered. "I'm wearing nothing beneath."

With a groan, he spread the robe open, slipped his hands inside and looked his fill. "You are so beautiful." Sinking to his knees, he put his mouth to her hip, kissing her softly. Then her belly button.

And then lower.

Her hands fisted in his hair. Her head fell back. Then his mouth moved southward—and hit her equator. One lick and she was panting for air, her senses on overload. *"Jacob."*

"Mmm," he said, his mouth full, his tongue... God. His tongue.

"What about the real room service? They might come," she gasped, her eyes rolling back in her head when he did something fantastic and wickedly wicked with his fingers.

"The only one coming is you."

Then he lowered her to the floor, and made good on that promise.

JACOB LAY FLAT on the floor, stripped naked, with an equally naked Em nibbling her way over his body. It was torture, but the best torture he'd ever experienced.

"You've got such an amazing body," she told him, exploring every inch. "Just looking at it makes me want to gobble you up." She licked his nipple, then lifted her head. "I've never said such a thing to a man before."

Oh, yeah. Torture.

"This is my favorite, right here." And she sank her teeth into his inner thigh.

When he jerked, she lifted her head, eyes luminous, breasts swaying. "Do you want me to stop?"

"God, no."

She resumed her activities, taking her mouth on a happy little tour, until she reached his erection and licked it like a lollipop.

He jerked again.

Once more she lifted her head, with an adorable concerned little frown puckering her brow. "Am I doing it wrong?"

Choking out a rough laugh, he slid his hands into her hair and guided her head back. "No."

"Are you sure? Because I can—"

"If you stop again, you're going to kill me."

She let out a slow, sex-kitten smile that had him groaning and his toes curling. He'd created a monster. "Come up here, Em, and let me—"

"No, let me," she murmured in the voice of a pure seductress. "Because this time, Jacob Hill, you're the one coming."

He'd wanted to be inside her when he climaxed, had planned for that with the unopened condom on the floor next to him, but she tore the control from his tightly held reins as no other woman had, with those fingers, with that incredibly soft, sweet mouth, both of which she used on him until his eyes crossed.

He was going to lose it. He was really going to lose it, right here, right now. "Wait," he gasped.

"It's okay."

"No, it's not that—" He couldn't think with the blood running out of his head and his entire body on high alert. "Em— Wait."

But she didn't, and there was something about her slightly fumbling hands and mouth, the endearing inexperience mixed with the sexual yearning that completely and totally undid him.

He exploded. And when he lay there, annihilated, still

quivering, humbled to the core and just as shocked, she put her hand on his chest and leaned over him until her face wavered in his view.

"Jacob?"

"Still here. Barely." He smiled.

Hers wobbled. "I love you," she whispered, and destroyed him all over again.

CHAPTER FIFTEEN

Note to Housekeeping:
Guest requested more silk scarves in room 1214.
There's some wild action going on in there!!

"LET ME GET THIS STRAIGHT." Pru blew the steam from her mug of Maddie's coffee and looked at Jacob. "You stood us up last night for that cute little TV producer you accosted a few nights back?"

Jacob had known this was coming. He'd stumbled home from Em's room at dawn. Pru and Caya had dragged him out of bed a short time later, bringing him here for the interrogation. He concentrated on not burning his tongue on his coffee and said nothing, silently pleading the Fifth.

At his lack of comment, Caya raised a brow. "Interesting."

"There's nothing interesting," he said.

"Uh-huh." This from Pru. "You went back for seconds. That's *very* interesting."

"Look, just because you two have found…whatever it is you've found—"

"Love," Caya said, and reached across the table to squeeze Pru's hand.

Pru smiled in a way Jacob had never seen, a soft special curve of the mouth. He sighed. "It doesn't mean everyone has to be just as happy as you guys."

"What's wrong with being happy?" Caya wanted to know.

He stared into his mug and thought about that. Thought about other things, too, things that started with "I" and ended with "love you."

Holy shit, had that really happened? Had he had the most mind-blowing orgasm of his life flat on his back in Em's hotel room floor, and then blinked back to consciousness to find her leaning over him, smiling with her entire heart in her eyes as she said "I love you"? "Nothing's wrong with being happy," he finally answered. "It's just not as easy for some."

"You think it was easy for us to get to the point where we know it's real, that beneath the passion there is enough to sustain us for the long haul?" Pru asked. "Because you know it wasn't easy, not at all."

"I do know. But—"

"No *buts*," Pru said. "Look, Jacob, I think you have this thing, like you believe you somehow don't deserve love and happiness the same as the rest of us." Her eyes were warm as she looked at him. "You're wrong, Jacob. You do."

He frowned at the both of them. "I thought we had an agreement. You two worry about your own lives, and I'll worry about mine."

"By your own words, that agreement was to be null and void once I got my own love life in order," Pru reminded him.

Caya's eyes shone brilliantly at her. "And your love life is most definitely in order."

The affection that shimmered back and forth between the two of them was so powerful it was overwhelming, and Jacob felt his throat tighten. He was really losing it here.

He'd had someone looking at him like that, and he'd walked. What did that make him?

A smart man, he reminded himself.

"Tell us about her," Pru said softly.

"Oh, I'll tell you," Maddie said as she came up to refill their cups. She smiled into Jacob's frowning face, utterly unimpressed by his silent imploring. "She's beautiful, of course. That's what attracted him."

"That is not what attracted me," he said in his defense. "I'm not that shallow."

"You're a man, aren't ya?" Maddie patted him on the head. "She's also sweet and smart, but the most important thing…" She leaned in as if departing a state secret. "She makes him yearn for things he didn't know were missing in his life."

"Maddie—"

She smiled warmly at Jacob's warning, then kissed him sweetly on the cheek. "Oh, luv. Just accept it. She's yours. And you're hers."

Pru and Caya were staring at him in shock as Maddie walked away.

"She *is* different from your other lovers," Pru said thoughtfully.

"Really?" Jacob asked, annoyed. "And how do you know that?"

"Because she lasted more than one night," Caya said.

Ouch. Was he really that quick to move around?

Yeah. He was.

"Tell us more," Pru said.

"Look, there's nothing to tell. She's leaving, so what does it matter?" Was that his voice, sounding shaken at the thought of Em going back to Los Angeles? Maybe he was just tired after the past few nights of incredible, wild sex.

Okay, not just sex. Sex he'd have been able to get past.

Whatever the hell they'd done had been more, enough to grab him by the throat and hold on good.

And then there had been those three shocking words he'd never heard directed at him before.

I love you.

"She loves me," he heard himself say.

Pru and Caya stared at him, then burst out laughing.

"What the hell is so funny about that?" he demanded.

"Because every woman falls in love with you," Caya said. "Hell, I'm half in love with you and I'm taken—" She broke off at the look on his face. "Oh. Oh," she breathed, and put her hand to her chest. Her eyes misted. "This one is different," she said softly. "She's different because you feel it back. Oh, Jacob."

"My God," Pru murmured in wonder. "It's happened. And I didn't even have to do a damn thing."

Jacob shoved his fingers through his short hair. "Not helping."

"Oh, honey." Pru grabbed his hand. "Why can't you just admit it?"

"Admit what? That you're a helpless romantic?"

"That you love her back."

"Maybe some of us don't like to wear our hearts on our sleeves," he said. "Maybe some of us have healthy caution inside and don't feel the need to rush into anything."

"Maybe some of us are terrified of feeling it at all," Caya said very softly, and leaning in, hugged him tight. "Is that it?"

"Damn it." He gently pushed her off him and went back to staring into his coffee and brooding.

"You aren't going to be stupid about this, right?" Pru asked. "You're going to go after her, this one-and-only woman who's ever turned your head."

She'd turned him upside down was what she'd done. "I'm not doing anything."

Caya and Pru looked at each other in dismay.

"Look, this little coffee get-together has been sweet, but…" He shoved to his feet and tossed down some money to cover everything.

"Jacob," Pru chided gently. "You can't just ignore it."

Sure he could. Especially when the alternative was something he couldn't even contemplate.

"You can't just walk away," Caya called after him. "You've always gotten away with that, I know, but one of these days it's going to catch up to you."

Maybe. But not this time.

ERIC AND LIZA flew home on an earlier flight than Em. With a few hours left before she had to leave for the airport, she sat in the lobby with her clipboard, trying to put some cohesive notes together for Nathan. Her cell phone rang. One glance at the caller ID had her wincing. The boss himself. "How's it going?" she asked him in the most chipper voice she could muster.

"That's my question for you."

"Oh, everything's fabulous," she said. Which was sort of the truth. Parts of this trip had been fabulous.

Mostly the parts when she'd had Jacob buried deep inside her, but that was definitely too much information.

"Have you got him yet?" Nathan wanted to know.

"Actually, I've got several candidates but I've decided to hold auditions in Los Angeles, as well."

"What happened to Hill?"

"He isn't interested."

"I thought you slept with him."

Em closed her eyes and winced. "I am never going to sleep with someone for my job."

Nathan sighed. "If you're going to be so damn empathetic, at least use it to your advantage. Have it help you instead of hurt you."

Though he couldn't see her, she lifted her chin. Being empathetic might have caused her more than a few embarrassing or uncomfortable moments, but it had helped her. It had helped her become the person she was. If he couldn't see that, then she couldn't make him. "I'll find someone just as good. Trust me."

There was a long silence. "You still have three weeks. Work on him."

Her stomach sank. "I'm not going to 'work' on anyone, Nathan." She couldn't. Wouldn't. But sometimes there were other ways, better ways. This was one of those times, she was sure of it. "But if you'd just trust me, I can do this."

"Your way, right?" he asked dryly.

Determination blazed. "That's right."

"I suppose you have ideas."

"You know it." Her mind whirled. "In fact…I wanted to talk to you about a few changes."

"I don't like changes."

"Just listen. I was thinking about a traveling cooking show."

"Traveling?"

"We'd still need a chef, but this person would be almost more like a host, coming to us from a different restaurant across the country each week." Her thoughts raced. "He wouldn't need to be a big celebrity chef. In fact if he's unknown, it'll be better for the ego of the chef at the restaurant we're visiting."

"Hmm."

Not exactly encouraging, but he hadn't said no yet so she went on. "With the spotlight on the variety of settings, people will want to tune in each week to see and learn

about a new place," she said earnestly, getting more and
more excited. Why hadn't she thought of this before? "No
stagnant studio. The restaurant will get promo, the sous or
executive chef at that restaurant will get promo, and we'll
get—"

"Drama." Nathan's voice became excited. "Love it. Do
it. Stay another day and keep thinking. New York is good
for you. Oh, and while you're there, find some New York
hot spots. You've got a gold ticket here."

She thought of Eric and Liza already cozy on a plane
heading west. She was on her own. But that was okay,
because she could do this. *She would do this.* She slipped
the phone back in her purse and dropped her head, needing
air. She'd been given another night here....

"Em?"

Her entire body reacted. Lifting her head, she faced the
man she couldn't stop thinking about, even with her career
on the line. He wore those battered black Levi's she loved
so much because they contoured his body to mouthwatering perfection. Old and clearly beloved, they were soft and
faded in all the stress spots, of which there were many. His
long-sleeved shirt was black with a caramel-brown stripe
that matched his solemn gaze. He stood before her, hands
shoved into his pockets, a frown marring that wonderful
face.

"What's the matter?" she asked him.

"I was going to ask you that same thing."

"Oh." She forced a smile, trying not to remember that
the last thing he'd done with that handsome face had been
to bury it in her hair, inhaling her as he squeezed her tight,
so tight that she thought maybe he never wanted to let her
go.

But he had.

And she had. "Nothing's wrong," she said, adding

another smile when he only cocked his head and studied her for a long heartbeat. "Really. In fact, things are great."

He hunkered down before her to take her hands, his gaze holding hers. "Great, huh?"

Oh, God. Physical affection. If she knew nothing else about him, she knew this much—for Jacob it was the same thing as waving a fifty-foot sign saying that he cared about her.

Her pathetic heart rolled over and exposed its underside and she fought an overwhelming desire to throw herself at him. "I'm fine," she repeated weakly.

"But—"

"Jacob. Do you really want me to tell you what's wrong? Really?"

He stared at her, and she could see that running through his head was the moment when she'd blurted out, "I love you," and he'd gone white as a sheet and said, "Thank you."

Thank you.

Yeah, that was what every girl dreamed of hearing from her prince after a lifetime of toads.

"Look," she said, pulling her hands free and standing. "I've got to get to work, which is finally going somewhere."

"You find a chef?"

"I sort of worked around the issue for now."

He nodded, slipping his hands back into his pockets rather than touch her again.

Good, she thought, even as her body missed the contact with every fiber of its being. She might as well get used to it.

"I thought you were leaving today," he said.

Which would make things easy for you, wouldn't it? "I thought so, too."

"But…?"

Was she wrong? Or had an odd flare of hope flickered in his eyes? "But it turns out I have one more day here."

Nope, definitely a flicker of emotion in those eyes. But the question was, was that flicker just sexual excitement at the thought of having her again? Or more?

"One more night is good," he said very quietly.

And damn if her body didn't quiver. "It's about work," she said. "The show, it's going to be a traveling cooking show. Same host, but instead of an L.A. set, we're going to hit different locales around the states. My boss thought that while I was here, we should be scoping out New York City to stack up a few restaurants."

"Ah."

"So I guess I need to run around to nail down some good places." They both knew he was the man to show her such spots. That Amuse Bouche should be, and was, at the top of her wish list.

Having a show set here, even only once, would be huge. But she had pride, too, and she couldn't, wouldn't, ask him one more time to disrupt the life he appeared to love.

"I have something I should show you," he finally said.

"Really?" She was afraid to read anything into that, into the way he was looking at her.

What did he have to show her? Himself?

"I'm due in the kitchen right now," he said. "But after—"

"Yes?"

"Meet me here?"

He was actually, in his way, asking, not telling. Unable to keep from melting just a little, she simply nodded. She'd meet him tonight.

CHAPTER SIXTEEN

JACOB FINISHED AT the restaurant late and, without taking time for his customary shower and late-night drink with the staff, rushed out into the lobby.

Em stood near the windows, hugging herself, looking out into the night. She wore one of those long flowing flowery skirts he loved on her, and a snug black angora sweater his fingers were already itching to touch. Remove.

As if she felt him coming, she turned slowly, her eyes unerringly meeting his across the filled lobby. And hell if his heart didn't start to pound.

Crazy. He was here only to give her the information he knew would help her search. When he reached her, she licked her lips as if nervous, and he couldn't help it, despite knowing he shouldn't, he leaned in and kissed her.

A little murmur of surprise came from her and for that perfect beat in time, her lips clung to his.

Then she pulled back and smiled at him, more sure of herself now. God, that was something, her sexual confidence. "Ready?"

Her gaze searched his. "I didn't know exactly what you had in mind or how to dress..."

A flicker of unease worked its way through him. "To walk to my apartment? To get the information I have for you?"

Her eyes never left his. "Information."

"When I was getting ready to hire on here, I had a stack

of offers. I still have all the files at my apartment. You can flip through them for the spots that interest you. For the show."

"Gotcha." Face carefully blank, she nodded. "Right."

She sounded funny, and that dread grew. "Em—"

"No, it's all good. Thanks," she added with extreme politeness, and turned away, toward the outside doors.

He pulled her back around, having to work at it because she was stiff as a piece of drywall. Searching her face, now so completely shuttered to his, he shook his head. "What did I miss?"

"Nothing." She gave him a smile, a surface-only smile that didn't come close to the warmth and wattage of her real one. "Let's go get the information then."

They walked. The night was chilly, and she refused his sweater, preferring instead to walk at his side, keeping her distance, arms crossed over herself. Through Bryant Park, pretty and peaceful at night, she said nothing. Across the street, toward his apartment building, where they were parted by a pack of teenagers on their way toward trouble, still nothing.

He stopped her at his building.

She looked up at the brick-and-glass front, lit with tiny white lights that no one had bothered yet to take down after the holidays. When he looked at the building, he always felt an odd surge, a sort of marvel that he'd found this place to call his, a nice, easy-on-the-eyes, classy yet warm and welcoming home.

Warm and homey had never been a requirement, and yet now that he had it, it was amazing how much he'd grown to like it. "Home sweet home," he said, and smiled.

She flashed him a quick one, and again it didn't meet her eyes.

More dread. "Third floor."

When he held open the front door for her, she went in ahead of him, careful not to brush any part of her against him, and he found himself leaning in to catch the scent of her. Pathetic.

They walked up the three flights of stairs, and at his door, he tried to turn on his legendary charm. "I can make a late-night snack, maybe a—"

"No, thank you."

He blinked. Had anyone, ever, since he'd begun cooking, turned down his offer of food?

Not once.

"Are you sure?" He nudged her inside. "Because—"

"I'm fine." Still hugging herself, she looked around the apartment without letting a thing show on her usually so vivid face. Not a single inkling of her thoughts.

He looked around, trying to see the place as a stranger would, a glimpse inside his world. And yet all he saw was the huge glass windows, the stark black lines of his leather couch and table, the utter lack of color.

And he saw something else, something more revealing. There was nothing of himself here, no pictures, no personal effects. It wasn't any different in the bedroom, where he had a huge bed, expensive furniture and barely anything else.

Had he thought the place warm and homey?

He showed her the kitchen.

"Oh," she breathed, stepping into the one room in the house he'd made his. Here he had his favorite pots and pans hanging from the ceiling within reach, his utensils in a big copper holder on the counter, his beloved cookbooks out for easy access.

All personal effects.

He felt like sagging in relief at the sight. He *had* put something of himself here. He walked over to a big, fat file near the phone and pulled it out. "This is pretty much a full representation of the best restaurants in the best locations in the city. There are brochures, pictures, reviews…"

She glanced at the file, and then without taking it, looked into his face. "Why did you keep all that?"

He scanned through it. "I don't really know."

"I do. You kept it because you didn't see yourself staying at Hush for longer than it took to get comfortable and settled. You never see yourself staying anywhere, even here."

"I like it here."

"Really?" She moved back into the living area, huge and lush and utterly devoid of…him. "Then where are the pictures of your friends? A fish? Even a plant? Where are the signs that a loving, caring, wildly passionate, beautiful man lives here?"

"You want a sign that I'm here, living and breathing and wildly passionate?" He hauled her up on her toes. "How's this?" And he covered her mouth with his.

THE MINUTE HIS MOUTH touched hers, Em's frustration melted. It had no chance against the onslaught of need and yearning and love she felt for him, none at all. His body was big, burning up with heat, and the easy strength of him such a damn turn-on.

"I need you," he murmured in her ear, then bit down on her lobe, sending waves of erotic desire skittering down her spine. "God, I need you."

A thrill raced through her. Not want, but…*need*. "Really? You *need* me?"

He went still, then pulled back. "I want you," he said carefully.

She shook her head. "You said need."

He stared at her. "I did not."

"It's okay to need me," she whispered, and touched his face. He hadn't shaved that day, and she loved the rough feel of his day-old growth. She ran her fingers over it and sighed. "Because I need you, Jacob."

Still, he just stared at her, stricken. His tough body quivered with tension; whether it was desire, or frustration, or even fear, she had no idea.

Nor did she have any idea how to soothe him, other than wrapping her arms around him.

Not a hardship when his body was like a pagan god's, and so perfectly suited to hers, so able to pleasure her that she was already wet for him as he reached for her sweater. "Want me," she said softly. "Need me. Just take me."

"Em—" he murmured against the tumble of her hair, sounding staggered.

She closed her eyes, absorbing that voice, memorizing it. This was it, their last time. It might have left her hollow but she'd save that for when she was alone again. For right now, feeling him was a relief and a pleasure she wouldn't deny herself. His body felt so good against hers, and that was because it was him. No other man would do. With a slow burn taking root deep in her belly, she put her mouth to his throat.

He made a sound, a rough one, his hands sweeping down her body to her bottom, palming it tightly, rocking her against him.

He was hard, so hard it made her catch her breath. His kiss was demanding, a little rough, as if he was not pleased with how much he wanted this, wanted her.

"Here. I want you here," he demanded gruffly, his hot mouth on her jaw as it worked its way back to her lips, then claimed them in a kiss, a fierce, untempered kiss. Finally his tongue stroked one last time along hers and pulled back. "*Now.*"

"Yes. Here," she gasped when his hands streaked over her already fevered body, beneath her sweater, her skirt, and his fingers slipped in her panties. *"Now."*

"Take it off, then. Take it all off." Then, before she could, he lent his hands to the cause, doing it for her, stripping her so fast her head spun.

Still fully clothed, he took her hands and held them out at her sides as he looked her over slowly, thoroughly, his eyes twin balls of heat. "You take my breath away," he said hoarsely.

Feeling incredibly vulnerable, she closed her eyes.

"No," he said. "Look at me."

Somehow she managed to open her eyes again.

"Amazing," he said in a reverent whisper, as if he couldn't believe she was here, for him. Then he slid his hands into her hair and tugged her close again, kissing her long and wet and deep.

She had to touch him. She slid her hand beneath his shirt, and he shuddered, breathing her name. She whispered his, as well, or at least she tried, though it came out more a moan than anything else because his hands were stoking the slow burn within her into flames.

Somehow she got his trousers opened. He was fully erect, hot to the touch, needing release as badly as she, and she wrapped her hands around him.

"God, Em. You slay me."

"Do I? Do I really?" she mused, and stroked him.

They were both lost then. He dropped to his knees and tugged her down with him, tumbling her to the soft rug in front of the fireplace. While he tucked her beneath him, she pulled his shirt open. His body was magnificent, and she had to touch, had to taste, one last time.

Because that thought threatened to intrude, to cool her down, she squeezed it out of her head and licked his nipple, scraped her teeth over it, absorbing the rough sound that came from deep in his throat.

Her insides were trembling, her fingers less than steady as they skimmed over his chest, over the hard muscles of his pecs, over the tapering line of hair down his middle, and the abs she could never get enough of, all the while finding herself more and more aroused. Because this was Jacob, this was the man who could take her right out of herself. She loved touching him, loved having him touch her, loved how his body was tense and trembling.

She loved him, and bit her lip rather than let it escape again.

He looked into her eyes and knew. "Em," he said in a ragged voice, lacing his fingers through hers, anchoring them by her shoulders. "Don't." He eased her legs farther apart. "Don't hold back because of me."

She looked into his eyes, knowing what she felt was reflected there. Heat and need and so much more it backed the breath up in her throat. Eyes burning, she shook her head. "I won't."

He squeezed his eyes shut, his face tightening in a grimace. "Tell me again."

"I love you."

His eyes opened, deep, dark and suspiciously bright.

"I love you," she said again.

He groaned, then thrust into her, keeping his gaze on hers, letting her see him, see into him, and there was so much there, she let out a small cry and arched up.

He sank into her, again and again, in a connection so heartbreaking and mind shattering, she lost herself. But he found her, held her, and seemed bent on rewarding her in the only way he knew how. Not with words, but with his body. He showed her how high he could take her, how much he could give. It was all too much, she couldn't hold back, and with a fevered cry, she came apart in his arms.

With her name on his lips, he followed her over.

EM LAY ON HER BACK, with Jacob sprawled over her. He was heavy but she loved the feeling of him, hot and trembly, heart still pounding against hers. She hoped he never moved. If they never moved she wouldn't have to face tomorrow.

Finally, with a low hum of pleasure, Jacob turned his head and put his mouth to her throat.

She wrapped her arms tighter around him and held on.

"You okay?" he asked.

"*So* okay."

"We could—"

"No." She tightened her arms on him. "Stay a minute. Right here."

"As long as you like," he murmured.

God, she hoped so, because though the truth burned, she couldn't deny it—she'd stay right here, in New York, in his arms, anywhere…if he'd only ask.

CHAPTER SEVENTEEN

IN THE END, JACOB didn't ask anything. Dawn came, and Em finally made herself get dressed and leave his apartment.

Though she'd asked him not to, he walked her back to the hotel to get her suitcase.

Then he caught her a cab for the airport and held the door open for her.

The cabdriver put her suitcase in the trunk and got behind the wheel. Em bent to get in, too, but Jacob wrapped his fingers around her arm and held her back.

"I've got to go," she said, unable to handle a drawn-out goodbye.

He kissed her, and everything else faded away, the sounds of the busy street outside the hotel, the irritated hmph of the cabbie waiting for her, everything except the feel of his fingers sliding into her hair to hold her head, the heat of his body as he pressed his to hers, and the way her heart took one bold leap.

This was not a tentative goodbye kiss, or a maybe-I'll-see-you-around-sometime kiss. It was a hard, emotion-packed I'll-never-see-you-again kiss.

It broke her heart.

Pulling back, breathing unevenly, he stared at her. She stared right back, willing herself not to lose it, not yet. God, not yet.

"Hell," he muttered, and dragging her up on her toes, kissed her again.

Her heart was a big knot in her throat, blocking words, breath, everything but this. She'd lifted a hand to ward him off but it settled on his arm now, digging in, holding on, clinging.

And then it was over. He pulled back, their lips making one last suction sound that pulled at each nerve ending in her entire body.

"Hey, lady, come on," complained the cabdriver.

"Coming," she said, without taking her eyes off Jacob. "Goodbye," she whispered, reaching up to touch his jaw.

He turned his face into her palm, kissed the soft flesh there, then looked into her eyes. And for that beat in time he let her deep inside himself, to a part she hadn't been allowed before. A softer, more gentle side. Quieter. To a place where he had doubts, fears.

But then he blinked and those weaknesses were gone. He again put up his confident, edgy, enigmatic front that nothing could penetrate or disturb.

"Goodbye, Em," he said, and it was as though they had never touched each other, tasted each other. It was as though they were indeed just TV producer and famous chef, two people whose lives had casually crossed.

Never to cross again.

"Lady," griped the cabdriver.

"'Bye," she whispered once more, and to the cabdriver's infinite relief, sank to the seat and shut the door.

She told herself she wouldn't look back, should never look back, but she did. She craned around, and when she couldn't see anything, got up to her knees on the seat and practically pressed her nose to the window, but it was too late. They'd pulled out into traffic, and Hush was gone from view.

And so was Chef Jacob Hill.

THE FLIGHT BACK to Los Angeles was uneventful, at least on the outside.

On the inside, a whole other story.

Hurting, Em sat there in her seat, forehead to the window, watching the country go by.

Somewhere over Arizona, she realized that the old adage that claimed time heals all wounds was full of crap.

Time was making it worse.

With every moment that passed, her heart ached more, her body mourned more. Her brain was having a field day rewinding the memories and playing them over and over and over....

By the time she landed at LAX, her eyes were gritty and grainy, her chest tight with the suppression of tears, and she needed the oblivion of a twelve-hour nap.

While waiting for her luggage, jostled by the other frustrated passengers, she accessed her messages. The first one was from her mom.

"Honey, I know you've been traveling, but you should call your father once in a while. He worries—" There was a sound like a scuffle, and then her father's voice came on the line. "What she really means is call your mother because she wants to ask you if you've been eating properly, sleeping properly and dating. She wants to know if you're married with kids yet—"

Another scuffle, and a helpless smile came over Em's face as her mother grabbed the phone back. "Honey," her mom said. "Don't pay any attention to him. He's a man. What does he know? Of course you're not married with kids yet. You wouldn't have dared to do such a thing without me. Now remember, call your father."

Em's throat felt thick. Her parents had been married thirty-five years and still acted like kids. Kids in love.

How had they managed such a beautiful thing? And why couldn't she come anywhere even in the ballpark?

That thought reminded her of what she'd done these past few days, which was fall foolishly in love with a man who couldn't even think about stepping into the ballpark.

God, she missed him already. She accessed her next message.

"Em, listen to me," came Liza's voice, full of excitement and adrenaline. "The solution has been in front of us all along. We can use *Eric*. Eric as our chef."

Em blinked. Huh?

"He's hot, right? And best yet…he really can cook. I just never thought of it before because, well, I was always too busy being pissed off at him."

Em's brain slowly switched gears from her own misery to her career, where it belonged. Eric. As their chef.

"Think about it," Liza said. "He's been right beneath our nose the entire time. He says he'll do it if being the host means a pay raise from being location director because he's tired of eating mac and cheese by the end of the month anyway."

A massive exaggeration. Eric, also a true food snob, would never eat mac and cheese. At least not from a box. He'd have it homemade.

"It's a perfect solution," Liza said. "Call us."

Us.

The two of them were an "us" again.

She was happy for them—she really was. More than happy. The two of them deserved everything they found together.

It was just that Em had never been so happy for someone else, and yet so utterly devastated for herself at the same time.

Three weeks later

"WELL, IT'S OFFICIAL." Nathan let himself into Em's office and tossed a stack of papers on her desk, his face utterly inscrutable.

Oh, God. Watching him, her stomach sank to the floor, where it had been a lot since she'd gotten into that cab and left New York and Jacob. She hadn't been sleeping or eating well. She hadn't been doing anything well, much to Liza's consternation.

"You need to get laid," had been Liza's solution.

"I've already tried that," she said.

"I meant with someone new. To forget Jacob."

But there would be no forgetting him.

At the look on her face, Liza had hugged her tight. "Oh, honey. I'm sorry. So damned sorry. I wanted you to have a happy ending, too."

"I'll have my happy ending when this show is a success."

"I meant in the bedroom."

Tell that to the fist around her heart. Ridiculous that one trip and a few days could change her life, but it had.

He had.

God, she missed him, so much.

But this was a new kind of dread now, watching Nathan. It was over. The past three weeks of bone-breaking hard work and traveling and planning and prepping had all been in vain. They'd filmed three out of the six shows the network had asked for, one in San Francisco, one in New Orleans and one right here in Los Angeles, each in a fabulous, exciting, chic restaurant, each with Eric presenting the featured chef.

They'd believed it was working, that Eric had charisma on camera, that the places they'd chosen had been fascinating and interesting, that the concept was a good one that they could continue with indefinitely.

If the network picked them up for a season.

But now, given Nathan's somberness, she had to believe that for whatever reason the network had pulled the plug before they'd even aired. No more filming, no order from the Powers-That-Be for a full season.

Bye-bye career, hello working at Taco Bell. "What's official?" she asked, and then held her breath.

Nathan pointed to the papers.

"Can you be more specific?" she whispered.

He looked at her, and slowly smiled.

Smiled.

"Nathan." It was difficult to hear her own voice over the roar of blood in her veins. "It's possible I'm going to have heart failure right here if you don't use words."

"You're pulling it off." He seemed surprised but inordinately pleased. "The reports I've gotten are all positive. Your early reviews are optimistic. The network is happy. And a happy network, Em, makes a happy happy me."

"So you're not saying we're canceled before we've even begun?"

"Nope."

"And I still have a job?"

"Yep."

"Oh, God." She let out a breath, then a relieved laugh, and then jumped up and threw her arms around him.

Just as she remembered—no hugging the boss.

Backing up with an apologetic smile, she did a little three-sixty dance, then sank back to her chair. "Okay, then. Whew. *Whew.*"

Nathan grinned. "What's the plan for the next few cities?"

"I was thinking Seattle, Miami, Chicago."

"What about New York? I don't understand why you haven't done New York."

Just the words caused a ping low in her belly. "Well, you know, New York seems so obvious."

"Don't be ridiculous, New York has got to be included. In fact, why don't you use Amuse Bouche, with Jacob Hill? I bet he'd love to have the opportunity to showcase his restaurant."

"I don't think—"

"Are you kidding? What kind of chef wouldn't want the publicity a show like this is going to offer?"

"The kind who could care less about publicity. Trust me." Em shoved her bangs out of her face, her hand shaking. This was not the conversation she wanted to be having. It was better when she didn't think about Jacob at all, which she managed to do for whole minutes. Sometimes. "He's not interested."

"A real shame." He patted her arm and left the office.

Em let out a pent-up breath and sagged into her chair, only to straighten up again when Nathan suddenly stuck his head back in. He had a funny look on his face, one she couldn't quite place as he held out a basket. "This is for you."

Standing up, she took the basket. When she saw the pale pink and black tissue paper, embossed with the word Hush, her heart kicked into gear. "Where did you get this?"

"Just got delivered," Nathan said.

She stared at him, the oddest sensations running through her: confusion, denial and, the worst, hope. "It's for me?"

"That's what it says." He merely winked at her and left.

Em stared down at the basket. If her hands had been shaking before, they were apoplectic now, almost a blur. It had to be from Jacob, but she hadn't heard from him, not once in all these weeks. She'd long ago despaired of ever seeing him again.

Why would he send a basket?

Probably it wasn't from him. Probably it was from the hotel itself, thanking her for all the money she'd spent while there. Yep, that had to be it.

She sat on the corner of her desk and peeled the pretty tissue paper back. At the contents, she let out a choked laugh as her eyes welled.

The makings of s'mores, Chef Jacob Hill style, with house-made marshmallows and the most expensive of chocolates along with fresh graham crackers.

What had he been thinking?

She was running her finger over the wrapped chocolate wondering what it meant, when she saw the note. Setting the basket down on her desk, she pulled out the paper.

Dear Em,
I'm hoping you're still interested in desserts. I'm hoping you're still interested in a lot of things. Enclosed is my résumé.
J

What? What did that mean? Em extracted the second piece of paper, and smoothed it out, her gaze running over the carefully printed page.

She sagged back, laughing as a tear escaped. It was a résumé, formally typed up. Not for the chef's position, but to be "your lover, your friend and bearer of your heart."

He'd gone on to list his qualifications, including being loyal to a fault, honest to the point of bluntness and willing to make sacrifices to strengthen the relationship.

At the bottom was a footnote that read:

Available for interviews upon request. And by the way, now would be a great time to request an interview.

Heart drumming, she stood up and opened her office door, gasping at the tall figure standing there.

Jacob.

He looked so completely overwhelmingly magnificently gorgeous that he took her breath. And then she looked closer and saw the strain in his beautiful mocha eyes, the tenseness in his jaw, the way he had his hands jammed in the pockets of those beloved battered black Levi's. His hair had grown out a bit, and looked dark and glossy under the harsh lights. She itched to sink her fingers into it. His scent came to her, so familiar her knees nearly buckled.

And as he met her eyes, she felt that fist around her heart loosen very slightly.

"You have a minute?" he asked in that quiet way he had.

Behind him the office staff, mostly women, were all watching with interest. Stacy, Nathan's secretary, was nearly falling off her chair as she tried to get a better look. She was speaking into a phone as though giving a play-by-play, which didn't make any sense, until Liza came skittering down the hall with her cell phone to her ear, stopping on a dime at the sight of them.

"Em," Liza said, shoving her cell phone in her pocket after a glance back at Stacy, who hung up her phone, looking guilty. "I need to talk to you."

Em gestured to Jacob. "I'm kind of in the middle of something—"

"I know." Liza came close and looked at Jacob. In a very low voice she said, *"Why are you here?"*

"Liza," Em said, horrified at the unfriendly tone.

"No, I want to know," Liza said in quiet fury to Em. "Because for three weeks you haven't been yourself, you've been sad and grieving and not eating and not sleeping, and just today I thought you were getting better, that you were getting over him, but now here he is, ready to sleep with you and then walk away again. I'm not going to have it, Em. You're strong, so very strong, and I love you too much to let an egotistical jerk-off—"

"Excuse me," Jacob said. "I'm right here."

Liza barely spared him a glance. "I mean it, Em. He's only here for the sex—"

"Until three weeks ago," Em reminded her, "sex was all you were interested in yourself. So, Ms. Pot, please. I think I can handle Mr. Kettle."

Liza looked at Em for a long moment, and nodded. Then she subjected Jacob to a long, withering stare.

Em thought he would offer Liza some pithy remark. She didn't expect him to speak with quiet earnestness.

"This is the second time I've said this," he said to Liza. "The first time was to Eric, and it turns out I was wrong. I'm not wrong this time. I'm not going to hurt her. Not ever again. I promise."

Liza stared at him for a minute more, then gave another nod and turned to leave them alone.

"Can we talk now?" Jacob asked.

The rest of the staff were pretending to work but hanging on every word.

"For someone bearing chocolate," she managed to say in a normal voice. "I can definitely talk." She brought him into her office and shut the door on their audience.

Em tried to keep it together as she lifted Jacob's résumé, silently asking him to tell her what it meant, even though she thought maybe she knew. God, she hoped she knew. "Impressive," she said.

"I was thinking we could discuss terms." He nodded to the résumé. "I still don't want to be on your show," he said very gently.

"I didn't think so." A lump blocked her throat at the worry in his eyes. "It's okay."

"You look great, Em."

She had black circles beneath her eyes, she'd forgotten to put mascara on that morning, and her hair…she couldn't bear thinking about her hair. She was wearing her last pair of panties because she hadn't had the energy to do laundry, and she thought that if he said one more nice word, she would do the unthinkable and burst into tears.

"I've missed you," he said quietly.

Oh, damn. She blinked hard.

"I was a fool." He took a step toward her. "A complete fool to let you go. A cowardly one, too." Another step, and then another. "All my life I've walked away from commitment, from relationships, from anything that was more than skin-deep." One last step put them face-to-face, only inches apart. "But when I was with you, Em, I realized something."

She could scarcely breathe. "What's that?"

"I don't want to be that guy anymore."

It was painful, so painful, to look at him because she knew she couldn't keep the hope out of her voice. "What are you saying?" she whispered.

"I'm saying there's a lot more between us than passion, though that's pretty damn great. I'm saying I love you back, damn it."

Oh, God. "Jacob—"

He put his hands on her arms. "And I know you're here and I'm there, but I'll take the executive chef position if I have to and only work once a week at Hush. Or I'll start over somewhere else, somewhere here—"

She put her fingers over his mouth, and then because words failed, she just looked at him for a minute. "That you'd even do that for me… The show is a success, Jacob. It doesn't need me every day anymore. I'll have to come up with a new show now to produce, of course, but I can do that anywhere."

He wrapped his fingers around her wrist and gently pulled her hand from his mouth. "Keep talking."

"I loved New York. Enough to maybe give the city a shot. I'm sure there's something I can do there, because I know how much you want to be at Hush. That is…if you'd like."

"I don't care where we are, as long as we're there together." His eyes glittered. "So, yeah. I'd like."

"So." She held up his résumé. "The job of holding my heart. You seem uniquely qualified for that."

Slowly his tension seemed to drain. And for the first time since he'd stepped inside her office, he let out a slow smile, one infused with obvious relief. "You think so?"

Nodding, she smiled. "And I am hiring you on the spot for all the above, to be my lover, my friend and the bearer of my heart. As long as I get to be the bearer of yours."

"Always," he whispered fiercely, his arms banding tightly around her as he lifted her up. "Always."

* * * * *

SHADOW HAWK

Being a writer can be lonely.
Thankfully, I have a support group.
Thanks to Steph for the sanity lunches.
Thanks to Laurie for the sweet enthusiasm.
And thanks to Gena for...well, everything.
Couldn't have done this one without you.

PROLOGUE

Cheyenne, Wyoming Regional ATF offices

SHE WAS ALL LEG, and Conner Hawk was most definitely a leg man. Hell, he was also a T&A man, but Abigail Wells, fellow ATF agent and communications expert, not to mention all around hot chick, was so well put together she could have made him a certified elbow man.

Too bad she hated his guts.

She walked—strolled—across the Bureau of Alcohol, Tobacco and Firearms' office, her soft skirt clinging to her thighs with every graceful swing of her hips. Her blazer hid her torso from view, but he knew she had it going on beneath that as well. Her honey-colored hair was pulled up in some complicated do that screamed On Top Of Her World.

As if she'd read the direction his thoughts had traveled, Abigail glanced over at him, those bee-stung lips flipping her smile upside down, her eyes going from work-mode to pissy-female mode.

Oh yeah, *there* was the frown, the one she'd been giving him ever since the day she joined the team six months ago. She'd come from the Seattle office, where she'd worked in the field. He tried to imagine her wearing an ATF flak jacket, guarding his six, and was halfway lost in that fun fantasy when she spoke.

"You." This in a tone that suggested he could, and should, go to hell.

"Me," he agreed, surprised that she'd even given him that one word. She usually avoided talking directly to him, as if he carried some new infectious disease.

Odd, since to everyone else she'd been personable, even sweet and kind. It made that steely backbone of hers so surprising. When she decided to dig her heels into something, watch out. He'd seen it over and over, people so shocked by the unexpected toughness that this pleasant, melodious little thing exhibited that she got whatever she wanted. She must have been a hell of a force out in the field, probably underestimated by every single scum of the earth who'd come across her, but here in Cheyenne she'd stayed behind the scenes.

"You're late," she said in a school-principal-to-errant-student tone.

Oh yeah, now *there* was a fantasy…. He pulled out his cell phone and looked at the digital readout. Two minutes. He was two minutes late, and that was because someone had taken his parking spot. And he might have explained that to her if she hadn't been giving him the look that people gave their shoe when they stepped on dog shit.

Even as he thought it, her nose slightly wrinkled.

Yeah. In her eyes—which were an amazing drown-in-me blue—he was about equal to dog shit. Nice to know.

"We're wanted in Tibbs's office," Abigail said.

We? Well, *that* was a new term. Hawk dutifully followed her into their supervisor's office, his gaze slipping down that stiff spine to her spectacular ass. Attitude or not, she looked good enough to nibble on. A little sweet, a little hot…nice combo—

Whoa. She'd suddenly stopped, forcing him to put his hands on her hips rather than plow her over.

Clearly hating even that small contact, she jerked free and sent him a look that said go-directly-to-hell-without-passing-Go.

Right. Hands off. Maybe he should write that down somewhere.

"Any news on the rifles?" she asked.

Great. The absolute last thing he wanted to talk about. The rifles. Everyone had heard about the 350 confiscated rifles, which had gone missing from ATF storage before they could be melted down. Stolen, from beneath their noses.

His nose.

She was asking, of course, because he'd been the agent on the raid, the one who'd brought the weapons in. He had no idea how they'd gone missing, but he knew why. They had a mole and Hawk was getting too close.

"No. No news."

"I see." And with one last cool glance, she knocked on Tibbs's door.

I see? What the hell did that mean? Before he could ask, Tibbs called out for them to enter.

Their supervisor stood behind his desk, which didn't make that much of a difference since he was maybe five foot four and nearly as round as he was tall. The balding man shoved his glasses higher on his prominent nose. "We got a tip on the bombers," he said in that Alabama drawl of his.

Hawk had been working on the Kiddie Bombers for the past two years. Some asshole, or group of assholes, was teaching teenagers how to put together bombs, then using the explosives to terrorize big corporations into paying millions of dollars. Twelve kids had died so far, eight of them under the age of eighteen, and the ATF wanted the bomb-makers and their knowledge off the streets.

Hawk wanted that, too, and also the man running the Kiddie Bombers. Eighteen months ago he'd nearly caught him in a raid on a downtown warehouse. In the pitch-black, on the hard concrete floor, they'd fought. Hawk had wrestled a gun from his hand, managing to shoot him before being tackled by another Kiddie Bomber.

Hawk had escaped with his life intact, thanks to his partner, Logan, and given that the gang had gone quiet after that night, it had been assumed that the Kiddie Bombers' leader had died from his gunshot wound.

But a year ago, the Kiddie Bombers had popped back onto the radar, pulling off two huge jobs with weapons that had been previously confiscated by the ATF.

Hawk had his suspicions, mostly because there was only one person who could be linked to all the raids—Elliot Gaines. But that was so crazy wild, so out there, he'd kept it to himself, except for Logan. What he hadn't kept to himself was his vow to get the Kiddie Bombers' leader.

In the past month alone, Hawk and Logan had confiscated two huge warehouses full of ammo and other supplies. But not a single suspect. "Tip?" he asked Tibbs.

"Suspicious activity, rumored arsenal. Orders came down from Gaines on this."

Elliot Gaines was the regional head. Or, as some put it, God. Word had spread that the Almighty was tired of the delays, tired of the false leads and *really* tired of the ATF looking like idiots.

"You're both heading out." Tibbs tossed a full file on his desk for them to read. "Bullet City."

Northern Wyoming, approximately four-and-a-half hours from Nowhere, U.S.A. Yeah, made sense to Hawk. Isolated. Cold, which was good for the materials the bombers used. And, oh yeah, isolated. Great.

"Word is tonight's the night they're testing some new

product," Tibbs drawled. "We'll need to catch them in the middle of their private fireworks show."

That worked for Hawk. He picked up the file and flipped through it, reading about the barn that'd been found loaded to the gills with incriminating equipment, complete with an elusive owner they hadn't been able to pin down.

Abby shifted closer to read over Hawk's shoulder, making him extremely aware of her tension as it crackled through the air like static electricity.

"You've got two hours," Tibbs told them. "You fly out together."

"Together?" Abby repeated, her voice actually cracking.

Surprised at the unexpected chink in her armor, Hawk looked at her.

"You'll run the show from the van, Abby," Tibbs said. "And Hawk from the field. There'll be a team in place."

Abby blinked. "But…"

Both men eyed her as two high splotches of color marked her cheeks. Interesting, Hawk thought. She was usually cool as ice. So what had her riled up? Him? Because she sure as hell got to him. He couldn't help it, beneath her veneer there was just something about her, something… special. Sure, he wanted to do wicked things to her body and vice versa, but that alone wouldn't have kept him on edge around her for six months. "Don't worry," he told her. "I've done this once or twice before."

"Ha." But her brow puckered, her kiss-me-mouth tightened.

Normally this would make him wonder how long he'd have to kiss her before she softened for him, but not now. "What is it? You don't trust me out there?"

"Hawk," Tibbs said quietly.

He heard the warning in his boss's voice, but he didn't care. "No, I think it's time, past time, that we get this out in the open. I want to know, Abby. What exactly is your problem with me?"

"Nothing." She hit him with those baby blues, which were suddenly void of any emotion whatsoever. "There's no problem at all."

Bullshit. But hell if he was going to keep bashing his head against a brick wall. "Okay, then. Fine."

"Fine." She gestured to the file in his hands as she gathered her control around her like a cloak. "Flight's at two." She said this evenly, back to being as cool as a cucumber. In a freezer. In Antarctica. "Be late and I leave without you."

CHAPTER ONE

Later that night
Twenty-five miles outside of Bullet City, Wyoming

ABBY ENTERED THE COMMUNICATIONS van, and the men stopped talking. Typical. Men complained that women were the difficult gender, but it seemed to her the penis-carrying half were far more thorny.

Not to mention downright problematic.

Not that she cared, because when it came to personal relationships, she'd given them up. A fact that made her life much simpler.

Sliding the door shut behind her, she shivered. Late fall in the high altitude Bighorn Mountains meant that razor-sharp air cut right through her, layers and all. As she rubbed her frozen hands together, her gaze inadvertently locked on Hawk, who had his long-sleeved black shirt open and the matching T-shirt beneath it shoved up so that he could get wired.

He stood there, six feet two inches of solid badass complete with a wicked, mischievous grin, topped with warm, chocolate eyes that could melt or freeze on a dime. From beneath the sleeve of his T-shirt peeked the very edge of the tattoo on his bicep, which she knew was a hawk.

The women in the office practically swooned at it, every time.

But not Abby. Nope, she was made of firmer stuff.

There was a four-inch scar, old and nearly faded, along his left side between two ribs, and another puckered scar above his left pec. The first was a knife wound, the second a bullet hole. She could also see his smooth, sleek flesh pressed taut to hard, rippled sinew. One long, lean muscle, not an ounce of extra on him.

Whew. Had she been cold only a moment before? Because suddenly, she was starting to sweat. She cursed her 20/20 vision.

Maybe she wasn't made of firmer stuff after all…. But regardless, she was over men. *So* over men. And seeing that she'd become so enlightened…she blew out a breath and moved to her communications station.

Where for the first time, she hesitated. That in itself pissed her off. So a year ago she'd nearly died out in the field. She hadn't. And she wasn't going to this time, either. Shrugging off her nerves, Abby looked around and caught the long, assessing look Hawk shot her as he pulled on a flak vest. He was sharp, she'd give him that. Clearly, he sensed her hesitation, but hell if she'd let him see her sweat. She lifted her chin and sat down.

But if she was a good actress, then he was a great actor, because she had no idea what he was thinking behind that perpetually cynical gaze.

And she didn't care. She was here for the job. She would remain in the van, in charge of communications, while the team made their way to the farmhouse, and then to the barn a half mile beyond that, where they'd execute the raid.

"There," Watkins said to Hawk as he finished wiring him.

Hawk shrugged back into his shirt. "You fix the problem from the other day?" he asked.

Abby's eyes had wandered again to Hawk's body—bad eyes—but her ears pricked. "Problem?"

"Bad wire." Watkins lifted a shoulder. "Happens."

"It shouldn't," she said. "Make sure it doesn't."

Watkins nodded.

Hawk let his T-shirt fall over his abs, hiding the wires as his gaze again met hers. One eyebrow arched in the silent question: *Were you staring at me?*

No. No, she wasn't. To prove it, she turned to her own equipment, trying not to remember the last time she'd been wired before a raid. Elliot Gaines, the head honcho, had done her up himself.

Of course he'd had a personal interest. They'd had a burgeoning friendship, at least on her part. For his part, he clearly wished for more, far more. In any case, he couldn't have known how bad it would all go....

And it had gone extremely bad. One minute she'd been listening to Gaines's quiet, authoritative voice in her ear, telling her she was doing great, just to hold her position while his team to the west "handled it," and then the next, there'd been a 12-gauge shotgun to her temple and she'd been taken hostage.

Now, a year later, in another time and place, someone murmured something in a low voice that she couldn't quite catch, and several of the men behind her laughed softly.

Releasing tension, she knew, most likely with an off-color joke that she didn't want to hear. Living as a woman in a man's world was nothing new, but she had to admit, tonight, it was grating on her nerves.

Granted, her nerves were already scraped raw just by being here, but that was no one's fault but her own. Gaines had transferred her at her request after a leave of absence. She'd wanted to prove to herself that she could still do her job, that she hadn't let the "incident" take anything from her.

But with damp palms and butterflies bouncing in her

gut, she wondered if maybe she had more to overcome than she'd thought.

"Hey."

With a start, Abby turned toward Hawk. He was geared up and ready to face the night, looking big, bad, tough and prepared for anything. She bet he didn't have any butterflies.

The others were engaged in conversation, but Hawk stood close, looking at her as if he could see her anxiety. "Ready?"

That he could see her nervousness meant she didn't have it nearly as together as she'd like. "Of course I'm ready."

"Of course," he repeated, but didn't move. "Listen, I know you're going to bite my head off for this, but I'm getting a weird vibe from you here, and—"

"I said I was fine." She swiveled back to her computer to prove it.

"All right, then." She could feel him watching her very closely. "You're fine. I'm fine. We're all fine."

She heard him turn to follow the others out the door, and glanced back to watch the long-limbed ease that didn't do a thing to hide the latent power just beneath the surface. Or the irritation.

Abby let out a rough breath. *Damn it.* He might be a hell of a charmer, but he was also a hell of an agent, and truth be told, she admired his work ethic even more than she secretly admired his body. And she wanted him to be able to admire *her* work ethic. "Hawk."

He looked back, his broad shoulders blocking the night from view, but not the chill that danced in on an icy wind. "Yeah?"

"Watch yourself."

A hint of a self-deprecating smile crossed his lips. "Thought you were doing that for me."

She felt the heat rise to her face, but he'd caught her fair and square. His smile came slow and sure, and far too sexy for her comfort.

As he left, she let out a slow breath and fanned her face.

"DAMN, IT'S BUTT-ASS COLD out here."

At Logan's statement of the obvious, Hawk blew out a breath, which changed into a puff of fog before being whipped away by the cutting wind. The two of them lay on their bellies on the battered roof of the barn that had been pinpointed as a bomb-processing plant.

And yeah, it was butt-ass cold up here, but he was more focused on the fact that he was thirty feet above the ground without a safety rope, with the wind threatening to take him to the land of Oz.

Christ, he really hated heights.

Logan lowered his binoculars to blow on his hands. "Maybe we could do this thing before we freeze to the roof like a pair of Popsicles."

Like Hawk, Logan was built with the capacity to do whatever, whenever. Tough as nails. Physically honed. Trained to be a weapon all on his own, with or without the aid of bullets. But he enjoyed complaining. Always had, and Hawk should know—they'd been together since they'd been eighteen and in boot camp. They'd gone from bunkmates to brothers and knew each other like no one else.

To get here, they'd drugged a pack of rottweilers, disabled the alarm on the farmhouse and stealthily made their way through the woods to the barn. The place was a nice setup for criminal activity. Surrounded by the sharp, jagged peaks of the Bighorn Mountains, there were also rolling hills and a maze of lakes and streams, all of which were nothing but an inky black silhouette in the dark night.

No neighboring ranches, no neighboring anything except maybe bears and bison and coyotes.

And the many cars and trucks parked behind the farmhouse.

Odd. It would seem that there was a large group of people here somewhere, and yet there hadn't been a soul in the house or in any of the small storage sheds behind it.

Which left the huge barn.

An icy gust hit Hawk in the face, burning his skin. He had to admit, things had definitely gone from interesting to tricky, because now the metal tiles beneath them were icing over. Any movement could be detrimental to their health, because slipping off here meant a thirty-foot fall to the frozen earth below.

Thanks to his goggles, Hawk had a crystal-clear view of the ground, and the distance to it made him want to puke. They'd been in far worse circumstances, he reminded himself, where his fear of heights had been the least of his worries. He and Logan had done some pretty ugly shit involving some pretty ugly people. On more than one occasion, they'd managed to stay alive on instinct alone, in parts of the world that didn't even warrant being on the map.

So all in all, things had improved.

"Hope it doesn't rain, because this baby'll turn right into a giant metal slide." Logan said this calmly, because he, damn him, did not have a height issue. "Like the one at the carnival—"

"Logan?"

"Yeah?"

"Shut up."

He laughed softly.

The temperature had indeed dropped to two degrees above freezing their balls off, and with that wind icing up their organs, Hawk wanted to get a move on. But they were stuck up here until they got the signal from communications, which happened to be Abby and crew parked in a van on the main road half a mile south of here. "We need to move closer," he said to her via his mic, over a noisy gust that whipped dust from the roof and into his face.

"Remain in position," she ordered, her voice breaking with static, but still sounding soft, warm…and sexy as hell.

At least in Hawk's opinion.

Just listening to her made him react like Pavlov's dog. Only he wasn't drooling. Nope, listening to her elicited visions of wild up-against-the-wall sex, which caused a much more base reaction than slobber. "Remaining in position isn't going to work," he told her.

"Soon as I hear from Watkins and Thomas," she said, the static increasing, "we'll move."

We. As in not her. He knew she used to be a great field agent, and yeah, so he'd read her files. But all her cases had ended abruptly a year ago, and no amount of digging could produce a reason. Then, after a six-month leave, she'd transferred from Seattle to Cheyenne, where Hawk had done his best to ignore his inexplicable attraction to her, because that had seemed to work for her.

But now he wondered, how was it she'd gotten so comfortable behind the safety net? Why had she given up being in the trenches with the rest of them for a computer screen?

"Watkins and Thomas are making their way to the east and west doors beneath you," she added, referring to Logan's and Hawk's counterparts on the ground. "Wait for my cue."

Uh-huh. Easy for her to say. She sat out of the slicing wind in that van, and Hawk would bet money she had the motor running and the heater on full blast.

She'd changed on the plane, out of her skirt, the one that had messed with his mind every time it clung to her thighs, which was only with every single movement she made. But her cargo pants and long-sleeved ATF button-down clung to her, too. Hell, she could wear a potato sack and do something to him.

Logan shifted. Probably trying not to freeze to the roof. Hawk did the same, but for different reasons entirely.

"Nearly there," Thomas said into their earpieces. "Hearing noises from inside, a steady pinging."

"Affirmative," Watkins said. "The windows are blacked out, going in southwest door— *Jesus.* It's full of ammo and workstations. Definitely bomb-making going on here, guys, but there's no one in sight." He let out a low whistle. "Seriously, there's enough blow in here to make Las Vegas prime beachfront property."

"Suspects?" Abby asked.

"None."

"That can't be," she murmured.

Hawk had to agree with her. Something was off, and not just because they'd managed to get onto the premises and up here, past the alarm and a pack of hungry rottweilers without being detected. But now they'd found the proof, right beneath their noses? It was all too easy. He flicked off his mic and looked at Logan.

"You thinking what I'm thinking?" Logan asked.

"That we're being set up, instead of the other way around?"

"Bingo."

"I'm guessing we got too close, and he's unhappy with us?"

"Let's make him really unhappy and catch the SOB red-handed."

"Watkins, search the interior," Abby directed, the static

now nearly overriding her voice. "Hawk, Logan, guard the exits from above."

"But where is everyone?" This from Thomas. "It's like a ghost town in here."

"There's got to be a building we haven't cased yet. Or a basement. Something," she insisted. "Find it. Find them."

"There's nothing," Watkins said from inside. "No one."

Logan cocked his head just as Hawk felt it, a slight vibration beneath them. It was hard to discern between the howling wind screeching in his ear and the sharp static on the radio, but he'd bet that they were no longer alone up here.

"What's going on?" Abby asked.

Neither Logan or Hawk answered, not wanting to give away their position in the icy darkness, which was so complete that without the night vision goggles, they couldn't have seen a hand in front of their faces. Unfortunately, the goggles couldn't cut through the heavy dust kicked up by the wind as they silently moved toward the ladder they'd commandeered and left on the northeast side.

Which was now missing. *Shit.*

"Problem," Logan said.

"What?" Abby repeated in that voice that could give a dead guy a wet dream. Hopefully Hawk wasn't going to get dead, but without the ladder there was no way down without taking a flying leap. Just the thought made him break out into a cold, slippery sweat.

Logan jerked his head to the left, and Hawk nodded. Logan would go left, and he'd go right.

"Logan," Abby said tightly. "Hawk. Check in."

"We've got company," Logan said, so calmly he sounded comatose. "We're separating to locate."

"Details," she demanded.

"Someone took our ladder."

There was silence for one disbelieving beat. "Watkins, Thomas," she snapped. "Back them up. Now."

She was sounding a little more drill sergeant and a little less sex kitten, thought Hawk. Which was good, except he must be one sick puppy because the sound of her kicking ass turned him on as much as when she'd sounded like she was kissing it.

"West side is clear," Logan reported via radio, right on cue.

"Hawk?" This from Abby. "Check in."

"Oh, I'm fine, thanks." He eyed the slippery roof, the distance to the ground, and gave a shudder. At Abby's growl of frustration, he let slip a grim smile as he looked left, right, behind him. Another gust blew through, wailing, railing, raising both holy hell and a thick cloud of dust as the icy air sliced right through him. He couldn't see anything, any sign of Logan behind him, or anyone else.

Which could be good.

Or very, very bad.

"Where are you?" Abby asked.

In hell. Of that, Hawk had no doubt. "Logan?"

"Hawk, get down now," Logan suddenly said, and then came a click, as if he'd been cut off.

"Logan?" Hawk tapped the earpiece. Nothing. The radio was dead, but he'd get off the roof because Logan's instincts were as good as his own. He couldn't see much, but he knew there was a tall oak nearby, with branches close enough to reach and subsequently shimmy down. *All* the way down. *Christ.*

A sound came from three o'clock, and Hawk whipped his head around. Logan or enemy? Going down.

To do so, he had to shove his night vision goggles to the

top of his head so that he couldn't see the ground rushing up to meet him, not that *that* helped much because he had a helluva imagination, and could picture it just fine.

The wind doubled its efforts to loosen his hold, blinding him with debris. All he could do was hold on and pray for mercy as he lowered himself, even though praying had never really worked for him.

When his feet finally touched ground, he inhaled a deep breath and nearly kissed the damn tree trunk. Instead, he drew his gun and backed to the wall of the barn. Just to his left was a window, boarded and taped, and yet he'd swear he saw a quick flash of light from within.

Someone was definitely inside.

Watkins?

Or his very secretive bomb maker?

The radio was still eerily silent, and foreboding crept up through his veins as he slipped the night vision goggles back over his eyes and turned the corner of the barn. There his gaze landed on a door low to the ground—a cellar entrance. Before he could try the radio again, the door flipped open, catching the wind and hitting the barn wall like a bullet.

A man crawled out, silhouetted by stacks of ammo behind him, and piles of guns, *rifles*, awfully similar to the ones that had been stolen from beneath his nose. Apparently the Kiddie Bombers liked to be armed. With ATF-confiscated weapons. Hawk steadied his gun and waited for the rogue agent to reveal himself.

The man's head lifted and all Hawk's suspicions were immediately confirmed. *Gaines.*

He managed to get a shot off, then a white-hot blast knocked him flat on his ass.

CHAPTER TWO

THE BASTARD HAD shot him, point blank, and given that it felt like his lungs had collapsed, he assumed he'd taken the hit in his chest. God bless the bullet-proof vest. Stunned, gasping for air, he tried to remain conscious, but his vision had already faded on the edges and was closing in as he lay on his back, staring up at the night sky as a whole new kind of hurt made itself at home in every corner of his body....

"Hawk? Check in," Abby said in his ear.

Check in? He felt like he was checking out.... But the radio was back, good to know, and man, did she sound hot. Too bad he was floating...floating on agony, thank you very much, and utterly unable to move.

Or speak.

"Hawk."

Ah, wasn't that sweet? She sounded worried. He was touched, or would have been if he could get past the searing pain. He needed to get up, to protect himself—

A foot planted itself on his throat, and then the fire in his body sizzled along with his vision as his air supply was abruptly cut off.

By Gaines. Regional director.

Traitor.

Hawk tried to lift one of his arms to grasp at the foot on his windpipe.

"Don't bother." Gaines pressed harder. "You'll be dead

soon, anyway. I just wanted you to suffer a little first, you know, for screwing with me for so long."

Hawk found himself shockingly helpless, an absolutely new and unenjoyable experience. He simply couldn't draw air, and good Christ but he felt like his chest was burning.

"Hurts like a mother, doesn't it?"

What hurt the most was that he couldn't remember if he'd managed to spit out Gaines's name before he'd gone down. In case this all went to shit, he wanted Logan to know they'd been right. That is, if the radio was even back up. "Logan—"

"Sorry. It's going to be a tragic evening all around. You're both going to die trying to double-cross the agency."

Through a haze of agony as he choked on his very last breath, he realized he was still gripping his gun. Now if only he could get the muscles in his arm to raise it. As he struggled, he heard everyone checking in.

Watkins.

Thomas.

Logan. Thank God, Logan.

Any second now they'd realize Hawk hadn't checked in as well.

That he couldn't…

"HAWK? COME IN, HAWK." Abby said this with what she felt was admirable calm, even as a bead of sweat ran between her breasts. Something was wrong, and it wasn't just that their equipment had failed—even the backup equipment—for five long minutes.

"I don't see him," Thomas radioed.

"Me either." This from Watkins.

"I'm going back up to the roof," Logan responded. "Maybe he never got down."

She expected Hawk to jump in here with laughter in his voice to say that everything was good. But he didn't. Oh, God. She needed to sit down. For several months. Because he would not joke, not at a time like this. He might be surprisingly laid-back and easy-going considering the constant, nonstop danger the job put him in, but he knew protocol. He'd been a soldier, Special Forces. He lived by the rules, and to her knowledge, always followed them. *"Hawk."*

When he still didn't answer, she visualized him. Her therapist had taught her that picturing the cause of her grievance helped.

Of course her therapist had meant the men who'd taken her hostage, but the idea behind it was the same. Hoping it would work, she concentrated on the image of Conner Hawk.

It took embarrassingly little time—like one-point-two seconds. He came to her shirtless, which she didn't—shouldn't—speculate about. The only time she'd ever seen him that way had been six months ago, on her first day. He and Logan had spent hours lying beneath a truck in the broiling hot sun, surveying a house. After the arrests, Hawk had come into the office for a change of clothing he kept in his locker.

Abby had been sitting at a table in the employee room eating lunch, her fork raised halfway to her mouth, her salad forgotten as he'd stalked past, eyes tired, several days worth of growth on his lean jaw, sunglasses shoved up to the top of his head. He'd ripped off his sweaty shirt and stood there in nothing but jeans riding dangerously low on his hips as he and Logan laughed about something while he fought with his locker door.

Ever since the hostage situation, her therapist had been promising her that her physical desire for men would eventually return, probably when she least expected it. She'd traveled a bit, visited her parents and sister in Florida, where they'd busily set her up on all the blind dates she'd allow, and yet nothing had really taken. But sitting there in that room, it had not only returned, it came back with bells and whistles.

Holy smokes.

Conner Hawk had it going on.

Unable to help herself, she'd continued to stare at him, soaking in his tanned, sinewy chest, the tattoo, the various scars that spoke of how many years he'd been doing the hero thing. His jeans had a hole in one knee and another on the opposite thigh, exposing more lean flesh.

Then he'd glanced over and caught her staring.

Unnerved, she'd dropped her fork in her lap. Unfortunately it had still been loaded with the bite she'd never taken. Ranch dressing on silk. Nicely done.

Those melting chocolate eyes had met hers, filled with that cynical amusement he was so good at. He hadn't said a word as he'd yanked a fresh, clean shirt over his head, the muscles in his biceps and quads flexing, his ridged abdomen rippling as he'd pulled the material down. His eyes, even heavy-lidded from exhaustion, had still managed to convey a heat that had exhilarated her in a way she hadn't wanted to think about.

After that, he'd never quite accepted her icy silence for what it was—a desperate cry for him to stay away, because she needed her distance.

Oh, boy, had she needed her distance. And she couldn't blame him for not really buying it. Hell, she'd definitely, at least for that one moment, given him the wrong impression. She'd given *herself* the wrong impression, because she'd wanted him—wanted his arms to come around her, wanted him to dip his head and kiss her, long and deep and wet as he slid his hands over her body, giving it the pleasure she'd denied herself all year.

But she'd come to her senses and hadn't let herself lapse again.

At least not publicly.

As the newcomer to the division, she'd made a big effort to fit in, to get to know all her co-workers, while definitely staying clear of Hawk. She'd been aloof and stand-offish with him and him alone because she'd thought it best for her to keep far away until she was ready for the feelings he evoked. Which she still wasn't.

That didn't mean she didn't care, because she did. Too much. Therein lay her problem.

From that salad-in-the-lap moment, Abby had taken one look at him, past the bad boy physique, past the knowing grin, and had known.

She could care too much for this man.

Now she sat in the van, with the night whipping around them, desperately visualizing Hawk checking in because she had to believe he was okay.

Please be okay.

"Someone's down," came Watkins's voice. "Repeat, *agent down.*"

Oh, God. Once upon a time, *she'd* been the agent down, and just the words brought back the stark terror.

Dark room.

Chained to a wall.

Cold, then hot, then fear like nothing she'd ever known when she'd realized her captors wanted information she didn't have, and that they were going to torture her anyway....

But this wasn't then. And what had happened to her wasn't happening now. *Concentrate*, damn it. *Focus.* "Where is he?"

The men behind her, Ken and Wayne, already in high alert from the equipment failure, worked more frantically, trying to get feed on him.

"Watkins," she said. "Clarify."

Nothing.

"Thomas, are you with Watkins?"

More of that horrifying nothing. Whipping around, she looked at the two men in disbelief. "Are we down again?"

Wayne's fingers tapped across his keyboard. "Fuck. Yes."

Was it possible for a heart to completely stop and yet pound at the same time? "They need backup." She stood to yank off her blazer.

"What are you doing?" Ken demanded.

"Getting ready." Abby tossed her useless headset aside.

"No. We're not supposed to—"

"We have at least one man down and no radio." She slapped a vest over her shirt, and then grabbed a gun, emotion sitting heavy in her voice. No cool, calm and collected now. No, all that had gone right out the window with her last ounce of common sense, apparently. "We're going in."

There was some scrambling, whether to join her or stop her she didn't know because she didn't look back as she opened the door to the van.

LOGAN BOLTED ACROSS THE ROOF of the barn, dodging the icy spots and the shadow he'd seen. Not Gaines, but one of his paid goons, coming back from where he'd last spotted Hawk.

He sped up, high-tailing his way toward Hawk, because that's what they did, they backed each other up. They'd been doing so for years in far tighter jams than this one. And in all that time, he'd never once felt anything but utterly invincible.

But at this moment, all he felt was terror.

Hawk was down.

Rounding a corner of the roof, Logan headed toward a vent. As he crouched down behind it to survey the situation, the air stirred, and he felt a blinding pain in the back of his neck. As he whipped around to fight, he was hit again, by a two-by-four, or so it felt, and then he was flying off the roof toward the ground.

Shit. Now both he and Hawk were down....

THIS WAS RIDICULOUS, ABBY TOLD herself as the cold, icy night slapped her face. She'd taken herself *out* of the field. She'd vowed that nothing could get her back to it. And yet here she was, off and running at the first sign of trouble because she couldn't stand the thought of an agent down.

Ken caught up with her, both of them gasping in the shockingly bitter wind. They took the long, winding dirt path up toward the ranch. The place sat on a set of rolling hills that looked deceptively mild and beautiful by day. But by night the area turned almost sinister, steep, rugged and dangerously isolated. Fallen pine needles crunched beneath their feet. The patches of ice were lethal spots of menace that could send them flying, but still they ran.

The wind didn't help. It was picking up, if that was possible, slicing through to the very bone, kicking up a dusty haze that nothing could cut through, not even the night vision goggles.

When they reached the dark farmhouse, they stopped to draw air into their burning lungs.

"Around the back," Ken said. "The barn's around the back."

She was already moving that way but came to a stop at the corner of the farmhouse, where she had the vantage point of what should have been a woodsy clearing, but with the dark and the driving winds, seemed more like the wilds of Siberia.

She knew the barn lay beyond the trees, but in between there were no lights, no sign of human life. Abby went left, Ken right, both skirting the edges of the clearing, using the trees as cover.

Where was everyone?

As she came through the woods, the barn loomed up ahead, nothing but a black outline against a black sky. And then she saw him.

Hawk.

He was standing, holding his gun pointed at someone standing in the door of the barn.

Abby watched in horror as the gun flashed, and she caught a glimpse of the man he'd aimed at flying backward like a rag doll.

Gaines? Elliot Gaines? What the hell? Why was he here? Everything within her went cold. Had Hawk just shot Gaines?

CHAPTER THREE

WINNING WAS EVERYTHING. Knowing it, Gaines pushed down harder on Hawk's windpipe, barely feeling the blood running down his arm. He'd been nicked before, a year and a half ago in Seattle as a matter of fact, while wrestling in the dark with one of his own ATF agents.

Hawk, in fact.

See, that's what happened when one hired the best, and Hawk was the best of the best. He was a fucking pitbull, and he'd all but publicly promised to stop at nothing until the leader of the Kiddie Bombers was behind bars.

He might as well have signed his own death certificate.

And goddamn, he'd actually gotten a shot off. That was a pisser. But the explosions Gaines's men had rigged would go off soon, and Hawk would be lost in them. Logan also, because it had become clear tonight that there was no other way.

And though it killed him, Abby, too.

No loose ends.

And there wouldn't be. Thanks to his crew, which included Watkins working on the inside, everything had been perfectly choreographed. Already Tibbs would have received an anonymous tip that would raise enough questions about Hawk's "role" in the theft of the rifles from the ATF to enable Tibbs to get a search warrant for Hawk's place. There he'd find a computer memory stick with Kiddie Bombers' information, including purchases, sales and contacts, password-protected and encrypted just enough to make it look legit.

Hawk framed, check. Hawk dead, almost check.

And then, retirement time. Good times. The only thing that would have made tonight perfect would have been if he hadn't been forced to take out Abby. He regretted that, and he'd miss her like hell, but he couldn't risk the rest of his life for a piece of tail, no matter how badly he wanted that piece.

He was so close now. Close enough to taste it. God, he loved to win. And tonight, he planned to win big. "Got any last-minute prayers?"

EVEN WITH HIS VEST, the after-effects of taking a slug in the chest were brutal. His muscles were spasming, his body twitching, and it was sheer agony to get his limbs to obey his mind. But Hawk managed to grab Gaines's ankle and yank him to the ground, leveling the playing field, though not by much. Jesus, even his brain hurt, feeling as if it'd been used as a pinball within his skull. Gathering his thoughts was an exercise in futility, but he had to fight off Gaines—then he caught the flicker from within the barn. Flames. Ah, shit, the whole thing was going to—

Blow.

The explosion knocked them both backward. The barn roof blew sky high, catching the grass in the clearing on fire, as well as the trees.

Surrounded. He was surrounded by unrelenting heat, scorching him both inside and out. Gaines came up on his knees, looking like death warmed over as he staggered to his feet, pointing his gun. "You're hard to kill."

"So are you." Hawk's gaze locked on the dark spot blooming out from the shoulder of Gaines's jacket. "Missed your black heart, unfortunately. I blame the hit to the chest. Threw me off."

The smoke rose from behind Gaines's head, making it look like steam was coming out of his ears.

"It's going to get worse," his own personal monster said.

It was true. If Gaines chose to shoot Hawk in the nuts, there was nothing he could do. His body was shit at the moment.

Gaines pointed the gun between Hawk's eyes.

"Go to hell," Hawk said.

Gaines grinned. "Tell you what, I'll meet you there."

Hawk's life flashed before his eyes. His parents, gone now, but so proud of him when they'd been alive. Special Forces, where he'd had a good run—no, make that a great run—before moving to ATF.

Another great run.

Until now.

Maybe he should have added some more personal touches to his life's canvas. A wife. Kids. But he'd always figured there was plenty of time for that.

Helluva time to be wrong. "Do it," he said, coughing from the smoke. "And die."

Gaines laughed. "You have no idea how right you are. Now give me your gun."

Hawk tossed it over, then attempted to keep breathing. Not easy when his chest was still on fire, and actual flames were leaping all around them. He had no idea why he was alive but just in case it didn't last, he kicked his foot out and again swiped Gaines's legs from beneath him. They rolled, and he got two strong punches into his superior's gut before he lost the element of surprise and Gaines clocked him in the jaw, and then his ribs.

Unlike Tibbs, Gaines had no soft middle. He was built

like a boxer, one who trained 24/7. On a good day, he'd be a tough opponent in a fight, but tonight, with Hawk in agony, was not a good day. They fought dirty and hard, and the bitch of it was, Hawk had no idea what the hell had happened—why had Gaines come after him? He fisted his hands in Gaines's shirt, and the material ripped, revealing...

A puckered scar over his collar bone. From a bullet. Goddamn, his proof had just literally appeared. "I did hit you that night," he breathed. "I did. I fucking hit you."

"But I lived." Panting heavily, Gaines grinned. "Guess you need more target practice, huh?"

The heat from the blast and the flames licking at them had sweat streaming into Hawk's eyes. He couldn't see anything but Gaines's face and a wall of flames.

They had to finish this thing off now, one way or another, or they were both going to die. Hawk swiped more sweat from his eyes and gasped to draw air into his taxed lungs. "So running the whole division wasn't good enough for you, you had to put illegal weapons back on the street? Why didn't you just kill a bunch of innocent people yourself?"

Gaines's jaw tightened. He was holding onto his shoulder with his free hand, assuring Hawk that he'd been hurt more than he wanted to show. "I'm going to kill you instead."

"I'm not dying tonight."

"We're both dying tonight. Only difference is that my death's going to be fake. Well, that and the fact that you're going out as the bad guy."

"You're insane. No one will ever believe that."

"Abby will."

Abby. *Abby?* What the hell did she have to do with this?

"She's out there, you know." Gaines jerked his chin in the direction of the clearing.

Hawk was just stunned enough to crane his head and look, but all he saw were those flickering flames coming ever closer, so close he could feel the hairs on his arm singing. "What are you talking about? She's in the van." Safe and sound.

God, please let her be in the van, safe and sound.

Gaines shrugged. "Let's just say the hero worship I've built up with her is going to finally pay off for me, however briefly. Along with the news that Tibbs has just discovered evidence that you've been running the Kiddie Bombers." He *tsked*. "Shame on you."

Hawk had no idea what the hell Gaines was talking about. He couldn't see Abby. Hell, he couldn't see anything beyond the smoke, but Abby wouldn't leave the van.

And yet he remembered how she'd lost her 1-900 voice when she'd sounded worried about him.

Or so he'd assumed…

He hadn't survived all he'd survived without seeing the ugly side of human nature. Maybe she hadn't been worried for him at all, but for Gaines. Ah, God, the thought of her in cahoots with the bad guy put a sharp pain right through him. A new pain, over and above the others, and that was saying something.

"Once Abby realizes I'm here and that I'm missing, she'll want to save me," Gaines mocked. "Too little, too late, of course."

Hawk willed his damn muscles to obey the commands his brain was sending. Get up. *Kick his ass.* "Abby's done with you. She turned you in," he improvised.

Gaines went utterly still. "Bullshit."

"Are you willing to gamble on it?" he taunted, biding time, trying to figure a way out of this mess.

Gaines straightened to scan the horizon, still holding his shoulder as he searched for someone.

Abby?

"If that's true, I'll have to up my timeline."

Oh, Christ. "You won't find her." Because Hawk would get to her first. He began to inch backward. He had no idea where he thought he could escape to, but it was time to go. He'd managed to get a foot away when another explosion rang out, raining down fiery fragments on top of them. The smoke was so thick Hawk couldn't breathe, couldn't see, but he sure as hell could keep moving, and he hightailed it as fast as he could.

"Goddamn you!" came Gaines's howl of fury at Hawk's escape.

Using the choking smoke as a screen, Hawk dodged into the woods, past the flames and grabbed a tree for support. Christ, he felt as if he'd been run over by a Mack truck.

Sinking all the way to the spinning ground seemed like a good idea. He did manage to roll to his back, where he studied the smoke-filled sky. Though he couldn't see anything without his night goggles, which had slid off, oh, somewhere about the time that Gaines had given him a nice one-two punch to the left kidney, he could hear sirens. Fire engines, probably cops, too. Lots of them.

Because somehow Gaines had managed to frame him for everything *he'd* done, which was plenty.

God, he was so screwed.

ABBY COULDN'T BREATHE. Yes, she'd just run a half mile in less than two minutes, and was now inhaling only smoke as she stared in horror at the barn, engulfed in flames, but that wasn't why she couldn't catch any air in her lungs.

Had she really seen Hawk shoot Gaines before the explosion? She'd left the van in such a hurry that she hadn't taken a radio. The only personal effects she carried were her gun, cell phone and the mini credit card she had attached to it in case of emergencies. She'd already called Tibbs. He'd told her that according to Thomas, Logan had fallen from the roof and was waiting for a helicopter to airlift him to Cheyenne Memorial Hospital. No word from Hawk.

God. The whole night had blown up in their faces. She'd asked Tibbs about Gaines being here, and he said he'd check and get back to her. In the meantime, gun drawn, she tried to get closer to the barn but the heat stopped her. She couldn't see a thing, and she couldn't get closer.

And then her cell vibrated. "Gaines *is* there," Tibbs drawled. "Apparently, he came to watch the takedown."

"Oh, my God." So if she hadn't imagined Gaines, then she probably hadn't imagined Hawk shooting him either. Still holding her phone to her ear, she took off again but immediately tripped, falling flat on her face and losing her grip on her gun. Twisting around to see what she'd fallen over, she saw a roof shingle, and…a rifle?

"Abigail?"

"I'm here, Tibbs. I'm okay." Crawling to the rifle, she picked it up, burning her fingers. She dropped it, but she didn't need to access her computer to guess that the serial number on this rifle would match one of the ones stolen from their storage.

Was that why Gaines had come—had he suspected the Kiddie Bombers had taken the illegal weapons for their own personal use?

And why had Hawk shot him?

"Gaines radioed his office that he'd gotten into the barn," Tibbs told her.

"The barn is on fire."

"Did he get out?"

"On it." After spending a few futile minutes trying to find her gun, she checked the rifle. Loaded. She slipped the leather strap over her shoulder and took a deep breath for courage. You can still do this. All around her the flames leaped and crackled and burned brighter, spurred on by the vicious wind.

Knowing she had to hurry, she moved deeper into the woods to get around the fire, staggering to a halt at the unholy howling of a wolf that sounded far too close. Could be worse, she told herself. Could be a grizzly.

Some branches rustled and she nearly swallowed her tongue as she rushed into motion, her shoes crunching on the frozen ground as she circled back in toward the barn, determined to get to the bottom of this crazy evening.

She passed no one, and not for the first time felt unnerved by that fact. How was the place so utterly deserted? None of it made any sense.

Unless.

Oh, God. Unless it had been a setup from the start. At the realization, her feet faltered, and she slipped on the rocky terrain but caught herself in time on a tree only twenty feet from the barn. Abby wanted so badly to wake up, to know that she wasn't losing her mind.

She thought she knew Hawk, and sometimes she'd even felt as if he knew her, which was exceptionally crazy because she'd never let him in at all. But, God, the thought of him being a bad guy was like a knife to the gut.

Again her cell phone vibrated. She flipped it open.

"Where are you?" Watkins demanded.

"I'm—"

"I know, I've handled it," he said.

Abby went absolutely still. "What?"

"Nothing, talking into my radio."

Wait—radio? He was talking into his radio? But the radios were down. And now her heart was in her throat. *I've handled it…*those three words brought her directly back to another raid, and another extremely bad time.

They'd been the words Gaines had spoken before she'd gone in that day, and then later, she'd heard those words from the men who'd held her. They'd spoken the words *handled it* into a radio to some unseen boss.

No. Had to be coincidental. Of course it was.

"Where are you?" Watkins asked tensely. "Why the hell did you leave the safety of the van? I need you to get back to the safety of the van, Abby. Do you copy?"

She opened her mouth to answer him but stopped herself.

Not saying a word was stepping over a line, a big one, but she didn't speak. Couldn't. Because who the hell was the bad guy here? Hawk?

Or...Watkins?

God, she was losing it.

"Abby?"

Yeah. That was her. But instead of responding, she quietly shut her phone and kept hugging the tree because suddenly her legs didn't want to hold her.

She'd seen Hawk shoot Gaines. Hawk, gun in his hand, shoot point-blank. That made it him.

Right?

Her brain hurt, physically hurt. She couldn't process it all, or make sense of it. Who to trust? Knowing she had only herself, she pushed away from the tree and ran—

And then tripped over...oh, God...a man sprawled on the ground, far too close to the flickering flames. "Elliot—" Dropping to her knees, Abby set her hands on his back and realized her mistake instantly.

This body was one solid muscle. With a moan, he rolled to his back, keeping his eyes closed beneath dark lashes and the straight dark lines of his eyebrows, which were furrowed together.

Hawk.

CHAPTER FOUR

ABBY CROUCHED OVER HAWK and checked for a pulse, which he had. Relieved, she got to her feet and peered through the trees that were providing them cover. Out there she could see the barn. The side door was open, fire ripping outward, drawn by the cold, chilly oxygen. Beyond them, she could see...oh, God...boxes and boxes of ammo. She ran back to Hawk. *"Hawk."*

"Present."

She had no idea whose side he was on, but she sure as hell wasn't going to leave him here to die. "Get up."

"Sure." But he didn't move. And in spite of herself, everything within her softened. It was nothing personal, she tended to soften for injured animals and wayward children, too. It helped that he didn't look like his usual strong, capable self all sprawled on the ground. "That was a direct order."

"I'm hearing ya."

She put her hand on his jaw and looked at his mouth, which was usually curved in amusement, at her, at himself, at life. But at the moment, it was tight. Grim. Reflecting pain. She never thought she'd miss that smile, but she did. "Come on, get up, you cocky, smug SOB."

He lifted his head, and she found herself leveled flat by his soft brown eyes that were so in contrast to his definitively unsoft demeanor. Even flat on his back, he looked lean and angular and startlingly attractive as that mouth curved slightly. "Abby."

How, while completely surrounded by such utter chaos, she could feel an odd zing, she had no idea. But just looking at him made her feel dangerously feminine. "Where's Gaines?" she asked.

Hawk's short, almost buzzed hair was dusted with dirt and ash and stood straight up, revealing his hairline and a nasty cut, oozing blood. "In hell," he answered, voice rusty. "If there's any justice."

Oh, God. So it was true. Regret, and a huge sadness welled inside her. Once Gaines had saved her. Picked up the broken pieces and helped her put herself back together again. And she hadn't been able to return the favor. "So he's—"

"Not yet, he's not." His face hardened, his eyes so intense on hers that she'd have fallen to her knees if she hadn't already been there.

"I saw you shoot him," she said.

"Did you?" He grimaced. "Trust me—"

"Are you kidding?" Abby managed a laugh. He hadn't even tried to deny it. "After what I saw tonight, I should trust a rat's ass over you."

"Look, whatever you're thinking, you've got it wrong." His gaze shifted past her as he carefully scanned the immediate area, making her shiver at the danger sparking from his eyes. "He set this whole game up tonight."

Okay, clearly he was delusional, but she still had to get him away from the flames. "What hurts?"

His laugh was short and harsh. "Only every fucking inch."

Well, that they could deal with. "Get up."

"Any minute now, I swear." He closed his eyes. "So, a cocky, smug SOB? Really?"

"Come on, Hawk." He might be eyeing the flames licking at them with an eerie calm, but she was not. She hoped like hell Elliot had indeed gotten out. "Get up!"

He shifted to do just that. "Check our sixes."

"What?"

"Our asses, Ab. Make sure we're not being made. Gaines has a crew out here tonight, somewhere. They're setting explosions and making merry."

She added *paranoid* to the list. Which, given his situation, made sense. "I've got your damn ass, Hawk." Fine as it was. Crawling around behind him, she slid her arms beneath his, wrapping them around his chest so that she could pull him to safety.

"Ah, that's so sweet," he murmured. "But now's not a good time for me."

She grated her teeth. This. This was one reason why she'd stayed her distance. The man exuded raw sex appeal. Only problem? He knew it. "Don't flatter yourself." She tugged. "Do you have to be so big?"

Though his eyes remained closed, he flashed a smile straight out of her very secret fantasies—pure wicked, mischievous promise. "You don't know the half of it."

Okay, if she ever got him out of here, she was going to kill him herself.

"You smell pretty," he whispered.

Her gaze swiveled back to his, but his eyes were still closed.

"You always smell pretty…"

"You're dreaming," Abby said flatly.

"Nah. If I was dreaming, I wouldn't be this close to begging you to finish me off." But he tried to stand up, then inhaled sharply at the movement and promptly choked on the smoke. "Yeah. You really do smell amazing. Sexy."

Now *she* choked. "Stop it."

"Really sexy. Even when you're blasting me with your glacial stare."

"Shut up, Hawk."

"You don't glare at Logan," he said thoughtfully. "Or Watkins. Or anyone. Just me."

Well, that was just true enough to have her drawing in her own sharp breath as he staggered to his feet. "You don't like me much," he told her, rolling his shoulder as if it hurt.

"That's not true. I like you plenty when you're not talking."

He sighed. "Now, see, I think I'd like you plenty if you were naked."

"You're such an asshole."

"Asshole Hawk. Yeah, that fits—"

The next explosion was small but way too close and very hot. Instinctively, she pushed him back, knocking them both down. Then she was enveloped in Hawk's strong arms and rolled, tucked into him while embers rained down.

When it was over, she realized that the muscles in his arms were quaking. He was a dead weight on top of her. "Hawk?"

A litany of swear words escaped him, blowing her hair back. He lifted his head, his eyes not even close to warm and soft, but hard as aged whiskey. "Don't ever do that again."

"What? Save your sorry ass?"

"Exactly. Save your own first, you hear me?"

"Then get moving!"

"Yeah." With a groan, he got to his feet and reached out a hand to help her. A considerate bad guy.

Where was Gaines…?

Having been in a bad situation before, the worst, Abby had a gut-wrenching need for everyone to be okay and accounted for, even knowing that someone on her team had caused all this. "Do you think Gaines—"

"Oh, that's right. You still need to rescue your Sugar Daddy."

No one at ATF knew that she'd dated him twice, she'd made sure of that. Their relationship mostly consisted of her miraculous rescue, and then a vague, uncomfortable friendship that she'd had difficulty maintaining because of her new "issues."

"Where is he, Hawk?" When he didn't answer, she shook her head and turned toward the direction of the barn.

"No, wait. Don't." Hawk grabbed her arm, his eyes dark with concern. For her. And though it shouldn't have, it touched her as he spoke. "Don't even think about going back—"

"I have to."

"Goddamnit, Ab—"

Yanking free, she was halfway to the barn when her cell vibrated. Pulling it out of her pocket, she flipped it open and saw "unknown" ID. "Hello?"

"It's me."

Elliot's unmistakable voice brought a wave of relief. *"Where are you—"*

"Listen to me. We've been betrayed. By Hawk."

She processed the words, but, damn, it was hard to swallow, despite what she'd seen with her own eyes. "Elliot, are you sure, because—"

"Have I ever been wrong?"

Okay, no. No, he hadn't. And she knew exactly what she owed him, but— "Whose phone are you calling me on, because it's not yours—"

"Trust me, Abby."

She wanted to. She knew he wanted her to. But just because she hadn't ever allowed Hawk's charm to melt away her panties didn't mean she didn't know that he was an incredibly good ATF agent, one who believed in what he did and believed in putting away the bad guys. There had to be an explanation for all of this. "Tell me where you are—"

Another explosion interrupted her, picking her up like a rag doll, tossing her once again on her ass in the dirt. *Damn.* Crawling back through the trees to where she'd left Hawk, she realized three extremely unsettling facts at once.

Gaines had disconnected.

Hawk was gone.

And she was all alone.

This night just kept getting better and better.

CHAPTER FIVE

HAWK STUMBLED THROUGH the burning forest, getting his
strength back as he made his way through the fiery night.
Things had gone FUBAR quickly— "fucked up beyond all
repair"—but he knew Gaines planned on somehow van-
ishing for good, and he couldn't let that happen. What he
really needed right now was Logan, and he wished like
hell he still had a radio.

But, really, he was lucky to still have his head.

He knew Abby was going to be pissed at the disappear-
ing act, but he'd have to deal with that later. And if it turned
out she wasn't in with Gaines, well, then he'd apologize and
they'd all go back to their regularly scheduled program.

Which was her ignoring him. One of these days he'd
figure out why her pissiness was such a turn-on….

Hawk made it around to the back of the barn before he
fell to his hands and knees hard. Staring down at the dirt,
he tried to gather his wits. Not easy, since they'd been
scrambled by the explosions and then again by the knowledge that his boss had been playing both sides, selling the
weapons they'd confiscated over the years on the black
market, in essence undoing all the good they'd accom-
plished by putting those weapons right back into the hands
of gangbangers, murderers and terrorists.

If he thought about it too long, it hurt his brain all
the more. But it sure made sense. No matter how hard

they'd worked at getting to the top of the Kiddie Bombers' hierarchy, they'd been thwarted at every turn.

But Gaines hadn't worked alone. No way. So who else was involved...Abby? And if not her, then who?

Watkins? Thomas?

Tibbs?

Not for the first time, he slapped at his pockets and his belt, but all forms of communication had been stripped from him in the fight. He'd even managed to lose his cell phone.

"We can't get in because of the explosions."

Hawk's ears perked at the male voice. Who was that? Thomas?

"On Gaines's last transmission, he said that Hawk did this, all of it."

No, not Thomas, Hawk thought as he used a tree to silently push himself to his feet and peer through the trees at the figures he could barely make out.

"Gaines is presumed dead."

Watkins. Watkins was the inside help Gaines had most likely needed.

"No," came an answering female voice. A shaken one. "We don't know that he's dead."

Abby. Sweet, hot Abby, with those gorgeous baby blues that softened whenever she smiled.

And hardened whenever she looked at Hawk.

He'd been looked at that way by women before, usually after a few drinks and an overnighter, when he'd made his excuses rather than stick around and explain that he was only saving the woman some time because he wasn't a good long-term bet.

Hell, he wasn't even a good medium-term bet.

No sweat, he'd always figured. He'd get back to the whole love game when he retired from the job.

Which wasn't looking so good right now.

Abby had pulled out her cell, and was listening. "Yes, sir." Slapping the phone shut, she let out a breath. "Tibbs found a memory stick in Hawk's house." She hesitated. "With information on the Kiddie Bombers."

Ah, Christ. He'd been set up but good. *Thanks, Gaines.*

"If Gaines is dead…" Watkins trailed off, but Hawk silently finished the sentence in his own head.

Then I go up for murder.

The men around Abby moved off, probably to search for him. Get in line, he thought.

Gaines had really gotten it together for this one. If he had his way, Hawk would die tonight. Probably Logan, too.

And…oh, Christ. If Hawk had succeeded in even planting a seed of doubt in Gaines's mind about Abby turning him in, then he'd screwed her.

Gaines would have to off her, too.

Whether she'd been in with Gaines no longer mattered, she was now a target right alongside Hawk. If something happened to her, it'd be his fault. *Shit.* Gulping in a deep breath, he pushed off from the tree and whipped around to pursue Abby.

To keep her safe.

But he only got about two steps before he plowed directly into a brick wall. A soft, perfumed brick wall.

Flying through the air, he realized the person trying to kill him had an instantly recognizable body and scent. Flowers, and some sort of sexy light spice that made him think of both sweetness and heat at the same time.

Of Abby, who'd wrapped her arms around him hard, and as they both sailed through the hazy air, heading toward the frozen earth, he had time to think one more thing.

Goddamn, but he was getting tired of eating dirt tonight.

ABBY SKIDDED ACROSS the unforgiving ground. She felt it digging into her legs, felt the damp chill her skin, but that was the least of her problems as Hawk rolled, pressing her into the ground with his body, which was taut and extremely primed for violence. Before she could so much as draw a smoke-filled breath, he clamped a hand over her mouth, completely immobilizing her, which promptly brought her back to another time and place. All her training flew out the window as terror took over, leaving her fighting like a wild thing, ineffective and serving only to drain her energy.

"Stop." Hawk's voice came low and gravelly, his mouth so close to her ear that she felt his lips brush her skin. "I'm not going to hurt you, but I can't vouch for Gaines, so save it."

The night and smoke combined to create an unwanted intimacy, as did his weight over her. They were away from the barn, in the trees, out of sight. But still, she held out hope that any second now Ken or Watkins or *someone* was going to help her. Then she'd find Elliot and get to the bottom of this crazy night.

"I'm going to take my hand away," Hawk murmured. "But we're going to stay just like this. Real quiet, okay?"

She nodded. Of course she nodded, but the minute he lifted away his fingers, she spit out *"Get off me!"*

He sighed and again covered her mouth, which made her struggle like mad beneath him. She was beyond frightened, but he was calm, breathing so normally she wanted to scream in frustration.

"Abby, goddamn it, *stop.*"

She tried to bite his fingers but he just pressed harder on her mouth. The low light cast his face in soft shadows, softening his features, making him seem almost vulnerable.

Which was ridiculous given that she was the vulnerable one here!

"Are you with Gaines?" he asked.

What?

He was watching her very carefully. "I need to know. Which side are you on?" Slowly he lifted his hand from her mouth.

"I'm on the *good* side!"

Hawk stared at her. "I have no idea if you're lying—"

"I'm not!"

His jaw brushed hers as he nodded, and she became extremely aware of how he held her. Tightly. Too tightly to move. And yet somehow, incredibly gently.

What kind of a bad guy cared if he hurt her or not?

"Just had to make sure." He said this lightly, as if they were having tea and cookies instead of lying on the ground. "So if you're not a bad guy, that means you—what came back to help me?"

"Yes," she lied, closing her eyes for a moment to protect her thoughts, which were that she wished she could help him. She wished she could connect what she'd seen to what her heart was telling her—that this man, this fierce, intense, wildly sexy man couldn't have possibly done what she saw him do. She gauged his weight. "I came back to help you." Take you in. "Hawk…" She had to, Abby reminded herself, and though she had no idea what made her say it, she whispered, "I'm sorry," and then came up hard with her knee between his legs.

When he slumped over her and let out his breath in a soft *whoosh*, she played the rolling game as well as he had a moment ago and ended up on top, straddling his hips, breasts pressed to his chest, hands entwined with his on either side of his head to hold him down. Then she made the monumental mistake of looking into his face.

His eyes met hers in the dark night, reflecting the fact that despite his easy-going tone, he was in some serious pain. "Good one," he wheezed and coughed. "Holy shit."

Remorse was a luxury she couldn't afford, no matter how much she was attracted to him or how good an agent she'd thought him to be. She wouldn't make the mistake of thinking she had the upper hand for long. He'd been Special Forces, and he was considered a deadly weapon even when completely naked, so she knew the truth—if Hawk wanted to get away from her, he could. "I'm going to have to call for backup," she said slowly, watching him, overwhelmingly aware of his body tensed with barely repressed aggression beneath hers. She hadn't been this close physically to a guy in a year.

A year, two weeks and three days.

But who was counting?

Why was he letting her hold him down?

She didn't know, but she needed the rifle, and began to reach back for it—

"Don't." He tried flashing a grin. "Come on. We don't need backup. You and I can rock and roll all on our own."

"I'm not hitting on you, and you know it. I've never hit on you."

"Really."

"Really."

"So that time I caught you staring at me changing shirts, you were, what—checking for moles?"

Okay, he had her there. "I was not hitting on you," she repeated stiffly. "Good God, only an idiot would think that!"

"An ass *and* an idiot." He sounded amused. "I had no idea how highly you thought of me."

"You shot Gaines," she reminded him, watching him

very carefully. She knew better than most how fast the man could move.

"So we're going to talk shop now?" he asked, as if he hadn't just held her down against her will. Maybe he'd decided she was no threat. That she wouldn't scream to get help when she needed it.

Too bad he was dead wrong.

"Because up until now you haven't been all that interested. Unless…unless it's the opposite. You've just been playing hard to get." Hawk grinned again, but it was forced.

And, yes, she actually knew the difference between his real smile and a forced one. But she'd obsess over that later. For right now, Abby wasn't going to let him distract her, not when he was as slick as rain, and she could feel him beneath her, gathering strength, his every muscle poised for action. She very carefully shifted her weight and…

He almost let her get the rifle, too. But then he locked his gaze on hers, his filled with a whole host of things she wished she couldn't see—regret, resignation and also sadness, which she didn't understand. The next thing she knew, he'd unarmed her and once again she found herself held down by six feet two inches of solid muscle.

"Where did you get the rifle?"

"I found it after the first explosion."

"Or you got it from Gaines, out of the barn. Damn it." He shifted, pressing down harder.

Her windpipe closed, her heart stopped and she thought maybe the world had slowed to a halt on its axis. Abby opened her mouth to scream, but again his hand came down over it.

"No, don't. I can't let you shoot me, or call for help," he said with real remorse in his voice as he threw the strap of the rifle over his shoulder. His eyes were black, fathomless pools, unwavering in their intensity as they fixed on her. "I'm sorry you're scared. I'm not going to hurt you."

Ha, she tried to say. *I'm not scared.* But she was so far beyond scared she couldn't even speak the lie.

Hawk sighed and leaned in a little closer. She could feel his chest pressing into her breasts, the powerful thigh he'd shoved between hers. He still had one hand on her mouth, the other gripping her wrists high above her head. He wasn't hurting her, though he outweighed her by a good seventy pounds. "Any more weapons I need to know about?" he asked, shifting slightly and releasing the hand on her wrists in order to frisk her. As he did, her nose brushed against his neck. His hand slid down her body intimately, choking a gasp out of her. His scent was a surprisingly good one given the night he'd had.

"No screaming," he reminded her. "Promise me."

She nodded her head. She'd have promised him the moon if he'd only get the hell off her so that she could draw air into her aching lungs. Besides, she was banking on someone, anyone, discovering them any second now.

He nodded in return. "Good. Because I'm having a major guilt attack here, and I really just need you to cooperate." That said, he lifted his fingers from her mouth.

Immediately, she opened her mouth to yell, but he stopped her but good.

This time with his mouth.

She was so stunned, it actually took Abby a moment to struggle. He was kissing her.

Really.

Kissing.

Her.

And, holy smokes, she had to work frantically to actually keep herself distanced…which turned out to be all but impossible with his lips slanting over hers, his tongue licking the inside of her mouth, consuming her, heating her up from the inside.

God. Six months of wondering how it'd feel to have his hands on her hadn't come close to the reality, but this wasn't the time to melt. No. No melting. This went against every thing she'd expected, against everything she'd experienced the last time a man held her down, and she didn't know how to react.

But Hawk did. Oblivious to her inner torment, he kept on kissing her. And if she'd thought accidentally brushing her nose against his neck had been heart attack inducing, it was nothing compared to mouth on mouth. His lips were surprisingly soft and yet somehow firm, and while she processed that realization, another came right on its heels.

She'd frozen like a scared little bunny, when she'd promised herself no more scared little bunny. It was why she'd talked Gaines into letting her come back to work after the leave of absence, it was why she'd chosen communications, where she could be in the action and yet not in danger.

Ha!

His tongue traced her lower lip, then slipped inside her mouth to tango with hers, reminding her she was in danger now, mortal danger of forgetting where they were.

Oh, no. Nope. Not happening. Again she came up hard with her knee.

But she'd lost the element of surprise, and he anticipated the move, shifting so that she caught him in the upper thigh instead as he kept kissing her.

She'd shoot him. Soon as she got her rifle back, that is. He still had one of his powerful legs between hers, pressed up high enough that she couldn't swallow without him feeling it, but she squirmed anyway. He merely pressed down harder, and unbelievably, it awakened parts of her that had been dormant for a long time.

Then he lifted his head, his breathing none too steady as he stared at her. "Two things. Gaines wants me dead, and I think he wants you the same. I need you to believe me."

"No—"

"Goddamnit—" Hawk bit back the curse, then shook his head. "Fine. You won't trust me, then I have no choice."

Reaching back, he grabbed something from his pocket. Handcuffs.

Abby met his gaze and at what she saw there, felt like she was straddling a steep crevice, about to plunge to a helluva fall. "Hawk."

"Sorry."

"Whoa. Wait a damn minute—"

He slapped the steel on one of her wrists and then on one of his, linking them together.

CHAPTER SIX

WATKINS STOOD ON THE EDGE of the clearing, feeling the heat of the fire toast his face. The wind lashed at him, the smoke stinging his eyes. He'd directed Gaines's men out of there now that the explosions had gone off, and the fire was out of control.

Their job was done. Permanently. Most would vanish completely now with the booty Gaines had given each of them, although it was inevitable that some, the greedy ones, would continue with their illegal forays.

Not his problem.

His cell vibrated. He looked down at the readout and grimaced. He debated not answering, but that could be bad for his health. "Yeah?"

"How the hell did Logan get onto a heli-transport?" Gaines demanded. "He's supposed to be dead. You were supposed to have him killed."

Watkins closed his eyes. He'd been paid extremely well over the years, and, as a result, he hadn't had a problem with how tonight was to go down.

But he hadn't agreed to off Logan.

Nor Abby.

Besides, there wasn't enough money to look into Abby's eyes and watch her die. There just wasn't. "Not my fault. Sam screwed up and didn't make sure he was dead before he tossed him off the roof. And then Abby ordered me to—"

"Christ. You let a woman run your show? You're worthless."

The back of Watkins's neck tingled. His heart lodged in his throat. He turned in a slow circle, making it half-way around before he came face-to-face with two hooded men.

Gaines's men. "I thought I told you guys to get out of here."

"Goodbye, Watkins," Gaines said in his ear, just as one of the men lifted his gun and pointed it at Watkins's chest.

J.T. LOGAN WAS DREAMING ABOUT floating on a raft, sur-rounded by a sea of gorgeous, stacked *Playboy* centerfolds there to serve his every whim. Even dead asleep he knew the utter ridiculousness of the fantasy, and exactly how politically incorrect it was, but, hey, it wasn't his fault, he was dreaming.

But it didn't last long enough. As he came awake in slow degrees, pain spread like knives stabbing throughout his entire body.

Holy shit. With a moan, he opened his eyes and found himself staring up at one of his *Playboy* centerfolds. *Huh?* Still dreaming? Hard to tell. She wasn't picture-perfect like the others nor magazine-cover ready, but there was something vibrant, something extremely real about her.

She wore blue, which contrasted with her siren-red hair, pulled into two haphazard braids on either side of her head. She was watching over him from behind black-rimmed glasses through which a pair of forest-green eyes, outlined by long, spiky lashes, blinked at him. These rather amazing eyes were narrowed, and her forehead was creased into a frown, with one eyebrow bisected by a scar that drew his gaze.

He couldn't look away. Oddly, he wanted to know what had happened to cause that scar more than he wanted to know why his head felt as if it'd been blown half off his shoulders.

She wore no makeup except for gloss on lips that were still frowning and also moving.

Asking him a question, he realized. Unfortunately, he couldn't seem to hear a thing.

Yeah, he had to still be dreaming. But what was this harassed-looking, slightly rumpled *Playboy* bunny doing in his dreams?

The others had all been naked, and yet here she sat wearing clothes. Scrubs to be exact, which wasn't one of his particular fantasies, though he was always willing to—

Uh-oh.

Turning his head, he took in the sky. Ah. Not a *Playboy* bunny but an angel. Yeah, that explained it.

Except he didn't want to be dead….

Then Logan realized he was looking at the sky from a small window. He was flying. In a pretty damn fine helicopter, too.

Oh, boy. Either he really was on his way to heaven, or he was in big trouble.

He'd take door number three instead, thank you very much.

Too bad that didn't appear to be an option.

His hearing was slowly coming back, though everything was sounding tinny and very, very faint, as if coming from miles away. And, damn, the pain had him gasping, wanting to curl into a ball.

Or hurl.

"What's your name?" the angel in scrubs was asking.

"J.T. Logan. Just Logan is good, though," he answered

automatically. Which was good, right? It was always good to know your name.

"Okay, J.T. Logan, how many fingers am I holding up?"

Now that stymied him, because, interestingly enough, he didn't see any fingers. Though he did see a lot of that red hair, escaping those messy braids. She had the kind of bangs that swept across her temple and down one side of her face, framing her jaw. Her ears were small, dainty, with two single gold hoops in one ear, and four in the other. Her V-necked scrubs were short-sleeved, revealing toned, tanned arms.

His angel liked to be outside, and she liked to be physical, which in no way took away from the fact that she was nicely stacked.

"How many fingers?" she asked again, bending over him to check one of the pieces of equipment behind him. As she did, her top gaped, revealing a pink bra beneath.

And a heart belly ring.

God bless the belly ring. "Two," he answered definitively, looking at her breasts. "Pink cotton-clad—*ouch!*"

His angel jabbed him with a needle, which answered his question about heaven. He definitely wasn't there. Proving it, she pressed something just behind his ear, which came away bright red.

Blood.

His.

Ah, shit. Pain continued to bloom through him.

"Nice gash there," she said, still frowning. "You'll need stitches after X-rays." Then she set down the blood-soaked cloth and ran her hands down his body, and he wished like hell he could feel them instead of the agony slashing through him because he'd bet her hands were warm and sweet and gentle—

"Besides the possible concussion, I'm going to guess at least two dinged-up ribs—" She paused, probing, while he did his best not to lose his dignity and throw up on her very clean, white athletic shoes. "Make that three."

"That's probably going to hurt pretty good when I stop floating," he said.

Again she leveled him with those green, green eyes. His beautiful, still-frowning flight nurse. "You feel like you're floating?"

"Better than puking, right?" Logan tried a smile and felt his eyes roll in the back of his head at the movement.

"Don't move." She ran her fingers over his ribs and fire burst through his veins instead of blood.

"Holy shit!" he gasped. "What else is injured?"

"I'm guessing some internal bleeding. I think your right leg's fractured. Not sure about your hip."

God. He stared up at the ceiling of the chopper and concentrated on breathing. At least he was breathing. And then it occurred to him that he had no recollection of getting there. "What happened to me?"

"You don't remember?"

He stared at her as his brain hit Pause, Search and then Play. But all he could summon up were the *Playboy* models floating naked on the ocean, pleasuring him however he wanted, when he wanted. Somehow he didn't think she wanted to hear about that.

"It's okay," she said, softening, her fingers touching his jaw. "Just relax, and—"

"Enjoy the flight?" He let out a laugh that definitely wasn't full of amusement. "That depends on what the in-flight movie is for today." Logan went to sit up, and found his vision hampered by yet another explosion of white-hot pain.

"Yeah, that's your ribs. Hence the not moving suggestion."

Got it. Not moving. Very carefully not moving. But as he lay back and went still, he wracked his brain for answers.

None came.

"What's your last memory?" she asked.

"Floating with the bunnies."

She arched that scarred eyebrow. "The fluffy white-tail kind?"

"Um…sure."

She eyed him, and he had a feeling he was slipping nothing by her.

"Huh," she said. "Wonder what *bunnies* were doing at your raid."

"Raid?"

She lifted up the flak vest she'd obviously had to cut off him. The big white letters across the back read *ATF Agent*.

And just like that, it slammed into him. Separating from Hawk on the roof. Hearing Hawk call out Gaines's name. Having it all make terrible gut-wrenching sense and then being hit over the head before being shoved off the roof. It hadn't been Gaines, he'd been on the ground, but one of Gaines's men. He knew it. "Hawk," he said hoarsely. "Where's Hawk?"

His angel/nurse gently set a hand on his chest. Yep, just as he thought, she had a sweet touch. Sweet and unyielding.

Because she wasn't letting him get up.

"My partner," he ground out, gasping as he lay back. "Do you know about him?"

Her eyes filled with compassion as she shook her head. "You're the only one we have tonight."

"Cell phone. I need my—"

"Whoa there, cowboy."

"I need to—"

"Breathe," she said firmly, nodding when he gulped in air. "Yeah, just keep doing that." She was leaning over him again, hands on his upper arms, holding him down. "That's it." She looked behind him to the pilot. "Ethan, ETA?"

"Twelve minutes."

"Almost there," she told Logan, stroking a hand down his arm and back up again, in a manner that was incredibly calming. "You've had quite the night, haven't you?"

"I need to call in—" He broke off at a wave of dizziness. "Shit, this sucks."

"Tell you what. You lie really still for me, and soon as we land, I'll find out about your partner, okay?"

He wanted her to call now. But there were spots swimming in his eyes and he thought maybe he was going to puke after all.

"So, do you remember how you got so dinged up?"

"Took a hit to the head." Which had hurt way more than he'd expected, but not as much as, say, taking a flying leap off a roof. "Then I took a tumble off a roof."

"You fell off a roof?"

"Not fell." His jaw throbbed with tension and all the pain. "I was pushed."

She shook her head. "And I thought *my* job was hazardous."

Logan let out a low laugh, which had him groaning in agony. Again she bent over him.

"Keep breathing," she whispered, eyes on his.

Yeah, he'd keep breathing, soon as he was done throwing up. He would keep breathing, just as long as he could keep looking at her....

HAWK WAS STILL HOLDING ONTO Abby, who was staring in horror at the handcuff on her wrist. He had to admit to feeling a little bit of horror himself, but he had to keep her safe, at all costs. Because that's what he did, he upheld the law, he kept people safe…

And she needed to be kept safe, whether she knew it or not.

God. He'd handcuffed her to him. And somehow he didn't think it would help to explain to her that sometimes to do the right thing you had to cross the line. Especially when he hadn't just crossed it, he'd stomped on it. But, God, she'd tasted so sweet, so hot, he wanted to stomp on that line again….

No. Bad.

Focus.

He was going to keep her safe, at any cost.

The wind had kicked the flames so that they were surrounded, as if in their own, intimate hell. They stared at each other, her glaring, him stunned. Kissing her had been everything he'd ever imagined and more, so much more, because the reality of her willowy body against his had been better than any fantasy. If he hadn't been bleeding all over her from the cut on his head, that is.

Oh, and if he hadn't *cuffed her.* Yeah, that had been the golden touch right there. Really, it was shocking that she wasn't falling all over herself to be with him.

She'd been right after all; he *was* an idiot, and an ass.

Abby tried to jerk free, and she was strong for such a little thing. He hadn't realized that about her. He'd known she was strong-minded, driven, that she enjoyed work, that she had a pair of eyes that cut through all his crap and saw the real him. Oh, and that she'd taken an instant dislike to him from day one.

Under normal circumstances, Hawk might have simply

turned up the charm and tried to figure out where he'd taken a wrong step, but Tibbs had warned him way back on her first day to leave her alone. And he had.

Now he was extremely sorry he hadn't cultivated more of a friendship with her regardless because he sure as hell could use her on his side at the moment. Big time.

"Abby, you have to listen to me." Grabbing her shoulders, he backed her to a tree and peered into her face. "You're in danger. We're both in danger. I need you to—"

"Uncuff me."

At the tension in her voice, he eased back. Normally she avoided him like the plague, but she did so with an indifferent disdain that was designed to turn him off, even though for some sick reason it always had the opposite effect.

But there was no disdain now. No, she had a look in those kill-me-slowly baby blues that spelled complete and abject terror.

She really believed him to be the bad guy.

Unbelievable. "Hey. Hey, it's okay. I'm not going to hurt you, I only need to—"

"Let me go, Hawk."

Her fear cut through him and broke his heart. "I can't do that."

"Let. Me. *Go.*"

"I hear you, believe me," he said with real regret, protecting her with his body when a blast of wind brought hot ashes drifting down on them. "But I can't do it, I'm sorry."

"Won't, you mean."

"Okay, yeah. Won't. Not until you listen to me."

She glared at him with so much emotion spitting from her eyes, he nearly did as she asked and let go of her. Usually put together, she now had dirt streaked down a cheek and along her jaw, and her shirt was torn. So were her pants, from knees to thigh, exposing one of her world-class legs and the scratches she'd sustained.

She looked like a wreck. A furious, undone, adorable wreck. And he wanted to kiss her again. God, he'd give a limb to do just that.

Scratch that.

He just wanted to hold her. Hold her tight until she was safe, and no longer scared.

Yeah, explain *that*.

"You're a wanted man," she said. "It changes everything, Hawk."

"Wanted for what, exactly?"

"For turning rogue!" Abby arched up with each word, bumping some interesting female body parts into many of his favorite parts. "For running the Kiddie Bombers! For shooting Gaines! Pick one!"

"I would, except for one thing. I am not running the Kiddie Bombers."

"But I saw you shoot him." Her voice quavered though her eyes did not. Nope, they were cemented to his, shiny with emotion and a self-righteousness, which normally made him want to wrestle her down and mess up her hair and wrinkle her clothes.

But she was already ruffled, which was just as well because he couldn't summon even a shred of playfulness or his legendary calm, not with his heart lodged in his throat. "You have to trust me," he said quietly.

She stared at him, then slowly shook her head.

Fine. *Christ.* Hawk was not a man used to explaining himself, but he gave it a go now, he had to. "Okay, I shot him, yes."

"Oh, my God."

"But it was in self-defense. This was all a crazy setup. Gaines has been running the Kiddie Bombers. He's been re-selling the confiscated weapons, putting them back on the streets, probably at a pretty profit. But I got too close, and now I've become a problem to him. He decided to lay the blame on me and then fake his death."

She stared at him like he'd lost it, and truthfully—he had. He totally had. "He's still very much alive, Abby. I didn't kill him, I swear it."

He didn't realize how much he needed her to believe him until she stared up at his face, her heart in her eyes.

"I know," she whispered. "He can't be dead because he called me."

"He *what?*"

"He wanted to tell me you were the bad guy." She stared down at the handcuff linking them.

"I'm not," he promised. "But he's feeling closed in by all the loose ends now." He touched her face. "You're a loose end, Ab. You're in danger. He means for me to die here tonight, and now, I think he means the same for you. Please, let's not let him win."

Abby swept her gaze down the length of him, and he knew what she saw. Blood. His. Gaines's. "I swear it," he whispered. "I won't hurt you."

"Then uncuff me."

"Do you promise to come with me, so I can keep you safe?"

"I'm not ready to promise you anything."

This evening was not going his way. "Where's Logan?"

"He was air-lifted out."

That stopped Hawk cold. "What? What happened?"

"He fell from the barn roof."

Christ. "Listen to me," he said, gripping her shoulders and giving her a little shake. "Logan didn't fall from any roof, he would never have fallen. Don't you get it? He's fucking with us, Abby, like we're toys."

"Then come in with me, and we'll figure this all out."

"By *in,* you mean turn myself in?"

It was all over her face, and he shook his head.

"Hawk—"

"I need to get to Logan, wherever they took him. He's in danger, too."

"Fine. After we go back, we'll—"

"No." He laughed harshly. "Let me save you some bullshitting time, okay? I overheard you and Watkins. If I go in, I go in charged for Gaines's murder. Even though you and I both know he's not dead."

He watched her eyes once again lock on the blood splattered down the front of his shirt. Watched as she stepped close to set her hand on him. The warmth from her body seeped right through to his chilled flesh, and he nearly shut his eyes, but then he realized she'd slipped that hand around him, reaching for the rifle he'd swiped from her.

That settled it.

Time for Plan B. And though his muscles screamed in protest, and every inch of him hurt like hell, he pressed her back against the tree. "Don't even think about it." Before she could find another way to kill him, he took off running, forcing her along with him.

"Hey!" Abby tugged, trying to slow him down.

"Later." He'd talk her into believing him later. He'd have to. "We're going on the run. Together."

CHAPTER SEVEN

WITH LITTLE CHOICE, ABBY FOUND herself racing alongside Hawk, whose endurance showed her she'd been stupid
to think she could ever win in a physical battle with him—
and, given that she'd put herself in a position to be caught
and handcuffed, possibly not even a battle of wits. They
dodged through trees, the heat of the fire following them.
Everything seemed to be engulfed. Flames flickered and
hissed and snapped all around them.

She wondered if the farmhouse had caught fire as well,
wondered if the others were looking for her, wondered
about Elliot. "Where are you taking me?"

"To get to the bottom of this unbelievably fucked-up
night."

She tried to slow him down and came up against the
restraint of the handcuffs, which reminded her. She had a
panic attack scheduled for, oh, right about *now*. "I can't be
handcuffed, Hawk," she puffed. "I can't—"

"Just run."

"See, that's the thing." She gasped for breath. "You're
just making this worse on yourself—"

"Shh."

He stopped so fast Abby blinked. She eyed the veins in
his temples working overtime. His jaw was so tight it could
shatter. "Do you realize you've spoken more words to me
in the past sixty seconds than in our entire relationship?"

"I need to know what's going on, Hawk. Now."

"I told you. The Kiddie Bombers have been run by an inside mole all along. Gaines. And I've apparently gotten too close. He's got no choice now but to stop me. And Logan. And you, Abby."

The situation was impossible, not real, and yet...

And yet his words reminded her that over a year ago, she'd also been suspicious about how the group seemed to know the ATF's every step. Then she'd been kidnapped, and had ended up being distracted by the events of that whole nightmare night, and then her rescue and leave of absence.

"Come on," Hawk urged. "He's not working alone, there are others. We have to get out of here."

The next thing she knew they were running again, through the trees, far from the fire, from the scene. "Hawk."

Ignoring her, he just kept pulling her along, and when she dragged her feet, he simply entwined his fingers in hers and tugged harder.

"Stop." Accompanying this demand, she dug her heels into the ground, but it was frozen and slippery, and all she did was trip.

"Jesus." The hands he put on her waist felt strong and very capable as he steadied her. She'd set something off in him, and if she wasn't mistaken, it was concern, not anger. "Don't be stupid."

"I'm not going anywhere with you, Hawk. Except back to the others. Now uncuff me." She nearly choked on her next word but spit it out anyway. *"Please."*

Hearing the crack in her voice, he grimaced, and so did she. *Oh, God. Don't be pathetic, Abby. Keep it together.*

"We both know what will happen to me if we go back," he said. "I'm being set up, Abby. And by the time the red tape gets untangled, it'll be too late. Gaines will be gone."

"Gone? Where?"

"Who knows. Some uncharted South Pacific island. But not before he makes us pay."

"You're wrong." Her chest felt tight. God, who to believe? "He wouldn't hurt me."

He let out a frustrated breath and gave her a little shake. "Why are you so loyal to him? What does he have over you?"

He'd saved her, and she'd never be able to forget that. "I owe him…everything."

Hawk stared at her for a long moment, opened his mouth, then closed it. "This is crazy, you know that? Gaines is after us, I swear it."

"And your proof of all this is…?"

Behind them came the sound of a man's shout.

"Shit. Run," he commanded.

"Hawk—"

He pulled her along. "My gut is screaming," he told her over his shoulder. "And my gut is never, ever wrong."

"But—"

"Jesus. Can't you just trust me?"

"No!" She was panting for air. "Because you're basing all this on your gut. That's not enough."

"Yes, I—" He took one glance at her undoubtedly mutinous expression and shook his head. "Ah, forget it." Ruthlessly he continued to pull her along, on a path only he knew.

So much was wrong, Abby couldn't even wrap her mind around the facts, or her feet, apparently, because she tripped again. She'd have landed flat on her face, too, if Hawk hadn't grabbed her at the cost of his own balance, and then they were falling anyway, hitting the cold ground. As luck would have it, her chin bounced off a patch of snow instead of dirt, which she supposed she should appreciate.

"Shit." Hawk was on all fours, head down, breathing hard. *"Shit!"*

"Yeah, you've already said that."

Turning his head, he leveled her with an extremely unamused glare. "If you could keep in mind we're attached."

"If you could keep in mind that you're kidnapping me!"

"I'm *protecting* you!"

"Then uncuff me." She was breathing as if they'd been running miles, instead of a quarter mile, tops, but she needed to be uncuffed. *Now.* "You don't need me," she gasped. "Just uncuff me and go do what you've got to do."

"You have to stay with me. Or—"

"Or what? Or I'll be safe?"

"Damn it, I told you, *I'm* keeping you safe!"

"Let me go." She heard the panic in her voice but couldn't help it. "I'm…I'm begging you, Hawk."

He closed his eyes. "Abby…" His voice was hoarse. "I have to do this. If something happens to you, I won't be able to live with myself."

"Nothing's going to happen to me—"

"Right, because I'm going to make sure of it. Besides, I know you. If I let you go, you'll go digging—"

"No." He didn't know her. He didn't know, for example, that she was an inch from meltdown. Or that she could scarcely breathe because of it. Or that she didn't understand any of this, not the way she'd broken protocol and left the van in the first place to run after him when she'd thought him in danger, not the way she'd let him kiss her for a good long time before she'd kneed him…

And now she was handcuffed to him, the man she'd been so secretly attracted to. Gee, what great taste she had. Clearly there was something seriously wrong with her. "So you want me to believe that this is for *my* protection?"

"Yes," he said, clearly relieved that she got it.

But all she got was that he was unbelievable. "What an overprotective, egomaniacal, stupid thing to do! I can protect myself, Hawk. My God, I'm a trained agent, too!"

He was already shaking his head, his eyes flat and stubborn. "No. You didn't see him tonight. You didn't see his eyes." He turned from her and studied the night. "He's lost it. Completely."

Abby tried to see whatever he was looking at, but she couldn't see a thing. She had no idea how he decided which way to go, but suddenly they were moving through the woods again. As they moved, she eyed his pockets, wondering which one held the key for the cuffs.

Because she was going to get free.

The wind continued to whip at them, cutting bites that nipped at her skin. The smoke was still thick, choking her. When she started coughing, Hawk stopped and waited for her to catch her breath.

A thoughtful captor. Too bad she still wanted to kill him.

He wasn't looking at her now, but was taking in their surroundings, an awareness about him, a physical readiness. He was primed and ready for more trouble, but then he turned to her, and his eyes changed. Softened. He pulled something from her hair. And something else. Twigs, she imagined. Pine needles.

Then he touched her face.

She jerked back at the uncomfortable, unfortunately familiar, claustrophobic feeling of someone being too close. "Don't."

Don't touch me.

It was too dark to see his expression clearly, but he went still for a charged moment, then stepped back as far as he could, considering they were still linked. "I told you, I'm not going to hurt you."

But that wasn't the promise she wanted. "So let me go."

Instead, he turned away. "Let's go. Almost there." And they were running again.

From the depths of her pocket, Abby felt her cell phone vibrate. Incoming text message. She glanced at Hawk. He was slightly ahead of her, watching where they were going. That, and the dark night allowed her to pull out her cell without his seeing. She flicked aside the mini credit card attached to the small chain on the antennae in order to see the screen. Watkins. Where are you?

She hit Reply, then hesitated because there was the little issue of trust. She had no idea who to believe. Abby shook her head. *No.* That didn't matter right now, all that mattered was getting free. She hit Send, and off the blank message went. As an SOS. It would have to do.

They came to a clearing that she recognized. They'd gone in one big circle, eastbound, putting them just south of the farmhouse.... She looked around but saw nothing with which to help herself. The woods were thick, black as the inside of Hawk's heart, but still not as scary as, say, being handcuffed to him.

Damn, she wished she had her rifle back. She'd get that, too, along with the key. She was determined.

And terrified.

She tried to keep the panic at bay. After all, tonight was nothing, nothing at all, like her nightmare.

The nightmare that had really happened.

First of all, it'd been daytime, at a gun specialty shop

where it'd been suspected the Kiddie Bombers were selling confiscated weapons out of the back. She'd been on duty the day of the raid. In hindsight, it had been just rotten luck. Not so agreeable to the raid, the men had fought back as if they'd known the ATF were coming. Abby had been taken hostage and held in a basement, a cold, dark, dank place that even now, a year later, she could still smell in her dreams.

"I thought you were hurt," she said bitterly to Hawk's back, forced to keep her feet moving or get dragged along.

"Just stunned."

"From?"

"Taking a bullet to the chest." Slowing to a walk, he grabbed her free hand and pressed it up against his vest, over his heart, forcing her to feel the hole in his vest.

A bullet indentation. "He shot you when you pulled your gun on him?"

"No. He shot me point-blank."

"He must have known you were wearing a vest. Why didn't he shoot you where he'd have had a chance at killing you?"

"He tried. But it was dark, and I rolled. Then I pulled a gun on him."

"That's not what I saw."

"Sweetheart, I am not trying to argue with you here, but maybe you should get your eyes checked."

"You're saying Elliot drew on you first?"

"Elliot?" Hawk asked, and stopped so unexpectedly that she plowed into the back of him. "You call him Elliot?"

"It's his name."

"Sounds pretty chummy."

Yes, well, after he'd busted into that basement, guns drawn, to find her stripped naked and staring down the thugs who'd just pulled out a set of jumper cables to torture her with, they were definitely on a first-name basis. "We have a…history."

Hawk just stared at her, his eyes gleaming in the night. Clearly this news had not made his day. "So, you were what, fucking the boss while he was stealing back the confiscated stolen weapons to re-sell them on the black market?"

"You really are an asshole."

"Just calling it like I see it."

"You don't know what you're talking about."

"No? Then enlighten me."

Abby pressed the fingers of her free hand to her eyes and tried to keep a level head. "Why? Why would he do such things, Hawk?"

"Well, connecting the dots, I'd hazard a guess that it's because he's the bad guy."

Rolling her eyes, she turned away.

He sighed and pulled her back. "You want me to believe that lover boy never mentioned any of this when you two were doing the tangle on his sheets?"

Staring up at him, she slowly shook her head, feeling frustration and anger push aside her fear. Good, because she'd sure as hell rather be pissed off than afraid. "You are way out of line, Hawk."

"Yeah? Then put me in line." He stood there, his eyes searching hers, not mocking now, just wanting the truth.

But she didn't have the words. "Just tell me what you think we're supposed to do now."

"We need proof of Gaines's indiscretions. Unfortunately, my rock-solid proof ran off."

"What?"

"Eighteen months ago I shot the leader of the Kiddie Bombers. It was dark, in a warehouse, but I got him.

Tonight, wrestling with Gaines, I saw the scar. Here." He pointed to his collarbone.

"A bullet hole? But lots of ATF agents have bullet holes."

"Not undocumented ones. But now we have this." He patted the rifle. "If the serial number on this baby matches one of the serial numbers on the ATF database, it's one of the pieces of the puzzle."

Her mind whirled. "But even if that matches—"

"Yeah, yeah, we still need to tie it to Gaines, I know."

"*If* it's him."

"Abby—"

"Because from where I'm standing…" She jangled the cuffs. "It sure as hell could still be you."

She waited for him to defend himself, and though a muscle bunched in his jaw, he said nothing.

"I'm not going to make this easy for you," she told him.

Rubbing a weary hand over his face, Hawk sighed. "Yeah. Tell me something I don't know."

CHAPTER EIGHT

"KEEP MOVING," HAWK DEMANDED, refusing to give in to Abby's resistance when he was this close. They were headed toward the farmhouse and the trucks he'd seen there. His plan—get to an ATF database.

"Damn it, Hawk. Slow down."

She was tugging again and probably going to yank them to the ground, which she'd done four times and counting. He had the bloody knees to prove it, which, considering how dead Gaines wanted him, was the least of his worries.

Jesus, he could hardly even wrap his brain around how badly the evening had gone. Logan, down. Gaines, rogue. Abby...definitely not on his side.

He wasn't sure whose side that put her on.

"Hawk."

He'd been trying to ignore her, but she sounded panicked and breathless. Not from running so much as hyperventilating, and while that fact brought out some sympathy, it also came with annoyance, because, for Christ's sake, he wasn't hurting her.

He'd never hurt her.

Too bad she wouldn't say the same. "Nearly there."

To her credit, she kept going, but he knew it wasn't for him but to get to wherever he was headed and get uncuffed. He appreciated the warrior in her, more than she could know, because his shoulder blades kept itching.

Gaines was out there, armed, gunning for them.

They had to keep moving.

At the edge of the woods, he finally came to a stop. Abby stood as far away as the restraints would allow, so that the chain was pulled taut and the metal was digging into his raw skin. She had to feel it, too, but apparently she refused to even breathe in the same vicinity as him.

Good to know tonight was no different from any other.

He could see the faint outline of the farmhouse that he'd circled around to, and just behind that was a handful of cars. All ripe for the picking because, as he now knew, tonight had been nothing more than a setup.

Which meant he should be able to commandeer one of those vehicles and get them the hell out of there. Exactly *where* he would get them the hell *to* was yet to be determined, but one thing was clear—he couldn't let himself be brought in. Not until he could prove his innocence and Gaines's guilt.

"I think the truck is our best bet."

Abby was breathing harshly but not fighting him, which was an unexpected bonus. She had more twigs in her hair and a nasty scratch on one cheek. Her clothes were torn and beyond dirty from wrestling on the ground with him. She'd started the day so neat, too.

Just looking at her had something inside him softening. In a different time and place, he'd have reached over and pulled her close, maybe burying his face in her hair, pressing his mouth to her skin…

But her attention was on the cuffs, as if she could remove them by glare alone. He wished she'd just let it go for now, but she was definitely not the letting go type. "Keep up, okay?"

"I have a better plan. Uncuff me."

"I can't."

"Won't, you mean."

"Okay, won't. You'll turn me in before I can prove I'm right."

"You know what? Don't talk to me."

Oh, good. She was definitely coming around, surrendering to his charms. "See that truck?" he asked. "We're going for that."

Taking that whole not-talking-to-him thing pretty seriously, she didn't answer. But she was looking at him plenty, sending icy stares that felt like daggers. Probably trying to decide how to murder him, slowly. Resigned, Hawk pulled her toward the fifteen-year-old Ford pickup painted a combo of forest-green and bad-weather rust. He pulled open the driver's door, which was blessedly unlocked. Putting his hands on Abby's waist, he bent at the knees to hoist her in ahead of him.

She balked. Of course she balked, but he didn't have time for this. Now that they were clear of the fire and the chaos, the night was quiet, *too* quiet, making him extremely uneasy.

"I vote we go back to the van," she said.

He shook his head.

"I'm not getting into this truck with you."

She was tired. Scared. He got that. But that would have to be taken care of later, say if they lived, so to that end, he pressed his body into hers, trying to get her inside the cab of the truck. Her hair jabbed him in the eyes, her ass ground into his crotch, neither of which was exactly an unpleasant sensation, but at the contact, she jerked as if shot and jumped away from him, pulling on the cuffs.

"Jesus, Abby. Just do this. *Please*. Just get in."

"Uncuff me."

"Soon as we're out of here, I swear. I have to jump-start it."

"Oh, God." She hunched over, covering her face with her free hand, breathing like a lunatic.

What the hell? He touched her shoulder, and she nearly leapt out of her skin, eyes wide. Wild. Like she was no longer with him.

"Hey." Hawk lifted his free hand and wondered what was going on. "Hey, it's just me."

Her hysterical laugh broke the silence. Up until right then, a part of him, admittedly a sick part, had been enjoying their close contact, the way her body fit to his, the scent of her hair, how when he'd tried to lift her into the truck, her breasts had pressed into his forearm. But this reaction from her, this genuine fear, made him feel like a molester. "I'm not going to hurt you, Abby. I swear it. Just get into the truck, and I'll—"

"No!"

He understood her reticence, he really did, but she'd screamed this, leaving him no choice but to slide his hand over her mouth.

Of course, because this was Abby, she bit him, and then she was fighting him like a feral cat, tooth and nail. She fought dirty, too, twisting his arm but good as she whirled and tried to punch him in the throat, instead catching him high on his bruised chest, which hurt enough to have him chomping down on both his lip and his frustration. "Abby, stop. I am *not* the bad guy!"

She stopped fighting and brought her head up, eyes still wide but not so wild. "I swear it," he whispered, smoothing his fingers along the curve of her jaw. He had no idea when his priorities this night had changed from kicking

Gaines's ass to seeing this woman safe, but they had. "It's going to be okay—"

Another harsh laugh, this one a half sob, and she yanked at their joined wrists so hard his teeth grated. He began to understand something he'd missed before in the rush to survive—she definitely had something else going on here, something that the handcuffs were only making worse.

But it would have to wait, because for now he had to get out of here before he was discovered, and she was coming with him, period. To that end, Hawk bodily lifted her into the truck, taking another kick to the thigh in the process, swearing as he bent beneath the console to hot-wire the car.

"Hot-wire," she gasped, still breathless from the fight, as the engine leaped to life. "Not jump."

"Right."

"You said jump."

Had he? "To jump-start it, I'd have needed another car."

"And cables."

"Yes." It was the way she said *cables* that had him trying to get a look at her face as he whipped the truck around. But she turned her head away, staring out the window into the dark night.

Exhausted, but pumped full of adrenaline, he headed down the road without lights, driving slowly enough to avoid kicking up dust, but hopefully fast enough that no one noticed them. The road was completely deserted, but he didn't breathe freely until the main highway. There he flicked on the headlights and hit the gas. He was aware of Abby sitting stiffly, as far from him as she could get, her hand dangling limply near the steering wheel.

Saying nothing.

There weren't many cars on the highway this late at

night. Hell, there were *no* cars. Out here, even the wide-open spaces had wide-open spaces.

In the daylight the view had been of wildflower meadows, fall foliage and towering peaks all around them, covered in deep forests.

But at night, the sky-scratching mountains were no more than a dark looming outline, creating a feeling of vastness, which only increased his sense of isolation.

It was many moments before they saw another vehicle, and then, in the oncoming headlights, Hawk glanced over at Abby.

She hadn't relaxed, not a single muscle. Her skin was pale, her hair wild around her face, her eyes huge and underlined with exhaustion. "Abby," he said softly.

No answer, big surprise.

"I realize you're pissed and probably going to castrate me at the first opportunity, but before you do, just tell me one thing."

Her eyes cut to his.

"What happened to you?"

She closed those eyes.

And his heart sunk, because he'd gotten the answer to his next question. Whatever it'd been, it'd been bad, very bad. And it wasn't hard to make a few educated guesses, none of which he wanted to think about her suffering through.

Abby didn't speak, just sat there silently stewing. Steam practically rose from her clothing, which was even more ripped and dirty now and made him feel like crap because he'd done this to her.

Shooting him another sidelong glance that had his death written all over it, she hugged herself with her one free arm, took a deep breath as if steeling herself against the craziness they'd left behind and what was to come, and thrust her chin to nose-bleed heights.

While Hawk loved the show of bravado, he knew no one could maintain it for long, and when she crashed, that would be his fault, too.

When she finally spoke, it wasn't what he expected. "You're on empty."

He looked at her, surprised she cared enough to notice. "I know. Believe me, I could sleep for at least a week—"

"The gas tank."

"What?" He looked at the gauge and thought, *ah, shit.* Just one more thing in a long list of things that were not going his way tonight.

CHAPTER NINE

Somewhere south of Bullet City, Wyoming

Was it good or bad that they found a gas station almost immediately? Abby couldn't decide as Hawk pulled the truck off the highway and into the parking lot. From her perch in the passenger seat, she searched for an attendant, a customer, anyone she could flag down for help.

But there was not a single soul.

The handcuffs clanked as Hawk shifted, and her hand brushed his, making her breath hitch. She was so used to avoiding a man's touch, she found herself startled by the fact that though she was still furious, she was not afraid of their close proximity.

Why was Hawk different from other men?

Didn't matter. Slipping her free hand into her pants pocket, she closed her fingers around her cell phone. Hawk was looking at the pump, his head turned from her. Now or never, she decided...

Thumbing open the phone, Abby tried to figure out who to call, then froze as her finger inadvertently pushed a key.

At the unmistakable electronic beep, Hawk's head whipped back to hers. "What was that?"

She shrugged.

"Goddamnit." Pressing her back against the door, he set his hand low on her ribs.

"Hey!"

But his hand merely slid further down, brushing her hip, inching into her pocket without qualm, his fingers closing over hers. "What are you doing?"

Momentarily stunned at how intimate it felt to have his fingers in her pocket, so close to her, with his big body holding her prone against the seat, it took her a moment to answer. "Nothing."

"Doesn't feel like nothing."

Nope. It felt like…like he had his hand down her pants. "I'm just keeping my hand warm." It was amazing how fast the lie rolled off her tongue.

It would have been better if she hadn't sounded so damn breathless.

In answer, he slid his thumb over her lower lip. "Did you text someone?"

She licked her lips, the tip of her tongue accidentally touching his thumb. In response, he inhaled unevenly, and as if connected to him, her stomach quivered.

"Abby? Did you?"

"Uh…" For some odd reason, she'd lost track of the conversation.

"Did you tell anyone where we are?"

Needing him to get off her, she rocked up, managing only to bump her hips to his. He was surrounding her, holding her down, and it left her feeling confused, muddled. Instead of fighting him, as she'd figured she would, her body was doing a sort of slow-burning awareness thing, complete with hard nipples and quivering thighs. *What the hell?*

Hawk didn't appear outwardly affected by their closeness at all. Instead, he kept track of the issue at hand with apparent ease.

Why couldn't she keep track of the issue at hand?

"Did you?" he demanded, then pulled out the phone himself. When he swore, she assumed he'd located her blank text message in the sent file.

Shutting the phone, he lifted his head. Their mouths were a fraction of an inch apart, and somehow fascinated by this, she stared at his lips.

"You lied," he said very softly.

"No."

Honestly, she had no idea why she kept lying. He had the proof in his hand. "I—"

"Stop." As if to insure she did just that, he covered her mouth with his.

This time, this second kiss, Abby didn't have to brace herself. She knew what to expect, an inexplicable onslaught of hunger and desire, so compelling that a low sigh fell from her.

At the sound, he went utterly still, then slid his free hand into her hair, tightening his grip, changing the angle of the kiss to better suit him as he ran his tongue along her lower lip.

Oh, God. Two things occurred simultaneously. One, her heart skittered into near cardiac arrest, and two…a horrifyingly needy moan escaped her.

Hawk pulled back. Though his lids were heavy over his eyes so that she couldn't get a read from them, she sensed his confusion matched hers. "I must be insane," he whispered. "Totally and completely insane."

Yeah, no argument there.

"Tell me again you're not in on this whole thing," he whispered, still holding her face. "Because if you are, you should just kill me now."

"You're crazy."

"Please answer."

Slowly she shook her head.

"Is that no, you're not going to answer, or no—"

"No, I'm not in on this whole thing."

He stared at her for a beat, then let out a breath as he levered himself up off her. "Okay. Okay, that's going to have to be good enough, isn't it? Come on, we're getting out."

She turned to the windshield and was shocked to find it fogged up, dripping condensation. Had they done that? Steamed up the glass with just a simple kiss? Except there'd been nothing simple about it at all…. "We'll freeze to death."

"Can't freeze to death in hell, and I'm definitely in hell." Sitting back, he shoved his free hand through his short hair, making it stand on end. His eyes were shadowed, his lean jaw scruffy, his clothes tattered and blood-strewn. The cut on his forehead had stopped bleeding, but she guessed from his uneven breathing that he still hurt pretty good.

She should be glad. Instead, all Abby felt was a sense of uneasiness, and—truthfully?—a secret wish that he'd go back to holding her. Because for some reason, in his arms she'd felt safer than she had in a very long time.

HAWK EYED THE GAS STATION. It was quiet and badly lit. Both things worked in their favor, or so he hoped.

But it'd only been an hour since the first explosion. Gaines's men couldn't be far behind them. "They'll have figured out you're missing by now. And we know they're looking for me."

Nothing from the woman cuffed to him.

"We'll have to hurry."

She raised an eyebrow, and wordlessly offered up her wrist to be uncuffed.

He had no right to continue to hold her to him, he had nothing but a gut instinct that said he'd saved her life. The best thing now was to get her to Tibbs. Tibbs would keep her safe.

But the thought of walking away from her killed him, though he had no idea why.

Okay, he knew why. He knew exactly why. It was her eyes, mirrors to his own soul. It was the way she brought something out in him, the best part.

And having her smoking body so close to his didn't hurt…. Clearly, kissing her had destroyed too many brain cells. "You're going to run screaming the moment I uncuff you."

More of her loaded nothing.

"Look, I took you with me for your own good—"

She let out a snort that managed to perfectly convey exactly how full of shit she thought he was.

"Jesus." He pinched the bridge of his nose. "I'm a lot of things, Abby, I'll give you that. Stubborn. Tough. Maybe even as asshole—"

She nodded in agreement, which worked wonders for his ego, it really did.

"But whatever you think of me," he insisted. "I'm not a liar."

She slanted him a baleful stare.

"Okay, name it," he challenged her. "Name a lie I've told."

Clearly unable to, she turned her head away.

"Okay, fine. Great. Don't talk to me. Just promise me that you won't scream for help." He unzipped a small pocket on his outer thigh, pulling out a key. "Promise me, and I'll uncuff you."

At that, she leveled him with a furious look. "So now you *want* me to lie?"

"Fine." He tucked the key away again. "We'll do this

the hard way. Why the fuck not? We've done everything else that way all damn night."

She went back to her stony silence, and he was back to talking to himself. "I'm going to slide out. You're going to sit in the driver's seat and give me as much slack as you can while I pump gas."

She didn't answer, big surprise. He reached for the door, then let out a breath at the renewed pain in his chest.

Abby looked at him, her gaze darkening with what he sincerely hoped was a tiny bit of sympathy. Some of her hair had slipped free of its bond, falling in silken curves around her face, framing those eyes he could look at all day.

"The effects shouldn't last much longer," she said.

He wasn't sure why, but something turned over inside of him, and it was all he could do not to haul her close and kiss her again, just hold onto her until this nightmare was over. Except she was sending out serious back-off signals, so he got out of the driver's seat to get the gas. She willingly shifted over, giving him enough arm room to maneuver the nozzle into the gas tank.

And that's when he remembered. He had no money.

His gaze locked with hers, and he could see she'd thought of the same thing, since her eyes were mocking him. Christ, he was tired of fighting with her. "You don't by any chance have a wallet on you?"

She simply arched an eyebrow.

Terrific. He hadn't died of smoke inhalation, his wounds, or the fact that his heart had been ripped out by everyone believing he'd gone rogue. Nope, he was going to die because he'd been stupid enough to take her with him, to protect her no less, when she'd as soon rip off his nuts. "Do you or do you not have any money?"

"I don't carry money when I'm being kidnapped."

Hawk understood her anger, he really did. But he was hurting, too, and cold, and just about beyond frustrated. "He's coming for you, too, Abby."

She turned her head to lock her gaze on his. As she did, the scent of her hair drifted over him like a sweet balm. He had no time to be feeling anything since he was currently up hell's creek without a paddle. And yet he felt plenty, mostly an inexplicable need to kiss her again. "I need your cell phone."

"No. Don't—" She choked as his fingers slid across her abdomen, trying to get to her pocket. "Don't touch me."

"Relax." His hand brushed the warm skin of her belly just above her low waistband. "I only want the—"

Her elbow clocked him in the nose, and he saw stars. "Jesus!" He fell back against the opened door. "Jesus Christ, woman!"

Breathing like a lunatic, she glared at him, eyes hot and furious beneath the hair that had fallen in her face. "I told you not to touch."

"Okay, yeah, getting that loud and clear. The phone, Abby."

Her jaw tightened. "It's almost out of battery."

The battery didn't matter, and they both knew it. She threw her cell phone at him, and thank you, God, the little keychain he'd seen with her mini credit card was attached to it.

"I can't believe you expect your victim to pay for your gas."

"No, what I expect is to wake up from this nightmare any second, but I'm not going to get that lucky." He swiped the card at the pump and nearly fell to his knees in gratitude when the gas began pumping into the truck.

Her cell phone vibrated in his hand. Incoming text message. His gaze locked with hers, then he looked at the caller ID. "Do you know this number?"

She looked and blinked.

"Abby?"

"It's an established line between Gaines and me. He got it after…it was just for us to communicate back and forth."

He flipped open the phone to read: Where are you?

"Interesting that he isn't concerned with making you think he's dead. Interesting, and very telling."

"Right." She closed her eyes. "Because if I'm on his short list for the evening, it doesn't matter if I know he's alive. Because I won't be for much longer." She slid him a glance that sliced at his heart as she waited for him to nod.

Hawk slapped the phone closed against his thigh and sighed.

She didn't say anything more, and after a moment he realized she wasn't being obstinate—her default mood of the night—but rather trying hard to control whatever emotion she was keeping to herself. Bending closer, he risked life and limb to see into her face. "Talk to me."

She just shook her head.

"Abby—"

"Please," she whispered, clearly trying with all her might to keep it together. "Don't. Just let me think."

Okay. He could do that. For a little while, anyway. But then she shifted in the seat at the same time he pulled back, and her shoulder brushed his chest. The accidental touch seemed to freeze her.

It sure as hell froze him, and he watched as very slowly her head came up. God, her eyes, they completely slayed him. He just wanted to look at her all night. Look at her and inhale her and touch her…. The yearning was nothing new. He'd been inhaling deeply to catch her scent for six long months now. Hawk breathed her in and tried not to lose it, but, God, she got him, right in the gut.

In the heart.

She had a strand of silky hair over one eye, and very, very slowly he reached out to stroke it away, wanting to do much more but unable to figure out how to further touch her without her gutting him. "It's going to be okay," he murmured. "Unfortunately, I don't know exactly how, but we'll get there, I promise."

Her gaze searched his, soft now, uncertain, leaving him just as uncertain what to make of the shadowed expression in her eyes. Was she still mad? Hurt? Was she feeling any of what he was feeling, which was that he wanted to kiss her again, for real this time, without anything coming between them?

Abby turned away.

And there was his answer. No, she was not feeling any of what he was. Still waiting on the gas, he pulled out the phone again and dialed Logan's cell. No answer. Damn… Glancing up, he found her watching him.

"Last I heard," she said quietly. "He was in the air, headed back to Cheyenne County."

He only hoped that wasn't as serious as it sounded. "Okay, so we go with what we've got. The rifle. I just have to match it to the ATF serial number list to place it as one of the stolen weapons. So we need to get into regional offices."

"Or to my laptop at home."

"Yeah, much easier. Let's go."

"There's that 'let's' again."

"We have to do this, Abby. Placing the rifle is evidence of the inside job."

"Still not enough."

"Well, we'll think of more then. We have to do this, you know we do."

"No, we don't. *We* don't have to do anything." But Hawk realized the heat in her voice was gone.

Best news all night, from where he stood, because whether she knew it or not, he was winning her over. "If I'm wrong, I'll—"

"What? Turn yourself in?"

"Yeah."

She stared at him. "Let's call Tibbs now."

"Not without the serial number. Not when he already has evidence against me."

"Hawk…"

"Look, if I'm wrong, you can call him. I promise."

She tugged on the cuffs. "Your promise is no good to me when I'm with you against my will."

Okay, good point. But he wasn't letting her go until they were back on the road, because he wasn't going to risk her getting out of the truck this close to Gaines. "I'm sorry."

"If that were true, I wouldn't be here."

"No, I'm sorry about whatever happened to you."

Abby went so still he doubted she was even breathing. Slowly she lifted her gaze to meet his, and then *he* wasn't breathing, because there, revealed for him to see, was such pain he nearly staggered backward.

In the loaded silence came the startlingly loud click of the gas pump, signaling that the tank was full, and she blinked and turned away.

Moment over.

By the time Hawk got back into the truck, with her hurriedly scooting over so that he wouldn't have to touch her, she'd regained her control.

And reestablished her silence.

He started the engine, but she cleared her throat and rattled the handcuffs.

Right. Hoping he wasn't being an idiot, he pulled out onto the highway before he tossed the key into her lap. She wouldn't do anything stupid at sixty-five miles per hour, he figured.

Hoped.

Abby grabbed the key. Bending her head, she set herself to the task of unlocking the cuffs, her hair falling over his forearm, her breasts inadvertently brushing his bicep. She'd probably have a heart attack if she realized but he had another reaction altogether.

Freed, she rubbed her wrist and stared out the window. Reaching over, he brought her hand close until he could see her skin in the dim light of the console display. She was bruised, abraded and raw.

"Don't you dare say you're sorry," she told him.

He closed his lips on the words and pressed his lips to her skin.

She didn't snatch her hand free, which he considered an excellent sign. Instead, her breath caught as if maybe she liked his touch after all, as if maybe she was finally going to surrender her aggression and fear, and soften toward him. At least in his dreams.

"Why would he show himself to you?"

His eyes met hers. So she hadn't decided that he was completely full of shit. He'd take that. "I think it was sheer cockiness, to tell you the truth. Sort of like, look what I pulled off."

"But to play both sides… It's so crazy dangerous."

"He's dying tonight, remember," he reminded her. "In essence, retiring."

"After getting rid of his loose ends."

"Yes."

"Like you."

"Yes."

She nodded, clearly holding it together by a string, and he wanted to touch her so badly, just to let her know she wasn't alone.

"I keep going back," she said. "To when I was working on the Kiddie Bombers in Seattle."

He slanted her a glance. "Something clicking?"

"There were several times when things went down like tonight, when Gaines showed up at raids no one expected him to be at. To watch the take-downs, he always said." She shook her head. "Once I questioned him on that."

"And he was thrilled."

"He brushed me off." Abby shook her head. "And I let him. I discounted all of it until now. But I'm thinking that on the off chance I was getting too close…" She closed her eyes. "I'm a loose end, too."

"Yes, but you're an alive one," he reminded her. "Let's keep it that way. First, your computer."

"And then what? We draw him out in order to prove he's alive?"

It was the first real sign he'd had that she might believe him. "I like the way you think, and yeah. He needs to be drawn out."

Which Hawk would do alone, because no way in hell did he plan on letting Gaines anywhere near her. In fact, he needed to find a safe place for her until this was over. And yet…and yet there was a small part of him that couldn't deny what it felt like having her with him.

Because with her here, he wasn't alone. As disastrously bad as the night had gone, as bad as it could still get, he wasn't alone.

CHAPTER TEN

Cheyenne Memorial Hospital

LOGAN WOKE UP IN A WHITE ROOM filled with beeping equipment and a sterile smell that made him groan in disgust.

A hospital.

He hated hospitals, always had. His asshole father had put him in several, until the state had finally decided, oh, gee, maybe we'd better do our job and remove the kid from his situation. Logan had thrived in foster homes, but thanks in no small part to his wild streak, he'd still managed to land himself in various emergency rooms all on his own.

Then there'd been Special Forces and the time he and Hawk had been nearly shot to kingdom come when their convoy had been hit in the Gulf.

Since then, however, he'd actually managed to stay hospital free, though he had a running bet with Hawk—one hundred bucks on which of them would run out of luck first.

And damn it, now he'd lost. Unless he could get himself checked out before Hawk found out....

Something rustled at his side, and a face swam in front of his. Fiery red hair, black-rimmed glasses, mossy eyes and well-glossed lips.

His sweet angel, who'd been with him when he'd been

dreaming about *Playboy* bunnies, and when he'd ended up tossing his cookies at her feet.

Oh, yeah, *that* had been a highlight.

Still the sight of her made him want to smile. When he did, a whole new kind of pain swam through him. "Oh, shit."

"Careful." She cupped his jaw, her hand blessedly cool on his burning skin. "Stay still."

He let out a raw laugh. "Yeah. Not so good at that."

"I'd suggest trying."

She'd seen him at his absolute worst and was still here. Other than Hawk, that was a rarity for him. And worth everything. He could look at her all day. Hell, all week. He felt dazzled. Dizzy.

But that might have been the pain meds. "You stayed."

She put her deliciously cool hand on his forehead. "I'm glad you're back."

"When was I gone?"

"You've been pretty out of it. Your boss called and he sounded devastated at what had happened to you."

"Tibbs?"

"I didn't catch his name. He said he'd see you soon."

"Southern accent so thick he sounds like his cheeks are filled with marbles?"

"No. Sort of a rushed, clipped voice."

At that, images flashed to him from the barn. Everything going to shit. The shadow on the roof with him. Looking down and seeing something, someone on the ground, looking up at him just before the hit to the head.

Gaines.

He knew that now. He'd looked into Gaines's eyes and yet had been hit from behind.

By one of Gaines's men. *Bastard.*

"You were out for a long time."

That sounded bad. He only vaguely remembered being loaded from the chopper into the hospital, but he definitely remembered this gorgeous angel hovering over him with those sweet eyes and that mouth that made him think of hot, sweaty sex. He tried to lift a hand to touch her and found it taped to a board with two separate IVs hooked up to his arm. Uh-oh. Locating his other hand, he slapped at his legs to make sure they were both still there, and a searing bolt of pain sang up his right leg. This time he couldn't even swear, much less breathe.

"Oh, Logan, don't." She ran a hand down his arm in a slow, comforting manner. "Just hang tight. And don't move."

He gasped for breath. "Just—give it to me straight. My injuries."

She looked him right in the eyes. "Well, you have some."

"Some? Or so many they can't be counted?"

Her lips quirked. Her eyes softened. "Somewhere in the middle."

A sense of humor. With eyes like that and a mouth made for sin, it was sensory overload. "Tell me."

"Let me get your doctor—"

Somehow he managed to grab her hand and hold her still. "I want to hear it from you."

"Well, you have quite a concussion."

"Okay, that explains why my head feels like it was stitched back onto my neck."

"Yep, eighteen stitches."

"Ouch."

"There was some concern about the length of time you were unconscious, but you're awake now, and that's all the matters." She stroked her fingers over his. "Right?"

He stared at her fingers. Long, strong, capable. Ringless. "Absolutely. Awake is good, but…? I thought I heard a big one at the end of that statement."

"Logan."

Oh, yeah. His humor faded. "Spill it."

"You fractured your right leg and three ribs in the fall."

"I've had worse." Which was true.

"There's some internal bleeding that's causing concern. They were worried one of your ribs might have punctured a lung—"

"Hey, I'm breathing just fine."

She nodded and smoothed his blanket, looking so touchingly concerned he wanted to pull her into his lap and kiss it away. Too bad he hurt so much that he was in danger of puking again.

She read his expression with alarming accuracy. "Do you need—"

"No." He would not throw up again in front of her if it was the last thing he didn't do.

"Well…I should probably go. I'll get your doctor first—"

"No." Logan tightened his grip on her hand, about to utter two words he'd never said before, to anyone. "Don't go."

"I really shouldn't be here."

"And yet you are."

"But I shouldn't be," she repeated with a helpless smile. "I don't know why. I just…"

"What?"

"Nothing."

"Come on. I puked in front of you. Give me something."

She glanced back at the door. "It sounds so silly, like a cliché, but I felt this…connection…"

"I know." He'd felt it too, and he didn't do connections. Not breaking eye contact, he pulled her closer until she sat on the edge of his bed.

"So you felt it, too?" She asked this casually, just like this wasn't the moment he usually ran like hell from. If he couldn't run, he typically backpedaled, scrambling to make up whatever it was that a woman needed to hear, whatever it took to get her back into bed, or into her clothes and out his door, whatever *he* happened to need at the time.

He could be, as Hawk liked to say, a real prick.

But Logan preferred to think of it like this: it took little to no effort at all to compliment a woman, to touch her the way she wanted to be touched, to listen when she spoke. They loved it.

And he loved being loved.

Normally, by the time he backed out of whatever budding relationship he had going, moving into different waters, the woman he'd been with felt great about themselves.

Both parties happy.

But staring into his angel's eyes, he suddenly had no fancy words, no moves. He had nothing, and as the silence grew, her smile faded. She stood.

"No, wait. I'm—"

"Sorry? Don't be. It's okay." She shook her head. "It's my fault. I shouldn't have stayed. You just rest now, and—"

"Your name," he said hoarsely. Christ, his chest hurt.

"What?"

She tried to pull free but he didn't let go of her, couldn't, because suddenly, seriously, his chest hurt like hell. And it wasn't from his fall. "I don't even know your name."

"I've got to go." Gently but firmly she broke loose and turned to the door, and Logan closed his eyes. The irony didn't escape him. When it came to women, he did the leaving, he always had. A shrink would have a field day with the reasons for his behavior, but he didn't care about any of that now, except that for the first time in his life, the roles were reversed.

She was leaving him.

It didn't matter that he'd known her for all of a handful of minutes. That he didn't even know her fucking name. That he was injured, and he had no idea where or how Hawk was, or how the take-down had turned out.

Nothing mattered but this, crazy as it was. "Please, wait."

Hand on the door, she went still but didn't look at him.

More pain in his chest. Ah, now he got it. Not his chest, but his heart. He stared at her slim spine, at the lush red hair that he wanted to bury his face in. *Turn around*, he silently willed.

She didn't. Of course she didn't.

Because for once, he wasn't in charge, and he had no choice but to reveal himself. "I felt it."

Pivoting around, she locked her eyes on his. "What?"

"The connection. If you meant this thing zinging between us at the approximate speed of sound, possibly even the speed of light, then, yeah." He cleared his throat, and did something utterly new.

Bared his soul. "I *felt* it."

She looked down at her feet, then back into his eyes. "Callen. My name is Callen O'Malley."

"Well, Callen O'Malley..." He held out his hand. "Now that I've puked in front of you, not to mention been delirious and probably an all around class A asshole to boot, maybe I could show you a different side of me. A better side."

She arched an eyebrow. "And what side would that be? I've already seen every inch."

One glance at the hospital gown he wore instead of his ATF gear was all the explanation of that statement he needed. "I hope they were the good inches."

She smiled, and he felt like he'd won the jackpot. And when she stepped back toward him, he thought he could just die right now, because for the first time in hours, hell years, he felt like everything was going to be okay.

"YOU GOING TO tell me the plan?"

Hawk glanced at Abby in surprise. She hadn't spoken to him in thirty-three minutes. He knew because he was still holding her phone and he'd glanced at the readout at least a thousand times.

By some miracle, they hadn't been followed, but they were on borrowed time. He had only until their pursuers caught up to them to figure out a concrete plan for getting Abby somewhere safe, and then to her computer. "She speaks."

"Hostages don't speak. We suffer."

He glanced over at her, but she was already shaking her head. "Forget I said that."

Yeah, okay. Except he never forgot a thing. Not how she'd gone running out into the night from the relative safety of the van into the woods because she'd been worried about him, or how she'd sounded when she'd found him slumped on the ground. Or the feel of her arching against him as he'd kissed her.

At the time he hadn't been sure if she'd meant to pull him closer or push him away, but he knew better now.

She'd meant to shoot him.

Only she hadn't.

"I need to make a stop," she said.

"Hungry?"

"No."

"Thirsty?"

She shifted in her seat, looking uncomfortable. "No."

"Then no stop."

"I have to go to the bathroom."

Damn it. The one excuse he had no defense against. Pulling off the highway at the next exit, he drove into the only thing around, a campground with a sign that read Lost Hills. The sign didn't lie, the place was rugged, remote. Indeed, someone could easily get lost here. The guard station was empty, and Hawk chose to take that as the first good sign in an otherwise entirely shitty evening.

Maybe his luck was changing.

He drove down the bumpy one-lane road, eyeing all the campsites, which were empty. Normal people didn't camp in northern Wyoming in the late fall, because it would freeze your body parts off cold. The road had plenty of turnoffs, and he picked an out-of-the-way spot. Pleased, he turned to Abby.

Who was distinctly not pleased. "I don't see a bathroom," she said.

"Well—"

"And don't you dare point to a tree."

Which was exactly what he'd been about to do. "I'll close my eyes."

"How do you know that I won't gut you when you do?"

He sighed, the exhaustion creeping up on him like a sledgehammer to the side of the head. "Because you're not crazy about blood."

She let out a disbelieving laugh.

"Look, kill me if you have to, I'm feeling halfway dead anyway." He scrubbed a hand over his face. "And if you don't, we'll take off again when you're ready."

"To go to my place for my computer, and then we flush out Gaines. Right?"

There was going to be an "and then." His head swam for a moment, probably from sheer exhaustion. That, and an odd need to ask her to repeat the "we."

There hadn't been many "we's" in his life. Not once a woman realized his long hours and dangerous work would keep him just a little too gone, and way too distant. Few had hung in there, seeing past the job to the man beneath.

"Right. We'll stick to the plan." Well, mostly. Except for the part where she was with him when he flushed out Gaines.

"And if the numbers don't match...?" she pressed.

It was a good question. A fair question. "The numbers will match."

"Right. And you know this because your instincts tell you so." Abby laughed, completely mirthlessly, and covered her eyes, leaning her head back against the headrest.

"You never explained. What's your attachment to Gaines, anyway?"

She shot him a look that said *none of your business*. Well that, and *go to hell*. Preferably yesterday.

"Look," he told her. "I can promise you, I am not the bad guy here." Hawk felt that bore repeating. Over and over. But when he took in her ashen face and the bruises forming around her wrist, he grimaced. "Okay, I didn't *mean* to be the bad guy."

She turned away and made him feel like shit. "Abby, please. Look at me."

After a hesitation, she leveled him with those wide baby blues.

"I woke up this morning and I *was* the good guy. I was on the verge of bringing down the Kiddie Bombers. Then I went to the raid and ended up fighting off our boss."

"It's just all so hard to swallow—"

He thrust her cell at her. "Call him. I guarantee you, you're never going to hear from him again."

Taking the phone, she flipped it open and stared down at the keypad. "What am I supposed to say? Excuse me, but are you the bad guy? Because Hawk says you are."

"And because you know it, too."

Her eyes met his for one long beat.

"Call," he whispered.

She hit a number and he realized she had Elliot on her speed dial, which gave him a ridiculous twist in the gut as the green-eyed monster took over for a moment.

"Elliot," she said softly, her gaze locked on Hawk's. "Can you call me?" Slowly Abby shut the phone, staring down at it as if she expected it to vibrate any second.

"So," he said, much lighter than he felt. "How long ago did the two of you…?" He waggled an eyebrow.

She sighed. "I'm not doing the boss, Hawk."

"You've dated."

"A few times," she agreed. "A very long time ago. A lifetime ago." She gazed out the window into the dark night, looking so sad it made him hurt.

"Look, obviously I'm missing a big piece of this puzzle. If we're going to figure this all out, I should know everything." Bullshit. He wanted to know for other reasons. Personal reasons. "Talk to me, Ab."

Letting out an uneven breath, she dipped her head down so that she was staring at her lap. "We need to sleep."

"Soon. Talk to me."

"Do you remember the Seattle raid last year that went bad?"

He remembered because it was the first time in several years that an agent had been injured on the job. A female agent, if he remembered correctly, who'd been caught and held captive, tortured for information—

Ah, Christ. "No—"

"It was me." She slanted him a quick glance to make sure she had his attention. As if he could do anything but look at her, sick to his very soul. "Gaines rescued me."

Stunned, he just sat there. She was telling the truth, at least as she knew it. No one could fake that look on her face, or the tinge of hero worship that the rescue had no doubt created. *Shit*, he thought, realizing how much he was asking of her to believe Gaines had done all he'd done.

"I didn't know," he said very quietly, staring at the raw skin on her wrist. In all likelihood it was nothing compared to what she'd suffered last year.

"Afterward, I took some time off," she whispered. "Gaines encouraged that. And then when I was ready to get back to work, he put me here because I could be in communications, out of the action."

"I'm surprised you came back to work at all."

"I know. Me, too. But I didn't want to let them take this from me. I had to prove something to myself."

And he'd put her right back into the nightmare. Knowing it, he hated himself. "Abby—"

"Funny thing is, I felt safe, too." She closed her eyes. "Until I left the van."

He wanted to kick his own ass. "Abby, God. I'm so sorry—"

"Don't." She shook her head, still very carefully not looking at him. "Don't be sorry. I'm fine."

She didn't want his pity. He wouldn't have wanted any either. But that didn't change the basic facts. She'd overcome one nightmare, and now was living a new one.

"I need to talk to Logan," he said. "And to Watkins and Thomas. To see exactly what we're up against."

She said nothing but fed him a long stare. *Right*. She didn't do "we," she didn't do trust either, at least not for him. "We're in this now, for better or worse."

"Through sickness and health?" Her eyes flashed in brief good humor. "Just don't even think about asking me to obey. Or to sleep in this truck with you."

If nothing else, he had to admire her sheer will and the inner strength he'd only suspected existed before. He couldn't imagine all she'd gone through—or maybe the problem was he *could*, in great detail, and it made him want to personally hunt down each and every single one of her demons and kill them for her. "No, we're not going to sleep in the truck. I have a friend with a B&B. We can grab some shut-eye there, and get to your place in the morning, okay?"

Abby stared at him so long he figured the gig was up, she was done with him. But finally she nodded. She wasn't over her mistrust of him, not yet, but neither was she still fighting him. And after the night he'd had, he felt grateful for the small favor. But first…

Hawk gestured to the nearest grove of trees with his hand. "Would you like me to escort you to the facilities?"

CHAPTER ELEVEN

Outside of Cheyenne, Wyoming

ABBY JERKED AWAKE. Sitting straight up, heart in her throat, she nearly leaped right out of her skin when Hawk set a hand on her arm.

"Easy," he said softly. "Just me."

She'd been deeply asleep, dreamless, which was a miracle in its own right, but that she'd actually for a moment forgotten where she was and who she was with and what they were doing…

The truck was parked and turned off. That's probably what had woken her. It was still dark but with the very hint of a lightening of the sky in the far east. Almost dawn. She probably looked like a disaster.

Hawk stroked a finger over her temple, pushing a strand of hair off her face. "You all the way awake?" he asked.

"Yeah." The dash clash read 5:05 a.m. "What I can't believe is that I slept." She pulled free of his touch and scrubbed a hand over her face. "Given our situation."

"Remember, we're the good guys. We've done nothing wrong."

"Except flee the crime scene."

"The crime scene in which we were the victims."

"It's still not okay that we just left—"

"It was that or die," he said flatly, and she took a good long look at him. His eyes were shadowed and so was his jaw. There was a weariness to the way he sat in the driver's seat that told her he was still hurting, still exhausted, and on the very edge.

"We're only forty-five minutes out of Cheyenne." He jutted his chin toward the outside of the truck, for the first time drawing her gaze to where he'd stopped.

They were on a long, wide street lined by huge oak trees, wooden sidewalks and old-fashioned cabin-style houses all clean and neat and exuding charm and personality. It looked like the wild, wild West all cleaned up. "Where are we?"

"B&B row, Old West style. They've done up this town like it was back then—for the tourists. I need to get a few hours sleep, Abby, or I'm going to do something stupid."

She slid him a long look. "Like?"

"Like…" He slid his thumb over her jaw, his gaze filled with things that made her swallow hard.

And there were other reactions as well, reactions that reminded her that he was a man, an exceedingly sensual, sexy, hot man, and that she was all woman.

Yowza. She'd nearly forgotten what lust felt like. "If we could just get to my computer—"

Hawk was shaking his head before she even finished her sentence.

"If you're too tired to keep driving," she said. "I'll do it."

"I don't think so."

Disbelief filled her. "Let me get this straight. I'm supposed to trust you, but you don't have to trust me?" She couldn't help but sound a little bitter at this one. "That's ridiculous! I'm the innocent one here. I'm the one to be trusted!"

"Because you promised to make this as difficult and painful as possible, remember?"

Okay, he had her there.

"And you haven't yet decided to finally trust me."

And there.

"What do you think I'm going to do, anyway?" she asked.

He laughed and rubbed a weary hand over his face. "Oh, I don't know. Turn me in to Tibbs before I can prove my innocence." He shrugged out of his flak vest and outer shirt, leaving him in just the black T-shirt. "I'm sorry, but I'm not going to go to sleep only to wake up to you driving me directly to the ATF. I left my Get Out of Jail Free card at home."

"If we just went to Regional and laid out all the events in the order that they happened, I'm sure—"

"Sure what? That I'll get a fair trial before death row?"

"If you're innocent—"

"If? Jesus, Abby." Sending her a stare that was filled with just enough hurt to stab right at her heart, he got out of the truck and slammed the door.

Abby shook her head at herself. Truth was, she believed him. Or she wanted to. How terrifying was that? With a sigh, she followed, the pre-dawn air slapping her face, stinging her skin. "Hawk, wait."

He tipped his head up at the still-dark sky, then turned to look at her, his expression pure resistance, frustration— and also reluctant affection.

God.

It was that, that got her. Because a murderer would not be looking at her as if he couldn't decide between kissing her and wrapping his fingers around her neck, would he?

"I didn't mean…" She trailed off, and he looked as if he was resisting the urge to thunk his head on the trunk of the truck.

Straightening, he drew in a deep breath and lifted his hands, stabbing them into his hair. The muscles in his shoulders and arms were tense, straining the sleeves of his T-shirt.

She'd experienced his strength firsthand last night and did not want to go another round with him.

Which did not in any way explain the little quiver that occurred low in her belly.

"I called about Logan while you were asleep," he said. "He's still in intensive care." Hawk shook his head. "He didn't fall from that roof. No way in hell." He dropped his arms to his side and let her see everything he was feeling, which was more of that rage, frustration, exhaustion and also an underlying need for her to believe in him. "He didn't call you back."

Yeah. She'd noticed. If Gaines was on the up and up, and alive, he'd have called her back. Unless, of course, he really was dead. "Maybe the fire did get him—"

"It didn't."

"How do you know he didn't die from his gunshot?"

"It was a flesh wound. Nothing more. And now he has the ultimate freedom."

Abby shut her door and came around to the front of the truck to face him. "You're certain he's not dead."

Fingers still shoved in his hair, he closed his eyes and drew a breath. "I'd stake my life on it."

His body was taut as an arrow. She came up only to his shoulders, and she knew damn well he could have used physical force to coerce her to do whatever he wanted, but other than when she'd lost it completely last night, he hadn't. In fact, he'd done everything within his power not to hurt her, even when she'd hurt him.

Then he opened his eyes and let her look at him, into him, hiding nothing at all. She peered into his face for a long beat and he stared straight back at her, as if he was hoping to hell she was finding the honesty she sought because he couldn't possibly lay himself more bare.

"The Gaines I know loves justice," she finally said.

"No, he loves to win."

Yes, that was true, too. He'd taken great pride in all the cases he'd closed, and that was no secret.

"I realize you have a bond with him." Hawk said this just a little too tightly, as if maybe he hated thinking about it.

"He saved me," she reminded him.

He shocked her by reaching for her hand. "I know."

She stared down at their joined fingers. "Hawk?"

"Yeah?"

"Just before I was taken, I'd been working on the Kiddie Bombers."

"Yeah? There were a lot of agents across the whole western region doing so."

"I felt like I was really making a breakthrough." Her voice trailed off and they stared at each other. "This is insane," she whispered. "You know that."

"Insane, but real."

"He saved me from the very men that you'd like to prove work for him. My God. He did this, he set all this up."

He squeezed her fingers. "Yeah. I think so. Abby, I'm sorry, but I will prove it."

Her gaze searched his. "He knew who had me. He let them have me." Images bombarded her, the terror, the overwhelming certainty that she was dead. And then being all too alive— "He ordered me held captive," she repeated in disbelief.

"God, Abby." His low, husky voice brought her back. "I don't want to dredge it up for you, I just—"

"You just want me to know that the reason I made it out

of there alive is the only reason that I was there in the first place." Sickened, she closed her eyes.

"I think he wanted to make himself the good guy. Your good guy."

The men who'd taken her had been well-versed in how to get the answers they wanted. And what they'd wanted from her was any concrete knowledge she had on the Kiddie Bombers, which hadn't been all that much. But she'd been chained up, then left alone in the pitch-black for four long hours before they'd come for her, knowing by then she'd be half out of her mind. And she had been.

They'd just begun to really have fun with her while she'd been trying desperately to pretend she was somewhere, anywhere, else, when Gaines had come in, gun drawn, taking two of her assailants out without blinking.

The other two had run like scared little bunnies while Gaines had freed her and carried her out.

She'd never questioned how he'd known, how he'd killed only two of the four and yet been able to get her out of there without either of them being killed.

It had never occurred to her to be anything but grateful. *Extremely* grateful.

"Abby."

She opened her eyes.

Hawk had stepped close. "I hate bringing you back there." He slid his hands in her hair. "I hate myself for making you think about it at all. But my life depends on it."

"I can't think this way," she whispered. "I'll fall apart."

"Then *I'll* think that way. All I'm asking you to do is give me a chance. Don't send me to the gallows yet."

"So what now? Do you think we're going to go in there and I'm going to sleep with you?"

"No, I think *I'm* going to sleep, and you're possibly going to stab me in my sleep. Which is slightly preferable to going to jail."

"Okay," she said softly.

"Okay, what? You're going to stab me in my sleep?"

"I guess you'll have to take your chances on that, won't you." She turned and headed up the front walk to the door. Her clothes felt damp and icy, though she knew that was more from shock than anything else because Hawk had been running the heater in the truck for hours.

But she felt as if she'd never get warm again.

He caught up with her with his long-legged stride, and reached out and took her hand in a sweet gesture.

Or maybe to keep her from running. Although where he thought she was going to run off to, she had no idea.

Opening the rough wooden gate, he let her in. There were several low lights lining the walk, illuminating an antique-covered wagon in the front yard and the house, complete with old-style shutters and white lace curtains hanging in the windows. The yard itself was thick with growth. She took her first deep breath in hours, and smelled fresh-cut grass and the scent of myriad different blooms.

Behind her, the gate clicked closed and she knew Hawk was right on her heels. Watching her closely. Was he looking at her wild hair? Her grubby clothes? She glanced back—

Um. Yes. He was noticing all the above, and more. When his gaze lifted and met hers, he didn't try to be coy or reserved, or anything other than who he was, and he had no problem letting her see him.

All of him.

Everything he felt, which pretty much ran the gamut. Oh, God. She'd never been so aware of another human being in all her life, standing so close she could feel his soft exhale on her temple, could see deep into his warm eyes. He was just so…overwhelmingly male. Did he know the confusion he aroused? Or that when he stared at her like that she had certain reactions she couldn't seem to help? She crossed her arms over her chest, because, seriously, she had a problem. How could her body react in this manner, when with the other side of her brain she was recoiling in horror at the evening's events? "This is crazy," she whispered. "I don't want to look at you and—"

"And what?"

"Hawk."

"And what, Ab? Want me?"

"I don't…want you." Trying to be casual, she dropped her arms to her side.

His gaze fell to the front of her shirt, which revealed her traitorous nipples, hard and pressing against the fabric of her shirt. She felt the heat rush to her cheeks. He should have at least pretended not to notice.

Instead his eyes blazed with a new awareness, and a staggering heat that almost equalled the explosions they'd faced earlier.

Oh, God. Was this really happening?

"Abby—"

But whatever he'd planned on saying was lost as the front door opened. There in the doorway stood a stunningly beautiful brunette in a cream silk bathrobe that hugged her spectacular curves. Her smile came slow and sure as she took in the sight of Hawk on her doorstep. "Well, look what the cat dragged in."

He smiled back. "Serena."

Serena tossed back her long, thick hair and crossed her arms, which as she undoubtedly knew, plumped up her substantial breasts from a D-plus to at least a triple-F. "My my. I guess hell froze over?"

"If you only knew." Hawk's smile remained easy and charming, and completely confident in the manner of a man who always got his own way. "Do you have a room available?"

"*Two* rooms," Abby clarified.

"One," Hawk repeated.

"Two, or nothing," Abby said through her teeth.

Hawk sighed. "Connecting. We'll take connecting rooms."

Serena divided a glance between them, then tossed back her head and laughed. "Oh, boy, Hawk. I think you've finally met your match."

CHAPTER TWELVE

STANDING IN THE pre-dawn chill, Abby craned her neck and stared at Hawk. She'd thought tonight couldn't get any more Twilight Zone–like. "Your match?"

"Serena has a very peculiar sense of humor." He shot Serena a long look. "Any second now she's going to let us in off her doorstep and put us in a room, and then go far, far away."

Serena smiled but didn't budge. "Oh, but this is so much more fun. So." She turned to Abby. "You been dating him long?"

Abby opened her mouth to correct that impression, but Serena went on. "No, it can't have been too long, because, after all, you're still with him." She grinned at herself. "That means you haven't discovered his character flaws yet."

Next to Abby, Hawk let out a sigh.

Abby shook her head at Serena. "You've gotten the wrong idea—"

"Oh, believe me, honey. I know how hard it is to give him up."

Abby doubted that greatly. Hawk was a handful, not to mention most likely walking/talking heartbreak. She could give him up just like that.

Probably.

"It's a little like walking away from double-fudge chocolate cake, isn't it?" Serena asked. "Harder than anything, but in the end, you save yourself the bellyache."

"I'm not all that fond of chocolate cake in the first place," Abby replied.

Serena let out a deep laugh. "You know what? I like you already." She elbowed Abby. "At least the sex is off the charts amazing, right?"

"Can we focus?" Hawk asked, sounding pained.

Off the charts? Abby had little reference for "off the charts amazing." She didn't want to know, she reminded herself. Okay, mostly didn't want to know....

Ah, hell. She wanted to know.

"If we could just get a room," Hawk said.

"Two," Abby corrected. "*Two* rooms." No off the charts sex today, thank you very much.

Serena looked at Hawk, and at whatever she saw in his face, maybe it was the grim set of his jaw, or, gee, maybe the cut over his eye, she nodded, stepped back and gestured them into the inn.

The main room was large and had a fire going, which Abby headed directly toward. Serena held Hawk back. "Sorry about the heckling," she said softly. "I couldn't seem to help myself."

"Forget it."

"Are you all right?"

"I will be."

Abby turned back to see her touch Hawk's cheek, her smile now tinged with fondness and some lingering heat. "Anything you need?"

"In spite of my character flaws?" he asked her drily, but he patted her hand with his.

Serena smiled and hugged him, the gesture warm and familiar, the affection unmistakable. "Food?" she asked.

"Sleep."

She nodded. "And a change of clothes."

"That would be—"

"Off the charts amazing?" Serena let out a low laugh. "Sorry about that, couldn't resist."

And Hawk blushed.

Blushed.

Huh. If Abby had set her sights on Hawk, which she so hadn't, she might have been flooded with jealousy at the obvious ease and warmth between them. As it was, she felt nothing.

Liar, liar pants on fire...

She concentrated on the pretty room. The hardwood floors were scarred and covered in throw rugs, the furniture was well used but large and very comfortable looking. Butter-colored walls carried old-fashioned black-and-white pictures from the Wild West. She stuck her hands out to the flames, listening to Hawk and Serena murmur to each other behind her. After a moment, he settled a hand on her shoulder, gesturing for her to come with him, and they headed out of the large room behind Serena, whose hips sashayed beneath that silky robe.

She obviously wasn't wearing anything beneath it.

Abby glanced at Hawk, sure he'd be staring at that lush body, but he was looking right at her. "You okay?" he murmured.

She nodded. She was okay. Maybe even more okay than she'd imagined.

Serena led them upstairs, down a hallway to the last door on the right, which she opened. Hawk nudged Abby in, and though she was drawn to the small but quaint bedroom with its huge rustic wood bed piled high in fluffy bedding, she immediately turned back. "This is one room."

"And a bathroom." Serena pointed to a door.

"But—"

Serena looked at Hawk, then back to Abby. "It's the only room available, hon, sorry."

She was lying. For Hawk's sake. Abby looked at his shirt. Most of the blood had been on the outer shirt, which he'd left in the truck, but there were still some dubious dark stains on his black ATF T-shirt as well.

Why wasn't she telling Serena she needed to use the phone, that she needed help?

Because there was a voice deep inside that said Hawk could be right. That Gaines was lethal, deadly, dangerous. *That* thought made it hard for her to breathe so she did her damnedest not to think at all.

After a minute, Serena left them alone, and when Hawk shut the door, silence reverberated around them nearly as loud as one of the explosions they'd lived through last night.

One room.

One bed.

One really beautiful, lush-looking bed that in no time at all was going to be holding a tall, leanly muscled man who drew her like no one else ever had.

But she didn't want to be drawn.

He let out a low laugh and kicked off his shoes. "You're thinking pretty loudly."

"Sorry."

"Don't be. But let's just say I can tell you're still half convinced you need to call the cops on me."

Not half, but certainly an eighth… "So who's Serena, a girlfriend?"

"An old friend."

"She didn't touch you like a friend."

That brought a ghost of a smile. She realized now that he'd put on that carefree, easygoing air for Serena, because he was not in a joking, light-hearted mood at all. "Jealous?"

"Ha," she said, without any real rancor behind it. Just when she thought she had him all figured out, he revealed another side.

Who the hell was he?

Proving he had more layers than an onion, Hawk pulled out her cell and checked on Logan's status again, clearly concerned. "I need to talk to him," he said to someone on the phone, then paused and frowned. "Yes, I realize he's gravely injured, but—" Listening, he pinched the bridge of his nose. "Okay, thank you." He disconnected. "Damn it. No change."

"But he's alive," she reminded him.

"True enough." He punched in a different number.

"What are you doing?"

"Calling his cell."

"But he won't—"

"No, but someone else might."

"Like who?"

"Like whoever is at his side—hello," Hawk said into the phone, looking surprised. "Who's this? Logan's nurse? Perfect. This is Conner Hawk, his partner, and—oh." He paused. "You know about me—he was awake?" He nodded. "Yeah, we're family. How is he?" After a few seconds, he visibly relaxed. "You've just made my day, Callen—no, I understand the severity of his injuries but, see, he's going to recover. Yeah, trust me, best news I've had in hours. Can I talk to him? It's urgent—" He listened intently. "Yeah, I heard him. Tell him to watch his six. It's in danger, too." He paused again. "Right. And no visitors. None, not even a high-ranking ATF official, can you manage that? Yeah, I'm serious. This is serious. As serious as it gets."

"Hawk. A nurse won't stop Gaines."

"Callen," Hawk said without missing a beat. "I need to get him moved. What are the chances of that?" He stalked the length of the room, his long legs churning up the space in two strides before he had to spin to walk again. "Yeah. It's life or death. Logan's life or death—yes, that would do it. Switch his chart, change his name. Disguise him, if you have to. Hell, put him where he won't be expected. No, definitely away from the ER—" He smiled. "Yeah. That'll work."

"Where?" Abby asked.

Hawk grinned. "Maternity," he whispered to her. "Callen? He's going to fight this. Tell him too fucking bad." He listened again, then nodded. "Okay. And tell him—" He stopped smiling. "Tell him to get his sorry ass healed, that's his job now. That I'll be there in a few hours. And thanks. I owe you more than you'll ever know." He shut the phone, then stood there for a long moment.

"Hawk?"

He looked at her. "He's bad off."

Shocked at an urge to wrap her arms around him, she hugged herself instead. "I know. I'm sorry."

"But still, he made sure I got the message."

"Message?"

"Someone called, said he was Logan's boss. Asked about his status."

"Tibbs."

"No southern accent."

As she processed that, he went on. "And then Tibbs did call, complete with accent. To tell him that they found a body at the barn. Unidentifiable, because it's burned beyond recognition. It's still crazy up there, the fire is uncontrolled, but they're presuming it's Gaines. Do you want the first shower?"

"No, we need my laptop, Hawk. We should go now." It would give her one answer at least, and she needed that.

"We'll get there." He began tossing the contents of his pockets to the nightstand—her cell phone... the handcuffs. He pulled off his shirt, which left him standing there in dangerously low-slung jeans and a pair of socks, which he toed off.

"W-what are you doing?"

"Stripping," he said as if that was the most natural thing in the world to be doing.

"Yes, but—"

Every breath he took seemed to threaten the decency level of his waistband. There was a gap between the denim and the most amazing six-pack abs she'd ever seen. In another time and place there was no way she could have resisted shoving her hand down that gap to go treasure hunting.

Well, except for one thing.

She'd never been that bold a day in her life.

He reached for the buttons on the Levi's. "I'm going to shower. Tell me I don't need to worry while I'm in there."

Pop went the first button on his jeans.

Pop went the second button.

Oh, God. He'd revealed a wedge of skin that was paler than the skin covering his chest and belly. "Um—"

Eyes serious but warm, he mercifully stopped the unbuttoning. "Look, I just want a shower and some shut-eye. I can sleep on the floor, you can have the bed, I don't care. I just have to recharge for a few hours, that's all. Tell me you're not going to steal the truck, Ab."

"You mean the truck that *you* stole first—"

Hawk acknowledged that with a slight nod of his head.

"I just need to know you and that truck are going to be here when I get out."

"Because you need my computer."

"Because I don't need to come out to be surrounded by the cops."

Pop.

She couldn't help it. Maybe once she'd been brave, but all that courage had left her, and she covered her eyes.

"Abby?" She felt him shift closer, and then his big, callused palms slid up and down her limbs in a gesture that was somehow soothing, yet made her want to leap right out of her skin. "Hey," he whispered. "Don't give up on me now." Up and down. Down and up.

The cold she'd felt only minutes ago had deserted her entirely. *What was the matter with her?* She opened her eyes and found her vision filled with his torso, the light from the lamp behind him blocked out by his broad shoulders. She had no idea what it was about a naked male chest that spun her wheels, had no idea such a shallow thing even could, but there it was. Lust, pure and simple, buzzed through her system and made her punch drunk.

"We're so close," he murmured, apparently clueless to what his hands were doing to her.

Yes. Yes, she was. Close to orgasmic bliss.

"After a quick catnap, we get your laptop," he said. "And then we draw out Gaines."

She dropped her gaze. Took in the scar over one pec. Without thinking, she ran a finger over it, eliciting a low sound from him.

"Abby." His voice was hoarse. "What are you doing?"

She had no idea. "Just standing here." She jerked her hand away from him.

"You were touching me. Looking at me. Like you wanted a bite of me."

"No." *Yes.*

Backing away, he lifted his hands in the air, then turned from her, once again shoving his fingers in his short hair. His unbuttoned jeans had slid down, revealing a line of black cotton and a sleek spine that was as edible as the rest of him.

Hawk headed to the bathroom, popping open that last button as he went. "Just…say you're going to be here when I get out."

Eyes glued to the seat of his jeans, which had slid to an almost indecent level, she couldn't quite have answered the age-old question of briefs or boxers, but any second now—

"Abby?"

Her gaze jerked up as he turned. Oh, God. And caught her staring. Eyes narrowed, he lifted a hand and pointed a finger at her. "That." He sounded more than a little off his axis. "What the hell was *that?*"

"N-nothing."

Walking back toward her, he let out a sound of disbelief. "No, that wasn't nothing. That was…heat. That was lust."

She covered her face. "I'm sorry."

A low laugh escaped him. "Abigail Wells, were you just lusting after me?"

"No." She winced. "A little, maybe."

He stared at her for one long beat. "Maybe or most definitely?"

Again she bit her lip.

"Look, you were just looking at me as if I was a twelve-course meal and you'd been fasting for two days. That, or you're plotting my slow, painful murder."

"A little of both, I think."

"Okay, I really need to go now."

"Hawk—"

But she was talking to his back. And as he walked into the bathroom, he kicked his Levi's to the floor.

Knit boxers.

Then the door shut, leaving her standing there, knees a little bit wobbly. Her kidnapper had just flashed her the best buns she'd ever seen.

HAWK CAME OUT OF THE SHOWER with some trepidation. He'd faced war, he'd faced gangs, he'd faced a whole hell of a lot just in the past twenty-four hours alone, but now his stomach actually hurt as he opened the bathroom door and waited for the steam to dissipate, because this time he had no idea what was waiting for him.

Utter silence and pitch blackness.

Clearly Abby had shut the shades, but he couldn't even hear her breathing, and he had some damn fine hearing.

Not. Good. "Abby?"

Nothing.

Christ. She was probably halfway to Cheyenne by now, with the police on their way here to take him to jail for a whole host of crimes he hadn't committed.

He'd trusted her. He'd trusted her and she'd stabbed him in the damn heart. God, he really was an ass. Pissed, and more hurt than he cared to acknowledge, Hawk stepped into the dark room and tripped over the bed, then nearly had heart failure when someone lurched off the mattress and hit the floor with a small cry.

Abby.

"Oh, God. I'm sorry." Rushing forward, hands out to find her, he felt a soft, curvy form and dropped to his knees at her side.

She was doubled over, hands on her knees, gasping for breath.

"Abby—" Eyes adjusted, he reached out to touch her, but was not surprised when she jerked back with another small cry, an animal sound really, that caused a sharp pain in his chest.

He'd felt pretty damn small several times in the past eight hours but that moment topped them all. It was the way he'd brought her here, of course, against her will. "Abby."

"Don't."

Don't what? Don't touch? Don't look? Don't do any damn thing, likely enough. "You were sleeping."

She didn't answer, just panted as if she'd been running.

"I startled you," he murmured.

"Not you," she said with only a hint of that bravado he loved in her. *"You* didn't scare me."

"Okay." Sitting back on his heels, Hawk studied her outline in the dark. She was still breathing heavily. "You were dreaming. Badly."

She lifted a shoulder. The only admission he was going to get most likely.

"Tibbs called." She said this so quietly that he had to lean in to hear her. When the words soaked into his addled brain, he froze.

Shit. "So should I expect to get my ass hauled out of here any time now?" He asked this with remarkable calm, given that his life was over.

She didn't respond.

"Abby?"

She sighed, and he shook his head. *Perfect.*

CHAPTER THIRTEEN

"ABBY," HAWK SAID AS CALMLY as he could, which wasn't all that calmly. He wondered how much time he had. Ten minutes?

Less?

He should probably get dressed in more than just a damn towel. Because no way did he want to go to prison in only a towel. But before he could move, someone knocked on the door, and pretty much took five years off his life.

In the dark room, Abby drew a deep breath. A sound that held a good amount of guilt.

Damn. He gripped his towel and wished for clean clothes at least. He couldn't even go out the window, they were on the second floor—

Another knock, which didn't help his heart rate any. The way the poor organ had been abused tonight, it was a wonder it was still ticking at all. "Shit," he said again, brilliantly.

"I didn't answer when he called," Abby said quietly.

He stared at her. What did she mean, she hadn't answered the call? Hard to tell in the dark since he couldn't read her expression.

The knock came again. Then Serena's voice. "Hawk?"

Okay, maybe he could get those five years back. Holding onto his towel, he opened the door to find Serena holding a stack of folded clothing. "Hey," she said, and looked him

over with frank appreciation before grinning. "Damn." She
waggled her eyebrows. "Almost makes me sorry I dumped
your workaholic ass."

"Serena—"

"Oh, relax. I know what's good for me and what's not.
And you are definitely not." She thrust the clothing at him,
which he struggled to grab and also keep a grip on the
towel.

Serena appeared to enjoy the battle. "Thought you could
use some of the clothes you left here. And I brought Abby
something, too. Also, I pulled the truck into my garage."

All irritation at her interruption vanished. "Thanks."

She tried to peer into the dark room behind him, but
couldn't. "Also, there's a first aid kit in the pile, for that
cut on your head. Do you need a doctor?"

He felt like he'd been hit with a Mack truck, but he was
fairly certain he was going to live. "Nah. I'm okay."

"All right, tough guy." Leaning in, she kissed his cheek.
"You're in it deep again, aren't you?"

"A little."

"Honey, with you, there's no 'little' anything." And with
a smile she walked away.

Hawk shut the door and turned back to the dark room.
There she was. Still by the bed.

"Did she love you?"

He couldn't believe that this was the conversation they
were going to have before he went to jail. "She used to say
she did."

"She still wants you."

He set the clothes on the foot of the bed. "She dumped
me."

"Maybe, but that doesn't change her feelings."

Hawk reached for the light.

"Don't, please."

Easing back, he tried to see her. "Abby—"

"You let yourself be loved. I'm just trying to picture this, the big, badass, tough as nails, elusive, edgy Conner Hawk, letting himself be loved by a woman."

"Badass?" With a harsh laugh, he scrubbed a hand over his face. "I don't feel so badass. With you, I feel…"

"What?"

Since she sounded sincerely curious, he decided to tell her. "Like a sorry-ass marshmallow. Am I going to jail, Abby?"

"No."

Relieved, he sank to the mattress. "And why is that?"

"Because while I retrieved Tibbs's message, I didn't speak to him."

"What did he say?"

"That I need to tell him where I am. He said that they found the murder weapon in the clearing near the barn with your prints on the gun. Oh, and the barn was a complete loss—a total burn."

That took some careful planning. Careful planning, and planting of explosives in the right spots.

Knowledge, of course, that Gaines had. "They have my prints because it's my own damn gun," he said tightly. "He took it from me. But how is it that the gun didn't melt in the fire? Pretty damn suspicious if you ask me."

"Agreed."

Hawk didn't know what hit him the hardest—that she'd stayed willingly when given a chance to leave or the quiet word that signaled she was beginning to believe him. It was a good thing he was already sitting, he was that shaky with relief. *God*. He hadn't realized how tense he'd felt, how unnerved, and frankly, how fucking alone.

But he wasn't alone at all. He leaned back against the

headboard, and with the same care he'd give a nuclear bomb, reached for her. "Come here."

Shockingly, she let him pull her in. He did so very slowly, not wanting to scare her off, but needing to feel her close. She sat at his side, but went still when he tugged her into the crook of his arm.

"Don't," she choked out.

"Shh. You're okay."

Instead of responding with a slug to the gut as he was more than half braced for, Abby absolutely devastated him by setting her head on his shoulder.

And then she finished him off by turning her face into his neck.

His entire body went still as stone because he was afraid if he moved, hell if he so much as breathed, he'd scare her and she'd scramble away. It shocked him how much he wanted her to stay, just as she was, curled against him, for, oh…the rest of his life.

Holy shit, if that wasn't a thought. His need for her surprised him, but not more so than her clear reflection of it right back at him.

Whether she admitted it or not, she wanted him, too.

She trusted him. An onslaught of tenderness hit him so hard he nearly bawled like a baby. Gently, because he couldn't resist, Hawk pressed his mouth to her temple, brushing his lips across her skin in a light caress, more for comfort than sex, though there were plenty of those urges as well. "You okay?" he whispered.

"I think so. It's the first time I've done this, gotten this physically close since…"

He closed his eyes and struggled not to squeeze her. "I wouldn't do anything to hurt you, Abby. I'd never do anything to hurt you."

"I hurt you." She was quiet a moment. "I hurt you and you didn't hurt me back."

"Yeah. The truth is, you could gut me right here, I'm that helpless when it comes to you. But not you. You are not helpless."

"I was last time."

He drew a careful breath to remain relaxed, as a shocking amount of violence suddenly coursed through him. "I'm sorry. So damned sorry."

"They handcuffed me."

Christ, he wished to God he'd never done that to her. He wished even more that he could go back in time and be there that day for her.

"To a wall. They took my clothes and brought out these jumper cables, which they said were effective in getting information out of people."

He needed to shoot something. That might help.

"But Gaines rescued me just in time."

He opened his eyes. "Before they—"

"Yes," she whispered. "I was okay."

"Yeah, you are."

"No, I mean I don't hate men or anything…" She let out a little laugh. "Contrary to how I've treated you."

"I can't tell you how very happy I am to hear that you don't hate men, since I'm one. But…"

"But why, if I don't hate men, did I treat you like crap from day one?" she guessed.

Hawk rubbed his jaw over the sweet silk of her hair. "Yeah."

"Apparently not hating men and letting them close are two different ballgames entirely. Up until moving to Cheyenne, it was easy to keep my distance from guys. Probably too easy. Then I met you."

He stopped breathing. "And…?"

"And I couldn't keep my distance. So I pretended."

"Okay, I have to do this." Still moving slowly, he shifted onto his side, pulling her in for a hug, melting a little when she let him.

"You should know…" she said a little shakily "…that contrary to our position, I intend to *keep* my distance."

He ran his jaw over her cheek, loving the softness. "Why?"

"Why?" She let out a little laugh. "Okay, so I'm not sure why exactly."

"You don't have to be afraid of me."

"I'm not."

"And as far as the physical stuff, we could go slow."

"Yeah, see, that I doubt."

Okay, she had a point. Reluctant or not, they had a chemistry, and he imagined if she hadn't been inhibited, they'd already have used at least one condom from the basket on the counter in the bathroom.

"It's been a long time for me, Hawk. A year. If I let us… if we sleep together, I'm not going to be able to take that lightly. And the opposite of not lightly? Not something I'm ready for, and I doubt you are either."

"Ah, Abby." With a sigh, he stroked a hand up her slim spine. "I'm so sorry you were dragged into this."

"I dragged myself in."

He was extremely aware of the fact that she hadn't returned the hug. One of her hands was in her own lap, the other had slipped down and was resting, fist tightly closed, against his abs.

A little higher and she could feel what she'd done to his heart.

A little lower and she'd feel another body part entirely.

But he couldn't help it. He was covered only by the towel, which was pretty insubstantial, and he was holding her.

And she believed him.

Hell, that alone had excited him. But then she let out a shuddery sigh, her breath fanning lightly across his neck in the most incredible sensation he could remember as a strand of her hair stuck to the stubble on his jaw.

He needed to get up, coax her into a shower of her own, and get some sleep, but he didn't want to.

"You can stop worrying about me turning you in," she said, her mouth still against his skin. "I can't do that now. I couldn't live with myself if it turned out everything you've said was true." She lifted her face. "We have to see this through to the end."

Because she humbled him to the core, because he didn't think he could talk through the sudden lump in his throat, he lifted a hand and gently swept back her hair, tucking it behind her ear, using it as an excuse to sink his fingers into her hair while his thumb slid over her cheekbone. "Yeah. We'll see it through. Together." Unable to help himself, he leaned in, but Abby lifted her hand and slapped it to his chest.

"Really, *really* bad idea, remember?"

"I think we're going to have to agree to disagree there, Ab."

"I'm not kidding, Hawk."

Yeah. Damn. He could see that.

"We…" She chewed on her lower lip and stared at his. "We shouldn't."

"So you keep saying. But I gotta tell you, you don't sound all that certain."

"Of course I don't. I'm lying through my teeth."

His heart literally skipped a beat, and unbelievably, he

wanted to smile. He wanted to cry and smile at the same time. A true first. Leaning past her, he reached for the lamp.

"No, don't—"

He looked into her eyes. "We've gotten past quite a bit tonight, let's get past this as well, and see each other. I mean really see each other. Okay?"

He could feel her thinking it over. Hell, she was thinking so hard the air shimmered with it, and he brushed his mouth past her cheek. "Come on, Abby. You've trusted me this far…."

"Yeah, well, there's trust, and then there's trust."

"What's the worst that could happen?"

She fell silent, then let out a small laugh that had more nervousness than humor. "I don't know."

"Never fear the unknown." And he flicked on the light.

CHAPTER FOURTEEN

As Hawk turned on the light, a warm glow bathed the room. The bed was tousled, and so was the woman in his arms.

"You're naked," she accused him.

"I'm wearing a towel."

"Nearly naked, then." Her breathing had changed, and she wasn't meeting his eyes. But that's because she was soaking him in, from his shoulders to his pecs to his belly, which she seemed to linger over, making the muscles there quiver like...well, like he was a horny teenager about to get lucky for the first time. He felt lucky, so goddamned lucky, even knowing he was crazy to be here, like this, with her.

Insane, he thought, even as his hands fisted in her shirt. Reckless, after what had happened tonight. But she did something to him, to his gut, his heart.

She'd spent six months being cool and icy, shooting him down with her superior disdain. Now he was suddenly beneath that tough veneer, and while he was here, he wanted to ruffle her up, see the real her. He should be running, yet instead he kissed her.

Pulling back, her gaze dipped down his body again, taking in the towel loosely wrapped around his hips and what it covered.

And what it didn't cover.

But there was the problem. The longer she looked, the less that it covered. Hawk didn't want to freak her out or anything but if she kept it up, which she appeared to be set to do, he wasn't sure that the entire bedspread could cover him. He needed to slow them down, somehow, and opened his mouth to say so, but her tongue came out and wet her lower lip, and he went harder. Great. Nice way to slow down. "Uh, Abby?"

"You're so beautiful," she whispered.

"Not like you. You take my breath." And now the Neanderthal in him wanted to strip her down and get to even more beautiful parts. He wanted it so badly he was shaking, but that was for him. For her…he didn't know what the right thing was, but he wasn't going to rush her, or make the first move. Nope, he was going to sit here and let her look her fill, completely still, nonthreatening, for as long as she wanted.

And if he keeled over from having all his blood between his legs, well then, he hoped she knew CPR. "The last thing I want to do is bring up bad memories."

"No." She shook her head. "I'm okay. I just forgot what it felt like, this…rush."

Okay, looking at him was giving her a rush. He liked that. He liked that a lot. In fact, knowing it gave him a rush of his own.

A big one. One she couldn't possibly miss. But she kept looking, and he kept letting her, for as long as he could, until it had to be completely obvious what she was doing to him, since his towel had become more like a tent. "It's sort of a direct ratio thing," Hawk murmured in his own defense.

Her eyes lifted to his, wide and questioning.

"The longer you look at me like that, the more turned on I get."

"Oh." She grinned.

He tried to laugh, and found his mouth touching her temple.

She lifted her face and their noses bumped. "Oh," she said again, even more breathlessly, and then he was stroking away her hair, which was poking him in the eye.

She smiled a little, but her gaze was glued to his mouth, which was a mere fraction of an inch from hers, and then suddenly she'd closed the gap. When her tongue met his, he thought he'd died and gone to heaven. Oh, God, he didn't want her to ever stop.

Cupping the back of her head with his hand, he deepened the kiss, which tugged a surprised, throaty moan from her and sent a flood of desire raging through him, one that seriously threatened the placement of his towel. Abby was curvy and warm in his arms, her soft sighs of pleasure causing a rush of emotion that nearly swamped him.

She had one hand on his chest, palm open, as if she might have originally planned on holding him off but had lost her train of thought.

Or changed her mind.

He hoped for that second option. She was battling her demons, and Hawk could appreciate that because he had his own. All his life, his job had always taken priority, over family, over friends, over everything. While in Special Forces, he'd lost most of those close to him because it was hard to maintain relationships with what he did for a living.

He'd felt a little regret—but there'd always been that elusive future when he'd stop working, settle down and get serious about letting someone in his life. For now, he was still driven to ferret out bad guys. Hell, he didn't even *know* how to do anything else, be anyone else. Women as a whole didn't seem to like that, and as a result, they'd come and gone, mostly gone.

But when Abby looked at him, he didn't have to try to

downplay his life, or hide how crazy his job was. She knew, because she lived it, too.

So freeing. Slipping his fingers into her hair, Hawk kissed her again, deeper now, trying to let her know it was okay to delve as long and hot and wet as she wanted. With a sexy-as-hell little murmur, she lifted one of her hands.

Oh, yeah, he thought. Touch me. *Do it*. Even the thought made him hard. Or harder, because he'd been hard, painfully so, since he'd pulled her onto the bed with him.

Her hand hovered in the air, then headed toward his shoulder, touched down, jerked back, then touched down again.

At the connection, he groaned and she jerked both hands off him and pulled her mouth free, lips wet, breathing ragged, body trembling. "I'm sorry," she gasped.

Sorry? Was she kidding? "No, I want you to—" Wanted so much he was afraid to even finish the thought. But she'd kissed him like he was better than air, like he was her lifeline, her only hope, like maybe that one kiss wasn't going to be enough, could never be enough.

Yeah, he could live off that fantasy alone. When he'd rolled around with her on that hard ground at the ranch, her body had moved against his, all curves and softness, and he'd sent up a desperate wish that someday they'd be rolling around and *not* fighting for their lives.

The need had surprised him then, but it didn't now. This thing between them had been building up for six months, six months during which he'd been frustrated and hot and bothered, and he hoped she'd been the same. Now there was nothing to hold them back.

Still staring at him with those wide eyes, Abby lifted her fingers to her mouth and slowly shook her head. "I'm sorry. I'm not ready—"

"Okay," he managed. He even smiled, though truthfully, he wanted to cry. "It's okay."

"It's just that you're so strong," she said very softly, staring at the width of his shoulders. His chest. The tattoo on his bicep. His belly...the tented towel. "Very strong."

That clearly was not a compliment. "Would it help to know that when you look at me, I feel like a two-pound weakling?"

She smiled, but shook her head. Hawk sighed. He *was* strong. Hell, he'd spent years toning and strengthening his body for his job, they both knew that. It'd been a matter of survival after all. "I'd never use my strength against you, Abby."

"Except, of course, if I was going to turn you in."

At the reminder of how he'd tumbled her around in the woods, he winced. "I tried really hard not to—"

"I know. And you weren't naked then, and I couldn't really see...but now..." She lifted a shoulder. "I guess I'm just wishing that you were very skinny, or maybe even fat. Yeah, fat would do."

He blinked. "You'd rather I was fat?"

"And weak. Instead of..." She eyeballed him again. "You know."

"Wow. Okay..."

"I'm sorry."

"No, wait. I can fix this." Grabbing the handcuffs on the nightstand, he snapped one on his wrist, the other to the headboard.

Abby stared at him in shock. "What are you doing?"

Arm stretched above his head now, he leaned back. "Just sitting here. Not fat, sorry, but weakened. One hand only, see?" Hawk wriggled his fingers. "You can take me one-handed, and we both know it. I'm at your mercy, Ab." He looked into her eyes. "You're in total control."

Something leaped into her gaze at that, gratitude, relief, and oh, baby, a whole bunch of heat that had his own blood boiling again. His fingers itched to move, to touch her, but he remained still as stone.

Well, except for the part of him that he couldn't make go still. Beneath the towel it gave a hopeful surge.

Her gaze dropped to it.

"Okay, well that part of me has a mind of its own. But the rest of me? Just sitting here. Restrained. So do as you will, Abby. Look, touch…" Taste. "Whatever you want, I'm yours."

Totally.

Completely.

Yours.

Obviously intrigued, she reached out to touch his chest, then pulled back. "But…?"

"But what? No buts."

"But what happens when we're back in the real world?"

"Now see, I sort of thought we *were* in the real world."

"You know what I mean," Abby protested. "The real world is different. We work together in the real world. We have to be professional."

"Hey, I'm the king of professional."

She laughed. *Laughed.* And it was the sweetest sound he'd ever heard. Then she leaned a hand on his chest, bracing her weight completely over him as she peered into his face. "You're going to stay just like this? Really?"

"Just like this."

If it killed him.

Which it might.

"It's not that I'm afraid of you…."

"I know."

"I'm just…"

"You need the control. It's okay, Ab. I get it." He jangled the handcuff to remind her how much he got it. She hadn't been sexually abused, but being stripped, helpless, had left its mark. They'd destroyed her confidence. They'd hurt her.

Now the situation was reversed.

She had a chance to be the one clothed, the one with all the power, and he was going to sit there and let her do whatever she wanted. "You're in the driver's seat."

"What should I do?" she whispered.

"Whatever you want."

"To you?"

"To me."

She stared into his eyes, torn between wariness and excitement. Just seeing it had his body leaping.

Down boy. He offered her a smile. "Just be kind."

"I will," she said very seriously, as if taking care with him was of the utmost importance, and for some reason that reached out and grabbed him by the throat. In his life, he was the one who took care of others, making places safe, taking out the bad guys...

But few, if any, had ever taken care of him, or even wanted to.

There Abby sat, fully dressed, her lower lip between her teeth as she contemplated him, arm stretched above his head, handcuffed to the bed in just a towel. As he waited there, not moving, hell barely breathing, she didn't move either.

But she was thinking, thinking so loudly he could practically hear her mind racing. Her face was flushed, and he could see her nipples pressing against the material of her shirt, two tight, aching peaks just waiting their turn for attention, which he was dying to give.

"I'm not sure where to start," she admitted.

He could guide her, even rush her. Everything in those wide eyes, in the way she was breathing, told him he could.

But he'd promised her all the control, promised her that she could go at whatever pace she wanted. And if she wanted more, and Hawk hoped like hell she wanted more, she needed to make this first move. "Wherever you want."

"Okay." Finally she lifted a hand and glided it over his chest, her finger brushing one of his nipples.

His muscles leaped, and feeling it, she paused, then arched an eyebrow and did it again. "You like that."

He was already sweating. "Yes."

Chewing on her lower lip in great concentration, she ran her hands down his torso. More quivering on his part. "And that," she noted. "You like that, too."

"Let me save you some time here," he managed. "I'm going to like everything you do."

"Really?" Again her fingers moved, lower.

Over his ribs.

Then his trembling abs.

All while she watched his face with great interest.

Hawk had fantasized about this and far, far more. But in those X-rated dreams, he'd completely underestimated the effect she would have on him. Hell, she didn't even have to be touching him to make him hard, just the sound of her voice could do it, and yet now she was pressed to his side, looking, touching…

Stay still, he reminded himself.

The hardest thing he'd ever done.

"Okay," she whispered, answering some unspoken question in her own head. Then she dipped her head and nearly, but not quite, touched her lips to his.

And then stopped.

He didn't move either, just did his best to keep breathing so he wouldn't pass out and miss something good.

And then, as if he'd somehow passed a final test he hadn't even seen coming, she licked her lips and kissed him.

Killed him.

Same thing.

CHAPTER FIFTEEN

Cheyenne Memorial Hospital

CALLEN SAT AT LOGAN'S SIDE. She'd been watching over the cocky ATF agent as she often watched over her patients, with one noticeable difference.

Her heart was in her throat.

Not a comfortable place for it to be, not for a person who was used to being in charge at all times. But all sense of control had deserted her. So had common sense. And for what? The one thing she'd always sworn she'd keep her head about.

A man.

His partner's call had shaken her to the core. Logan was in danger; it sounded crazy, but she'd believed him. So much so that she'd switched the charts, and now Logan was Stephen Caudill. At the next shift change, he'd be making yet another chart change.

To Annabelle Levin, a thirty-year-old woman, nine months pregnant, five centimeters dilated.

He'd be so thrilled.

God. She'd risked all tonight. For a man. Her sister would not be happy. Kate had raised Callen because their parents had been hardly more than kids themselves, and not the sharpest tools in the shed, either. And she had warned Callen—*when love hits, it's like a ton of bricks upside the head. Either wear a helmet or accept that at some point, you're going to get clobbered.*

Heeding those words, Callen had made her way through life without getting overly involved.

Until now. Now she'd been clobbered, and as tough as she was, as careful as she'd been, she'd had no warning.

Kate had been right. It made no sense, and Callen had no explanation for it, but Logan was The One.

She knew it.

And she'd been so careful with her heart, too, only giving it away when she was quite certain it was safe.

Ha! Now she'd handed it over to an ex–Special Forces ATF agent who was currently embroiled in a situation where some high-ranking official wanted him dead. Just about as unsafe as it got.

But, good God, the man had charisma in spades. All he had to do was look at her. Hell, even lying there prone and far too still, she felt the space around her heart constrict, making it almost painful to be near him.

How did that happen in a matter of hours?

And then there'd been his obvious connection to his partner, and the frank concern he'd felt over leaving him alone to face the mess they'd found themselves in. She'd always had a thing for a man with a hero complex, and this man was definitely hero complex worthy.

She watched his face for signs of pain, because that she could handle, there she knew what to do, but his eyes were closed, his drool-inducing body motionless.

He was out cold.

So why her heart pounded, she had no clue. She couldn't seem to find her cool reserve, the place in her head where she kept her fears and panic at bay. There she could treat and care for the sickest of people, and still remain a little bit distant, just enough that she didn't lose a piece of her heart to each and every person who came into her life.

Because a lot of needy people came into her life.

But with Logan she hadn't been able to retreat. It wasn't just his physical attributes. She was immune to good looks and easy charm; in her line of work, she'd seen both erased by pain and suffering, leaving only the soul beneath.

Maybe it was his wit, which in spite of the pain, he'd shown in spades. Or maybe it had been the way he'd looked at her, as if she was the only woman he'd ever really seen.

Yeah, Callen thought, letting out a shaky breath. That'd been it.

She sat, at his side, watching him sleep as if she could keep him alive by willing it. But his injuries weren't going to kill him, he was merely sleeping off the pain and the load of meds he'd been given. By daylight he'd open those melting eyes and be on his way to recovery.

And then she'd go.

Deep in his drug-induced dreamland, Logan let out a long sigh. He could be dreaming about anything, she knew, given the dangerous life he led. Shifting closer, she set her hand on his arm and stroked, hoping her touch was soothing. "Don't let the bad dreams get you."

"I'm not asleep."

She nearly jumped out of her skin.

Turning his arm, he snagged her fingers in his. "Sorry."

He had a cut on his thumb and his palm was rough, callused. Warm. Leaning over him, she looked into his eyes. "Why aren't you sleeping?"

"Fighting the drugs." His voice was low, raw. Rough. "Callen—"

"Right here."

"If the worst happens—"

"Hold it." Her stomach dropped. "The worst is not going to happen."

A ghost of a smile touched his lips. "If you really believed that, you wouldn't have changed my chart."

Damn.

"I just want you to know," he murmured. "I could have fallen for you. The can't-eat-can't-sleep-can't-do-any-fucking-thing kind of fall."

Well, if that didn't grab her by the throat. She swallowed. "That's the drugs talking."

"Hell if it is." He lifted his arm, revealing the fact that he'd pulled out his IV.

The man was fighting a massive concussion, three fractured ribs and a wrecked leg, with no drugs. "Logan—"

"I want you to believe me. I could have fallen in love with you."

Her eyes filled. "Shut up and save it, because no one's dying."

He tried to smile but failed. "Shit."

"Damn it, let me redo the IV."

"No. I'm good. I'm still breathing, remember? Tell me again what Hawk said."

"You need to rest."

"I'll rest when I'm dead. Listen, I know he needs help—"

"You need help. And I'm here to give it."

"No. I'm not dragging you into this any more than I already have. I can handle this. You need...you need to go."

He said this with his eyes still closed, and he held onto her hand as if he didn't intend to ever let go. "Callen?"

She couldn't tear her gaze from his face. "Yes?"

He licked his dry lips. A decidedly un-nurse-like longing filled her. "You're still here."

"Yeah."

"Why?"

"Because I'm a nurse."

"That's not why."

She was glad he hadn't opened his eyes. "Maybe I don't want you to wake up alone. Why were you faking sleep?"

"Honestly?" He finally opened his eyes. "I was waiting for you to leave so I could break out of this joint."

She stared at him. Laughed. "Come on."

He didn't smile.

"Logan. You're not going anywhere."

"Want to bet?"

Her smile faded. "You're not kidding."

"Hawk needs me, Callen."

"He's going to have to wait for you, then. And don't even think about shaking your head, it'll hurt like hell."

"Jesus," he gasped, and lay back. "Okay, you're right."

"There, now see? You just keep saying things like that, and we'll be good."

Logan laughed, low and a bit hoarse. "What the hell are we doing?"

"About your health? I don't know, but I'm prepared to sit on you if that's what it takes to keep you here."

Swiveling his head, he looked right into her eyes, his own suddenly heated in spite of all the pain he must be feeling. "Maybe I'll try to get up so you can do just that."

"Probably sleeping would be a better use of your time." Callen managed to sound normal in spite of the fact her entire body had reacted to his words. The man was a walking, talking sex toy. But she had a vibrator, thank you very much, and didn't require a man for such simple pleasures as sex.

Although it'd been awhile, maybe she wasn't remembering it clearly.

"I can't sleep," he said. "I can't do anything but think about what I should be doing."

Logan needed a distraction. So many inappropriate things came to mind she had to stand up and flick on the television.

"What's that?" he asked.

She glanced up at the screen. *"Friends."*

"I meant what are you doing?"

"Distracting you from trying to break out of this joint, when you're still so hurt you can't even take a deep breath."

Reaching out, he snagged her hand. "Looking at you is distraction enough. You're so pretty, Callen."

"Stop it." But his words did something they shouldn't have, they warmed her from the inside out. "You're just trying to charm me into complacency so you can get out of here."

That he didn't deny that sent a frisson of alarm up her spine. He was. He was still going to try to get out of here and head back into danger.

"How many patients like me have you had to babysit since you've been a nurse?"

"Like you?" She laughed. "Exactly none. You're fairly different." As in off-the-charts different.

"I don't want to watch TV," he whispered, and very, very carefully, he sat up.

"You're not leaving."

"Callen—"

"I'll stop you," she warned.

He eyed her. "How?"

Good question. She opened her big old purse that held just about everything except a kitchen sink and sifted through for inspiration. She pulled out the book she'd planned on reading tonight if there'd been a break.

Logan took a look at the nearly naked earl on the cover, the one pulling off some maiden's dress, and laughed. "Okay, but could you skip to the good parts?"

Hmm, maybe not reading. Again, she searched the depth of the purse and came up with a pair of playing cards.

"I'm not a big card player."

She was running out of options. "Are you telling me you're not a gambling man?"

That caught his interest. "Poker? You'd take advantage of a man when he's down?"

If that's what it took. "What's the matter, you chicken?"

His eyes heated with the challenge. "Lock the door."

"What?" She laughed, though inside something leaped to attention. "Why?"

"Because if we're playing poker, we're going to do it right. Lock the door, Callen."

As if she was having an out-of-body experience, she got up and locked the door. "This is crazy."

"Now who's chicken?"

"You're suggesting we play strip poker?"

His eyes flashed. "I hadn't suggested anything. But since you've brought it up, sounds great. I'm in."

She opened her mouth, then closed it again, not wanting to analyze the way her bones felt sort of loose, and her skin too tight. At least he was no longer thinking about breaking out of this joint….

Oh, God. She was actually going to do this. Good thing she had a great poker face and was incredibly lucky. Not to mention fully dressed, while he had on a hospital gown and nothing else. It was a win-win situation for her. "Five card stud," she said, shuffling. "Deuces wild."

"I'm beginning to think that's not all that's wild."

Her gaze met his. "If in the end—"

"You mean when you're naked."

"Actually, I meant when *you're* naked." Just the words brought an illogical thrill, since she'd already seen everything there was to see when they'd cut off his clothes. Except that hadn't counted because at the time she'd actually been working on him, and truly had been focused on that. She wanted another peek, and the time to enjoy it. "If I win," she went on, "you stay here."

"And if *I* win…"

He paused and Callen felt like she was on the edge of a cliff, with her toes hanging off, a wind blowing at her back, and the earth rocking and rolling beneath her. "If you win, what?"

He full out grinned. "Winner's choice."

"You're not going to name it?"

"I'm going to keep it a surprise."

Oh, God. Okay. No problem. She pretended like that hadn't gone straight to all her good spots, and dealt the cards. A pair of tens. Not great, but not bad. She looked at him. He had no expression on his face whatsoever, and asked for two more cards. She took three.

And got a deuce. Oh, yeah. She kept her grin to herself and let him call her. "Three of a kind," she said, and fanned out the cards to show him.

He nodded, and with absolutely no expression on his face, revealed his hand—a full house.

Callen stared down at the cards in silence. Oh, boy. "Well," she finally said, and stood. "That was fun, but maybe this episode of *Friends* is a good one—"

"You have to lose an item of clothing."

Right. No problem. She pulled off her scrub top. Beneath she wore a pink bra. More coverage than her bikini, really, but here in this hospital room, with the light on dim, she felt extremely…naked.

He let his gaze dip from hers and slowly took her in, from the scar on her shoulder—result of rotator cuff surgery several years back—to her belly ring, to her hard nipples.

And it wasn't cold in the room. Quite the opposite, actually.

After a long, charged moment, he let out a long breath. "Consider me distracted."

Yeah, her, too. She reached for the cards and shuffled. Dealt. Stared at her hand without seeing a thing, because he hadn't taken his eyes off her, and it was all she could do to breathe.

Nothing could happen. He was too injured, and they were in a hospital room for God's sake…and yet she'd never felt so aroused in her entire life.

He took two cards, and so did she, both of them inhaling just a little too heavily, the silence so charged she could almost see the current sparking between them.

The only item of clothing he had to lose was his gown. She still had her scrub bottoms and bra and panties to strip, and suddenly the idea of doing that held far more appeal than winning.

Logan was looking into her eyes, not at his cards, waiting for her move.

"Call," she whispered, her voice tight.

Without breaking eye contact, he revealed…a pair of fives.

She set the cards face down and stood.

"What did you have?" he asked.

A pair of jacks. Which beat him, but she wasn't going to mention that.

"Callen?"

"You win." Gaze locked on his, she pulled on the tie of her scrub bottoms and let them fall.

He stared at her panties with the U.S. flag on the little triangle of material and let out a breath. "God bless America."

A shaky laugh escaped her.

"You take my breath, Callen."

"That's your injuries."

"No, it's you. Come here."

"Our game isn't over. I'm trying to make sure you're good and distracted."

"Oh, I'm good and distracted, all right. All the blood has drained south for the winter. Please come here."

Her feet took her forward until her thighs bumped Logan's bed.

He tossed back his covers, revealing his wrapped leg, the hospital gown, and pressing against it…

A most impressive erection. "Oh, my," she whispered.

"Yeah, unfortunately I can't move, so there's not much I can do with it."

She wanted to tell him he didn't have to move, that she'd do all the work.

Oblivious to where her thoughts had gone, he patted the spot next to him. And then she did as she'd never imagined she'd actually do. She climbed into bed with him and slid into his arms as if she'd been made for them.

Putting her face into his throat, she wrapped her arms carefully around his neck and just breathed him in. "This is new," she admitted.

"Cuddling in a hospital bed?"

"Cuddling. Period."

"I knew it. You're a serial heartbreaker, aren't you? A love 'em and leave 'em kind of woman. Damn." Logan sighed with mock hurt. "Be kind to me, will you?"

Her heart absolutely melted, and she knew she planned on being anything he wanted…. Lifting her head, Callen held his gaze while she reached behind her for her purse.

"What are you doing?"

She unzipped an inside pocket and pulled out a—

"Condom." He stared at it, then her. "Callen. Are you sure—"

"Very."

He took it from her, then let out a frustrated breath. "I'm going to hate myself for saying this, but I don't think I can—"

"No, but I can."

Logan stared into her eyes as she pulled the sheet, and then his hospital gown, from his body. He let her see every reaction as it hit him—arousal, hunger, desire, all for her…. And when she was finished, they were both sweating a little, both laughing a little, even before she carefully straddled him, slipping her panties to one side so she could slide down over him without hurting his leg.

"Ah, God, Callen…" he said roughly. She hugged his hips with her inner thighs and lifted up, until he was nearly out of her, before sinking back onto him.

Heaven. On. Earth. Her eyes drifted shut as she rocked on him, moving her own hands down her body.

"No," he whispered, voice hoarse. "Stay with me."

Startled, she opened her eyes. Arching backward, she fisted her hands in the bedsheets to avoid accidentally touching his chest and jarring his ribs. "Yeah," he murmured. "Like that." As she continued to move on him so that he slid in and out of her in a dizzying rhythm, Logan danced his good hand up her damp body, cupping a breast, rasping his thumb over her nipple, then gliding over her ribs, her belly, and lower, where they were connected, gently stroking, stroking…until she was coming completely undone for him.

Completely.

Undone.

She only vaguely heard his broken groan as he followed her over.

Wow. Just…wow…

"Callen," he whispered a long moment later as they both slowly came back to themselves.

She separated their bodies, realizing that he probably needed to breathe, and went to dismount from the bed, but he tightened his hand on her arm and drew her down beside him.

"Don't." He nuzzled at her neck, sounding sleepy, and so sexy she wanted another go at him. "Don't leave."

No. No, given the danger he was in, she wouldn't. And a small part of her was grateful for the excuse to stay. She curled up as he drifted off, feeling the last of the tension drain out of her limbs.

It'd been an incredible day: nerve-wracking, terrifying and exhilarating all at once, and she sighed, exhaustion creeping up on her as well. She'd let her defenses down with this one, and no doubt she was heading toward Hurt City, but right now in his arms, sated, content, she didn't care.

CHAPTER SIXTEEN

Serena's B&B Crack of dawn

THE HOTEL ROOM WAS WARM, COZY and shockingly intimate, but that wasn't what caught Abby's breath. No, that came from the sight of Hawk, naked except the towel, stretched out for her perusal.

Or for whatever she chose.

Handcuffed to the headboard, eyes dark and full and steady on hers, he made quite the sight. If she thought too much about what she'd like to do to him, she'd probably die of embarrassment.

So she didn't think.

She just did. "I saw you," she whispered. "That first day on the job, without a shirt. I wanted to touch."

"That would have worked for me."

"But I didn't know you then."

His eyes met hers. "And you think you know me now?"

"Yes."

"I'm not talking about the ATF part, Abby."

"Me either."

"Most people don't see past that, you know."

Something in his careful tone caught her. Softened her. "Yes," she whispered. "I can see why. As an ATF agent, you're pretty impressive. But that's not what draws me to you."

Again, his gaze met hers, and for the first time ever, she saw a hint of vulnerability. She thought maybe that was the most arousing thing about him, even though he was built like a pagan statue, all golden skin stretched taut over defined muscle.

Like her, he wasn't good at showing people what was beneath the exterior. Probably that drew her more than anything.

He had scars, lots of them, some old and some very new. A dark bruise bloomed over his ribs. Several inches below that, he had another on his hipbone, partially hidden by the towel.

She found herself wanting to touch each and every single one. So she reached out and lightly put the pad of her finger to one of his pecs. He made a low sound and went very still, so very carefully still she knew he was exercising every bit of control he had. She was running the show, and he wanted her to know it.

A rush of gratitude and warmth flooded her at that. He understood.

People had tried to understand in the past year. Friends. Family.

Men.

Gaines had tried to understand, had claimed to get it, and yet there'd remained something far too aggressive about him, and she hadn't been able to get past that.

Hawk, too, was a big, bad, aggressive alpha guy, through and through. In work, in play, even in rest, everything about him suggested that he could be ready for anything in a blink of an eye.

And yet he hadn't aimed that aggression at her. Hell, he hadn't even done so when she'd been wrestling him down to the ground in the midst of explosions and fire. He'd rolled her beneath him, yes. He'd held her down, yes. But never to simply exert his superior strength over her.

Now he'd given her free rein to do as she would to him. And, God, the things she wanted to do… She'd started out at his side, but somehow after she'd kissed him, she'd ended up sprawled out, half on top of him. Abby could feel the power of him beneath her, latent, edgy power, all contained and controlled. It was intoxicating. It made her tingly and uncomfortably hot.

He made her feel…sensual. Yeah, that was it. He made her feel sexy in a way she hadn't expected to feel again, at least not now, not with him.

So she kissed him again. He was aroused, she could feel that, too, nudging at her hip, and instead of worrying her, she felt a rush of excitement. Real, true lust. She was damp with it, even. Their mouths were touching, they were breathing each other's air, but it wasn't enough.

She opened her eyes and found his open as well, filled with heat, patience and amusement.

"What's so funny?" she asked.

He gave a shake of his head. "I thought I was dead tonight. Several times. But that was nothing to this."

"What do you mean?"

"You're killing me, Abby. Killing me with your sweetness, your heat—no, don't stop."

She'd begun to pull away, but saw that he wasn't making fun of her.

He wanted her to keep going.

And shockingly, she wanted to do just that. Cupping his face, she slid her finger along his rough jaw, tilting it a little before kissing him again.

"Deeper," he urged so very softly she might have imagined it. She opened her mouth, then ran her tongue along his lower lip, an action that wrenched a guttural groan from him. His free hand came up, gripping the headboard next to his bound one, as if he didn't trust himself not to touch her. But she trusted him, so she did as he'd asked and deepened the kiss, getting a little lost in the heat of him, in the taste, in the way they were moving.

And then she found she yearned for his hands on her. "Hawk, touch me."

"Abby—"

"Please? Touch me."

He let go of the headboard to stroke his hand down her back in a languid, sensual motion that had her stretching and nearly purring like a cat. She'd missed this. Being touched. Although she couldn't ever remember a man's touch making her want to melt into a puddle at his feet. Needing more, she kissed him again and his fingers tightened on her shirt, fisted in the material at the small of her back, urging her a little closer.

When she ran her tongue along his, he made a low sound and slid his hand beneath her shirt. His fingers were callused, and his touch curled her toes as they stroked up and down, catching on her bra strap. And then somehow she was fully on top of him, kissing him wildly, spiraling out of control.

With another of those low sexy noises deep in his throat, he rocked his hips to hers, nestling his erection against her core. Surprised, she jerked.

"Sorry," he gasped, and pulled back, removing his hand from beneath her shirt, slapping it back on the headboard next to his bound one, face tight, body tighter. *"Sorry."*

"No—"

"I'm going to close my eyes," he said in a hoarse voice, doing just that. "It might help if I can't see how you look sitting there touching me, the feel of you on my skin, the look on your face as it hits you what that touch is doing to me—" He winced. "Christ. Even my own words are turning me on."

"Hawk, I'm not that fragile."

"I know."

"I just didn't know if I was ready for this—"

"I know that, too. It's okay, I have a grip now." A white-knuckled one. "Let's try again."

Abby wanted to. More than anything. Because something had occurred to her. She felt no sense of panic, no claustrophobia at all as she let her fingers fall from his jaw, over his throat, down his chest, damp now, and rising and falling more quickly than when he'd run through the woods. She skimmed his abs, those amazing, sexy abs, which she wanted to trace with her tongue, then touched the edge of the towel where it was tucked into itself. It loosened.

Gaped away from those abs.

And her mouth watered. "Hawk, can I—"

"Anything," he said hoarsely, his eyes closed, his Adam's apple bouncing as he swallowed hard. "Any-god-damn-thing you want."

Biting her lower lip, she scooted back on his thighs so that she could bend down and press her mouth to his chest.

Feminine power surged through her, and she opened her mouth and licked him. He let out another rough sound but didn't move. She watched as his nipples puckered.

Hers did the same.

And then, almost without her brain's approval, her fingers tugged on his towel. It slipped free, and then *whoops,* look at that, spread wide, falling away from him.

"Oh," she breathed. He was bigger than she'd imagined. Just looking at him made her thighs tingle, and between them, much more than tingle. The sensation felt so wondrous, she went very quiet to savor every single second. Then she wrapped her hand around him.

A strangled sound tumbled from his lips, but he held still.

Warm metal. That's what he felt like. "You're big all over," she noted a bit shakily.

A harsh laugh escaped him. "Normally, I'd take that as a compliment, but—christ, Abby!"

She'd bent over and kissed him, on the very tip. "Do we have a condom?" she asked, then nibbled him again.

Another wordless sound rumbled from his chest, and his body arched up from the mattress, seeking her lips. "Bathroom," he gasped. "Basket on the counter."

She rushed into the bathroom, staring for one beat at the rosy, sensual woman in the mirror, then raced back to Hawk, galvanized by the golden, sinewy body stretched before her, flexed and taut with need. "Hawk."

"I know." He gulped in air and quivered. "I swear I'm trying to just sit here—"

"I need the key." Abby climbed back onto the bed. "I need you to touch me with both hands."

His head whipped up, his eyes connecting with hers. "Are you sure—"

"*Yes.*"

Nearly before she'd gotten the word out, he'd grabbed the key on the nightstand and freed himself, his hands immediately going to her hips, pulling her over him. Feeling him beneath her brought a rush of heat and more excitement, and, helplessly, she rocked her hips, frustrated by her clothes.

"How do you want me to touch you?" His hands danced up her ribs, his fingers not quite touching her breasts, though they ached for him to. "Here?" His thumbs scraped lightly over her belly.

Now *her* head fell back, and with her hips in motion, slowly rocking, oscillating, she was nothing but a bundle of raw nerve endings, racing toward the finish line.

"Abby?"

"Everywhere."

His fingers reached for the buttons on her shirt, and for a moment, she froze, because, oh, yeah, this was where she'd have to get naked...

In the warm circle of light from the lamp, his gaze met hers. "Just me, remember?"

"I know." She did, she really did, but she'd liked this a lot better when she wasn't thinking about losing her clothes.

So gently it nearly brought tears to her eyes, Hawk cupped her face. "We can stop here, Ab. I'll probably cry but we can stop."

She smiled, as he'd meant her to.

"Yeah," he whispered. "Love that look on you. Trust me, Abby...."

Oh, God, she really wanted to, but she wasn't ready to bare herself, and she couldn't force that. Twisting, she wrestled with a shoe, finally kicking it and one leg of her pants off before straddling him again.

"Wait. Abby, wait—" His hands on her waist tightened as he looked down her legs, opened over his thighs, at what she'd exposed. "Oh, God, look at you—"

"I need you inside me, Hawk."

"God, you're beautiful. So wet." Lightly, oh so devastatingly lightly, he stroked a thumb over her, right where she wanted him to sink into her body.

"Now," she nearly sobbed. "Please now."

"Yes, all of it, but first—" He stroked her, right at the center of her world, making her tremble, making her pant for air while with his other hand, he began to skim up her top, leaning in as if he planned on putting his mouth on the places he exposed.

Only she didn't want to be exposed, didn't want to tremble. She didn't want his tender gentleness now, she wanted him inside her, pounding until she exploded, until this desperate, almost unbearable tension left her. So she rose up on her knees and sank down over him—

"Abby, Jesus. Wait—"

Not stopping until he was fully seated within her.

CHAPTER SEVENTEEN

BURIED DEEP INSIDE ABBY, the woman of his dreams, Hawk gripped her hips and tried to keep a grip on himself as well.

She hadn't removed any of her clothing except the absolute essentials to get him inside her. She'd barely let him touch her, and certainly hadn't let him put his mouth on her, which he was absolutely dying to do.

Nope, she just wanted to get to the big bang, and you know what? He was going to let her. He was going to let her do whatever she damn well wanted to do to get off, and then, when she was soft and sated and damp and dewy, he had plans, big ones. He'd lay her back, strip her out of those clothes she was using as armor, tasting every inch he exposed, making her forget every nightmare she'd had over the past year, everything but this.

Him.

Even his thoughts were making him hot, and he pushed up deep inside her, and, oh, God, yeah, his groan co-mingled with hers, a sound that was music to his ears. She was right there with him. Not lost in unhappy memories, but here, with him. To keep her so, he slid his hands forward on her thighs, urging her up again, guiding her nearly off him before letting go so that she sank back down, panting in a matching rhythm that shot right through him.

Again she did it, while rocking those hips, setting him on fire. Staying still was all but impossible now, and he pushed up inside her, deep as he could get, and nearly lost it right then and there.

Leaning over him, she fisted her hands on his chest, getting a few chest hairs in the mix, but, hey, she could rip them all out one by one for all he cared. He wanted to watch her come undone for him, listen to her cry out his name, feel her spasm around him and know he'd brought her there. Sliding a hand through her hair, he tilted her head back, exposing her sweet neck, which he kissed, making his way down to her collar. Nudging it aside as far as he could, he licked her skin, then dipped his head and kissed her breast through the material of her shirt and bra.

"No," she gasped. "No, I just want to—" She broke off with a frustrated sob, her hips rocking, arching, her hair in her face, her skin damp and overheated. "Please, I just need to—"

Come. She was so desperate to get there that she was blocking herself. "Abby." He slid his hands to her hips and slowed her down, meeting her thrust for thrust, but going deeper now, harder, more controlled.

"I can't—"

"I'm hard as a rock," he murmured, kissing her jaw, her throat. "You do that to me. Can you feel me?"

Panting, she nodded.

Dipping his head, he rubbed his jaw over her breast, teasing the nipple through her shirt. "You do it for me, Abby. Completely. Let me do it for you."

"I can't—"

Pushing up her shirt, he rasped his tongue over her nipple.

She let out a sweet, shuddering sigh, and tried to move her hips faster again but he was holding them now, coaxing her to a slower rhythm, where she'd feel. Every. Single. Thing.

"Hawk," she whispered, clinging to him as if making sure he wouldn't let go.

He wouldn't. Ever. "Right here…"

She was panting again, warm and sweet and soft, murmuring his name over and over in his ear. The sound was the most erotic, most sensual, most heartfelt thing he'd ever heard, and just a little terrifying.

She felt it, too.

"Hawk?"

"Right here with you," he promised, breathing with her as he thrust up deep inside her, loving the feel of her breasts pressed to his chest, her thighs hugging his. His hands slipped down, cupping her ass, pulling her in, absorbing her soft gasp with his mouth.

She was going to come for him now, he could feel it in the desperate clutch of her hands, could see it in the way her eyes turned glossy and opaque. And then, with his name on her lips, she shattered, her body shuddering in his arms with so much sweet bliss it triggered his own release, dragging him under the wave of searing pleasure with her. He plunged into her one last time, trembling as he came from the tips of his toes, from every cell in his body, from the depths of his heart.

And as he went over, he had one thought—God, don't let me fall in love.

Yet as his vision faded, as an almost painful heat poured through him endlessly, he knew that whatever it was, it was much, much more than simple lust.

ABBY CAME BACK TO HERSELF in slow degrees, lethargic, replete, and more sated than she had any right to be, given their situation.

She was sprawled over Hawk's lap, her pants hooked on one ankle, her shirt half-opened and one breast revealed, the tip of which he was absently rasping with one callused thumb.

She had her face plastered to his throat, and as she took stock, she was very glad he couldn't see her face. Her legs were spread wide over his, her hands clutching him as if she never intended to let him go free.

As for his hands, well, he'd gotten quite comfortable with her body, hadn't he. His other one was intimately gripping her bottom, lightly gliding over her skin, making her want to, even now, stretch like a damn kitten and expose her belly for more.

Good God.

His face was buried in her hair, and with a long, pleasure-filled sigh, he lifted his head. His eyes were heavy with sleep, and extremely sexy as he smiled at her, looking quite pleased with himself. "Hey."

"Hey." She had no idea what to do or say, a definite first.

"You okay?"

"I think you know damn well that I surpassed okay."

He grinned.

Oh, yes, very pleased with himself, wasn't he.

Tucking a strand of hair behind her ear, he let that finger do the talking, stroking it down her throat and over her bared shoulder, where it caught on her shirt.

"Maybe next time, we could lose a few clothes," he murmured.

"You're not wearing any."

"I meant you."

She looked down at her bedraggled self and sighed. "Yeah. I guess I stupidly thought that leaving them on would be like wearing armor."

His smile faded. "No stupid. You had quite a bit to overcome."

And speaking of that…she had come. Probably if he so much as touched her again, she could do it again in a blink. "I didn't expect it to be so…" She searched for a word, and failed to find one that suitably did the job. "Wow."

"Me either."

Okay, so she wasn't alone in that. That was good. It might have been a little more embarrassing if she had been.

"Abby?"

She worked on meeting his gaze.

"You don't need armor with me."

No. No, she hadn't. And if that wasn't completely unnerving, Abby had no idea what was. She held his sincere gaze and sighed again. "I know. But I also know we don't have time for this."

He looked as if he might argue, then nodded instead. "Sleep?"

"Shower first." And using that as a reason to escape, she got up, somehow managed to ignore the urge to cover her good parts, and headed to the bathroom mirror.

Oh, boy.

Her cheeks were rosy, her eyes glowing. And so was her body.

Who'd have thought that damn fine sex would be part of the cure?

Not just sex, she told herself as she got into the shower. She'd had a healthy sex life before the raid, and what she'd just done with Hawk, while very hot and very unexpected, wasn't it.

It was something much, much more.

Which made this the scariest part of the entire past twelve hours.

CHAPTER EIGHTEEN

AFTER HER SHOWER, ABBY LOOKED at her filthy clothes and sighed, then held up what Serena had brought her. A black and sparkly sweater, low cut. Jeans, which had been made to fit like a glove.

She turned back to her clothes, but yep, they were still disgusting. Worse, her panties had somehow ripped and were useless. With another sigh, she pulled on Serena's clothes, knowing she'd never fill them out the way their hostess did. But her goal here was survival, not winning a beauty contest.

Abby opened the bathroom door, and found herself hesitating. She was embarrassed at how she'd let go with Hawk, and wasn't sure she could handle looking at him.

He'd left a light on for her, and that alone was enough to warm her from the inside out. She opened her mouth to thank him, but closed it again.

Oh. My. Goodness.

There he was, right where she'd left him, sprawled face down on the bed.

Completely in the buff.

Eyes closed, back rising and falling with his deep breathing, he was out cold.

He hadn't even pulled the covers over him, not that she minded the chance to stand there and look her fill without him being aware of it. Good God, but the man had it going on. Legs that went on forever, long, sleek, smooth back, broad shoulders, rippled arms that knew exactly how to hold onto a woman….

And then there were the good parts. She let her eyes linger in all the NC-17 spots until he suddenly rolled to his back, one arm flung up and over his eyes. She spent another moment taking in the new and even better view.

"Are you going to get over here?" he murmured in a sleep-roughened voice. "Or just stare at me all night?"

Crap. "I, um…"

Eyes still closed, he patted the mattress at his side.

Her feet made the decision for her, carrying her across the room until the mattress bumped her thighs. Without looking, he unerringly flung out his hand and caught hers, pulling her down to his side. "Just an hour," he said, and tugged her into his arms, apparently unconcerned by the fact that once again he was naked and she fully dressed.

Well, it hadn't bothered him earlier, she told herself, and let herself relax into him. And not just relax, but press her face into his throat. She might have also inhaled deeply, and then snuggled even closer.

In response, he sighed with pleasure and ran his hands up and down her back in the most soothing gesture she'd ever experienced. So why her body tingled, suddenly hopeful that it was going to get another man-made orgasm, she had no idea.

"Still fully clothed," he murmured, and she could hear the smile in his voice.

Along with exhaustion. "Sleep," she ordered.

"I know…I am…" He snuggled in. "Abby?"

"Yeah?"

"Maybe next time, you could be naked, too…."

Yeah, she had to admit, lying skin to skin with him would be pretty damn amazing. "Maybe…"

He let out a shuddering sigh.

"Maybe even…" She was crazy. "Now…"

Another sigh, but no words.

Lifting her head, she stared down into his face.

He'd fallen back asleep.

The irony did not escape her. She was finally ready to shed the last of her armor, and what happened? The guy she was ready to share it with was dead to the world.

HAWK AND ABBY MADE IT INTO Cheyenne two hours and twelve minutes later. Hawk had allowed himself to pass out for an hour and a half before he'd gotten them back on the road.

Now they were in Serena's borrowed SUV, only a few miles from Abby's condo, and he still hadn't figured out a safe place to leave her while he retrieved her laptop. She'd adamantly refused to stay at the B&B. "Do you have family in the area?"

She turned and leveled him with those baby blues. She wore Serena's clothes, and having discovered her ripped panties in the trash, he knew she was currently commando, a situation that was wreaking havoc with his thought process.

"Don't even think about ditching me."

"Maybe I was just asking." He did his best to put on his Sunday church face. The one that said he was an American hero, a man who'd never lie.

"My parents sold their house a few years back and retired to Florida," she said. "My sister moved there, too, with her kids."

"Sounds cozy."

"And too far for you to take me to."

He sighed, and dropped the innocent expression. "I just want you safe."

"If you're going to my condo, then so am I."

"If anyone's watching—"

"Then we move to Plan B."

This time the sound of the "we" didn't thrill Hawk. He couldn't stand the thought of how he'd dragged her into this entire disastrous mess.

She'd called Tibbs, briefly, letting him know she was alive and would be calling back with concrete evidence that would point to someone other than Hawk.

Where to take her?

"Stop trying to think of a place to dump me," she told him.

"Abby—"

"Look, don't make me use those handcuffs again."

He slanted her a look. "I might like that. Later."

She shook her head. "Men."

"Yeah. We're something."

"Something all right. What about *your* family?"

He glanced at her. "You going to ditch me now?"

A ghost of a smile crossed her mouth. "Maybe I'm just curious."

"My parents are gone."

"So you don't have family to be close with either."

"I have Logan." His heart squeezed just a little at the thought of what Logan was going through right about now. He'd called when they first hit the road, and Callen had promised she had him good and protected. Until he could get there, which would be right after he got the laptop, it would have to be good enough.

"Turn left here," Abby told him.

Her neighborhood was very suburban. Clean, cozy, sort of white picket fence meets the upscale set, complete with tennis court, pool, rec center… He wondered if she fit in here, and what she did on her time off. Did she wear a little white skirt and play tennis? Or slip into a bathing suit and swim laps?

"Up until last year, I never took any personal time for myself," she said as if she'd read his mind. "I was all work, work, work."

"And now?"

"Things have changed. I live my life. When I was on leave, I took tennis lessons. I could kick your ass all over that tennis court."

"Now that I'd like to see."

"Any time."

Her smug smile was the sexiest thing he'd ever seen. "I'm going to ask you to prove that one," he said.

"You play?"

"Well, it's been a while. In high school—"

She laughed. "I could take you."

"What do you wear when you play tennis?"

"What does that have to do with it?"

"Well, if it's a little tiny skirt, then I might have some trouble concentrating. I'll need a handicap."

She blinked, then smiled and shook her head, as if baffled.

"What?"

"You have this way of making me feel more like a woman in my grubbiest moments than I've ever felt in my entire life."

"Yeah, well, you have a way about you, too, Ab." Reaching for her hand, Hawk brought it up to his mouth. "Last night, I thought my life was over. Several times. You came through for me. I didn't realize it would be more than that, or that I'd get so much more than I bargained for. But I have."

"I'm more than you bargained for?"

"Hell, yeah. Aren't I for you? Isn't this?"

She stared at him, then let out a low laugh. "Wasn't even in the ballpark," she admitted. "But I can still take you on the court."

He laughed, suddenly feeling lighter than he could have imagined, given all they had in front of them. "You're on. You're so on."

If they lived.

"Take another left," she said. "Don't go to the gate."

They passed the front entrance, going around the block. "Back way in." Abby pointed. "They're doing construction here, adding another park. The fence is down. If we walk in from there, there'll be no record of us entering."

Hawk liked how she thought. He liked how she did just about everything, including the way she stared at him, as if maybe he was worth a second, even a third look.

And he especially liked how she clutched him when he was buried so deep inside her he didn't know where he ended and she began.

Yeah, he liked *that* a lot.

"Park here," she said, jerking his thoughts out of bed, pointing to a handful of trucks. Construction trucks, by the looks of them, toolboxes and equipment in the back of each. "We'll fit right in."

"How about just me fitting in?"

"You want me to wait here?"

"Yes."

"No."

"Well, glad that's settled." They got out, and just as she'd said, no one stopped them. They walked over the downed fence, through the tall grass and trees that were being turned into a greenbelt area behind the condos, and right past the pool and tennis courts, directly into the court-yard along the back of the condo units.

"You shouldn't stay here during construction," he said. "It's not safe."

"A fact for which we're grateful, remember?"

No one paid them any attention as they walked the length of the courtyard. Abby gestured to the second to last unit. "Home sweet home."

He stopped her at her back slider door and took her key. "Let me go in alone."

"For what, you to do the caveman thing and check the house?"

"Damn it. We're not going to fight about this, are we?"

She sighed. "We left the rifle in the car."

"Yes." He slid his hand up to her ponytail, lightly tugging her head back so he could cover her mouth with his for a short but effectively hot kiss.

"What was that for?" she asked, just a little breathless.

"You tend to stop arguing with me when I kiss you."

"It's because you're destroying my brain cells."

He ran his thumb over her lower lip.

She looked at the condo. "Hawk—"

"Look, what if I promise to argue with you later, your choice, will that work?"

Abby sighed again. "My laptop is on the little table by my bed, upstairs."

He let out a breath. "I'll be right back."

"Okay. And, Hawk?"

He turned back. Her eyes met his, those full, irresistible orbs, and in them he saw something that made him swallow hard. Oh, God. *Don't say it,* he thought. Don't bring in the L-word, because I'm not going there. So far he'd managed to keep his heart intact.

But this time, with her, he wasn't sure he could keep it that way.

She smiled, and that organ he'd been protecting rolled over and exposed its belly. *Huh.* Maybe… maybe it wouldn't be such a bad thing to have someone love him, truly love him, the way few had ever done. Because looking into this woman's eyes, he could see a future, could almost admit he was ready for it. "Yeah?"

She patted his arm. "Watch the second step. It creaks."

GAINES THREW HIS CELL PHONE across his office, and all three men standing in the doorway ducked.

It hit his crystal clock and shattered. "I've got three loose ends," he said calmly, and looked down at his computer screen, from which all of Tibbs's communications transcripts blinked back at him.

Tapping into Tibbs's computer had been nothing short of genius, if he said so himself, as it allowed him to keep track of all the players and the events. *Win.* "We need to take care of them, or I'll take care of you."

"Sir, yes, sir. But Logan wasn't supposed to get transferred to the hospital," Benny said in their defense. Benny had worked beneath Watkins.

Had.

Watkins had become dispensable the moment he'd balked at taking care of Abby. He'd had no problem betraying Hawk, but when it came to a pretty woman, he hadn't had what it took.

Gaines, however, did.

"Logan should never have been transferred," Benny said again. "But Watkins—"

"*Is* dead." Gaines looked at each of them. "As you will be if you don't fix this." He turned back to the computer screen. Abby had called for her voice mail, from somewhere near the city limits. Somehow he just knew Hawk was with her. The knowledge that they'd taken seven hours to get into Cheyenne instead of the usual four told him that they'd stopped.

Probably slept.

Together?

No. No, deep down she had a thing for him, he was certain of it. He'd cultivated the hero worship in her, had carefully honed it. No, his Abby hadn't slept with Hawk. She was too cautious—as he knew all too well. How many months had he put into trying to get into her pants? He'd wined and dined the hell out of her, managing only a whole lot of restless nights.

Until the raid. Of course he'd been behind it. Mostly because she'd come damn close to exposing him, more by accident than design, but still. She was a smart cookie, and with a little more time she'd have figured it out.

He'd had to throw her off, at any cost. So he'd finagled a way to scare her and indebt her to him at the same time. Ingenious, if he said so himself. And yet he'd played the goddamn hero for her and she'd *still* not given it up for him.

Had she given it up for Hawk?

If so, it was only one more damn good reason to kill the son of a bitch. And then, unfortunately, her as well. It was going to disappoint him as much as it hurt her, but some things just had to be done....

Abby's condo complex

ABBY STOOD ON HER BACK PATIO, hidden behind a tall potted ficus, staring at the glass slider, but unable to see more than her own reflection.

The ficus needed watering.

Story of her life. Oh, she'd been a big talker back there in the SUV, telling Hawk that she was living her life.

Liar.

She was still hiding. Still keeping herself closed off to feelings. But she hadn't kept herself closed off to him, had she? Nope, she'd let him inside both her body and her heart. Come on in, steal the china. Sighing, she pressed her forehead to the potted tree and closed her eyes. What was she doing? Did she have any idea at all…?

No. No, she did not.

Lifting her head, she eyed the glass door again. Hawk had been gone just long enough to get up the stairs. Hawk, who'd put her life ahead of his.

Several times last night alone.

Last night…God, last night. It'd been the wildest night of her entire life. A shuddering sigh went through her. There'd been a moment, several of them, when she'd wanted to stay in his arms forever, as implausible as that wish had seemed.

Implausible and very, very unlikely.

It had just been one night. She was positive there'd been no more to it than fear and adrenaline and need, creating a desire she hadn't been able to ignore. Very soon now things would go back to the way they'd been.

And yet, some things would most certainly change. Her, for one. She'd forever be different for the experience, for discovering that she was every bit as strong as she'd hoped, that she could absolutely be a woman in every sense of the word. That maybe, just maybe, she could even learn to trust her heart again.

Had he entered her bedroom yet?

Had she made her bed?

Why was she standing out here wondering? Clearly,

there was no trouble, she'd have heard something by now. Abby let herself inside. In the past, where she'd slept at night had never really been a home. She'd never had the time, nor the inclination to make one. But when she'd come here, she'd tried hard to create a haven, using warm colors, soft, cushy furniture and landscape photos of her favorite places on the walls.

She headed for the stairs, and in the doorway of her bedroom came face to face with the man who could both stop and kickstart her heart.

"Hey," Hawk said. "I heard you coming. I thought we decided you'd wait outside."

"No, you decided."

"Abby."

"Hawk." She repeated his tone, which made him laugh a little and reach for her.

She stepped right into his arms, and felt...amazing. Like she wasn't just standing in her home, she'd come home. Tilting her head back, she looked into his eyes, thinking she'd never had a man here, in this bedroom.

She'd never even given it a thought.

And yet this man, this quick-witted, smart, funny, sexy man, looked utterly and completely at home in her space.

It was a good fit.

"What?" he asked softly. "What is it?"

So damn much… "Later," she said.

Nodding slowly, he dipped his head and kissed her. Just a short, sweet kiss but their lips clung, and then opened, and then tongues got involved, and then…and then they were both panting and sort of arching into each other.

"The laptop," he murmured, his breath ragged, his hands beneath her shirt. "We're here for the laptop."

Right. With a steadying breath, she backed out of his

arms and pointed to it on the small table by her bed. "And get the locked box out of the drawer underneath it."

"What's in it?" He grinned at her. "Condoms?"

Abby rolled her eyes. "Something even better for protection—my backup gun and ammo."

Hawk looked impressed. "A woman after my own heart."

He headed for the nightstand while she did her best to get her racing pulse back under control—but *whew*. The guy's kiss packed a punch. Past him, on the floor, she could see the clothes she'd tried on yesterday and discarded, and then tried on again before deciding what to wear to a raid with the man she'd been secretly lusting over, as if it had been a date. Which was a joke, because she hadn't dated since...

Since Gaines. And their last date hadn't exactly been a rousing success—

Oh, God.

It all came back to her. He'd taken her to his second home, a luxurious ranch outside of Cheyenne, a "secret haven" he'd called it.

Secret haven.

"Abby?" Hawk put his hands on her arm. "What is it?"

What was it? Suddenly, she knew where to find Gaines.

CHAPTER NINETEEN

Cheyenne Memorial Hospital

LOGAN OPENED HIS EYES WITH some trepidation, but to his relief the blazing pain in his head had faded to a dull throbbing.

He could live with that.

Another thing he could live with? The woman curled up at his side.

Callen had stayed. Well, mostly because she hadn't wanted him to leave the hospital, but he knew it was more than that. Any woman who held his head while he tossed his cookies on a helicopter, risked her job to hide him, then played strip poker just to make him listen to her, was interested in more than just a patient/nurse relationship.

Or so he hoped. He stroked a hand down her side and she jerked straight up, eyes clear. "You hurting?" she asked.

"Yes."

Leaning in, frown in place, she put a hand to his forehead, but he took it in his and brought it to his chest.

There. That felt slightly better. But he wanted to pull her entirely inside him. "Here. I hurt here."

Still frowning, she yanked his hospital gown down to stare at his chest, her fingers running softly over his skin. "I don't see anything. Let me call the doctor—"

"No, it's not that kind of injury. Listen, Hawk's going to call—"

"He already did. He's coming for you. But—"

"No buts. We won't have time for this once he gets here, and before I go—"

"If you're in pain, we should rethink you going at all."

"Before I go," he repeated, "and make a really big fool out of myself here, I just want to ask you something. About last night." He met her gaze. "It was different, right? I mean, for you, too—"

"I've never been with a patient like this before, if that's what you're asking." Callen looked down at their clasped hands. "Never. In fact, I haven't…with anyone…in a long time. I haven't met anyone that I wanted— I've been working a lot, and—" She bit her lip and shook her head. "No, those are lies. A year ago I got out of a long relationship, and I haven't wanted to risk my heart again."

"Makes perfect sense, since I feel the same way. Or did, until about twelve hours ago."

"Logan—"

"Look, I know this is ridiculously fast, but I've just got to tell you, before today goes straight to hell—"

"No. No going straight to hell. No going anywhere."

"Actually, yes, I am. With Hawk, but—" He blinked, as he realized something. "I'm not in the same room as before."

"No."

His old room had been white, stark and smelled sterile. This one had soft pastel painted walls and different equipment—very different. Stirrups, for one. *Huh*. "Where am I, Callen?"

"I moved you. You're under a different name, on a different floor. Hawk's idea."

Good. It didn't matter where he was, as long as he got out to help Hawk. "I'll need clothes."

"Logan, this is crazy. *You're* crazy."

"Crazy. Yes. Crazy for you. You should know, I have no idea where this thing is going between us. I only know that I don't want it to end when I leave here."

"Oh." She breathed this softly, with no hint of whether that was a good or bad *oh*. So he swallowed hard and did the only thing he could, which was lay it all out for her.

"I want to see you again after this is over."

"You want to see me again."

"Tonight, if possible."

"Tonight."

"And tomorrow. And the next day. And—"

"I…get the idea."

"But do you like the idea?"

Her smile warmed his heart. "Okay, but Logan? I'm coming with you—"

"No. No way."

"You'll need a nurse. Especially one with access to stimulants that can keep you on your feet long enough to get somewhere safe, and take care of you when you collapse after they wear off."

"No, Callen. I'm not risking you."

She let it go while she brought him clothes. And when he saw what she brought him, he shook his head. "*Hell*, no."

"If the entrances and exits are being watched…" She smiled cajolingly. "A brand new momma is the perfect disguise to get you out of here undetected."

Logan stared at the huge tent dress, wig and bag of makeup. "Fuck me."

She grinned. "Ah, honey. Maybe later. But for now, let's pimp you up." She helped him pull the huge dress over his head, fussing with it, then standing back to admire it.

He shook his head. "You're enjoying this way too much."

"Uh-huh." She placed a dark blond frizzy wig on his head that made him look like a white RuPaul. "Cherry or strawberry?" she asked.

"Huh?"

"Lip gloss."

"Uh—"

"Strawberry," she decided, and stepped between his legs to apply the makeup.

His hands went to her hips and he pulled her in snugly, or as snug as she could get with his cast up to his thigh. It wasn't close enough. He spread his legs wider and let his hand slide down her back to squeeze her ass.

"Well." Callen laughed. "I've never been come on to by a woman before."

"It's different for me, too, believe me." He let his hand slip into her scrubs, then beneath the edging of her panties.

Her breath caught. "It feels kinky."

He'd like to show her a whole bunch more kink but not in a damn dress, that was for sure.

Then she brought him a mirror and he stared at the female version of himself.

He was the ugliest woman he'd ever seen. "I can't believe you let me touch you."

She snorted, then pulled out a wheelchair.

"Uh-uh. I don't need—"

She shoved a wrapped bundle into his arms. He stared down at the fake baby. "Okay, this is weird."

"What, the clothing?"

"No. The baby. I've never really seen myself with kids."

"Never?" She crouched to add booties over his very male feet.

"I guess I never figured myself as the kind of guy who'd

settle down and have a woman love him enough to give him a kid."

Callen glanced up into his face, her hand on his thigh. "You know what that means, right?"

"No, what?"

"That you've never been with the right woman."

He stared into her eyes, and suddenly found his throat tight. "Is that right?"

Gaze latched on his, she slowly nodded.

"So would you have any idea where I'd find the right woman?"

Her eyes went suspiciously shiny, but she only smiled.

Abby's condo complex

"I THINK I KNOW WHERE GAINES IS," Abby told Hawk. "He's got another piece of property he doesn't tell people about, an upscale ranch house about thirty minutes from here."

Hawk absorbed this as they quickly moved back through the gate and along the path, her laptop tucked beneath his arm, her gun in his waistband. He kept one hand free as they headed to the SUV, watching all the angles, his expression dangerous.

She couldn't take her eyes off him. Somehow she'd been caught up in this perilous game between two men capable of doing whatever they needed done. Just days ago she'd have said she didn't trust either of them fully.

But she couldn't say that now. Scary as Hawk seemed as he led her back to the relative safety of the SUV, she knew the truth.

She trusted him with her life. "Hawk."

He opened the driver's side and urged her in. "Yeah?"

She waited until he'd pulled out of the parking lot. "Do you remember the first thing I said to you last night?"

He sped down the road. "The part about you trusting a rat's ass before you could trust me?"

"Um, yeah." She winced. "That." They'd both been Gaines's victims. But no longer. "I've changed my mind."

He glanced at her with an arched eyebrow. She'd surprised him.

"I can trust you. With anything."

"Hold that thought," he said, and whipped them onto a side construction road so fast her hand slapped on the dash. He steered them behind a cluster of trees and yanked on the brake.

"What are you doing?"

"This." Hauling her to him, he covered her mouth with his.

Yeah, this. This was what she needed. She sank into the kiss, wrapping her arms around him, running her hands up and down his back, over his shoulders, up his neck into his hair, everywhere she could reach. She couldn't get enough of touching him. In this spinning, out-of-control world, he'd become her anchor, her rock.

And given the way he clutched at her, his own hands fighting with hers for purchase, skimming up her sides, her spine, then back to the front, beneath her shirt now, skin to skin, he felt the same way. "I don't want anything to happen to you." His lips brushed her skin.

"It won't." She cupped his face as he gently set his forehead to hers. They stayed that way a moment before Hawk drew a deep breath and lifted his head to look into her eyes.

He'd shifted gears already, and she took a moment to catch up.

"Abby."

She sighed.

"Gaines's ranch. Can you tell me where it is?"

"That would be a really bad idea."

"Or a really good one."

She understood the problem. Without ever wanting to, she'd become his soft spot, his Achilles' heel. Whether she was with him by choice or not didn't matter to Gaines, that she was with him at all made her a problem. A dispensable one. If he didn't get to Gaines, Gaines would likely get to him. And her. "I can draw you a map," she admitted.

"Good." Hawk punched some numbers into her cell phone. "Callen? Is he ready?" He listened, and his brow raised as he glanced at Abby. "I can talk to him? Great, thanks." There was a pause. "God, Logan, are you ever a sound for sore ears—"

His voice was so husky with emotion, she felt her throat tighten.

"Are you sure you're up for this, Logan, because—yeah, I hear you. Jesus, am I glad to hear you."

Abby looked out the window, concentrating on breathing as she listened to their reunion. They spoke in short, clipped sentences that spoke of the long-time ease between them, and an ability to guess what the other was thinking.

She'd never had a relationship like that in her entire life, because she didn't open up. She had started to with Gaines, and look what had happened. He'd set her up to be tortured.

How was she supposed to ever trust her judgment again?

She peeked at Hawk, still talking to Logan. He was trying to line up a secure place to dump her. Was she going to let him do that?

"I want her safe."

The words did something to the cold spot in her heart. The truth was, in spite of herself, she *had* learned to trust again. She knew Hawk was innocent. She knew he cared about her, and the knowledge warmed her in a way she'd never experienced.

She wished they were still at the B&B and she was back in his arms, where everything was okay as long as he kept holding her. Because with him, no matter what was going on, she felt safe. "Hawk, I'm staying with you."

Eyeing her, he said into the phone, "Are you sure, because Christ, Logan—yeah. Okay. We'll be right there to get you. Yeah, 'we.'" With a sigh, he closed the phone and reached behind him for her laptop, which he handed to her. "Serial numbers."

"What's the matter?"

He shook his head. "In a minute. Look up the serial numbers."

She started up her computer and her e-mail program automatically opened. On a hunch, Abby opened some old files, then leaned back and shook her head.

"What?" Hawk leaned over her to try and see.

"You said you shot Gaines on that raid eighteen months ago."

"Yes."

"You didn't know it was Gaines at the time."

"I didn't come to suspect so until later, no."

"Eighteen months ago he took a one-month leave." She flipped through several e-mails from him from that time. "Emergency appendicitis." She looked at him. "Too bad I don't believe in coincidence." Feeling overwhelmed by how big this was, she rubbed her hands over her face. "My God."

He reached for her, but she straightened and shook her head. Not the time to fall apart. "The serial numbers."

While she pulled up another file, he grabbed the confiscated rifle and read her the number.

Abby's stomach thumped as she matched it to her list. "It's here. Now tell me what Logan said to put that look on your face."

"Tibbs called again. They know the body wasn't Gaines."

Their eyes met. "Then who?"

"Watkins."

"Oh, my God." So Gaines had killed one of his own. Knowing it rammed home another certainty—Gaines would stop at nothing to get what he wanted.

"Gaines had Logan pushed off that roof to kill him," Hawk told her. "He needs us dead."

"Which is a very good reason *not* to go to his ranch."

"Or *to* go." There was knowledge in his eyes and acceptance.

Oh, God. He was going there to end this, one way or another, for her. So she'd be safe. "Hawk," she said. "You are not going to go there to die."

"Not me, no."

He sat there, so serious, so determined, she felt her heart just give in. From the very beginning he'd evoked myriad emotions from her—annoyance, lust, more annoyance, awe, affection, the ever-popular annoyance…and now, love. "We need to go to Tibbs."

Hawk let out a low laugh. "So he can hold me while they sort this out?"

"He won't—"

"He would, yes. That's his job. We'll call him, but when it's too late to stop me from finishing this with Gaines." His eyes were hard, his voice tight. "Which we do today."

CHAPTER TWENTY

Cheyenne Memorial Hospital

HAWK AND ABBY PULLED INTO the hospital parking lot just as a nurse wheeled out a large woman and her baby.

Hawk hopped out of the SUV, squatted before the wheelchair and grinned for the first time in two days. "Congratulations on your new arrival."

"Fuck you," Logan said from beneath his Vegas showgirl–style wig. He looked at Abby, then back at Hawk. "Huh?"

"What?"

"I just never thought you'd ever land yourself someone as classy as Abby, that's all."

Abby's brow shot up. "And how do you know he 'landed' me?"

"It's all over your face. Both your faces."

She blinked, then looked at the pretty nurse behind Logan, who smiled and held out her hand. "Hi, I'm Callen. And don't worry, I don't see anything but a lovely glow."

Abby put her hands to her face. Hawk looked over Logan's multitude of injuries, then glanced at Callen. "You didn't do so shabby either."

Logan reached for Callen's hand. "Yeah, I did pretty darn great."

Callen smiled dreamily, but that faded as two police

cars pulled into the lot. "I wonder if that's related to our new problem?"

"New problem?" Hawk asked.

"Later. Run now." They all piled into the vehicle, with Logan looking a little green despite his grin, which told Hawk he was hurting much more than he wanted to let on.

"New problem?" Hawk demanded from behind the wheel. "And the cops? What do they want? My head?"

"On a platter," Logan said. "The ATF has large sums of money going in and out of your accounts. *Out* being the key operative here, apparently. Supposedly you've just withdrawn a huge sum of money. Then there's the memory stick Tibbs found. And, wait for it…in spite of the fact that they do not have Gaines's body and all the evidence is looking right at *him*, they're charging *you* with kidnapping Abby."

"Is that all?" Hawk asked in tune to Abby's gasp. "Hell, that's not too bad." He met Logan's gaze in the rearview mirror. "We'll go to Gaines's ranch in two hours."

"Why two hours?"

"Because nightfall will be a better time to get close to Gaines."

"We can go to my place," Callen said.

It seemed as good a plan as any, especially since Logan really did look like death warmed over and Abby seemed ready to shatter. They'd take a few minutes, hopefully get their game plan together and finish this.

One way or another.

Callen's condo

HAWK PACED CALLEN'S SMALL spare bedroom while Abby sat on the bed watching him. "Okay," he said. "So he's got the money, freshly laundered through my account. He's going to vanish, and soon. Unfortunately, he's run into a snag. Me."

"If he sees you, you're dead."

"Right," he agreed. "Which is option number one."

"And option number two is?"

She sounded pissed, a front for her fear, which he appreciated, but he didn't plan on dying. "Me turning myself in on the mercy of the legal system."

Abby's eyes were conflicted. "I've been thinking about that. Given how he's handled everything so ruthlessly, that's not a good option. He'll try to have you killed while you're waiting for justice."

"Probably."

"So we move to option three," Abby said tightly. "Which is me offering myself up."

He stared at her in utter speechlessness. Finally, he managed to say, "Over my dead body."

"No, listen. We both know he has this obsession with me. He's got an ego the size of Texas, right? And he thinks I worship the ground he walks on, that's what keeps that ego going. You know it," she continued when he opened his mouth. "I'm the one thing he never got, and it's eating at him, Hawk, you know it is. I offer to go with him if he leaves you alone. It might work."

"Abby." His belly felt hollow. That she'd even suggested it after what she'd been through last year told him how much she meant to her. Touched beyond words, he ran a finger over the cut on her cheek, then leaned in and kissed it. "Not happening."

"I don't want you to die."

"Makes two of us."

She looked into his eyes, her own soft and sweet and heartbreakingly open. "Remember last night, when you said you'd do anything to make this all up to me?"

"Of course."

She backed to the door and hit the lock.

"What are you doing?"

Her hands came up and pulled off Serena's sweater, beneath which she wore her own bra. "I just figured out how you can do that."

"Oh, yeah?" Hawk's voice was no longer so steady, and neither were his hands as he shoved them in his pockets to try to keep them off her. But God, she stood there, offering him everything with her eyes, her body....

She reached for the zipper on the jeans. It was a tribute to how much she'd stunned him that she managed to shimmy out of them before he moved. Good Christ, she *was* commando. "Abby—" He reached for her but she slapped a hand to his chest.

"No, I'm not naked yet. I want to be naked with you."

His mouth went dry. All of his blood rushed to his groin so fast he got dizzy.

"Please, Hawk," she murmured, unhooking her bra and letting it drop, standing before him, gloriously nude. "Love me."

The kicker? He already did. So goddamn much he could hardly breathe. Gently pulling her in against him, he slowly backed her to the bed, following her down, down...ah, yeah, ending up right where he wanted to be, between her legs.

Home.

Her lips were soft, receptive and made for his, and kissing her was like heaven on earth. So was touching her. Never in a million years had he expected her to offer this again, to want him in the way he wanted her, and it hit like a freight train. "Abby."

She was busy, her mouth spreading hot, sweet kisses

down his throat, her hands shoving his jeans down at the same time so that she could wrap a leg around him, opening herself up so he could sink inside her.

God.

Yeah, he might have spent six months fantasizing about her, but those dreams had nothing, nothing at all, on the reality of being with her, feeling her body move with his, hearing her pant out his name as if there was no one else on earth who could do her right. The only sound in the room now was their harsh breathing as they struggled to keep their wordless pleas and moans from being overheard. Being with her like this was beyond his dreams, so sensual, so earthy and erotic as hell. It was also oddly unnerving because he knew...

She was it for him.

Her breasts were cushioned against his chest, her belly to his, her body soft against his hard, ungiving one. He had his hands on her ass, with each thrust driving them higher and higher, and he looked into her face, watching her go over for him, shatter with his name on her lips. Lost in her shudders, so sweetly encased in her body, he came right along with her, with only one thought in his brain.

Oh, yeah, he'd fallen. He'd fallen good and hard, and couldn't get up.

THE PLAN WAS SIMPLE, BUT STILL struck terror into Abby's heart. She'd described the lay of the ranch for Hawk and Logan. They'd wait until they were nearly there to call Tibbs and give him directions. That way he would be too late to stop them, but not too late to help.

Hopefully.

The possibility made Abby sick to her stomach. So many things could go wrong. Gaines could kill Logan and Hawk or her before admitting anything. Tibbs could not show up in time, or worse, show up too soon and take Hawk into custody.

The whole thing was one big crap shoot, and Abby hated gambling.

Logan, changed out of his maternal wear, got into the passenger seat of the SUV, looking far too weak for Abby's peace of mind, but there was no stopping this. He leaned out the window and gave Callen a kiss good-bye. "I'll never forget you," he said more solemnly than Abby had ever seen him.

Callen shook her head, eyes fierce. "Oh, no. Hell, no. Don't you dare say good-bye to me like you're not coming back."

Logan didn't smile, or try to reassure her. "Callen—"

"You know what? Forget this bullshit." And she climbed into the backseat. "I'm in as much danger if I stay behind. I gave Gaines my name when I thought he was your boss, and by now they've probably noticed you disappeared just before I left the hospital."

Hawk looked at Abby. "This is crazy."

Callen lifted a small tape recorder. "Not crazy. I can help. Hey, I might get something useful for you all to use later, right?"

"Absolutely crazy," Hawk repeated.

"There's no doubt of that." Abby gestured to the wheel. "You driving, or am I?"

"Shit." But he opened the backseat for her, and then got behind the wheel.

The plan was in motion now, and nothing could stop it. Abby met Hawk's gaze in the mirror and realized one thing she'd forgotten to do, one thing that was going to haunt her if things went bad.

She'd forgotten to tell him she loved him.

Gaines's ranch was high in the hills, in rough terrain, and extremely remote. Hawk didn't take the turn into its long dirt driveway. Instead, he took them on a four-wheel tour through the woods, entering onto the property from the back.

At the edge of a clearing, he stopped the vehicle. Down a ravine, about a half mile ahead, sat the ranch house, completely isolated. It was surrounded on two sides by running streams, and a third side by a rocky, sheer cliff.

Terrific.

"We're going to have to hike in," he told Logan.

They all looked at Logan's cast.

"No problem," Logan said confidently, and lifted his cane. "I'm feeling no pain."

Hawk doubted that but he knew he couldn't keep Logan from going—he'd follow him anyway. Abby was another story. He got out of the car and stopped her from doing the same. Leaning in, he put his hands on her face just to touch her, waiting until she slayed him with those eyes. "Someone needs to stay behind and protect Callen. I'll leave you the rifle. If we don't come back, get behind the wheel and drive the hell out of here."

"Hawk—"

"Go directly to Regional. Plant yourself there to protect yourself from Gaines's revenge, tell Tibbs I kidnapped you against your will, if necessary—"

"I am not going to put that nail in your coffin—"

"Abby, listen to me. If I don't come back, you won't need the nails. Show him your cuts, your bruises, the rifle, okay? Go back to Selena's and get my cuffs. The truck. With all the evidence they'll believe you."

Her eyes filled. "If you don't get out of that ranch house, I'll kill you myself."

He smiled, though he knew his eyes were shiny, too.

"That's a deal." Hawk smoothed back her hair, and kissed her once because he couldn't resist, letting their lips cling for a beat. "See you on the other side, Ab." He wanted to drop to his knees, take her hand and ask her to love him forever. Yeah, he really wanted to do that. But he had to survive the next hour before he asked her for her heart and soul, that seemed only fair. So he turned, and with Logan, walked away.

But he left his heart with her.

FIFTEEN SWEATY MINUTES LATER, Hawk and Logan came to one of the streams.

"Oh, boy." Logan weaved unsteadily.

Hawk reached out to grab him. "You okay?"

"Ask him."

Hawk followed Logan's gaze to a big-ass moose, who stood twenty-five yards away, watching them balefully. Between his huge palmated antlers, his elongated snout wriggled as he took in their scent.

"Just keep moving," Hawk said. "I've got your back."

"Why do I have to go first?"

"Because you're the injured one. The one most likely to get eaten. Jesus. Just go!"

The moose wriggled his nose again but was too lazy to chase them. It took another fifteen minutes to get down to Gaines's house. Gaines's deserted ranch house.

"Think the bastard already took off?" Not looking so hot, Logan sank to the porch swing.

"No." But it was so still as to be eerie. "He's here, somewhere."

Any minute, Tibbs and company were going to burst in with a blaze of glory, and damn it, having Gaines here would be ever so helpful. Hawk stepped into the yard and turned in a slow circle. "He's probably watching us."

"If that was true, we'd already be dead."

"Then he's watching something else." Narrowing his gaze, he turned again, stopping short at the sight of a surveillance camera mounted in the tree off the right side of the porch. A matching camera was on the left. And he'd bet every last cent he had, there were many, many more. *Shit.* He whipped back to Logan. "Abby and Callen."

"What?"

"This place is surrounded by cameras. He's been onto us since we first arrived. He's probably already at the car."

Logan swore and got to his feet, huffing and puffing. "Jesus. I'm worthless. The drugs are wearing off. Just go."

Hawk came back to him and shoved a shoulder into one of Logan's armpits, working as a human crutch. "Like I'm going to leave you behind now, after all these years that I've been carting your sorry ass around."

"Shut up and run."

It felt like it took them an eternity, but in twelve minutes they were back at the top of the hill, where they separated to circle around. Hawk came in from the east and hugged up to a tree. Damn it, he couldn't see. He'd have to climb the tree, which led him twenty feet straight up into hell before he had a good, dizzying, oh-holy-shit view.

God, he hated heights. But he hated what he saw even more. In front of the SUV, Callen was crumpled on the ground, eyes closed.

And Gaines. The bastard was leaning back against the car as if he had all the time in the world, Abby held tight to him, a gun to her temple.

"Might as well come out and join the party," Gaines called out.

Bullshit. Hawk aimed his gun directly between Gaines's

eyes, which unfortunately put him damn close to between Abby's as well. "Let her go."

At the sound of his voice, Abby gasped and looked up until she locked gazes with him. "I'm sorry," she said. "He got the jump on me."

"Of course I found you." Gaines pressed his cheek to hers. "I always will. Now, here's how this is going to work, Hawk. You're going to put down your gun. And, Logan? I know you're out there. Might as well show yourself."

Logan did not appear. Hawk had no idea if this was strategy, or if he hadn't made it around yet. "Let her go," he repeated, his gun still sighted right between Gaines's bloodshot eyes. "Do it. Or I promise you, this will hurt."

"I'm sorry." And actually, Gaines did look sorry. He sported a bandage around his shoulder that reminded Hawk he'd shot the bastard last night. "I can't always be looking for you over my shoulder. You have to die."

"No," Abby gasped, terror filling her gaze, terror for Hawk. "Elliot, don't be stupid, you'll never get away with this."

"You'd be surprised what I can get away with." Again, he ran his cheek over hers, his eyes softening. Then he shifted the muzzle of his gun from her temple to just beneath her jaw, and Hawk's heart just about stopped. The guy's hands were shaking, he was a loose cannon who was going to go off and shoot her in the process.

No. He wasn't going to let that happen. If he could get Abby to go limp and drop, he could get a clean shot. "Do you remember that one thing I wanted from you?" he asked.

She nodded. Trust. It was there in her eyes for him to accept, take. "Good," he told her, and nodded his head once, trying to signal her to drop. "That's real good." As his finger applied slow pressure, she looked him right in the eyes and mouthed "I love you," and on that stunning revelation, she didn't drop but shoved back with her elbow, landing it hard in Gaines's windpipe. A harsh sound expelled from his lungs, and then Abby dropped, in that split second giving Hawk the free target he needed.

Except that before he got a shot off, a different gun rang out, and both Gaines and Abby crumpled to the ground.

Hawk slid down the tree, racing toward the pair as Logan burst out of the woods, limping toward them, his gun in hand.

Hawk had never been so petrified in his life as he was in that very moment, that single moment of clarity, when he knew he was never going to be the same. Abby had just come into his life. With her smile, with every breath she took, she'd made it better.

She'd made him whole.

Goddamn, but he'd been waiting for that without even knowing it, and now that he'd experienced it, he was afraid he couldn't live without it.

Without her.

CHAPTER TWENTY-ONE

BEFORE ABBY COULD DRAW A breath into her compressed lungs, the heavy weight was lifted off of her, and she was yanked into a pair of strong, warm arms.

Trembling arms.

"Jesus, Abby." Hawk pulled back only enough to look down into her face.

"Hey," she told him. "Good shot."

"It wasn't me, it was Logan." He gulped for air. "Tell me you did not just say you love me when I had a gun pointed at your head."

She smiled as her eyes filled. She couldn't help it. "I did."

His eyes went misty, and he hauled her back into his arms.

She let him squeeze the air out of her because that was where she needed to be, in his arms, tight, face plastered into the crook of his neck, inhaling his scent, feeling as if she'd just come home for the first time in her life. They might have both been victims, but no longer. They had survived, because they were stronger together. "Is Gaines—"

"I don't know." He palmed her head in his hands and held her face to his throat. "Are you—"

"Fine," she promised. "Callen—"

"Logan's got her, she's coming around." They both turned.

Logan was holding onto Callen the same way Hawk was holding onto Abby, but Callen was shaking her head. "I'm fine, he got me from behind, knocked me out cold, but I'm good now." She managed to pull the tape recorder out from beneath her shirt. "Like me and the Energizer Bunny, this kept going."

From behind the SUV, Tibbs, Thomas and Wayne appeared, running.

"About time," Hawk said.

Tibbs held out his hand for the recorder. "Can I see that?"

Callen handed it over, and Tibbs tucked it away, nodding to first Logan, and then to Hawk, who visibly tensed.

But Tibbs didn't shoot him, didn't handcuff him, didn't do anything but let out a slow nod of approval. "Should have trusted me, Hawk. I'm not stupid enough to believe you'd leave incriminating evidence lying around your house. Luckily I was only half a step behind you."

Thomas and Wayne crouched at Gaines's side and turned him over. "Still breathing," Thomas noted.

Wayne radioed for the ambulance. "He's not going to thank us."

Logan hadn't taken his eyes off Callen. "He could have killed you. I'll never forgive myself for—"

"But he didn't kill me. And you're still alive, too," she pointed out. "So now that no one's dying today, maybe we can make plans, and do things right."

Logan looked shaken to the core, and as if he'd been hit by a bus. In a good way. "You mean we didn't do things right before?"

Callen smiled. "Well, you not being hooked up to any machines will be a bonus."

"True." He snagged her close, pulled her into his lap and just sat there. "Except I'm too tired to move."

"Don't worry. I have enough energy to keep us both moving."

Hawk tipped his head down to Abby, not looking nearly as ready to joke as Logan and Callen.

"You climbed a tree for me," Abby marveled. "A really tall pine tree."

"Thanks for noticing." He ran a hand down her hair, cupping her jaw. He couldn't stop looking at her.

"I'm really okay you know."

"Good." He sank all the way to the ground, holding her tight to him. "That's good, because I'm not."

"What? Did you get hurt?" Panicked, she ran her hands over his chest, his face, his arms, until he caught them in his.

"No, listen. I love you back, Abby. So much I don't even know what to do with it all."

She stared up into the face of the man she'd given herself over to so completely. "Really?"

"God, yes."

She felt so much joy she could hardly breathe. "Well, I have some ideas on what to do with it."

"I knew you would," he said fiercely, and beneath the setting sun, he kissed her to show that maybe he had a few ideas of his own.

EPILOGUE

ABBY CLOSED HER CELL PHONE and smiled. She also purred and stretched like a kitten because there was a pair of big, strong hands spreading suntan lotion on her back, smoothing it up and down in a delicious motion as she lay sprawled out in a large, comfy beach chair beneath a palm tree, the gorgeous crystal-clear ocean hitting the shore only five feet in front of her.... "Mmm."

The South Pacific was definitely all it was cracked up to be.

The fingers dug in a little, loosening up her muscles, and she let out a heartfelt appreciative moan. Then a mouth skimmed her ear.

"What did Tibbs want?" that mouth asked, her own personal cabana boy. God, she loved it when he sounded like that, all low and sexy. She flipped over and smiled up at Hawk, who was pouring more lotion in his hands.

Her body tingled in anticipation.

Since she wore only bikini bottoms, he could see exactly what he did to her. His gaze settled on her bare breasts, watching her nipples harden, and he let out a slow smile that had other reactions going on in her as well. She knew that heavy lidded look, knew what it meant.

Then he settled his hands on her belly and began smoothing in the lotion. Wearing only a pair of board shorts low on his hips, his hard body bronzed from two weeks in the sun, he could have passed for one of the natives here on this South Pacific island.

"Abby?"

Right. He'd asked her a question. "He wanted to make sure we're enjoying our entire forced leave—" She broke off when his hands began their ascent, heading up her ribs…

"It's tough, of course," he said. "The forced leave. But someone's got to do it."

They grinned at each other, and Hawk's hands continued to glide up her torso to her breasts. They were on their own private little beach, with their own private little luxurious hut behind them, only a quarter of a mile away from Logan's and Callen's equally private hut. Tibbs had given the four of them the trip that Gaines himself had planned to take, in reward for their service to the ATF. They'd been ordered to spend the time recouping, recovering and relaxing.

Abby was doing all three, with flying colors. "He also wanted to remind us that we still have two weeks left and he doesn't want to see us early. But that when he does, there's going to be a little change. We're getting raises."

"I like that part."

"Me, too."

"But I have a change of my own."

Hawk's thumbs slowly circled her nipples, and her breath caught. "Ch-change?"

"Of status." Nudging her to scoot over, he slid onto the lounger and pulled her close.

She shifted so that one of his thighs was between hers but when he cupped her face, looking so serious, her heart skipped a beat.

"I love you," he said solemnly, fiercely.

Ah. She was never going to get tired of hearing that. "I love you back, Hawk. So much."

"My own miracle…" He stroked a strand of hair from her face. "I know this might seem fast to you, but I've been finding myself feeling…well, old-fashioned and proprietary."

"Old-fashioned? Proprietary?" Abby looked down at her bare breasts, which were plumped up against his chest. "Meaning what, we have to stop getting naked?"

"Meaning I want to marry you. And live happily ever after."

She blinked as a warmth spread outward from the very depths of her soul.

"So…what do you think?"

"That I could get used to old-fashioned and proprietary."

Hawk let out a breath and pressed his forehead to hers. "Abby."

Cupping his face, she pulled back to see into his eyes. "Just thought of something. Old-fashioned…does that mean we can't sleep together before we make it legal?"

A slow, wicked grin pulled at his mouth, and he slid a hand down her spine and into her bikini bottoms, his fingers dipping low enough to make her shiver. "If I said yes, would you—"

"I'd find a way to get married right here and now," she declared unevenly as he stripped off her bottoms and his fingers got very, very busy.

"You know…" Lowering his head, he began to kiss his way down her neck. "Did I ever tell you that Logan is an ordained minister? He did it online several years ago as a joke."

"I love Logan."

"But you love me more."

Abby arched back as Hawk rolled, tucking her beneath him, gasping when he slid into her. "I love you more," she agreed. "I love you for always…."

* * * * *

REQUEST YOUR FREE BOOKS!
2 FREE NOVELS PLUS 2 FREE GIFTS!

♦ Harlequin®

Blaze™

red-hot reads!

HB11

Fan favorite author
TINA LEONARD
is back with
an exciting new miniseries.

Six bachelor brothers are given a challenge—
get married, start a big family and whoever does
so first will inherit the famed Rancho Diablo.
Too bad none of these cowboys is marriage material!

Callahan Cowboys:
Catch one if you can!

Harlequin *Romance*

Don't miss an irresistible new trilogy from acclaimed author

SUSAN MEIER

IN THE BOARDROOM

Greek Tycoons become devoted dads!

Coming in April 2011

The Baby Project

Whitney Ross is terrified when she becomes guardian
to a tiny baby boy, but everything changes when
she meets dashing Darius Andreas, Greek tycoon
and now a brand-new daddy!

Second Chance Baby (May 2011)
Baby on the Ranch (June 2011)

HRI7721